"LEIGH DRAWS READERS IN TO HER STORIES AND TAKES THEM ON A SENSUAL ROLLER COASTER."*

Praise for

HARMONY'S WAY

"Leigh's engrossing alternate reality combines spicy sensuality, romantic passion and deadly danger. Hot stuff indeed."
—*Romantic Times*

"I stand in awe of Ms. Leigh's ability to bring to life these wonderful characters as they slowly weave their way into my mind and heart. When it comes to this genre, Lora Leigh is the queen."
—*Romance Junkies*

Praise for

MEGAN'S MARK

"A riveting tale full of love, intrigue and every woman's fantasy, *Megan's Mark* is a wonderful contribution to Lora Leigh's Breeds series . . . As always, Lora Leigh delivers on all counts; *Megan's Mark* will certainly not disappoint her many fans!"
—*Romance Reviews Today*

"Hot, hot, hot—the sex and the setting . . . You can practically see the steam rising off the pages."
—*Fresh Fiction*

"A fast-paced romantic suspense that will have readers hungering for more. Like all the wonderfully erotic and exciting books in Leigh's Breeds series, *Megan's Mark* has at its core characters that you just want to sink your teeth into . . . Powerful, passionate and explosive."
—**Love Romances*

P9-BZG-337

continued . . .

Dawn's Awakening

Lora Leigh

BERKLEY SENSATION, NEW YORK

THE BERKLEY PUBLISHING GROUP
Published by the Penguin Group
Penguin Group (USA) Inc.
375 Hudson Street, New York, New York 10014, USA

Penguin Group (Canada), 90 Eglinton Avenue East, Suite 700, Toronto, Ontario M4P 2Y3, Canada
(a division of Pearson Penguin Canada Inc.)
Penguin Books Ltd., 80 Strand, London WC2R 0RL, England
Penguin Group Ireland, 25 St. Stephen's Green, Dublin 2, Ireland (a division of Penguin Books Ltd.)
Penguin Group (Australia), 250 Camberwell Road, Camberwell, Victoria 3124, Australia
(a division of Pearson Australia Group Pty. Ltd.)
Penguin Books India Pvt. Ltd., 11 Community Centre, Panchsheel Park, New Delhi—110 017, India
Penguin Group (NZ), 67 Apollo Drive, Rosedale, North Shore 0632, New Zealand
(a division of Pearson New Zealand Ltd.)
Penguin Books (South Africa) (Pty.) Ltd., 24 Sturdee Avenue, Rosebank, Johannesburg 2196,
South Africa

Penguin Books Ltd., Registered Offices: 80 Strand, London WC2R 0RL, England

DAWN'S AWAKENING

A Berkley Sensation Book / published by arrangement with the author

PRINTING HISTORY
Berkley Sensation mass-market edition / February 2008

ISBN: 978-0-425-21975-1

BERKLEY® SENSATION
Berkley Sensation Books are published by The Berkley Publishing Group,
a division of Penguin Group (USA) Inc.,
375 Hudson Street, New York, New York 10014.
BERKLEY SENSATION and the "B" design are trademarks belonging to Penguin Group (USA) Inc.

PRINTED IN THE UNITED STATES OF AMERICA

10 9 8 7 6

Dawn's Awakening

They were created, they weren't born.

They were trained, they weren't raised.

They were taught to kill, and now they'll use their training to ensure their freedom.

They are Breeds. Genetically altered with the DNA of the predators of the earth. The wolf, the lion, the cougar, the Bengal; the killers of the world. They were to be the army of a fanatical society intent on building its own personal army.

Until the world learned of their existence. Until the council lost control of their creations, and their creations began to change the world.

Now they're loose. Banding together, creating their own communities, their own society and their own safety, and fighting to hide the one secret that could see them destroyed.

The secret of mating heat. The chemical, biological, the emotional reaction of one Breed to the man or woman meant to be his or hers forever. A reaction that binds physically. A reaction that alters more than just the physical responses, heightening the sensuality. Nature has turned mating heat into the Breeds' Achilles' heel. It's their strength, and yet their weakness. And Mother Nature isn't finished playing yet.

Man has attempted to mess with Her creations. Now She's going to show Man exactly how She can refine them.

Her males are strong. They bend, they never break. They are the pinnacle of strength from birth. Built to fight, to survive, to protect.

To protect their females, be they lovers, mates or sisters. And it is their sisters who suffered far more than they. Females created by men as objects, as little more than tools to kill, and to satisfy their own craven, horrific lusts. And it is these females who suffer the most enduring pain. The females who must, now that freedom has been attained, rise above the nightmares to become mates.

Mother Nature will accept nothing less. And their hearts flow with the blood of the greatest creatures on earth: the female, the Amazon, the lioness, the cougar, the giver of life, the caretakers and the hunters. It is these females who must now face the nightmares, the fears and the burning memories of pain to find the life Mother Nature intended for them all along.

Man created them. But God has adopted them. And now Mother Nature will see to their ultimate survival.

· PROLOGUE ·

Seth Lawrence stepped into the office the Breed Enforcer directed him to and stared back at the Breeds gathered together. He knew them, not well, but well enough. He backed them, his companies supported them. His father would have betrayed them all as well as the sister that now lived among them. The sister Seth had never known he had, but loved anyway.

Callan Lyons, pride leader. He stood by the window, the late evening sunlight spearing through the heavy mane of hair that fell to his shoulders and cast his expression in shadow.

Beside him was Seth's brother-in-law, Taber Williams, who watched him with quiet anguish, a look in his eyes that had Seth tensing, preparing for the worst.

Kane Tyler, brother-in-law to Callan Lyons and Sanctuary's head of security, was resigned, somber. And Jonas Wyatt, the arrogant, forceful enforcer who had been steadily moving up the ranks of Security, stood at a scarred desk.

"Is she okay?" Seth asked the question, his voice gruff, fear squeezing his heart.

She was Dawn. Dawn Daniels, the little Cougar Breed female that he couldn't get out of his mind, that he couldn't forget. She had been wounded when Seth's chauffeur had attempted to kidnap a Breed child, Cassie Walker, and Seth's half sister, Roni, months ago.

She was too tiny, too delicate to be as reckless and fearless as she was in battle. To be so haunted when touched by a man.

In the few glimpses he had managed of her in the past months, she had looked haunted. And Seth wanted nothing more than to wipe those dark shadows from her eyes.

"She's fine, Seth," Kane answered after glancing at the others, his ice blue eyes flickering in indecision.

"Then why am I here?" He crossed his arms over his chest and stared them down. If they had brought him here to warn him away from Dawn, then they were wasting their time.

Nothing, no one, could change the course he had set for himself. In all his life no one had belonged to him. He hadn't loved anyone since his mother's death, until Dawn.

"I won't be part of this." Taber suddenly stiffened his shoulders and shook his dark head.

The Jaguar Breed was tall, leanly powerful and obviously not in agreement with this meeting.

"Taber." Callan kept his voice low. "None of us like it, but it has to be done."

"Then let's get to the damned point," Seth demanded coldly, his voice sharp, brisk. "I'll assume this is about Dawn?"

Callan almost snarled. Taber jerked his head to the side and Kane rubbed at the back of his neck.

"Mr. Lawrence, we've only met briefly." Jonas Wyatt, with his weird silver eyes and savage features, stepped forward to lean against the front of the desk, a television remote control in his hand.

"I remember you," Seth answered, his voice clipped.

"Dawn concerns us," he said then, his voice gruff, arrogant. He was one of those men that other men naturally never get along with. They might respect him, might admire his power and cunning, but he wasn't a man others could be comfortable around.

Seth knew the type. He was the same way. Control and power came with an innate arrogance that naturally didn't fit well when it came in contact with those who were similar.

"Dawn concerns me as well, Mr. Wyatt," Seth informed him. "For some reason I've been barred from seeking her out, and no one wants to talk to me about her. Damned inhospitable, if you ask me. Considering the aid Lawrence Industries has offered to the Breeds."

"Dawn isn't for sale, Lawrence," Callan growled then, the sound rumbling in his throat.

"I didn't ask to buy her." Seth sent him a cold smile. "I believe I made my intentions clear to you, Lyons."

"And that's why we're here." With a flick of his hand toward them, two silent enforcers slid the heavy curtains over the windows, leaving the room in shadows.

Seth noted the movement, a part of him, an instinctive part of him, warning him that what was about to come was something he didn't want to know.

"I'm out of here." Taber's growl was more animal than man and had Seth tensing for action.

Seth caught the other man's arm as he passed, ignoring the flash of dangerously sharp canines as Taber turned to him.

"What the hell is going on?"

"You'll find out soon enough." Taber jerked away from him and strode to the door. He jerked it open then slammed it behind him.

Callan turned his back on him. Kane shook and lowered his head.

"Dawn's the same as his sister," Jonas said then. "You've made your intentions clear where Dawn is concerned. We're going to show you, Mr. Lawrence, the battle you have ahead of you. Every soldier should be prepared for the war he's going to face. Wouldn't you agree?"

He pressed the remote, and the viewing screen on the wall behind the desk flared to life. Jonas kept his back to it and watched Seth.

There was no need for an explanation. He saw the number that flashed on the screen, the date, time, subject. Cougar Breed Female, six years of age. Listed number 7.036. They held the child to a cold metal table and branded the numbers on her hip.

The screams that filled the room had Seth stepping back, his fists clenching, rage shattering through his head. But if that was hard to watch, what came later would scar his soul for life.

He couldn't turn away. He wouldn't turn away. She had endured hell and he loved her to his last breath. She had lived through it, he could do no less.

He loved her. He already knew he loved her. He ached for

her. He would kill for her, and he would have given his own life to have saved her from the dark brutality the monsters that created her had taped.

Number 7.036. Age six. Age ten. Ah, God. Ah, God. Age thirteen. So tiny. So fucking tiny she looked like a doll as those bastards raped her. Sweet merciful Jesus. His guts cramped with pain, everything inside him howled with rage, and hopelessness filled him.

They strapped her to a cold, steel table. Metal restraints at her neck, her arms, her thighs and ankles. She strained against them, she fought them until blood seeped from beneath the edges and ran down her fragile limbs.

She screamed. She begged for God, and they laughed at her. Laughed at her and told her God didn't care about Breeds, and then they tore into her helpless, fragile body.

The images flickered through those first thirteen years of her life in a matter of minutes. A collage of brutal, horrifying flashes. Of abuses that should have killed her. Twenty minutes of the most horrific nightmares that could be inflicted on the female body. On a child.

When they winked off, no one moved. No one spoke. Seth continued to stare at the now-dark screen, seeing the child she had been in the woman she was now. The dark eyes flashing with nightmares, with pain each time she looked at him, each time she realized what he wanted from her. What he needed from her.

He tried to swallow, and couldn't. He blinked back moisture. Fuck, tears. He hadn't shed a tear in more years than he could remember. And he hated his father more than he ever had in his life.

His father and Lawrence Industries had helped fund those monsters before Seth took over. They had helped pay for the brutality committed against the woman who held his soul. The woman he could never have.

Seth finally managed to work up enough saliva to swallow, to force his vocal cords to work. Callan turned back from the closed window, his expression heavy with grief as he watched Seth. And now Seth understood why Taber had refused to stay.

He had never felt pain so deep, so intense as he felt it now. Agony that resonated through every part of his soul, that tore through his heart, his very spirit, like a jagged dagger, ripping pieces of his being to shreds.

"I love her," he whispered.

"And we're aware that an anomaly known within Breed physiology called 'mating heat' has begun showing in both of you. Dawn's blood is already showing the presence of minute quantities of the hormone released during this. It's like an aphrodisiac, Mr. Lawrence; it creates an arousal so strong that the mating pair can't deny it. It's something we're desperate to keep quiet until we can understand it and find a way to control it. In Dawn, it could be destructive, mentally and emotionally. You saw the images. You saw what they did to her, both with the drugs and without. At this time, none of us believes it's something she can endure. Had the atrocities ended there, perhaps she could have healed. Perhaps. But once Callan rescued them, unknown to him, their pride brother, Dayan, festered the memories inside her to control her. She was brutalized within the labs, and later, outside them. She's had less than a year to come to grips with true freedom, and she's making incredible progress. None of us want to see that progress experience a setback. None of us who love her, that is."

Seth stared back at Jonas, feeling the icy knowledge that what the other man said was no less than the truth.

"Should Sanctuary require anything of Lawrence Industries, you have only to contact my assistant." He moved to the door, opened it and stared back at them. "Should Dawn need anything, I, personally, expect to know immediately."

He moved from the room, closed the door carefully behind him, then came to an abrupt stop. The child who stood before him was the same one who had run so courageously from the estate house months before and thrown herself into the back of the limo Seth had been riding within. Little Cassie Walker Sinclair, with her thick black hair and too-solemn little face.

There was a smidgen of chocolate at the side of her mouth, and her big eyes stared up at him sadly. She had just returned to Sanctuary, coming ahead of her mother and stepfather in advance of her mother's release from the hospital.

He couldn't speak to her; instead, he moved to go around her.

"Seth." Her little girl voice was eerie, filled with compassion, heartbreaking in its gentleness.

Seth turned back to her, cleared his throat and tried to speak. He couldn't.

"She'll come to you," Cassie whispered then. "When she awakens."

Seth shook his head, watching her, seeing the odd glow that came to those spooky eyes.

"Who, Cassie?" She was a strange little girl, but adorable. Innocent.

"Dawn," she said softly. "Let her awaken before you give up on her."

Fuck. He'd heard rumors, whispers of this kid's strange knowledge, her sometimes spooky advice. He shook his head, believing them now.

"She'll come to you." Her smile was sad. "And you'll both hurt. Remember that, Seth. You'll both hurt. But she'll be whole then."

Then she turned and walked slowly down the hall to the curved staircase and down the stairs. Seth felt a chill race up his spine, freezing his insides with the knowledge that Dawn would never come to him.

He waited, then followed slowly, moving to the marble foyer and turning to stare back at the entrance to the stairs that led to the infirmary. Where Dawn was under the doctor's care. Where she was hurt. Where she lay alone, wounded, without him.

He had imagined hanging around Sanctuary for a while. Getting to know her, finding ways to make her laugh, to just once see a smile in her eyes rather than that soul-deep sadness that seemed to permeate every part of her.

He wanted to take her on a picnic. He wanted to take her to the mall. He wanted to take her parking and kiss those perfect pink lips and he wanted to lay her down in the bed at his home and love her until she screamed for more.

And it wasn't going to happen.

He could have never imagined doing what he did next. He turned and slowly left Sanctuary, and the woman he knew would never come to him.

And in doing so, he left his soul behind.

· CHAPTER 1 ·

It was the dreams that brought her awake, sweating, snarling, terror and rage snaking through her system with icy chills and harsh, violent shudders.

Dawn cringed, flinched, her flesh crawling at the feel of icy hands ghosting over it, pinching, probing. She tightened her thighs as she fought to scream, feeling the touch there, hating it, snarling in rage at the pain she knew she was coming.

She prayed. God wasn't for her. He didn't care. He didn't listen to Breeds, but still she prayed. *Oh God, make it stop.*

She could hear the laughter at her ear, the hands prying at her legs, forcing them apart, securing them with the metal restraints as the cold steel bit into her thighs and warm flesh moved between them . . .

Her eyes snapped open; savage, inhuman growls were still tearing from her throat, rasping it as it clogged with the tears she couldn't shed. Her hands bunched in the blankets around her, her arms straight at her side, her legs stiff, the muscles cramped.

She felt restrained. She stared into the darkness, feeling the metal restraints cutting into her flesh, her blood seeping from her, agony resonating through her thighs, her stomach, as a stark red haze met her vision and a feline scream tried to tear from her throat.

She jerked upright, sightless, fighting to breathe, fighting to see what she couldn't see, to remember what she refused to remember. To breathe. Hands clenched on her flesh, fingers dug into the muscle, and laughter, always the laughter echoed in her head.

"Dawn's rising soon. It won't be dark any longer."

The soft, sweetly pitched voice whispered through the room as Dawn came from beneath the blankets in a surge of violent fury, crouched and snarling, feeling her lips peel back from her canines as she prepared to attack.

The enemy sat curled in the chair across the room, a long linen gown shrouding her figure, her waist long, pitch black curls framing her heart-shaped face, and her eyes eerie, brilliant blue glowing points in the darkness of the room.

It took Dawn a moment to realize that her weapon, never far from her side, was trained between the child's eyes. Her finger was trembling on the trigger, sweat pouring from her body, dampening the thin tank top and gray boxer panties she wore as she shivered in reaction.

The chill of the air conditioner washed over her flesh, sending a harsh shudder racing through her body as Cassie Sinclair stared at the weapon.

"You shouldn't have to wake in the dark alone," Cassie said gently, reaching out to turn on the light by the chair. Dawn flinched at the movement.

Growls vibrated in her throat, and a distant part of her screamed out in horror at the animal that had pushed ahead of her and stared at the kid with ruthless savagery.

She had to fight back the rage, the memories that weren't memories, that screamed in her head and refused to show themselves. The ones that the animal, determined to survive, refused to let the woman confront.

"Dash." The word was savage, guttural. "Where's Dash?"

The girl's father should never have allowed her there alone. He should watch after his daughter better, rather than allowing her to slip into a room with a beast that could already taste blood.

A single tear slipped down Cassie's cheek as her lips trembled. But there was no fear. No scent of terror, just of pain, compassion. And Dawn hated it.

She forced the weapon down. She forced herself to ease out of the crouch, but she couldn't force back the screams echoing in her head. A child's screams, an animal's screams, horrific in their terror and pain.

"Dad is still asleep," the girl said gently, her hand moving to indicate a tray that sat on a nearby table. There was a steaming pot there, two cups. "I thought we'd have some hot chocolate before you had to get ready and begin your day, Dawn. I didn't want you to have to wake alone this morning."

"Are you fucking crazy!" Dawn stared at the girl, well, young woman, really. Cassie wasn't a precocious child any longer. She was eighteen and still eerie as hell. "Don't you know better than this, Cassie?" She slapped her weapon to the bedside table as she collapsed on the side of the bed and stared back at her in horror. "I could have fucking killed you."

Cassie shrugged. "Death isn't that scary, Dawn. And better your bullet than a Coyote's rage, yes?"

Eighteen. Cassie was fucking eighteen. A baby. Innocent, sheltered and protected since the moment the Wolf Breed Dash Sinclair had found her and her mother in the middle of a freak blizzard and rescued them from the monsters chasing them ten years ago.

She was still a virgin. She had never been wounded, slapped, beaten or raped. And she spoke more casually of death than any mature, lab-raised Breed ever had.

Dawn jerked her shirt from the floor and wiped the sweat from her face before running the jersey material over her damp hair and shoulders. She needed a moment, just a moment, to get herself under control.

"I brought hot chocolate." Cassie uncurled herself slowly from the chair and moved like a wraith, like the ghosts it was said she spoke to, to the small table by a window.

She poured two mugs of the sweet, rich brew, turned back slowly and set one on the table beside Dawn. Dawn's hands were shaking so badly, the effects of the nightmare still so much a part of her, that she couldn't have held the mug if she'd had to.

Cassie retreated back to her chair, sat down and curled her legs under her once more. She was so tiny, Dawn thought. Barely five-three, delicate. She had so much damned hair flowing around her that sometimes Dawn wondered how she held her head up.

Dawn ran her fingers through her own short locks. She kept them hacked off. If her hair wasn't long then there was nothing for the enemy to grip. To hold her down with. A woman with long hair might as well extend an invitation to every bastard out there that would hurt her. Hold her down. Force her.

Bile rose in her throat.

"A new day is beginning," Cassie said, looking toward the still-dark window. "Today will begin a new adventure." A small, sad smile shaped her lips as she turned back to Dawn. "Every day is an adventure though, isn't it?"

"Is that what you call it?" Dawn snorted as she glanced at her, slowly finding the control she had fought for so desperately over the years.

"Mom and Dad always give me the same look when I tell them that." Cassie's lips tilted in a strange, knowing smile. "Kenton rolls his eyes at me." Kenton was her brother, barely nine, but already showing the advanced intelligence and strength of a Breed child.

"Cassie, now isn't a good time." Dawn sighed roughly. "I need to shower and get some things done."

Cassie stared down at her own drink, steam rising from the cup as her lips tilted in saddened resignation. "I hear that a lot too."

Dawn knew she did. Cassie was an anomaly among the Breeds. Her DNA was Wolf and Coyote as well as human. She'd been distrusted and often avoided as she grew older and her eyes deepened to that hypnotic blue. Centuries before she would have been burned at the stake as a witch.

Dawn cared for the girl though. She had been a regular visitor at Sanctuary over the years, first as a precocious child and now often as a prankster and teasing teenager.

"This is a bad time for me," Dawn gritted out, knowing that sometimes Cassie needed explanations, despite the spooky air of knowledge she carried with her.

"That's why I came." Cassie suddenly smiled, as though Dawn had given her the invitation to stay, and that smile lit up her eyes, making their glow brighter. "I knew it would be bad. And the dreams always make you grouchy. Today, you have to look forward to the adventure, Dawn. So I came to cheer you up before you could begin stressing over what you don't remember."

Dawn swallowed tightly and couldn't control the flinch at the reminder of things she didn't remember.

"Cassie . . ."

"Dawn. You helped save me when I was little. You and Sherra put your lives on the line for me. You were hurt then just as you've been hurt over the years defending Sanctuary. Let me do this."

"Do what?" Dawn shook her head in confusion. "What can you do for me, Cassie? Can you wipe the dreams away? Can you take away the past or change it? How in the hell do you think you can make this better? Sweetheart, if you want to make it better, go away and let me get control of myself."

"Like everyone else does?" Cassie sighed. "Everyone goes away so you can think, so you can work, so you can sleep and so you can dream alone. Even Seth went away, didn't he?"

Dawn stilled. She felt something inside her, something that had been relaxing, freeze. She didn't want to hear about Seth, she didn't want to think about Seth. He was better off away from Sanctuary and away from her.

"What does Seth have to do with anything?"

Seth Lawrence of Lawrence Industries, one of the Breeds' greatest proponents and supporters, and he was one man she couldn't afford to think about.

"He was here the other day, arguing with Jonas. Did you hear?" Cassie tilted her head to the side. "He doesn't like Jonas much, you know."

"No one likes Jonas much." Dawn inhaled slowly, the irrational terror slowly easing inside her.

"Everyone likes Seth though." Cassie waggled her brows as she uncurled from the chair and moved to the bed.

Dawn watched as Cassie Sinclair plopped at the bottom of the bed, crossed her legs and leaned forward intently.

"Seth is *hawt*," she drawled.

Dawn winced. "Seth is too old for you, Cassie." She forced herself to keep her voice calm, unemotional. What the hell did she care who found Seth sexy? It was nothing to her. She wouldn't let it become something to her.

"He's still hot." Cassie wrinkled her nose. "For an old man."

"He's not an old man." And Dawn assured herself she hadn't just gritted the words out.

"Give it up." Cassie laughed. "Though I have to give him credit: He doesn't look like he's aged a day in the last ten years. You know, he was voted one of the world's most eligible bachelors last month on one of those society shows I saw on television."

Dawn clenched her teeth. She didn't need to know that. At the very mention of Seth's name her entire body seemed to respond. Her flesh felt more sensitive, her tongue itched and the tiny hairs along her body lifted almost sensually.

And fear knotted her stomach.

She knew what Seth Lawrence was to her, and to her body. She also knew what he was to her mind. He could break her like nothing that had ever happened in the past.

"I don't want to talk about Seth, Cassie." She rose from the bed and moved to the closet, where she pulled out her uniform for the day. Snug black mission pants and a matching tank top.

"You never want to talk about Seth," Cassie said then. "He asks about you though. Every time he sees me he asks how you're doing."

Dawn froze. Cassie always knew more than others. She saw or sensed things no one else could.

"And what do you tell him?" she asked almost fearfully.

"I usually tell him the same thing. You haven't awoken yet."

"You tell him I'm asleep?" She turned back to the child incredulously.

"I tell him you haven't awoken yet," she repeated, a mysterious smile playing about her lips. "It's enough for him."

"And what did you tell him this time?" Dawn tilted her head, not certain why she asked.

Cassie watched her for long seconds before answering.

"This time, I told him I was certain you would be awake soon." She frowned and looked down at her hot chocolate. "Sometimes though, it doesn't matter if you wake up, does it?"

She shrugged her thin shoulders before giving her head a shake and sipping at the chocolate.

"Cassie, are you trying to tell me something?" Sometimes, Cassie talked in riddles. A person had to know when she was doing it or they would walk around with more confusion than they needed.

"It's time to wake up," Cassie said softly, looking toward the window, and the faint hint of dawn that peeked through the curtains, before turning back to Dawn. "The nightmares are getting worse, and so is the mating heat."

Dawn turned away and stalked to her dresser, where she jerked serviceable black panties from one drawer and a bra from another. There was nothing fancy, nothing seductive. Black socks followed, and after she showered and dressed, she would lace black hiking boots on her feet. She was a Breed Enforcer. Inside and out. She was strong, powerful; she commanded and she led. She no longer whimpered and cowered from the horror of whatever she fought to keep hidden within her own mind. Or the man that haunted her like one of Cassie's ghosts.

"I'm not talking about Seth." And she sure as hell wasn't talking about mating heat.

"Fine." Cassie shrugged. "We'll talk about Styx. Or we could talk about Stygian. They're totally hot too. Though I have to be careful if Dad is around. He gets pretty pissed when Styx flirts with me."

Dawn wanted to shake her head at the abrupt change of the conversation.

"He wouldn't flirt if you didn't force him into begging for that chocolate you carry around."

Cassie's smile was all woman now. A hint of mystery, of feminine knowledge. "He could get chocolate elsewhere if he wanted to."

The red-haired, bolder-than-brass Scottish Wolf Breed was a shameless flirt. He had been inducted into the Bureau of Breed Affairs months before and had been assigned to Dawn's team just weeks ago.

"Styx isn't the serious type, Cassie."

"I'm eighteen. I'm not a child any longer, Dawn," Cassie pointed out.

"Tell that to your dad, not to me." Dash Sinclair was serious about protecting his daughter. Both her physical safety and her heart.

"As if Dad would listen." Cassie shrugged then rose from the bed and glanced at the window again before turning back to Dawn. "Dawn is awakening," she said again, and a chill swept over Dawn. "Are you ready for it?"

Dawn licked her lips, glanced at the window, then back at Cassie.

"What's going to happen, Cassie?" she finally asked, knowing, sensing that the girl knew so much more than she was saying.

"An adventure." Cassie suddenly smiled. "Come on, Dawn. It's a new day. And we're going to have lots of fun."

Fun. Dawn stared at the girl as though she had lost her mind. "Cassie, I'm going to work."

"For now." She tossed her head, throwing the long, loose curls behind her shoulder as she moved for the door, ethereal in her long gown, like a precocious fairy. "You're working for now, Dawn. But . . ." Cassie glanced to the window once again before turning back to her. "It's time to wake up."

With those last words eerie Cassandra Sinclair slipped out of her bedroom and closed the door behind her, leaving Dawn alone.

Just as Seth had left her alone.

◆　◆　◆

Time to wake up, her ass. Well, she was sure as hell awake now and madder than hell. Men. She hated men. Men were a plague on the female species and their arrogant, know-it-all attitudes were hampering her job on every side. And now. Now, to add insult to injury, her own brother, Callan, was joining their detestable ranks.

Dawn slammed into the communications bunker set into the mountain that rose above Sanctuary and slammed the heavy metal door behind her. Inside, radar, infrared, electronic maps and locator pinpoints beeped and flashed along the walls. There was a map of the mountain, the town, the surrounding lands and even a display of the cave system that ran within the mountains surrounding them. One of those systems was incomplete and getting more incomplete by the day.

"Micah, move into position."

Dawn's head swung around at the sound of Callan's voice, a spurt of surprise filling her that he seemed to be overseeing a mission. Callan rarely had time to involve himself in the actual missions that Breeds now hired themselves out for. Yet it seemed he had made time for one.

She moved closer, remaining quiet as she stared at the image displayed on the viewing screen in front of him.

The girl that had been kidnapped in the Middle East, she remembered now. She was the daughter of one of the Tyler Clan's friends, family of Callan's mate and wife, Merinus. A Breed unit had been sent in to rescue her.

"Flint, you have a go," Callan murmured into the communication link, a slender mic that curved around his cheek and attached to the ear-bud receiver at his ear.

"I have a visual." The Breed's voice echoed hollowly from the communications speaker at the side of the viewing screen.

Onscreen another image popped in alongside the main image. The image was hazy, but they could see the inside of a cell and the small, huddled form of the young woman.

"Guards are out." Another voice came through. "I'm on the locks."

Dawn watched as the small team moved with coordinated control. The cell door opened slowly and the young woman's frightened whimpers into the filthy mattress where she was huddled echoed through the intercom.

Dawn flinched at the sound, echoes of it drifting through her head. She could feel her chest clenching at the remembered feel of her dreams, and that very sound tearing from her own lips.

"You're safe." Flint McCain moved into position beside her and quickly tested the area and the woman for explosives. "We're clear."

He turned the girl over, putting his fingers to her lips before she could cry out. "Your father sent us. Can you walk?"

Her clothing was torn. The T-shirt was ripped down one shoulder, and her jeans were crusted with dirt and what appeared to be blood along one side.

She nodded quickly. Her face was heavily bruised, one eye nearly swollen shut as she tried to scramble to her feet.

Her leg gave out from under her. Before she could cry out in pain, a black-clad hand covered her lips and the Breed pulled her against him.

"They'll tie you to my back," he whispered into her ear, the words drifting through the intercom. "Then we're good to go, okay? Your dad is waiting back at base. Just a quick little run around the block then we'll jump into a jazzy little jet we have waiting. We're out of here."

He kept talking as two other Breeds quickly strapped her to his back; then they were easing out of the block cell and fading into the night.

Callan pulled the earpiece from his ear, tossed it to the table

and turned to his brother-in-law and the head of Sanctuary's security, Kane Tyler.

"Keep me up to date," he told Kane quietly. "I want to know
the second they reach base. Have them cancel layover there and
head straight back here. We're going to need them."

Kane moved into Callan's position with a nod of his dark
head, his expression intent as he watched the images that flipped
in and out in their own small boxes within the screen.

"You're with me," he told Dawn as he turned away.

He was angry with her. She always knew when Callan was
angry. Before, the thought of that anger would have had her
heart knocking in terror. Now it had her lips tightening in frustration. She didn't have time to deal with his irked mood.

"What the hell is going on?" she hissed as they made their
way through the long steel-and-cement bunker beneath the
ground. "I was halfway through those caves when you pulled
me out. Do you have any idea how long it's taken us to clear out
those explosives and lay the sensors through there?"

"I'm aware of the order I gave you a week ago to find another project," he growled as they turned from the main bunker
and headed down a short corridor to another large map and im-
aging room. "Do you think we need to lose six of our women,
our sisters, to those fucking explosives, Dawn? Son of a bitch,
what the hell has gotten into you?"

"You pulled me out because we're women?" Outrage raced
through her. "That is so damned bogus, Callan."

"You're damned right I pulled you out because you're
women. The fact that you're not the only one that would suffer
if you died didn't occur to you, did it, Dawn?" he snarled. "You
hide your head in the shadows and try to pretend it's just you.
What happens to your mate if you die?"

"I haven't mated."

"And I don't want to hear your lies to yourself," he snapped
as they turned again.

This was Mission Central. It was larger than the other room;
the murmur of voices—electronic, Breed and human—filtered
through it as they strode along the central walkway.

She bit back the enraged words trembling on her lips and
fought to use logic instead. He liked logic. It had swayed him
before.

"My team is specifically trained for just what they're doing," she hissed. "Those are still my people, my team, Callan."

"I need those women elsewhere. They were to be trained for new missions and you knew it," he growled as they stood aside for the black-clad operators working to get one of the viewing screens operational.

"That's my team, you agreed. And those caves were my project."

They moved into another corridor, heading she knew for the top secret mission control room. Here, the operations going out weren't mercenary in nature, but those of national security.

"Those women need to learn to work with the male members of this community and I'm tired of asking you nicely to obey those commands," Callan snapped, his head swinging around to glare at her. "You don't make the decisions around here, little sister. I do. I needed you to train a new team—"

"Of men," she sneered. "Come on, Callan, you know that's not going to work."

"I know you have no choice now." He stopped at a metal door, slid the secured card along the sensor and stepped inside when the door unlocked. "I'm short on teams and we have an emergency. That means you're up. And, by God, you better hope you're ready for it, because failure on this one is not an option."

The door clanged shut as one particular scent threatened to overwhelm Dawn's senses. She stared across the room, unable to move, to speak, to do anything but soak in the heat, the nectar of his scent and the regret that filled her.

"Hello, Dawn." Seth Lawrence rose from the long table in the center of the room. "It's been a while."

CHAPTER 2

Dawn's Awakening.

Dawn stared at Seth, and felt the animalistic side of her nature give a slow, sensual, mental stretch. Her body tensed as her muscles wanted to soften. She tightened her thighs as they threatened to weaken. But nothing could shut down the scent of him moving through her pores.

He stood across the room, dressed elegantly. A silk suit, dark of course. Today it was a dark gray, to match his eyes. Thick dark brown hair was conservatively cut; he was clean shaven, the strong planes and angles of his face showing arrogant aristocracy. The sharp blade of his nose, the strong set of his chin, the hewn lines of his jaw.

Beneath the silk his body was powerfully corded. She could sense it. She could feel his strength pouring off him, and the female animal inside her responded to it. He was a strong, able mate. He would be a protector and a partner. He was virile, he would have endurance. He would breed strong children and ride her through the storm that mating heat brewed inside her body.

Her breath shortened. She felt as though she couldn't drag enough air into her lungs, she couldn't focus, couldn't see anything but the man watching her so solemnly from across the shadowed room.

"Why is he here?" She was amazed that her voice sounded so calm, so confident as Callan moved around her.

"If you had hung around the house the last week instead of deliberately defying me, you would know," he snorted. "Come over here. I'll explain everything."

She flushed at the subtle ass-chewing but did as she was ordered. Callan could be pushed sometimes. When it came to family, he had an incredible amount of patience. But she knew she had pushed him as far as she dared. And she knew she wouldn't be here unless something was about to go seriously wrong.

Moving across the room, she took the seat farthest from Seth, and closest to the vent that provided ventilation and air-conditioning. His scent wasn't as strong here, the elusive smell of an aroused male, powerful and in his sexual prime, didn't torment her as it would farther down the table.

There were others in the room; she knew they were there, her senses picked them up and identified them. But she only saw Seth, even as she forced her eyes to lower, she kept sight of him from the corner of her eyes.

Jonas was at a smaller viewing screen farther back in the room, talking on a link. Mercury Warrant, Lawe Justice and Rule Breaker, his personal security force, stood silently, not far from him.

Styx was there. Stygian Black, the huge, dark black Wolf Breed, stood beside him. Stygian was darker skinned than most Breeds, his DNA having come from a rogue black wolf it was said, and possibly a voodoo priestess from New Orleans. The records found in the lab he nearly destroyed bare-handed had hinted at a broad selection of DNA mixed into his genetics.

One of Dawn's Lionesses was in attendance, Moira Calhoun. She was Irish, and a hellion if ever there was one. And standing closest to the door was Noble Chavin, a mysterious, less-than-social Jaguar.

"Meet your new team, Dawn." Callan waved toward the Breeds her senses had picked up.

Dawn glanced at the four then stared back at Callan.

"I'm command?" She rarely commanded men. They rarely got along with her, and she sure didn't get along with them.

"You're command." He nodded his head, his long hair feathering over his shoulders, more like a lion's mane than a man's head of hair. But he was pride leader for a reason.

"And we're here why?" She pushed back her anger, showing him the respect he deserved while in front of others.

"Because every other team is currently out busting their asses around the world and we have a major situation on our hands." Jonas moved forward as the other Breeds took their seats around the table.

Dawn slid her PDA from the protective holster at her side, jacked it into the connector set within the table and waited for the mission information to load.

She scanned the stats as they came in, fighting to keep her eyes off Seth as he watched her. She could feel his eyes caressing her.

Then the information loading into the small, palm-sized screen had her stiffening, restraining a growl and fighting back primal fury.

Her eyes lifted to Seth, her gaze tracking over him, making certain he was unharmed, that nothing showed of the attack that had been made on him. Her gaze rolled over his face, his shoulders; she inhaled carefully, desperate now to detect any sign of injury.

"As you're seeing, the situation is pretty damned imperative," Jonas bit out. "We've had one attempt made on Mr. Lawrence in the last week, and intel has come in that we can expect another."

"Cancel the meeting." Dawn didn't look at anyone else. She made the demand of Seth, her voice resonating with the fury building inside her. "You can't afford to take this chance."

"And if I hide now, then I may as well lock myself into a bunker and hide for the rest of my life." Those sensual, seductive lips curled in disgust. "The meeting stands."

"It's two weeks," she snapped. "How can you possibly expect us to cover you during the house party from hell, Seth?"

"I don't, Dawn," he admitted frankly. "The team is Jonas and Callan's idea. I won't back down. The board of directors to Lawrence Industries meets biannually to discuss the policies of the company as well as any other issues that come up. This year, a motion to dismiss the funding of Sanctuary is on the table by several of the older members. If we cancel the meeting, you can bet that funding will be placed on hold until the next meeting."

Could Sanctuary do without that funding?

"Jonas, there's no way to do this." She glared back at the director of the Bureau of Breed Affairs. "Not one team alone, and not with the area laid out to defend against." She waved her hand to the property that showed up on the viewing screen across the room.

"Lawrence Estate is reasonably secure—"

"It's a security nightmare," Dawn bit out.

Seth let a mocking smile curl his lips as he tilted his head in acknowledgment.

"Be that as it may, if I alter the location or the current plans, it will be a sign of weakness. If the Breeds' enemies want to get rid of me, they'll have to come to me. Jonas's intel suggests they'll make the attempt during this time. It's our best chance to control the outcome and learn why they've decided the support of Lawrence Industries to the Breeds is a threat to them."

"And it could be someone totally unrelated to the company that just doesn't want you supporting Sanctuary," Dawn argued.

Seth shook his head. "This is about someone within Lawrence Industries or close to it. Someone who believes they can take control if they can kill me."

"And you're playing right into their hands," she snapped.

"Enough." Callan's voice was calm, but the warning edge to it wasn't lost on Dawn. It wasn't lost, but it was ignored.

"Cancel the meeting, Seth."

He pursed his lips and watched her for a few moments, his long, powerful fingers tapping silently against the table before he slowly shook his head. "Canceling the meeting will only allow my assassins to catch me by surprise. If I'm going to die, Dawn, I'm going to face my murderers." He turned to Jonas then. "But she won't be part of the operation. Choose someone else or the deal is off."

He rose to his feet as though it were a board meeting. As though he could decide whether she was there or not.

"Choose someone else and I'll shoot him myself," Dawn snarled, jumping to her feet and slapping her palms against the table as she glared back at Seth. "What's wrong with me heading this operation?"

He tilted his head and stared back at her as he buttoned his jacket casually, his movements unconsciously graceful.

"You're a woman," he stated. "This isn't a mission I want a woman involved in."

"Well isn't that just too bad for you, sweetcheeks." She threw her hip to the side, propped her hand on it and regarded him with mocking sweetness as she wrinkled her nose back at him insultingly. "If you're insane enough to go through with your own execution, then I want to at least watch. I haven't seen a good comedy flick in a while."

His eyes narrowed back at her.

"Dawn, sit down," Callan ordered.

"When he does."

"As far as I'm concerned, this meeting is over." Seth turned to Jonas. "When you have the proper team formed, let me know."

"Callan, have an enforcer collect my travel bag, I'll be heading out with Mr. Lawrence."

She was insane, that was all there was to it. Where the hell were these words coming from? Shooting out of her mouth as though she somehow controlled the situation.

No one spoke. Dawn could feel the tension building in the room as all eyes settled on her and Seth.

"You will not—"

"Let you walk out of here into a firing squad," she snapped.

"Dammit, Dawn, I know what I'm doing," he snapped back.

"Oh, do you?" she drawled. "Well, Seth, why don't you just instruct little ole me and my team while you're doing it. Because you're not doing it alone. And you're not doing it with another team."

She wanted to be as far away from him as possible. Being in the same country with him was bad enough. Being stuck on an island, a sultry, heated island, was going to be hell. Dawn could feel the sweat beginning to crawl down her back, the fear that knotted her stomach and the arousal that throbbed deep inside her sex.

And she felt fear. Fear that someone, that something, would take him out of this world and then she really would be alone.

His lips tightened as his eyes swirled with anger, the gray darkening like a violent thundercloud.

"You heard me, Jonas," he stated, his voice commanding.

"Callan, have you sent that enforcer after my travel bag yet?" she asked.

No one spoke, and she didn't risk tearing her gaze from

Seth's long enough to see how far she had pissed her pride leader off.

"I'll tell you what we will do." Callan rose to his feet slowly. "We'll leave you two alone to discuss this for a few moments before we return to finalize the mission." His voice was carefully bland as the others rose to their feet and began to move toward the door.

Dawn could feel the amusement. Male amusement, of course, as she continued to face down Seth. She couldn't tear her eyes away from him, couldn't make herself back down.

How long had it been since she had been close enough to really smell him? So close that his scent was almost a taste against her tongue.

So long. Too long. She had avoided him during the rare visits he made to Sanctuary. She had refused the occasional missions that would have placed her anywhere close to him. She had fought her need for him, her body's need for him, and every demand that roiled inside her that she rub against him, stroke him and share the hunger that ate her alive.

She could have continued to avoid him, she told herself. This meant nothing. She was just concerned about him. He was her sister-in-law's brother. That was it. She latched on to the excuse like a life preserver. Seth was family. She had to protect him. She would never forgive herself otherwise and neither would Roni ever forgive her.

Seth had to live. The thought of anything less terrified her.

As the door to the room closed, leaving her and Seth alone, she continued to stare back at him, refusing to break eye contact or the connection she could feel inside her. Even furious with her, he was connected to her. Why hadn't she known that before? All the years she had watched him from afar, hoping to catch a glimpse of him even as she told herself she didn't want or need him, why hadn't she known what she was feeling when their eyes locked as they were now?

Instinct fought a battle with her conscious mind, the animal and the woman struggling to agree on their needs, what they could and couldn't have. She couldn't have him. But that instinctive part of herself, the animal, screamed out for the man it knew was her mate.

"You've grown more stubborn," he said softly, breaking that contact, and she drew in a harsh breath at the loss of it.

He shoved his hands in the pockets of his trousers and regarded her solemnly. "You know this isn't going to work, Dawn." He shook his head, as though regretting that fact. "I would be too busy trying to protect you. Too busy worrying about you. I won't be focused."

"Then we'll die together." She shrugged as though it didn't matter.

She could feel the waves of anger pouring off him, despite his calm. Yeah, Seth was controlled. Nearly as controlled as she was, perhaps more. He was steel, inside and out, hard and strong, and sometimes, she thought, invincible. But he was still human. Still flesh and blood. And he could still die.

"You say that so casually," he drawled. "We'll die together. Excuse me while I sneer, sweetheart, but I think you've been watching too much television."

"I don't watch television." She shrugged. "I don't listen to romantic music, and I don't tell ghost stories around campfires. What I do, and what I do well, is protection. You'll not be the first spoiled little rich boy I've had to babysit."

She expected an explosion with that one.

"I won't be the one to get you killed either," he stated coldly. "I'll inform Jonas the mission is off."

She stared at him furiously as he turned and moved to the door, something inside her breaking at the knowledge that he was serious.

Heedless of the consequences, Dawn moved around the table quickly and reached for him. But before she could touch, before she could feel, the warmth of his flesh through his clothes, he turned on her.

Dawn stared back at his face in fascination. The anger that tightened his features, the pure fury that darkened his eyes.

"Don't touch me, Dawn." His eyes were as cold as ice. "I've spent ten years getting over the effect you have on me. Ten years getting my own life back. I won't allow you to destroy the progress I made."

And it hit her then. She inhaled, her lips parting as she realized Seth was no longer in mating heat.

Dawn stumbled back at half step, the breath suddenly slicing into her lungs at the realization that she had lost him. Completely lost him.

"That's not possible," she whispered, suddenly horrified. "Mating heat doesn't just go away."

His lips twisted mockingly. "Not when mates are together, perhaps. Not when they touch, when they love. Not when there's something more binding them together than the brief little contacts we had, Dawn." His gaze flickered over her, regret shimmering within the anger. "There wasn't even a kiss to bind us, was there, sweetheart? Just my determination and arrogance. That doesn't get a man far, does it?"

But she was still his mate. The thought was disjointed, unconnected, as her gaze went over him, her senses reaching for him. There was none of her scent on him, no sign of the mating heat or of arousal. She was only barely aware of the furious little growl that came from her throat.

"There you go. Another reason you won't be part of this operation. Because I'll be damned if I let your effect on me destroy me again. Do us both a favor, Agent Daniels. Stay the hell away from me."

He jerked the door open and stalked out of the room, brushing past the others while she stared at his back in horrified awareness.

He wasn't her mate any longer. She felt her nails biting into her palm as Jonas turned slowly to stare at her.

"Delay his departure," she snarled.

The corners of his eyes twitched, as though he had only barely held back the widening of them.

"If he's refusing protection, Dawn, there's nothing we can do," he told her reasonably.

Dawn didn't want to hear reasonable. She didn't want logic and she didn't want an argument.

"Delay his departure an hour. Let him think he won. Lie to him, I don't care, you're good at that. But do something."

"And where will you be?" he asked.

"I have to talk to Ely." She had to stop shuddering. It wasn't showing on the outside, but on the inside she was coming apart and she couldn't handle it. "I have to talk to her now."

She brushed past the group, barely restraining a flinch each time her flesh came into contact with their bodies, reminding her that Seth might have gotten over her, but she was a long way from being cured.

She was aware of his eyes on her as she stalked through Mission Control. She knew exactly where he was, standing to the side, where he discussed one of the satellites he had given the Breeds free use of. His voice was low, but she heard him. Heard him beneath the other voices that filled the cavernous room as she hurried through it.

When had this happened? When had Seth stopped reacting to the mating heat that she had been warned had begun in him ten years before? It had to have been recently. As Cassie had stated, he hadn't aged a day in ten years. The mating heat slowed down the aging process considerably. He still looked in his early thirties. He was still strong and powerful, but he no longer carried her scent.

It was all she could do to keep from running from the communications bunker back to the estate. When she reached it, she slammed into the back door, ignoring the women sitting at the table, the children laughing and playing as they ate.

There were three Breed children now, and Tanner's wife and mate was carrying twins to add to them. Dawn hadn't thought she would want children, had never given them consideration. But regret sliced deep as well. She felt bombarded from all sides, rage and pain, regret and aching need racing through her as she made her way to the basement level of the estate house and pushed her way into Dr. Elyiana Morrey's office.

Ely looked up in surprise from the files she was reading as Dawn slammed the door behind her.

"It's not time for another treatment, Dawn."

It had become a battle between them. The hormonal treatments had had to be adjusted almost weekly to keep the effects of the mating heat from driving Dawn insane.

"Why didn't you tell me?" The words rasped from her throat, hollow and filled with pain.

Ely blinked back at her. "Tell you what?"

"Why didn't you tell me that you had found a cure for my mate?" she sneered, enraged. "You can cure him but you can't cure me?" The accusation was unfounded, and it wasn't the point.

The animal part of her was screaming in pain, in rage. It didn't want a cure. It wanted the mate. The touch, the bond, the connection to what belonged to it. To her.

Ely sighed heavily and shook her head as she rose to her feet and carried a file to the large wood cabinet on the other side of the room.

"I didn't think you would be interested, just to start with." She shrugged before brushing the thick strands of her dark brunette hair back from her face and adjusting her glasses on her face. "And it's an anomaly I'm still studying."

"How long have you known?" Something inside her was breaking apart, shattering.

Ely took a deep breath. "Almost a year for certain. The hormonal levels began leveling off in him nearly four years ago. There are only minute quantities showing up in his system now. Within a few months, I expect his system will be completely free of the heat."

Dawn sat down slowly in the upholstered chair closest to her and stared back at Ely. "Why not in me?" she whispered, feeling strangely hollow now, alone, in a way she hadn't felt in ten years.

"I don't know, Dawn," Ely said softly. "I suspect it's because it began in you. Your Breed physiology may not allow for the hormone levels to recede."

She stared back at Ely, her breathing rough, while inside—inside she felt the Cougar that so often lay dormant rising furiously. It snarled. Rage tore through the instinctive Breed synapses and shot through the woman's mind.

She wasn't just a woman. A woman who had lain alone, ached and fought the nightmares of a past that she couldn't escape. She was also a mate, and the man she had claimed so long ago was breaking the bonds that held them together.

"Dawn, you should be happy for this," Ely told her gently. "I know it's bothered you that Seth suffers . . ."

"He's mine!" She came out of the chair in a burst of furious energy.

Ely stared back at her in surprise for long seconds. "Not any longer, Dawn. Seth is no longer your mate. And hopefully, in time, the mating heat will recede from your system as well."

• CHAPTER 3 •

Dawn remembered, ten years before, when Seth and his father had arrived at Sanctuary to claim Taber's mate, Roni, as their family. She was Aaron Lawrence's daughter and Seth's half sister. They had been searching for her for years, and had found her during a newscast that reported that Roni Andrews, a known associate of the Breeds, carried a mark on her neck similar to that which was rumored to be a mating mark.

They had crashed through the gates of Sanctuary, and Cassie Sinclair had run through the Breeds surrounding their limo, careless of her own safety, and jumped inside to ensure that these unknown people were protected.

Dawn and her team had been assigned to guard them in one of the guest houses during that week, and she had gotten to know Seth in a way she had never known another man.

His dominance and power lay beneath the surface of the man. He was steel hard on the inside, but he knew how to smile and how to laugh. He knew how to tease her gently, how to brush against her or touch her without making her stomach contract with terror.

He had been the perfect gentleman, to a point. What he didn't say or act on was always in his eyes though. A simmering heat, a promise of wicked lusts, of a man that knew all the ways of pleasure.

Dawn didn't know pleasure. She had never known a lover's touch, never felt a lover's kiss, until Seth. Until his lips had brushed against hers and for the first time in her life she had been close to a man without being sick with fear.

And then everything had gone to hell. The chauffeur/body-guard Seth had with him had been a Council spy, and he'd caught her and Seth by surprise. He had managed to knock Seth out and secure Dawn to a chair under the threat of killing him.

And then he had touched her. While Seth had watched, en-raged, he had fondled her breasts, slapped her, taunted Seth and threatened to rape Dawn in front of his eyes.

But it wouldn't be the first time she had been raped, the man had sneered at her. Wasn't she no more than a plaything for the guards at the lab she had been created in?

And she had seen Seth's eyes when he said it. Seen the flash of horror and of pity, and she had hated them both. Before he left, the chauffeur had decided to make certain she was de-fenseless by hitting her in the head with something. The butt of his weapon she was told. She was unconscious for days. When she awoke, the nightmares began again, and she learned that the simple brushing of Seth's lips against hers, the touch of his hand against her neck, had begun the mating heat.

And she had cursed it.

Until now.

As she packed her travel bag the next day, a heavy duffel nearly half her size, rage was beating a harsh tattoo in her views. Jonas had sent Mercury, Lawe and Rule, along with the rest of the team he had chosen for her to command, with Seth to his little island estate.

And horrifyingly enough, Dash Sinclair, his wife, Elizabeth, and daughter, Cassie, were going to be in attendance as well. The two-week-long biannual meeting was no more than an ex-cuse for a huge house party. It was going to be a nightmare. Why in the hell Dash would take Elizabeth and Cassie there, she didn't have a clue.

And tonight, Sanctuary's heli-jet would fly her in. She would be taking command of the team under the watchful eye of the enigmatic Dash Sinclair, and pulling that one off had taken a lot of fancy talking.

Dash was one of the few Breeds who hadn't been raised completely within the Council labs they were created in. He had escaped at the tender age of ten, been placed in the foster system and joined the army at eighteen. When he found his mate and her daughter, he had taken the skills he had learned and used them to benefit the Breeds, and Sanctuary. He had been a major force in aligning the Feline, Wolf and rebel Coyotes together into a power that was slowly being accepted within the world.

"Are you sure you want to do this, Dawn?" Callan stood in her open doorway, his expression creased into lines of worry as she swung around to face him.

She shoved an extra weapon inside the bag, and stored the clips of ammo in the side before answering him.

"Ely said he's not my mate anymore." She was grieving and she knew it. Just as she knew she had no right to grieve.

She had stayed as far away from him as possible over the past ten years, suffering, knowing he was probably suffering too. Knowing he hadn't been just pissed her off now. She had suffered alone. Hurt alone. She had been alone, just as she always was.

"Dawn."

She flinched as he touched her arm, then moved away from him.

"Are you sure you want to do this?" he asked her again. "You're not focused."

"I'm second command." She shrugged. "And with Jonas's team there, I feel more confident. I . . ." She swallowed tightly as she avoided his gaze. "I can't not go."

"Dawn, why didn't you tell me what Dayan was doing to you?"

She flinched violently. It was so long ago. In a life she didn't want to remember. Her pride brother, Dayan. He hadn't been sane, but he had hid the insanity so well. He had worked them all to one degree or another. Playing Callan against the soldiers sent after him, betraying his whereabouts to them so he spent more and more time away from the home base they had established. And while Callan was gone, he had worked insidiously to destroy her and Sherra.

Sherra had been stronger though. She'd had the memories of her mate, Kane, to hold on to. Dawn had only the nightmares that Dayan had preyed upon. And the fear.

"I didn't know what he was doing to me," she finally whispered, lifting her head, feeling the shame that filled her as Callan's amber eyes darkened painfully. "The Council taught him well, Callan. That wasn't your fault. You can't take the blame for what he did anymore."

For how Dayan had maneuvered the men of the pride, how he had built upon her and Sherra's fears. Sherra had her memories though; Dawn had somehow managed to repress hers, and nothing she did now revealed them.

"He didn't rape me, Callan," she whispered.

"Yes, he did," he said heavily. "He raped your mind, Dawn. If I could kill him daily for the rest of my life, I would. I'd make him suffer as he never could have imagined."

Dayan had been his pride brother. Callan had risked his life for all of them, gave his life for them in the years he had protected them. All of them. And Dayan had betrayed him at every turn.

"It doesn't matter." She drew in a hard, deep breath. "The heli-jet's waiting on me. I have to go."

"Dawn." His voice sharpened, stopping her as she moved to jerk the duffel from her bed.

"What, Callan?" she snapped back. "What more do you want me to say?"

"He's going to want more from you than that part of you that refuses to let him go," he warned her harshly. "Do you understand me? Seth isn't a monk. He won't take vows of celibacy for you. And running to him, restarting the mating process without the clear intention of sleeping with that man is wrong. I have half a mind to order you to stay here." He pushed his hands through his hair in frustration. "Dammit, he doesn't deserve this any more than you do."

"He's mine!" The cry ripped from her throat.

"And he will demand your presence in his bed," he snarled. "I'm a mate, Dawn, I know what the mating heat does to a man. And God's truth, I would have committed suicide rather than do to my mate what Seth knows he's going to do to you. Let him go."

"Is this why you're here?" She felt her face contort in pain, her chest tighten with it, as she waved her hand at him in agitation. "To order me away from him?"

"He's making a life for himself. A chance to be a man, Dawn. A husband. A father."

She froze as she read the truth in his eyes.

"He has a lover." Her throat felt closed off, as though she were strangling on her own pain and rage.

Oh God, he was touching another woman? Sleeping with her? Holding her?

"Dawn—"

She jerked her hands up, shaking, the pain rising inside her until she was surprised it didn't bring her to her knees, didn't send her into an agony so intense she was screaming from it.

Her flesh, every cell in her body, was raging in denial. It couldn't happen. It wouldn't happen. He was her mate.

"He intends to announce his engagement during the gathering at Lawrence Island," he told her softly. "He didn't want to hurt you. He didn't want to make this painful for you, Dawn. I want you to stay here. I want you to let him go."

◆   ◆   ◆

Callan stepped back slowly at the expression that contorted Dawn's face, and the furious, inhuman growl that left her throat. She was shaking. He could see the muscles in her upper arms and chest twitching beneath the skin. Her upper lip curled back at one corner to flash those small, delicate canines.

Everything about Dawn was delicate, except the rage and pain that he saw flashing in her eyes, in her expression. Tears gathered and fell down her cheeks, and he stared at the sight in awe. Dawn had never cried. From the night he had carried her from the labs, to this second, Dawn had never shed a tear.

But two eased slowly down her cheeks now and he doubted she even realized it.

He could see the sense of betrayal she felt, and the agony. He knew himself as Merinus's mate—if he ever realized the mating had reversed and she longed for another, he would have shed blood. His and the man who held his mate's heart. It would be too much to be borne. And it was because of this that he and Jonas had decided to wait until Seth left to tell her what they had learned. What Seth hadn't told them until he learned Dawn would be on Lawrence Island.

As he watched, her expression stilled, froze, and he expected her to do as she had always done. Go hunting. Go chasing explosives in caves or council soldiers somewhere else. He didn't expect what came.

"My mate," she said coldly. "He might have a lover now, but he won't have one for long."

She jerked her duffel bag from the bed.

"And if he loves her, Dawn? What then? Do you love Seth enough to let him go? Or just enough to make both of you miserable?"

She paused, her back to him, the muscles jumping beneath the skin.

"Would you walk away?" she asked. "Could you?"

He debated lying to her. She sounded lost, lonely, more so than he believed he had ever heard in her voice. She deserved nothing less than the truth.

Callan sighed wearily. "If Merinus had suffered the hell you've suffered, I wouldn't have a choice. Her happiness would mean more to me than the knowledge that I could claim her without giving her the benefits of that claiming."

"He's mine," she whispered again and he heard the tears he knew she was now hiding from him.

Her voice was ripping his heart in half though. God, she was the baby of their family, the one most abused, the one he had wanted to shelter the most. She was more to him than a sister, nearly as dear to him as his own son. And the broken, agonized sound of her voice made him plead to God to ease her path, because he knew she wouldn't.

"Dawn. He deserves more than a claiming," he said gently, hating Seth Lawrence now more than he had ever hated him, for the pain Dawn suffered over him. But the man deserved more, just as Dawn did. Unfortunately, Callan feared Dawn would break rather than accept the memories she hid from.

"He started it," she cried out, and the sound of her voice was painful to hear. "He touched when he was warned not to. He touched when I whispered the risks to him. He touched me . . ." Her voice broke. "Now he can suffer as well, by God. Because I'll be damned if another woman will steal what's mine."

She jerked the strap of the duffel over her shoulder and strode from the room. The little warrior, that was how he always thought of her. Dressed in her uniform, too delicate to do the things he knew she did. She fought full-grown Breed males and she could put a hurting on them. She faced explosives and Council soldiers and drew blood with a sneer. But she couldn't face her own past.

He lowered his head and shook it before moving from the room and entering the hall. There he saw Jonas, standing silent and solemn as he watched the stairs Dawn had disappeared down.

The other man sighed heavily, ran his hands over his short black hair and shook his head as though weariness had settled over him.

"Call Dash," Callan ordered the other man. "I don't want this getting out of control."

"I should have killed Lawrence ten years ago," Jonas bit out. "I nearly did. I had him in my sights and had my finger on the trigger. I could have saved her from this. I wanted to save her from this."

Callan felt a chill race up his back. He knew Jonas could be cold, efficient, and took the preservation of the Breed society as a whole with exacting seriousness. Seeing it though, hearing him speak so easily of killing an innocent man, grated on Callan's sense of honor.

Jonas looked at him and smiled mockingly. "You would have never known, and neither would she. But she wouldn't be suffering now. And neither would you."

With that, Jonas followed behind Dawn as he jerked his satphone from the clip at his hip and contacted Dash.

Callan stood where he was, feeling Merinus near him, then feeling her arms sliding around his waist, her head settling comfortingly against his back.

"I can't save her this time." His voice was rough, husky with the knowledge that Dawn had to save herself now.

"She's grown, Callan." Her hands tightened against his stomach, holding him close to her. "Let her do what she has to. She'll never forgive you otherwise."

He turned to her slowly. "How do I forgive myself if she fails?"

Merinus's lips trembled as she reached up and cupped his jaw. "You won't," she admitted. "But you'll know you did all you could to protect her. Everything you could, Callan. A man can't ask any more of himself than that."

❖   ❖   ❖

A man couldn't ask more of himself than his own honesty, honor and pride.

Seth stood on the upper balcony of the two-story, sprawling mansion situated in the middle of Lawrence Island, just off the California coast, and stared into the ocean of blue that surrounded them.

He was a man who had everything other men wanted, but the core of sadness that had cemented inside his soul never abated. The mating heat had gone away; the torturous arousal for a woman he couldn't have was no longer like a cancer growing inside him. But a man didn't stop loving with the same ease. And Seth had never stopped.

Ten years was a long time to grieve over the loss of one woman. A long time to obsess over the things he couldn't have. Though, he admitted, she had grown in those ten years. She hadn't been timid during that meeting at Sanctuary. She had been strong—a smart-ass, but strong. And it had turned him on. Even without the mating heat, with nothing abnormal or preternatural, he had been so fucking hot for her he'd nearly melted his chair.

But those shadows were still in her eyes, and there was still a hint of fear there. And she was still the one woman he couldn't have. All he had now was this and, maybe, the hope of someone to leave it to later. A child perhaps rather than a fucking board of directors.

The island was lushly vegetated, private and fairly large. Cliffs fell into the ocean from the north, while the southern edge was a tropical paradise ringed by white sand beaches.

Helicopters were landing on the eastern edge, along the helipads, and the additional house servants were collecting the guests in four-wheel-drive all-terrains, which would negotiate the rough roads to the house.

Except for once every two years, Lawrence Island was a retreat rather than an entertainment center. Then, every two years, each room in the mansion and outer guest buildings was filled.

They were filling up now, even as he watched. The pool behind the house was already in use, the billiards and cinema center being prepared for the arrival of the families of the board members, as well as the guests invited to enjoy the island.

His father had begun the tradition of inviting more than just board members to the island during the meetings, and it was one Seth knew he wouldn't keep up long. He was already looking at scheduling the next meeting at the home offices of Lawrence

Industries in New York City rather than using the island any longer.

He leaned his arms against the smooth railing that ran the length of the upper story, clasped his hands and watched as the Breed heli-jet settled on the private helipad closer to the house.

Dash Sinclair and his family were arriving. He watched as Cassie climbed out behind her father, the waist-length trails of thick curls whipping in the wind as she stared up at the house.

He couldn't see her expression, but he knew she was staring directly back at him. Next came Elizabeth. Seth knew the Breed had left his young son at Sanctuary, his preferred location for the protection of his children when needed. He couldn't understand why he had brought his daughter.

He wiped a hand over his face and fought back the regret that burned through his mind like wildfire. Dawn could have been here, where he had dreamed of seeing her over the years. She could have filled his mansion with her spirit, and her haunted sadness.

Fuck. Ten years.

He stared out at the ocean again, the blue so intense it almost hurt the eyes, and imagined her there with him as he had a thousand times over. By his side. In his bed. Sharing his life and his passion. That had been his dream, his hope, and it had followed him even after those horrifying minutes that he had stood and watched the graphic, nightmarish proof of the life she had led in those labs.

Which was one of the reasons the board members were now bucking the amount of time and money Seth was putting into Sanctuary and the fight against the supremacist groups rising against them. Because of what he had seen. Because of what he had lost.

He moved a hand to his chest and rubbed at it absently. Right there over his heart, where the ache centered. Where he couldn't forget the years he had spent so tied to her that his flesh had crawled with the need for her touch.

"Darling, your guests are arriving. We should greet them."

He didn't tense when Caroline moved to him and pressed her barely covered breasts against his back, her arms snaking around his waist and burrowing beneath the loose white cotton shirt he wore.

His flesh no longer crawled at another woman's touch, and he no longer stalked away, unable to draw so much as an ounce of interest in a sexual relationship with another woman.

In ten years he hadn't aged, but the other effects of the mysterious mating heat had slowly worn away with the absence of the woman who had initiated it.

Caroline was but one woman among many that he had taken to his bed in the past years. Someone to warm the nights, to spend the excessive sexual release he needed more often than he had before meeting Dawn.

He was considering a more permanent relationship with her. He had given himself these two weeks as his deadline to make that decision.

She was young enough to have children, was socially adept, and would be an asset among his business contacts. If he could only force himself to actually spend a full night in her bed rather than just a few hours.

He moved from her touch, placing several inches between them, unconsciously drawing away from her even as he caught himself.

And she noticed it as well. She always noticed it. Her lips tightened in anger, and rather than deal with the tantrum he could feel brewing, he placed his hand at the small of her back and led her toward the outside staircase to the first floor.

"Why are all these Breeds arriving, Seth?" There was a snap to her voice as Lawe and Rule discreetly moved in protectively.

"The Breeds provide security for all my functions; you know this, Caroline." He restrained his impatience.

He reminded himself that Caroline was no different than millions of other people who were uncomfortable with the Breeds' presence, especially those who had foolishly or unknowingly supported the Genetics Council that created them.

It was one of the reasons he was having so much trouble with the board of directors now. They wanted the funding toward the Breeds halted and for Lawrence Industries, and Seth in particular, to break ties with them. Only a few of those members backed Seth at the moment. He was hoping to draw more to his side before the two weeks were out.

"Mr. Lawrence, Mr. Vanderale and Mr. Desalvo have arrived. You asked me to notify you when they reached the house." The house steward stepped from the path leading to the front of the house, his bland expression belying the excitement in his hazel eyes.

Richard loved the house parties.

"Thank you, Richard." He nodded as he turned Caroline toward the path leading around the house. "We'll be right in."

Richard hurried ahead of them as Lawe and Rule came in behind them. Caroline's body was tense now, offended sensibilities clearly demonstrated in the tap of her heels against the stone walk.

"We should have been awaiting them in the foyer," she snapped. "This does not make a good impression, Seth. And you haven't even changed clothes yet."

He restrained his sigh. Women always bitched about changing clothes and the right impression, didn't they? He seemed to remember that.

"I'm sure Dane won't mind the casual attitude," he assured her.

"Of course not. Dane Vanderale and his little sidekick are known for their eccentricities. It doesn't mean you have to follow suit," she hissed.

He was glad to see the end of the path and the wide front porch where Dane leaned casually against the railing, a slim cigar clenched between his teeth.

Dane Vanderale was an enigma, even among enigmas. With his rough, almost savage good looks, overly long light brown hair and mocking brown eyes, he could have been a Breed himself, instead of merely a supporter. Beside him, darker brown and lazily relaxed, his bodyguard and friend, Ryan Desalvo, watched as Seth and Caroline stepped onto the porch.

"Caro, sweetheart, you get prettier every time." Dane flashed her a smile before pulling her to him, smacking a kiss on her glossy red lips and smearing the brilliant lipstick.

"Really, Dane!" She pushed away from his chest, but the offended tone of her voice held a shade more interest than Seth was certain she wanted known. "You're insane."

Dane replaced the cigar between his teeth and chuckled before holding his hand out to Seth and glancing over his shoulder at the Breeds.

"Pulled in reinforcements, did you?" he questioned. "I wondered if you would."

Dane was one of the few people aware of the attempts on Seth's life over the past months.

Seth grinned back at the Breeds, his eyes twinkling in amusement.

"It's good to see you, Dane." Seth restrained his own grin at Caroline's obvious attraction to Dane.

"Seth, sweetheart, I'm going to go make certain everyone is settling in. I'll see you later." She reached up, kissed his cheek and moved to the opened doors leading into the mansion.

Seth's jaw clenched at the feel of her lipstick against his skin. He couldn't wipe it off fast enough, though he pretended nonchalance as he did just that.

Dane watched closely, his eyes narrowed. "Made up your mind yet?" he asked, and Seth knew what he was talking about.

"I might as well." He shifted his shoulders loosely. "I'm not getting any younger."

Dane shook his head slowly. "Some things a man has to fight for, Seth."

"And sometimes a man has to know when the battle is done," Seth said softly.

"I bet Dawn would be beautiful here."

Seth swung around, his eyes narrowing as Cassie stepped onto the landing to the porch, dressed in jeans and a tank top, her parents following close behind.

He heard the emphasis on "Dawn." She wasn't talking about the fucking sunrise.

"Cassie. Dash, Elizabeth, meet Dane Vanderale, heir to the Vanderale Legacy in Africa. His sometimes bodyguard and friend Ryan Desalvo."

Cassie paused in front of Dane, her eyes so blue they glowed as a little smile tugged at her lips and Dane seemed to tense.

"Hello, Cassie," he drawled, the African accent thickening his words and giving them a lazy, almost sensual sound. "Dash Sinclair. We met at Scheme and Tanner's engagement party. And his lovely wife, Elizabeth." He shook Dash's hand, but he was careful to not touch Elizabeth as he made a show of brushing her cheek with his lips.

"Dane, you're a flirt." Elizabeth smiled as Dash's dark face creased into a scowl.

Dash was a Breed. Fully mated. But even fully mated Breeds were known to be intensely jealous over their women.

"He likes to live dangerously," Dash commented mockingly,

though he pulled Cassie back as she edged closer to the other man.

Cassie flipped her hair over her shoulder and shot her father a frown that had Seth grinning. Cassie was inquisitive, sometimes too much. And Seth hadn't missed it.

"So I've been told regularly," Dane laughed. He flipped the fire off the end of the cigar and tapped it into his palm before sliding it into the worn pocket of his bush shirt. "And I believe we'll let the delectable little Caro show us to our rooms now. We'll catch up with you later, Seth. Dash." He nodded to both of them before strolling back into the house.

All eyes turned to Cassie as she narrowed her gaze and watched him silently. The girl often saw things . . .

"He's like, cute. For an old man." Her brows lifted as she quickly sidestepped her father's swatting hand and laughed in delight.

"Richard." Seth motioned to the house steward lingering close by. "The Sinclairs are very special guests. Make certain they're comfortable."

"Seth." Dash nodded in acceptance of the compliment. "We'll talk later."

Yeah, they would.

Seth inhaled and turned back to stare out along the private drive and the vehicles rolling to a stop. Another Breed heli-jet flew overhead. Hopefully a few additional security members, Seth thought. Damn, he didn't like this. The threat, the intel that another attempt would come here, within his own private fortress. And he had pushed Dawn away.

Ten fucking years he had dreamed of her, dreamed of having her here, by his side. Letting it go was the hardest thing he had ever done.

"Seth." Lawe stepped up to him, his expression somber, but his eyes gleaming. "Dawn's just arrived to take command of the group. Good luck, man."

She was just entering the wide, sheltered portico of the mansion, her duffel slung over her shoulder, when she saw him.

The door jerked open and he stepped from the house, his expression livid, his gray eyes dark and firing with fury as he slammed the door closed.

Dawn smirked. It was completely unlike her; everything rolling through her senses and her emotions was completely un-Dawn-like since she had learned Seth had a lover.

She stopped, cocked her hip and stared back at him as he stalked over to her, gripped her arm above the hem of the long-sleeved light jacket she wore and steered her to another entrance.

Steered her nothing—he was dragging her. The heat of his palm raced through the thin material of the black jacket, fired against her flesh and sent erratic impulses rushing through her body.

Past arousal was nothing compared to what she felt now. It wasn't arousal—it was an imperative, all-consuming hunger and a need that she couldn't survive without fulfilling.

He was hers. He was a part of her soul. When had that happened? Other than those brief days ten years before, she hadn't allowed herself to be alone with him, hadn't allowed herself the hope that she could have more than the nightmares.

She didn't want the pity. She didn't want the knowledge in his eyes of what she had been, but she couldn't bear to lose him either.

He pulled her into another door, slammed it closed, then swung her around to face him.

Dawn smiled mockingly as she looked around the huge, deserted laundry room.

"Isn't this just a little too clichéd, Seth?" She drawled. "And here I'm not wearing my little French maid outfit. Should I change for you?"

My God. His eyes. For a second, the hunger, the lust that fired inside them wiped the thoughts from her head and the saliva from her mouth, and not in fear. She could smell the lust pouring from his body, his pores, filling the room with the subtle scent of male musk and heated flames. It was the most erotic scent she had ever known.

"Who the hell are you and what did you do with Dawn?" he snarled. "Better yet, why the fuck are you here?"

"What, didn't want me to witness you going to your knees in surrender when you propose to your little bunny of the month?" she shot back, and watched as his nostrils flared, his head jerking back in surprise. "Didn't think Callan would tell me, Seth?" She wrinkled her nose as she had watched Cassie do a dozen times when slapping down one of the Breeds for impertinence. "Didn't think poor little Dawn could handle the sight of it?"

His lips thinned as she watched the anger build inside him. Well, that was fine with her. Let him get mad. Let him get as mad as she was and let him burn inside.

"You're right." She lifted to her tiptoes and almost, just almost managed to get right in his face as she dropped the duffel bag, placed her hands against his chest and pushed furiously. "You have a problem on your hands, stud. See how you can fix it."

He fell back a step, his expression frankly incredulous as she felt, scented, knew, the hunger that began to whip through his system.

The power of it slapped around her, tore through her like lightning and left her struggling to breathe as they glared at each other like combatants.

"You don't want to be here," he snarled. "God damn you,

Dawn. I won't let you fuck me up again, and I won't let you fuck my body up again. Get your ass back on that heli-jet and get out of here. I don't want you here."

"Liar," she growled furiously. "I can feel how much you want me here. I can smell it. I can feel it like flames burning over me, so don't even try to tell me you don't want me here."

His hands clenched at his sides; anger pulsed off his body in waves and fired her own, just as the arousal did. She could feel the familiar dampness growing between her thighs, feel her nipples hardening beneath her light summer-weight tank top and feel her hands and tongue itch.

They itched like a rash. Worse than a rash. Or what she had heard a rash felt like. She wanted to touch. Touch his skin. She had to touch his skin, had to rub her tongue against it and infect him with the same insanity crawling through her.

"I don't want you here," he bit out again, furious, sincerity ringing in his voice as it sliced across her soul. "I don't want to look at you, day in and day out, and ache for something I can't have, Dawn. You won't rip through me like that again. I won't allow it."

He didn't want her? Had he ever really wanted her or had it just been the mating heat?

Pride had her head lifting, her chin jutting in the air as she snarled back at him. "Then stay away from me, Mr. Lawrence. Keep your ass safe, and let me and my team find your irksome little assassin and I'll just be on my way again."

"Why?" Frustration, fury, lust—they all filled his voice.

"Why? Because it would look excellent on my résumé, of course." She shrugged, the sarcasm in her voice thick enough to slice through. "Just think of all the nifty little government assignments I'll get after this. Commanding my own team? In the thick of the danger?" She drew in a hard, sensual breath through clenched teeth. "Mr. Lawrence, I could command my own price. All because I managed to save your very tight, very sexy ass." She flicked her eyes over his body slowly and smiled. "Oh, and maybe your little mistress while I'm at it. Tell me, Seth, does she scratch and beg for more, or does she lay there like the little ice princess she portrays herself to be?"

Oh yeah, she had checked up on Miss Caroline Carrington herself. She had a nice thick file residing in her PDA and more information due at any time.

"Do you care?" He was breathing hard, staring at her as though she were some alien creature he had never seen before. Well, let him stare, because she didn't know herself anymore either. But she would figure it out before she left, and when she left she would make certain she had freed herself of Seth just as easily as he had managed to free himself of her.

"Do I care?" She flashed a canine at him furiously. "Not for much longer I won't, if I ever did."

It was killing her. It was breaking her soul in two, and she could feel the screams of agony ricocheting through the very core of her being.

She had dreamed of him, ached for him. She had watched him every time he had come to Sanctuary and inhaled his scent the moment he left a room. She had fought herself, and she had lost. Now she was losing here too, and something inside her was screaming out at the pain of it.

"If you ever did," he growled, flashing a look of male disgust. "That's the problem, Dawn. You never did, until now. Why now? Because someone else might have something you didn't want to begin with?"

"And when did you bother to ask me if I wanted it?" She wanted to scream. She wanted to rage and pound her fists at him. Because he hadn't. He had never come to her. He had flirted, he had teased, and she hadn't known how to handle it, so she had run. And within months he had stopped doing even that. He stopped seeking her out, and he stopped caring. And she had continued to hide, because as God was her witness she had no idea how to tell him she needed him when all she could see was that flash of pity in his eyes.

"I followed you around like a lovesick puppy for months," he bit out in self-disgust. "When I could find you."

"Months." She waved her hand mockingly. "Poor little Seth didn't get instant gratification. Isn't that just such a shame? Bad Dawn, being so mean to him."

Seth stared at her incredulously. Who the hell was this woman? This was not the shadow he had watched slipping around Sanctuary for ten years. This was not the woman who, on the rare occasions they were in the same room, avoided him like the plague.

He clenched his hands again, fighting against the nearly overwhelming need to just touch her. To run his hands down her arms, to feel her hands against his chest again. To take her lips.

He didn't want a cool little brush of lips as they'd had before. He wanted to take her lips, he wanted to devour them, he wanted to lick against them and suck that pretty little tongue into his mouth.

Arousal, almost violent in its extremity, rushed through his system. He could feel the thickening of his cock, the blood pumping furiously to it.

Damn her to hell. He hadn't been this aroused in his entire fucking life. So aroused he could feel the need in every cell of his body.

"Dawn, don't push me." He leaned forward just enough, just that extra bit that would have made the Dawn he knew run for cover.

This one didn't run. She stuck her chin out further, braced her hands on her hips and smirked. Son of a bitch, she was smirking at him.

"You're so hot you're going to catch this room on fire," she snarled. "Tell you what, Seth, don't you push me and I won't push you. And get the smell of your lust out of my face before I have to tell your little girlfriend just how hard you get for me."

"Dawn, don't do this." He wiped his hand over his face, more to wipe the betraying sweat from his brow than for any other reason. "This has been hard enough. For both of us. Let's just walk away from each other and thank God neither of us ended up too hurt in the process."

But he saw the pain flash in her eyes, for just a second. It was there, then gone so fast that he couldn't be certain it had even been there to begin with.

"Of course you didn't get hurt, Seth," she murmured, her voice cold, her lips twisting in amused contempt. "You would have had to invest something first, wouldn't you? As I said, just stay out of my way so I can keep that tight ass of yours alive, and I'll consider my job done. Now, can I get out of your laundry room? I'm tired of the scent of your dirty laundry."

Anger and lust beat a tattoo inside his head and his balls. He fisted his hands, fought against the flames racing over his body and knew if he didn't get out of that room, if he didn't get away from her, he was going to take her. He would rip her pants from her body, bend her over the fucking folding bench and take her with all the pent-up fury of a lust he thought he had finally conquered years ago.

He would do that to her. Even knowing the hell she had endured as a child. Knowing the brutality those monsters had
used, he would still do it and he knew it. He knew it and it sickened his gut.

"Stay out of my way," he snapped.

She lifted a brow and flashed those pretty little canines in a
smile that almost had him drooling with the need to take those
lips.

"Stay out of *my* way," she amended. "I'd hate infect you
again. Wouldn't that just suck, Seth?"

"More than you fucking know." He gripped the handle to the
door, gave it a vicious twist and slammed out of the laundry
room before he ended up doing something that would scar his
conscience forever.

◆   ◆   ◆

"Here's your room." Caroline Carrington was icy, contemptu-
ous and corrupt.

Dawn followed her into the room, her brows lifting at the
size of it and the clear knowledge that it was a servant's room.
She knew for a fact the Breed Enforcers were being placed
closer to Seth's suite.

"This won't work." She turned on the other woman, flashed
her canines and watched as Miss Carrington's eyes flickered
with disgust.

Aww, poor little Caro, she didn't like Breeds.

Too fucking bad.

"I beg your pardon?" Arrogance and imperious demand
filled every pore of the bitch.

"I think you heard me, Miss Carrington. Breed Enforcers are
being placed on the upper floor, closer to Mr. Lawrence's suite.
You can escort me there now, or I can find it on my own." She
shrugged. "I really don't give a damn which way it goes, but
I'm heading there."

Put her in the basement, would she? The basement? As
though she were a dirty little secret that needed to be kept out
of the public eye.

"Security members are employees, not guests," the black-
haired snake snapped.

Dawn ignored her, shifted her duffel on her back and took
the stairs to the upper floor two at a time. She could smell her

way; she didn't need Miss Caroline Carrington to show her anything.

The wicked witch of the universe had spied Dawn the moment she stepped into the house and with an arch little voice had informed her that her room was waiting.

Dawn had snorted at that. She had followed her just to see what the hell she was up to, but Dawn knew she hadn't been expected at all. And what was more, she knew this woman was the one Seth intended to announce his engagement to.

Not on a bet, Dawn thought. If he was sleeping with this black-haired snake in the grass then he wasn't doing it often enough to leave more than the most subtle of scents on her. He hadn't claimed her, and he hadn't marked her. Not with the scent of his passion or of his emotions. But she could smell his lust on her, and that was enough to make Dawn see red.

Fine, she had known they were both in mating heat over the years and she hadn't done anything about it. Well, where the hell had he been? What the hell had happened to the guy doing the chasing? Was it now a mortal sin? Somehow unmanly? Had the rules managed to change while she was learning how to survive?

"Agent Daniels, this is uncalled for," Miss Carrington snapped behind her.

Dawn looked back to see the black-haired witch making rather good time up the stairs in those mile-high shoes and that too-short skirt. She wondered if the other woman would split the side of that skirt trying to rush after her.

"Sure it's called for," she retorted. "It's called my job. Check with Seth, he'll okay it."

A gasp sounded behind her. "That is Mr. Lawrence to you."

Dawn snorted. Mr. Lawrence, her ass.

She turned as she reached the landing, followed her nose and, within minutes and, along two different hallways, she found the rooms she was looking for. And if she wasn't very much mistaken, there was an empty room right beside Seth's suite. Oh my, how lucky could one little Breed female get? Let him hump and roll while she was sitting right next to his room snarling in fury. It wasn't going to happen.

"You will not." Miss Carrington's voice went from angry to pure fury.

A second later talons gripped Dawn's arm and the flash of

fiery distaste had her jerking back and turning with a feral, enraged snarl, her hand slashing out, gripping Miss Carrington's
throat and, in a second, pulling her to her knees in front of her.

Dawn hadn't had time to think. There had been no thought.
There had only been instinct.

"What the hell is going on here!" Seth's voice, enraged, furious and incredulous, sliced through the room as Dawn snapped
her hand back and glared at him.

"Seth." The bitch. Carrington whimpered, her face pale, her
hand gripping her throat as she stumbled to her feet, pretending
shock. "Oh my God, Seth. She tried to kill me."

"Oh, get real," Dawn muttered and stared back at Seth as
that black-haired weasel ran to his arms.

Ran to his arms. She stared at them, seeing his powerful
arms surround another woman, hold her close. As though it
were happening in slow motion, as though the world had shifted
and ended right there in front of her eyes.

Dawn stepped back, and she stared. Just at his arms. Just at
the powerful, corded muscles flexing beneath the tanned flesh,
tightening, holding the woman to him. Arms that should have
been around her earlier. That should have been holding her.

What was she supposed to do now? She lifted her gaze to
Seth's, seeing the chill in his expression as she swallowed
tightly.

"She caught me unaware," she whispered, dazed. She felt as
though she had taken a blow to the head that she couldn't recover from. "Behind me. She grabbed my arm." She lifted a
hand, then dropped it as she shook her head.

"Caroline, what the hell happened?" Seth was coldly furious
and, Dawn realized, he couldn't believe her explanation.

She ran her hand down her arm and watched, no longer furious, no longer enraged. He was holding the other woman as she
cried, as she babbled . . . something. Something about being confused, she hadn't done anything, blah blah blah.

Dawn stared at his hands now. The way they curved over the
other woman's shoulders. So gently. He was holding her gently
and the animal inside Dawn was screaming, howling, fighting
to break free as agony seared it like a red hot whip.

"Dawn!" The crack of Dash's voice had her jerking to attention, her gaze swinging to where he and Elizabeth were standing in the doorway. "Is that true?"

"True?" She blinked back at him.

"Did you attack Miss Carrington? Unprovoked?" Dash's amber-brown eyes were flat and hard, commanding.

"I didn't." She shook her head slowly, concentrating on Dash's eyes. "She grabbed me, from behind." She turned her gaze back to Seth.

"Dawn!" Dash's voice jerked her back. "Why would Miss Carrington grab you from behind?"

She swallowed and fought to get a grip on herself, but, God, it was hard. Rage was twisting inside her, instinct screaming, clawing in pain.

"I'm second command," she told Dash, breathing in roughly. "I need to be upstairs. She tried to place me in the servant's quarters and I ignored her direction. I followed the scent of my unit." She indicated the room. "This will be my room."

She was unaware of her voice strengthening, but Dash wasn't. He stared at her, terrified he was going to lose her to the instinctual rage of the animal he could see firing in her eyes at the sight of another woman in her mate's arms.

They were so close. If they lost Dawn, everything she had fought for in the past ten years would be lost.

"Dawn!" He jerked her attention back to him as she turned to stare at Seth again.

"Seth, you have to get Miss Carrington out of here," Elizabeth whispered at his side. "Now."

"No!" Dawn snapped, now more tense than ever before, her eyes snapping back to Seth and Caroline Carrington with so much naked agony that Dash wondered how such a slight body could contain it all. "I apologize, Mr. Lawrence. Miss Carrington." She seemed to sway as the words passed her lips. "I'll . . ." She stared around the room. "I'll change rooms with one of the others."

She was moving toward the door when Caroline gave a little shriek of dismay and threw herself back into Seth's arms. Dawn froze. Dash watched the transformation, saw the enforcer's lips curl, watched as the Feline mate fought for freedom, fought to destroy the woman stealing her place in life.

"Now," Dash snarled, aware of Seth pushing Caroline toward Elizabeth with a hard, cold voice order to "Go." But Seth didn't go with her. He stared at Dawn, watched her carefully, his expression brooding, angry.

"I'll switch rooms with Lawe." Dawn inhaled deeply, shaking her head as though trying to shake off a drug. She moved for the door again.

"Stay here." Seth's voice was rough, as agonized as the pain tearing through Dawn's eyes. "Just fucking stay here."

He turned then and moved from the room, obviously ignoring a distraught Caroline as she rushed after him. Dash turned back to Dawn, his heart aching for the little Cougar Breed that fought so valiantly for the control that meant so much to her.

Her expression flinched and her lashes drifted over her eyes as she turned to him.

"I'm fine," she whispered. "I'll be fine."

And he had to believe it, because he couldn't order her back to Sanctuary, no more than Callan or Jonas could. Breed Law forbade interfering with mates. And despite the reversal of the hormone, Seth and Dawn were still mates. Though it was Dash's guess that that reversal was making a sudden turn to renew itself. He had smelled the scent of the hormone on Seth's flesh, and he had seen the flinch Seth couldn't control as Caroline threw herself against him.

"Dawn's awakening," he heard his daughter whisper behind him, and he turned to her quickly, his eyes narrowing suspiciously as a single tear slipped down Cassie's pale face. "She'll wish she had continued to sleep."

· CHAPTER 5 ·

Seth couldn't get the look on Dawn's face out of his mind when Caroline ran to his arms with her obviously false tears and accusations. It was in that moment that he knew an engagement to the heiress wasn't going to happen. Hell, he hadn't even been in her bed for more than a month and the thought of going to it now was more than he could stand.

He sat in his suite, his head resting on the pillowed back of the couch, and stared at the ceiling.

In that one moment, he had seen so much agony in Dawn's eyes that he had been shocked to his soul. Or what was left of it. It had burned in her eyes, like live coals stoked to a bitter flame. A pain he couldn't bear seeing there.

Seeing it—he closed his eyes. Seeing it had destroyed him. He had thought Dawn had gone blissfully through the past ten years unaware of the hell he had endured himself, but looking in her eyes he suspected something far different.

His questions regarding the mating heat had gone largely unanswered over the years. The doctor that monitored the hormone in his blood and attempted to regulate it and bring the symptoms under control hadn't answered his questions. Jonas had refused, and after that, Seth had just let it go. He had lived in hell; if Dawn had hurt the same, then she would have come to him. Cassie had warned him to let Dawn come to him. To wait. And he had waited, and waited.

He rose slowly to his feet and paced to the balcony doors. Dawn's room was beside his, but he knew she wasn't there. She had gone out with the rest of the team earlier to survey the island while Seth and his board of directors met together.

Lawe, Rule, Mercury and Dash had stayed behind to provide security.

Those meetings were finished for the day now, and he had nothing left to do but watch for her. Which wasn't entirely true. He could have been with Caroline fulfilling his role as host. He could have been reassuring his board members, socializing and attempting to regain control of the company that thought it could outwit him.

A five-year-old could outwit him right now with no problem.

He needed answers and he needed them quickly, before she returned, before she stared at him again with that broken gaze and that soul-deep agony. Because another woman was in his arms.

He shook the image away before pushing his fingers through his hair and pulling himself up from the settee. He moved quickly to his door, left the suite and strode down the hall to where he knew Dash and his family had been assigned.

He knocked quickly on the door, not giving himself a chance to hesitate. If he hesitated, he might act first and ask questions later. And he was suddenly more terrified of adding to Dawn's pain than he was of living the rest of his life alone.

Dash opened the door and stared back at him quietly. "Cassie said you'd show up." He stood back and waved Seth into the small sitting room.

"Where is she?" This wasn't a conversation he wanted to conduct in front of a teenager. No matter how grown-up she thought she was.

"She went out with Dawn." Dash's lips quirked somberly. "She's worried about her."

"Cassie's not the only one," Seth said quietly before turning to Dash's wife. "Hello, Elizabeth."

Black-haired and blue-eyed, she was a mature vision of her daughter, and just as lovely, though without Cassie's more delicate build.

"Hello, Seth." Her voice was gentle, compassionate. "Would you like me to step out of the room?" She indicated the bedroom next door. "You two could talk."

He shook his head quickly. "I need to talk to both of you." He needed to know. What was Dawn feeling? Why was she here after all this time? And why was it beginning not to matter to him why she was there?

"Let's sit down. Would you like a drink, Seth?"

Seth nodded, requested a whiskey, straight, and moved to the seating arrangement as he watched Elizabeth sit down slowly.

Dressed in tailored, cream-colored slacks and a sleeveless blouse, she looked more like Cassie's sister than her mother. And he knew the why of that. It was the mating heat and the delayed aging it caused.

"Her eyes—" He stared at Elizabeth. "I saw her eyes." He shook his head bleakly. "Hell if I know what to do now. I stayed away from her as they asked me to. I waited for her to come to me, and she never did."

Elizabeth frowned and glanced at her husband. "Who asked you to stay away from Dawn?" she snapped, frowning darkly. "Dash, were you aware of this?"

"It happened before Dash came to Sanctuary." He inhaled roughly. "Just before. I was trying to . . ." He grimaced. "I was trying to court her. Two of Jonas's enforcers showed me to an office in the estate. They showed me what those bastards did to her." He lowered his eyes as he took the whiskey from Dash. "The videos the Council made." He could still feel the rage tearing through him. "What they did to her."

"Who did this?" Dash asked.

"Jonas, Callan." He shook his head. "They knew what the mating heat would do to her, and once I saw it, I knew as well. It was already strong, Dash."

"They had no right to ask you to stay away from her," Elizabeth accused gently. "It's been ten years. Too long for her to have to fight the effects of the heat alone."

His head snapped up, his jaw clenching as he stared back at her suspiciously. "The doctor, Ely. She said the heat wasn't in full effect without the exchange of a full kiss, or more intimate contact than what we had had."

They were staring at him; Dash's expression was dark, Elizabeth's shocked as she looked to her husband.

"Ely has known better than that for several years," Dash told him. "And I know for a fact Dawn has been in full heat for as long as I've known her, Seth. I knew you were her mate, but I also knew that other female Breeds had taken longer to struggle against their pasts enough to go to their mates. I didn't ask questions." He shook his dark head sharply. "I should have, but I didn't."

Seth came violently to his feet. "She's suffered like that?" he demanded roughly. "As I did? All these years?"

"Probably worse," Elizabeth answered him then. "It's always harder on the women, whether they're Breed or not. And I can tell you from experience, there's nothing worse than being in full heat alone. But why would Callan do this?" He watched as she turned to her husband again in disbelief. "He loves her like his own child, Dash, why would he not let Seth know?"

"Unless they thought it would recede in her as it had in Seth." Dash leaned back in his chair and watched Seth with narrowed eyes. "How intimate was the first contact with her?"

Seth shook his head as he stalked to the doors, much like his own, that led out to the enclosed, private balcony. "Not much. Barely a brush of lips, a touching of hands." He shrugged. "I was . . . courting her."

"Impressive, considering your reputation at the time," Dash pointed out in amusement.

Seth shot him a glare as he ran his fingers through his hair again.

"What now?" He shook his head at the thought. "I'll be honest, I don't want her here. It's too dangerous, and I'm . . ." He frowned, fighting the knowledge even within himself. "My control is shot, Dash." He turned to the other man, frustrated and aware of his own weakness. "I don't know if I can hold back with her here, in the house."

Dash sighed roughly. "Jonas and Callan had no right to show you the footage taken from those labs."

Seth frowned. "I needed to know. The heat was already getting hard to deal with. I would have made things worse." He wouldn't have stayed away, and he would have only made her nightmares worse.

"What are you going to do now?" Dash asked.

Seth stared back at him fiercely. "I'll break off my relationship with Caroline tonight. But I want you to get Dawn back to

Sanctuary. Order her back. Kidnap her and lock her in her room. I don't care what you have to do, Dash, but get her away from this island."

Dash was silent for long moments. Finally, he nodded his head slowly. "I'll order her back to Virginia."

Dash's compliance had been too easy. There was no argument, no attempt to persuade him otherwise. Seth nodded again in relief. "Thank you. I'll let you enjoy some peace then, before the party tonight."

He left the suite, rubbing his chest as he did so, aching at the sense of loss he already felt.

◆   ◆   ◆

Dawn's tongue was itching. Her tongue and the fingers that rested on the sidearm strapped high on her thigh as she watched the couple moving gracefully through the crowded ballroom.

Seth Lawrence and his hostess. She snorted silently. Hostess her ass, that woman wanted in his bed so bad that Dawn could smell the stink of her arousal even across the crowded ballroom.

And once again, it was close to destroying her control and her mind. If she thought for a moment that Seth had had sex with the Carrington witch anytime recently, she would have to tear the witch's throat out.

But it didn't change the fact that Seth was hanging on to her like a baby to a pacifier. And it wasn't changing the pain that was growing in her by the moment.

"Lawe, move in on Lawrence, see if you can't keep him inside," she ordered the enforcer standing by the doors that led into the cool, sheltered gardens.

"The gardens are secure, Dawn," Lawe reminded her quietly through the earpiece she wore.

"I don't care if they're ringed shoulder to shoulder with guards, do as I said," she snapped into the wire-thin mic that curved over her cheek as she continued to survey the crowd. "We can't afford to lose him or his prissy miss."

Her fingers curled over the butt of her gun as her eyes narrowed on the woman's bare back. The dress she wore was little more than a scrap of cloth covering her ass. And Seth's hand was riding on the bare flesh of her lower back as they moved through the crowd.

Were his fingers caressing the woman's flesh? Her eyes narrowed on the strong hand touching another woman, and the growl that rumbled in her throat couldn't be held back.

She glanced around quickly to make certain no one else had heard the sound, then she grimaced furiously. She shouldn't be watching Seth. She was supposed to be watching the crowd, directing the enforcers assigned to guard Seth Lawrence's ass while he made a fool of himself romancing the hostess with the mostest bare flesh showing.

She hated this. She had no business dealing with this man; he made her insane, he made her want to claw his eyes out and taste the blood of that vapid little witch he kept laying his hands on. If he didn't stop—

She forced herself to inhale, to control the pain burning inside her. She didn't have a choice. Seth had made his feelings clear, and he clearly didn't want her.

"Excuse me, Mr. Lawrence." Lawe's voice sounded in the earpiece once again. "Agent Daniels has requested that you remain inside."

Dawn winced. She was going to have to have a talk with Lawe about the best way to handle these situations, especially with Seth.

"Has she now?" Seth drawled, his voice coming through the link and sending a surprising shiver racing down her spine as she heard the mockery in it. "Please inform Miss Daniels that I specifically required that the entire island be well secured. If she ignored that request, then she can personally play escort as Miss Carrington and I enjoy the gardens."

The son of a bitch.

Dawn gritted her teeth as she moved along the side of the room, aware of the bodies that slid quickly out of her path and the wary looks she was given as she passed by. She made people nervous, she knew she did. Especially non-Breeds. They watched her like they expected her to turn and snap at any moment. Just as she had earlier when that Carrington person had surprised her.

"Merc, do you have him in sight?" Dawn murmured into the mic as she headed for the doors Seth had passed through.

"In sight." Merc's gravelly voice came across the line. "He and Miss Carrington have taken the stone path toward the pond."

To the grotto and the intimate little padded bench set beneath a vine-covered arch.

Dawn's stomach tightened at the knowledge that Seth had every intention of marrying that woman. That he wasn't Dawn's. It was inconceivable that he wasn't hers any longer. Especially when every part of her cried out for him.

She slid past the garden doors, ignoring Lawe's mocking look as she took the stone path with a determined stride. She could hear the murmur of their voices farther ahead, and her lips thinned with irritation at the seductive drawl Seth used. His voice was edging into arousal, she could hear it. It was ripping through her. She didn't know how to bear this pain. It took everything she had not to howl out in agony.

"Mr. Lawrence." She kept her voice smooth, emotionless, as she rounded the curve of the path to find them standing next to the grotto.

Her hand clenched on the butt of her weapon again. Seth was leaning against the arched shelter, one elbow braced on the wooden post as he brushed back a stray strand of raven-black hair from Miss Carrington's cheek. The other woman flicked her an irritated, enraged glance. Anger filled the air here. Blazing, furious rage, and for a moment Dawn wondered if it was her own.

Dawn smiled back, satisfaction thrumming through her as the woman's gaze flickered warily at the sight of Dawn's canines flashing in the early evening light spearing through the sheltering branches overhead.

"Miss Daniels." Seth lifted his head, his gunmetal gray eyes flickering over her uniform, the hand on her weapon, then to her eyes.

She met his gaze with a cold smile. "I believe the chairman of Foreman Motors is looking for you inside, Mr. Lawrence," she announced, a blatant lie. "I told him I would be more than happy to hunt you up and send you right to him."

Seth's lips quirked bitterly. "I see," he murmured before glancing down at the too-lovely Miss Carrington. "It appears our discussion will have to wait, Caroline. Would you like to accompany me inside?"

"Well, I don't want to stand out here alone with her." Caroline's red lips thinned in displeasure. "Really, Seth, I've been here for days and each time we get a moment alone, we're disturbed." She flicked Dawn an accusing glance.

Yeah, yeah, yeah, it was all her fault. Dawn crossed her arms over her breasts and stared back at the other woman coldly, and fought to remind the bitch that she had just arrived today. If she hadn't been able to screw Seth in the days before, then that was her own fault.

She didn't like Miss Caroline Carrington. The woman was the worst sort of opportunist. And she was ovulating. Dawn narrowed her gaze, inhaling slowly. And she wasn't using birth control.

Dawn began to shake, and fought to hide it.

Son of a bitch. She had been trying to get into Seth's bed tonight for a reason, and it wasn't just lust. She was fertile. She thought she was going to trick Seth into giving her a child? Forcing him into marriage? Of course, Seth would marry the bitch.

"Dawn, are you growling?" Seth was staring at her in surprise.

Dammit. "No I'm not growling, Mr. Lawrence," she bit out. "I'll escort you back inside." She gave him another tight smile.

Seth's gaze narrowed on her. "Come on, Caroline, I'm sure we'll find time to talk after the party." His voice was harder now, determined.

"I'll need to meet with you first, Mr. Lawrence," Dawn informed him. "There are a few security matters we need to discuss when you have the time." She flashed the woman another cold smile. "If Miss Carrington can do without you that long."

"If I must." There was a challenge in the other woman's brown eyes, one Dawn recognized. She was staking her claim on Seth, which was fine and dandy, but first she had to get through the Breeds that were going to be placed around him like a living barrier. She would be damned if she would let Seth walk into such a trap.

Roni, his sister, would never forgive her. She would make Dawn's life hell if she allowed it. And Roni was her friend. Dawn had known her forever. Roni would pout for years if Dawn allowed Caroline Carrington to end up tricking Seth into knocking her up.

She was doing this for Roni. And for herself. Otherwise, she would end up killing Miss Caroline Carrington.

She followed the two back into the party. As Seth moved

through the crowd, she glanced around to make certain she wasn't overheard.

"Keep Lawrence and the bimbo from doing the nasty at least until after the party," she growled into her mic.

Lawe snorted into the line. "Hell, let the man get some, Dawn. It's been a long dry spell for him, hasn't it?"

Her lips thinned. Fat lot he knew. "Who's lead on this little party, Lawe?" she snapped. "According to my information, I'm commanding here, not you."

"Didn't know Seth's sex life was included in your area of jurisdiction," he stated mockingly. "But sure, I'm all for fun and games. I'll keep him high and dry until you can meet with him."

She caught her lip on the edge of a snarl before her gaze tracked the room again, only to be snared by Seth's. He was standing next to the president of Foreman Motors, his gray eyes watching her with mocking knowledge and an edge of anger. She could see the anger in the tight curl of his sensual lips, in the narrowed, dangerous gaze.

Her heart began to race, her mouth dried out and her tongue itched. It itched to the point that she ran it over her teeth to ease the irritation. She was jumpy, agitated and too aware of the way Seth continually glanced at her. There was a hint of retribution in his gaze, a promise of retaliation in the hard set of his expression.

He was angry with her, and he had good reason to be. She avoided him like the plague whenever he came to Sanctuary, and through the years had fought every assignment Jonas had tried to give her in Seth's vicinity, until now. Because she knew the danger in being around him. She knew the nightmares, the fears and the incomprehensible pain of turning away from him. But could anything hurt more than this? Right now?

He affected her, and she couldn't allow that now, because he didn't want her.

He made her flesh tingle, her tongue itch to kiss him, and her body ache for his touch. And Dawn didn't enjoy touch. No one's touch. And it had only grown worse over the years. It was irritating. It made her flesh cringe and old nightmares resurface. She couldn't stand the nightmares. She couldn't face them.

But she also didn't know if she could live another day without his touch. Without his tongue along hers, his body pressed against her flesh.

She fought back another shiver as Seth's gaze raked over her black uniform, pausing at her breasts, her thighs, before moving back to her eyes. She could feel the response beating through her bloodstream, tightening her nipples and her sex, making her clit awaken with the dampness that only he could call forth, to torment her.

Sexual response. She knew what it was. She knew and it terrified her even as it sent blood pounding through her veins as though in anticipation. Anticipation of something he had no intention of giving in to now.

She forced herself to turn away, to return to the party and the headache of ensuring his security. Seth wasn't big on helping with that. As one of the Breeds' leading proponents and supporters, the Breeds took his security very seriously. His death, right now, would be a major inconvenience.

She ignored the little voice inside her that howled in fury at the thought of anything happening to Seth. Her palms were sweating, her instincts going into overdrive. Nothing could happen to Seth. It was her job to protect him; she didn't fail. Not anymore. She had failed when she was younger. Failed to protect herself and to warn others of the danger coming. Failed to find the strength she needed to fight back.

She was strong now. She knew how to fight back. She knew how to protect herself and those she was assigned to protect. And Seth could hate it, and her, all he wanted to. But she would protect him. With her life, if need be.

◆　　◆　　◆

The door closed with a bang that would have caused a lesser woman to flinch. Dawn merely glanced at it, then at Seth as he tore his tie from around his neck and glared at her from the center of his home office.

"What the hell was so damned important?" he snapped at her, his gaze roiling with anger.

Dawn's lips thinned. "Your precious Miss Carrington just slipped naked into your bedroom. Were you aware of this?"

His eyes narrowed. "I didn't know it, but what business is it of yours?"

"She's ovulating and she's not on birth control. Fuck her and she's going to end up conceiving." Her fists clenched at the thought.

"For God's sake, do you think I leave such protection up to the women I fuck?" he asked her incredulously, his voice rising as he glowered down at her, his sharply defined face set in savage, arrogant lines. "And I'll ask you again, what business is it of yours?"

Dawn could feel the anger, and the arousal, rolling off him in waves now. It stroked over her flesh, heated it, made her jumpy. This was why she hated being around Seth; he made her jumpy. Made her too aware of the fact that she was indeed a woman, and that she had never touched a man in pleasure. Had never known a lover's touch.

She stepped back. "You're right, not my business."

Something exploded in her head. Some sensation, some instinct that she couldn't make sense of. She shook her head, feeling her lip twitch into a snarl as a blistering curse left Seth's lips.

"Is that all you wanted to tell me?" His dark voice was colder, more arrogant now.

Dawn could smell the arousal coming from him, and it pissed her off. She had no right to be angry with him. She had no right to care whom he fucked.

"Eager to head to your bed, Mr. Lawrence?" She was shocked at the snarl in her voice then, at the anger that surged through her. "A willing sacrifice to Miss Carrington's plans for impending nuptials?"

"Well, I'm not getting any younger, Agent Daniels," he sneered in return. "And I'm sick and damned tired of a lonely fucking bed."

Dawn flinched at the accusation in his voice even as something primal, something she couldn't understand, began beating in her heart. The blood was racing through her body, awareness spiking in her head. He was going to do it. He was going to go to that woman's body, spill his seed inside her. He was going to actually let another female touch him.

She didn't try to stop the growl that pulled from her chest this time.

"No."

"Excuse me?" He arched a brow as sarcasm echoed in his voice. "You have no say in the matter, Agent Daniels. Your job is to keep me from being kidnapped during the act, not keep me from the act itself."

Her fingers clenched, itched. Her tongue felt thick, swollen within her mouth. A strangely spicy, heated taste began to fill her senses as she tried to draw enough air into her lungs to keep from strangling on her fury.

"She doesn't love you. You don't love her," she hissed.

He laughed at that, a jeering sound that raked over her nerve endings like shards of glass.

"Love isn't required," he informed her.

Heat spilled to her womb, spasming through it as denial raced through her brain.

It wouldn't happen. She wouldn't let it.

"If there's nothing else you require, Agent Daniels," his voice was clipped, tight with anger, "I believe I have someone waiting on me."

Someone waiting on him? A fertile bitch with every intention of sucking his seed from his body and conceiving a child that would bind him to her forever?

"No."

His lips thinned as his eyes darkened ominously. Seth might not be a Breed, but he was still dangerously powerful. An ex–Special Forces soldier who took over his father's company, he had learned how to fight in the most violent gutters of the world.

He shook his head as his lips thinned with disgust. "Jonas made a mistake assigning you here. Go back to Sanctuary."

She was shaking her head. She couldn't believe this. She couldn't believe him.

"You would let her trick you like this?" Her voice was unrecognizable, even to herself. She couldn't think. She couldn't breathe. A haze seemed to fill her vision, her mind, making it hard to find the hard-earned control she had fought to achieve for eleven years now.

"It's only a trick if you don't know about it," he pointed out mockingly. "I'm not getting any younger, Dawn, and I'm damned tired of going to bed horny. At least she's woman enough to go after what she wants."

He turned away from her.

He was leaving. He was going to walk out? Go to that ovulating cow waiting naked in his bedroom?

The hell he was.

She didn't know who was more surprised by the vicious

snarl that left her chest, Seth or herself. He turned to her quickly, surprise flashing across his expression as her hands gripped his upper arms, powerful arms, muscular and steel-hard. She was on her tiptoes, against his chest, one hand gripping his neck and pulling him to her.

Her lips met his. They were parted just enough to allow her tongue to slip past them. Spicy heat filled her mouth and she shared it. Sweeping over his lips, against his tongue as she felt his arms surround her, jerking her to him as he bent his head closer. His lips caught her tongue, and a shattered cry filled her throat as he began to draw the fiery hormone from her.

It filled both their mouths. It pumped into her bloodstream, sent lust tearing through her system, pleasure quaking through her body. She wanted to crawl inside him. No, she wanted him inside her. She wanted his hard body covering her, the thick length of his cock, which was presently pressing into her belly, fucking into her.

She wanted him now. Hard. Hot. Deep.

She wanted her mate.

· CHAPTER 6 ·

He hadn't meant for this to happen, Seth thought hazily. He had been furious when she followed him and Caroline outside. He wanted to send the other woman home without too much anger, without hurting her, without humiliating her.

Caroline had been a friend. He didn't love her, she didn't love him, and they both knew it. They would have made a society match, little more. But there would have been children, a legacy, someone he could love and receive love from unconditionally. He had known the second he saw Dawn earlier that day that it wasn't going to happen.

He had known, and he'd made the deal with Dash. Now look at him. Ah, God, she tasted so fucking sweet, so hot. He licked and sucked at her tongue, then groaned with desperate pleasure as she sucked at his.

And he was touching her. Jerking her shirt from her pants, groaning against her lips, nipping at them as her hands dug into his hair and held him closer to her.

She was kissing him. Her lips were moving beneath his, she was moaning for him. Rich, earthy moans that vibrated with purring little growls. The sounds of it went straight to his dick and had it fully engorged. He was harder, hotter than he could ever remember being in his life. And he was tearing her shirt from her. He heard the material rend and cursed himself. He cursed himself but he couldn't stop, couldn't keep himself from revealing that plain little bra, the one that held her breasts perfectly for him.

"Seth." She whispered his name, a thin, hungry sound that he couldn't believe he was hearing. That he couldn't believe was falling from her lips.

And her hands. As he pushed her shirt from her shoulders and his lips moved down the graceful column of her neck, he felt the buttons pop on his, heard cloth tear.

Hell, he had never been so desperate for a woman. Never felt a hunger burn so deep inside his gut.

Then her hands were on his chest. Her fingers were pushing through the mat of hair that covered it, and she purred. A real, fucking honest-to-God purr left her lips, and he almost came in his trousers from the sound.

Seth jerked his head back, stared down at her, and God help him, he knew, from this moment on, if he wasn't touching Dawn, loving her, tasting her, then he would be completely alone. Because no other woman's touch would do.

◆　◆　◆

Dawn stared at where her hands pressed against the soft, short curls on Seth's chest. The light pelt was warm from his body heat, the short curls tickled her palms, the heat of his flesh warmed them.

She stared at her fingers, so small against the expanse of muscular flesh and male hair, and felt her knees weaken at the knowledge that she was finally touching him. Touching him, kissing him. And she could taste him.

She leaned forward and put her lips against his flesh, opened them, let her tongue lick at it. The muscles beneath the skin flexed and jumped and a hard groan tore from his chest.

"You like my touch?" she whispered in awe as she looked up at him, saw the dark thunderclouds in his eyes and the flush on his cheekbones.

"Like isn't a good word." His teeth were clenched as she let her fingers circle the flat, hard discs of his nipples.

No, like wasn't a good word if it felt anywhere as close to as good as his hands felt on her.

"Seth?" She was panting, just trying to breathe as so many sensations tore through her, unknown sensations, pleasure unlike anything she'd thought she would know in his arms.

"Anything, Dawn." He must have heard the question in her voice; maybe he heard the longing she couldn't disguise.

"Touch me." She tried to breathe.

She felt light-headed, off balance. His hands were at her hips, his fingers clenching, caressing, but she needed more. She ached in places that she didn't know how to ease, didn't know how to describe.

"Dawn." His head lowered as though he couldn't stop the action, and hers fell back with a cry as he bent over her, his lips moving to the swell of her breasts above her bra. "Sweet God, Dawn. You taste like life itself."

Shuddering, racing arcs of pleasure ripped through her as his tongue licked over the swell of flesh. He wasn't even touching her aching nipples and she was ready to scream from the pleasure.

"Seth, I need more." She arched into his arms, feeling them surround her, feeling his hands flatten on her back, draw her closer to him, loosen the clip to her bra.

She was going to pass out from lack of oxygen. From pleasure. Her hands gripped his shoulders as his tongue swiped over a nipple. Her nails bit into his flesh as his mouth covered it and he sucked her into his mouth.

And still it wasn't enough. Before she lost consciousness, she wanted to know it all. Because she knew she was going to faint. Rapid, white-hot streaks of sensation were tearing from her nipple to her womb. She could feel the juices easing from the swollen, sensitive flesh between her thighs, felt her clit throbbing, her heart racing.

And if she didn't get some ease—she had suffered arousal in the past but nothing like this.

"Seth, please." She arched in his arms as he moved from one breast to the next, as he sucked and licked, rasped with teeth and tongue and sent her senses spinning.

"It's not enough," she panted, trying to get closer, trying to crawl into him. "Seth, help me. It's not enough."

One hand slid from her back, over her rear. It jerked at her thigh then slid forward and cupped her between her thighs.

They both stilled. His breathing was harsh, heavy in the still air of the study, his forehead pressed against her breast as his hand moved, his fingers pressed into the humid flesh.

"I won't stop," he groaned, his voice agonized, tortured. "Dawn, if we keep this up—"

"Don't stop," she breathed out roughly. "Seth, please."

She felt close, so close, to a pleasure she couldn't define. One that had eluded her, but had tormented her for so many years.

Before she had time to cry out at the defection, he slid his hand from between her thighs as the other moved from behind her back as well. They met at her stomach, jerking, tearing at the metal buttons that secured her pants and sliding his palm inside.

Dawn froze, staring up at him as his head lifted and his hand slid inside her panties. His fingers inched over her lower belly, slowly, so slowly.

"I can already feel your heat." He grimaced, his expression tight, savage. "I know you're wet. So wet for me, Dawn. I've dreamed of touching you like this. Dreamed of feeling your sweetness against my fingers."

She jerked, jumped as his fingers slid into the thick, slick juices that coated the bare folds. They slid between the lips of her sex, stroked, and she came to her toes as a long, desperate wail left her lips when his palm pressed against her swollen clit.

"God, yes!" Savage, guttural with arousal, his voice tore across her senses and wrapped them in eroticism. "Fuck. Dawn. It's not enough." His other hand was working her pants down, pulling her panties with them.

He jerked them over her butt, struggled to push them over her thighs, then went to his knees in front of her.

"What are you doing?" Wide-eyed, uncertain, so hot she could feel the perspiration pouring down her back, she stared down at him.

His shirt, expensive silk, hung on his shoulders, gaping open to reveal his chest as his hands gripped her thighs and encouraged her to part them.

"Just a taste," he whispered, his expression twisted into lines of sensual desperation. "Just a taste, Dawn. Right here." And he lowered his head to that wet flesh.

"Seth, unlock this door." Striking, furious fists pounded on the door to the office as a snarl tore from Dawn's lips and a curse jerked from Seth's.

He was staring at her thighs, at the wet flesh, plump and swollen and aching for him. She didn't know what this felt like; she had dreamed of him almost touching her there, almost bringing her ease, and now the dream was so close.

He licked his lips and leaned forward.

"Open this door or I'll find someone to open it for me. Are you hurt? Has that feline bitch hurt you, Seth?" False hysteria echoed through the panel as Seth surged to his feet, jerked Dawn's pants to her hips and just as quickly rebuttoned them.

Dawn stared back at him in shock as he tried to draw her shirt back over her shoulders.

"Hell, I ripped your fucking shirt." He stared at it as though horrified.

"Seth. Open this door."

"Seth, don't touch her," Dawn pleaded. She stopped him as he tried to fix her shirt, staring up at him, feeling the agony, the burst of pain that ripped through her at the memory of him holding the other woman. "Please. Not in front of me. Don't touch her."

His lips tightened.

"Seth, damn you!" Pure rage flowed into the room.

A bitter curse slipped from his mouth as he strode forcefully to the door, unlocked it and jerked it open.

Dawn stood where she was; she couldn't have moved away from the desk if she'd had to. She didn't pull the shirt over her black bra, and she didn't flush as Caroline's eyes landed first on her, then Seth.

She took in their undress, the ripped shirts and the scratches on Seth's shoulders. And he did have a fine set of scratches, Dawn thought in satisfaction.

Caroline had a bloodred wrap tied around her overblown body, and her breasts were heaving in fury as she stared at Seth in disgust.

"I can't believe you," she sneered. "Ripped clothes, scratches." Her fingers flipped toward his shoulders. "You're in here messing around with that trampy little animal when I was waiting for you upstairs."

"That's enough, Caroline," Seth snapped, the anger building in his voice now. "What happened here was my fault. Not hers."

"I believe I kissed you first." Dawn smiled tightly at the other woman as her gaze jerked back to her.

"Dammit, Dawn." Seth turned to glare back at her.

She met his look head-on. If he didn't get rid of that black-haired slut, she was going to use her nails to scratch her eyes out.

Caroline's fingers clenched at her sides. "We need to talk," she ordered Seth imperiously. "Now."

"He's busy," Dawn informed her as Seth parted his lips to speak. "Or hadn't you noticed?"

An unattractive splotchy red filled the other woman's face as her eyes bugged out at Dawn.

"That thing." She pointed a shaky finger back at Dawn. "Get rid of her now."

"She's so melodramatic, Seth," Dawn drawled despite the gut-wrenching agony ripping through her body. Seth stood between them, staring at Dawn as though he had never seen her before. "How do you stand it? I'd have pitched her off a cliff by now."

"Seth." Bloodred nails uncurled and latched onto Seth's arm.

Dawn's eyes jerked to the contact and she saw red. She saw blood rushing across her gaze as a haze of pure fury began to flow over her senses.

"Dawn!" Seth's voice, commanding, sharp, jerked her gaze back to him. "We'll talk later."

She scowled back at him as she straightened against the desk. "Excuse me?" She could barely force the words past her lips.

"I said, we will talk later," he snapped. "Much later."

He turned, grabbed Caroline's wrist and pulled her from the doorway as Dawn watched in shock and betrayal.

They would talk later?

She moved to the door, hearing Caroline's fishwife voice screeching at Seth as he pulled her up the back stairs. Dawn followed slowly, stalking, moving with catlike stealth as she followed them.

Instinct, honed and sharpened over the years, guided her. The mating heat was blazing inside her, the animal so close to the surface she could taste the wildness in her mouth. And that animal was enraged, furious that her mate was moving away from her in another woman's presence.

God help her if he took her to his room. If he closed that door to his personal space and took that woman with him. She wouldn't be able to control the pain or the rage. Even now it was tearing through her with the same gut-wrenching intensity that the arousal had torn through her moments before.

She was still wet for him. Her flesh was still screaming in need for his touch and he was opening a door to another room and pushing Caroline into it.

She paused, eyes narrowed as he turned back and saw her. He paused in the doorway, his expression inscrutable, his eyes almost black with hunger.

She could smell his arousal even from the distance that separated them. She could smell it, she could almost taste it, and it was hers. He was hers.

Then he stepped into the room and slammed the door closed behind him as Caroline let out an enraged string of curses.

Dawn walked along the hall, unaware of the predatory movements in her body, the violence that almost shimmered on the air around her.

"Caroline is a bitch, isn't she?" a male voice responded with amused drollery from a doorway just ahead of her.

Dawn paused as the male stepped out, and barely held back the snarl that pulled at her lips.

He smiled, the curve arrogantly placating, holding his hands up as his eyes roved over her with a bit more familiarity than she liked. As though he had the right. He had no right.

Dark blond hair was cut close to the scalp, almost hiding the fact that it had begun to gray. Brown eyes, bloodshot and showing the influence of liquor, encouraged amusement, she guessed, in some people.

She stood carefully and watched him, like a snake, a rattler poised to strike. Her hand lingered on the butt of her weapon and she growled warningly.

"Yeah, Caroline pisses us all off like that." He smiled as he leaned a bare shoulder against the wall. He was dressed in slacks and nothing more, his tanned chest and abs flabby and unattractive. "I was getting ready to turn in when I heard her cursing Seth." He raked his eyes over her again. "She has a reason to be pissed."

He was flirting. She didn't belong to him, she belonged to the man who was currently in another woman's bedroom.

"Would you like a drink?" He indicated his room with a jerk of his head. "My names Jason, Jason Phelps. My old man was a friend of Seth's father's. I'm harmless, I promise."

"And I'm taken," she told him dangerously, moving slowly to pass him.

"Might want to remind Seth of that pretty soon." He grinned as though he hadn't taken offense. "Caroline can be persuasive."

Dawn smiled, a baring of her teeth, a flash of the promise of violence. "Don't worry," she told him softly. "He'll remember."

The mating hormone was speeding through Seth, just as it was through her. She had felt his discomfort when that bitch had touched him, and again when he had been forced to touch her. No, Caroline wouldn't be the least bit persuasive. Tonight.

She kept her eyes on the stranger as she passed him, and afterward she kept her senses open, tracking him as she moved to her room.

He wasn't to be trusted. She couldn't put her finger on why. Perhaps it was the liquor that he had obviously drank too much of, or the lust he didn't bother to disguise as he stared at the open edges of her shirt. She didn't know what it was, but it sent a chill up her spine.

"Hey, wait."

She turned, pivoting on her heel and almost coming to a crouch as he stepped from his room. Her hand rose hard on the butt of her weapon and she could feel the sense of violence rising inside her now.

"Hey, come on, kid." He lifted his hands and smiled again, almost laughing at the response as she slowly straightened. "I just wanted to talk. Hell, everyone downstairs is either plastered or talking business. You're sober. You might not be sane, but hey, none of us are perfect, right?"

"Stay away from me, Jason Phelps," she told him, rising slowly to her feet. "It's not a good night."

"PMS?" He waggled his brows.

"You have no earthly clue," she drawled coldly before turning again and moving past the room where Seth was obviously trying to placate Caroline.

She couldn't hear what they were saying, but Caroline was raging over his voice. Dawn smiled tightly and moved down the hall, made the turn to the next hallway and moved to her room.

As she went to grip the doorknob, she paused. She inhaled slowly then pulled the communicator link from her back pocket and attached the ear bud to her ear.

"We have contact. My room," she reported into the link as she drew her weapon from her side, locked it in ready and braced it against her side.

"Are you in the room?" Dash's voice came through the line.

"No."

"Stay in position. I'm on my way."

"I'm moving onto the balcony," Lawe reported.

"Covering the stairs," Mercury spoke softly into the link.

Each of the Breed Enforcers had reported in by the time Dash slid into the hallway beside her, his weapon held ready at his thigh as his gaze tracked over the condition of her shirt.

He moved to the door, laid his head against it and inhaled slowly as Dawn moved to Seth's door. She checked it, clenched her jaw, then nodded. Someone who shouldn't have had been there as well.

The scent was off, odd, as though something were covering it, barely disguising it.

"Moira, Noble, move in on the main room, balcony and back stairs," she ordered into the link.

Dash gave her a hard look when she indicated his attention to her room, and hers to Seth's. Her mate's room. Someone had dared to invade it.

Dash nodded slowly.

He counted to two, gripped her doorknob then swept into the room like a shadow of death. Dawn moved to the side, waited, gave Dash time to secure the room and move to the connecting door before she did the same. She jerked Seth's door open, went in at a roll and came up ready, her gaze scanning the darkness of the sitting room and moving unerringly to the open bedroom door.

The scent was strong here as well, causing her nose to wrinkle. There was a human scent beneath it, but something astringent and musky covered it.

"Clear," Dash spoke into the link. "I'm moving to the connector."

Dawn moved to the side of the door. "In position." Her voice was barely a whisper. "One o'clock." She gave her position in relation to the door.

Dash came through it a second later and she barely saw him. Even with her night vision, enhanced by years of working in the darkened forests, he almost slipped by her.

When she caught sight of him, he was giving her a silent order to cover him as he moved toward the bedroom.

They moved in aggressively, weapons held ready at their sides, their senses tracking the odd smell straight to the double French doors that led to the balcony outside the bedroom where the scent slowly dispersed in the night air.

"We've had visitors," Dash murmured as they holstered their weapons and let Mercury begin his sweep for explosives and listening devices.

"So it would seem," Dawn matched the near silent tone of his voice as they moved back into the bedroom and came face-to-face with Seth.

The light flipped on. The side of his face was a bit red, a long scratch scouring his scowling countenance as Dawn growled in fury that another had dared to slap her mate.

"If I hear another growl out of you, I'm going to tie you, gag you and throw you on that fucking heli-jet to be transported back to where you belong." His gaze sliced to Dash. "I covered my part. Now you take care of yours. And get the hell out of my bedroom."

Dawn stared back at him silently, painfully.

"Did you hear me, Dawn?" His voice was dangerously soft. "Return to your room, and do so now. I don't have time to deal with this mess, or the hell you're trying to throw me into, so let's just call it quits now and get it the hell over with."

He didn't wait for her to answer but stalked through the bedroom into the large master bath and slammed the door behind him.

"Cold showers don't work," she said sadly as Dash moved past her.

"Something worked the first time," he reminded her, his amber gaze warning. "Be careful if you're of a mind to hold on to him, Dawn. It might work a second time."

• CHAPTER 7 •

Seth lowered his head and braced it against the shower wall as the stinging spray attacked him from front and back. He was breathing harshly, almost shuddering from the exquisite pleasure of the water's caress against his flesh.

He hadn't forgotten what this felt like, but it was worse this time. He could taste Dawn in his mouth now as he never had before. On his tongue as he licked his lips, in his senses as he tried to take a breath without feeling her on his skin.

It was the worst agony, a bittersweet pleasure enfolded in an ache that bit straight to the bone and filled him with a furious arousal.

His dick was as stiff as a poker, heavy and engorged with blood as it stood out from his body. He lowered his hand and palmed the stiff sac of his balls, grimacing as he braced his hand tighter against the shower wall at the pleasure that sang through his sensitive flesh.

Even in the most hellish nights of those first few years after making the commitment to stay away from Dawn, the arousal hadn't been this intense. Nor had the discomfort in simply touching another woman. Something so simple as Caroline's hand against his arm, his against hers, sent shards of blistering pain through his flesh.

He forced his hand from between his thighs, forced back the need to grip the iron-hard erection and pump it to release. Because there was no relief in it; that was another lesson he had learned so long ago. He could jack off 24/7 and it wouldn't him do a damned bit of good.

He bit back a curse and straightened, shoving his hands through his wet hair and grabbing a waiting cloth from the rack beside him.

He soaped and washed, feeling every thread of the washcloth as he moved it over his body. And it made him think of Dawn. Of her hands, strong and sure as they gripped his shoulders, her sharp little nails as they raked across them.

He could feel the sting of the spray against the slight scratches. He hadn't even cared when she made them. All that had mattered was the taste of that kiss, like a drug, like power flowing into him, a tidal wave of arousal and strength as he devoured her lips and tongue.

And when he moved lower—he shuddered at the memory of kneeling before her, staring at the swollen bud of her clit as it peeked through the lush, glistening lips of her silken, hairless pussy.

He ground his teeth to hold back a moan at the remembered smell of that intimate flesh. Like sunrise. Like standing on his balcony at dawn and tasting the ocean. Fresh, clean, tempting.

His mouth watered at the thought of tasting her, at the anticipation that had rolled through him as he almost, just fucking almost, tasted the most lush flesh that God had ever created.

And he couldn't have it. He was a fool to kiss her. Demented if he thought he could have her now any more than he could have had her ten years ago.

What the hell was he supposed to do when he had her beneath him and the past rose in her mind and he saw the fear in her eyes? That was his nightmare. One that had chased him through ten years of fitful sleep. Dawn's eyes widened in fear, tears filling them as she begged him to stop, and he was so aroused, so desperate to fuck her that he paused at the gates of paradise and cursed her.

As he closed his eyes, he could still see the images from the disc Jonas had played years before tearing through his mind. Dawn, no more than a baby, mindless in agony and fear, begging God as those bastards told her God didn't exist for her. And they raped her anyway. They raped her as the most inhuman sounds he had ever heard came from a child too small for the monsters that took her.

If there were tears left inside him to shed, he wondered if he would shed them now.

The woman he had held in the study downstairs hadn't been a child though, and there had been no fear. She had been a temptress, wild, seductive, hungry. She had been wet and desperate for his touch, whispering his name and begging for more as he tore at her clothes.

As he bit her. He hissed in a breath. He had bit her neck, sucked at it, marked it. That mark was still there for the world to see, and they would see it.

Caroline had seen it and been enraged. And he refused to feel guilty over it.

He had been considering more than the occasional fuck with Caroline, but he hadn't made her any promises. To the contrary, he had warned her a year ago that he had no promises to give her and she had refused to listen.

Tomorrow, the Lawrence heli-jet would take Dawn off the island and return her home. That was the best place for her, not here, not where Dawn could stare at him again with betrayal and agony filling her eyes because Caroline had thrown herself into his arms.

He couldn't get that look out of his head any more than he could get the taste of her out of his mouth.

Getting over her this time would be worse than hell. Worse because he knew her kiss, knew the unique flavor of her hunger, the silken feel of her flesh, the sight of her need glistening between her thighs.

But he would get over it. He had beaten it the first time; he would beat it again.

But sweet merciful heaven it hadn't been this bad the last time. Even during the worst nights, the most aroused agony he had gone through, it hadn't been this bad. His skin hadn't itched with the need for her hands alone. His cock had never been so engorged, so violently aroused that even the wash of the water over it was an untold pleasure. But it was nothing compared to her lips against his chest. Her nails raking his shoulders.

Before he could stop himself, he struck out, slamming his fist into the ceramic of the shower wall as an enraged snarl tore from his lips.

Damn her. Fucking damn her, he hadn't asked for this. He'd stayed away from her, and by God that was what she had wanted from him or she would have sought him out.

Tomorrow. Dash better get her on that fucking heli-jet tomorrow or he wouldn't be responsible for his actions. Ten years was long enough for a man to torture himself over a woman. He wouldn't be tortured any more than he had been already. If she wasn't on that heli-jet, then she was going to be on her back with his dick buried so deep inside her she wouldn't know where he ended and she began. And God help them both if it wasn't what she wanted.

◆   ◆   ◆

Dawn didn't sleep that night. She tossed and turned in the bed, listened to Seth pace the floors, and she stared at the ceiling, a frown furrowing her brow at the scent of arousal and fury that wafted from his bedroom.

She wanted to feel regret. It was obvious he didn't want her there, even more obvious that he truly had been ready to begin a life, of some sort, with that corrupt little witch he had had at his side.

She couldn't feel that regret though, and she couldn't make sense of what she was feeling. As though a veil had fallen between the old Dawn and the one that had emerged at the knowledge that Seth had a lover, Dawn no longer knew herself.

As morning peeked over the horizon and she rose, showered, despite the extreme sensitivity of her flesh, and dressed in the more socially acceptable formal uniform that the Breeds wore when working social functions, she was still frowning.

She wore a silk undershirt beneath the baby-soft cotton of the short-sleeved black dress shirt. She tucked that into snug black slacks and strapped on her utility belt before securing her weapon holster to her thigh.

A Cougar emblem with the initials B.B.A., Bureau of Breed Affairs, was stitched to the right sleeve. Under it were four small silver stars, announcing her status as commander.

On her feet she laced dress boots that went to her ankle rather than hiking boots, and tucked a dagger into the sheath at the side of the right one. Then she moved to the mirror that sat on the chest of drawers across the room.

She saw a woman she didn't know.

She hadn't had her hair cut in a while. The short strands were whispering around her face, a few inches longer than normal, almost falling to her shoulders. The tawny gold color was mixed with hints of red and darker brown, shades of sunlight and earth. Like the cougar. Like the animal she could feel rising inside her.

She was still short. Nothing could change that, barely five four, but she made her stature work. What she couldn't accomplish with the advantage of height, she had been taught to make up for in calculated treachery. She could take down a Breed twice her size without getting a bruise, because she could move around him, below him, she could hit him where it mattered and use his height against him.

But she was still a woman. Her breasts were about the right size for Seth's hands. He had filled his fingers with them the night before and groaned at the fit. Her stomach was flat, her legs well toned. She wasn't a beautiful woman, nothing compared to the cool, dark beauty of Caroline Carrington.

But Seth belonged to her.

She felt her breath hitch at the thought of losing him. She had suffered; she had fought to strengthen herself, fought to get past the dark nightmares enough to gather her courage and maybe, one day, arrange to be where he was, to see if there was a chance.

She had tried to find a way to be a woman rather than the frightened child Dayan had used so easily, but maybe it had taken too long. Love could turn to hate, she had heard. Had the heat that tormented her tormented him until that had happened?

She wiped her hands over her face before staring at her image again. She had almost feline features. The high cheekbones, the narrow face and stubborn chin. Her nose was narrow and a little short. And it turned up at the end like a perky teenager's. She had always hated that. And she had never cared about her looks, so why was she standing here now as the first rays of the sun slid across the sheltered balcony outside?

Shaking her head, she pulled the communications link from

her utility belt, unfolded it and attached it to her ear before activating.

"Report," she spoke into the slender wand of the mic quietly.

"Someone needs to pull your mate in off the balcony," Moira said with her faint Irish brogue. "He looks better than that coffee he's drinking."

Dawn's lips tilted sadly and she thought longingly of a cup of coffee. She knew the hazards of it. She would probably end up ignoring the hazards, but she knew them.

"Down, Moira," Dawn murmured when she wanted to growl in possessive anger.

"Morning recon of the island is complete," Lawe reported in. "Merc and I have just made our way back. There's no sign of unauthorized landings or wandering guests."

"We're moving from the house to begin morning security protocol." Noble Chavin's rough growl filled the link.

"And wit'out me mornin' cho'olate," Styx said mournfully. "Lass, ye need to be talkin' to him about this."

The Scots Wolf Breed was a true anomaly within the species. Not so much in his love of chocolate, but in his overall attitude. Styx didn't get temperamental; he could be savage, he could kill, but he did it with a smile. He had fun, no matter what he was doing, and he drove the rest of the team crazy in the process.

But he had an instinctive sense of danger that no other Breed could touch, and a sense of smell when it came to tracking that couldn't be beat.

"Did you beat Styx out of his chocolate, Noble?" She chided him mockingly.

Noble snorted. "Some blond-haired vixen fed him chocolate most of the night in his room, Dawn. I'm amazed he can still walk today."

Styx chuckled. "He be jealous."

"And we've reached radio silence," Noble announced, indicating the boundary of the main grounds around the estate they would patrol that day. "Contact in two."

Two hours, unless extreme circumstances occurred. Dawn braced her hands on her hips and paced over to the duffel bag that she hadn't unpacked the night before. From within it she pulled free the sat laptop. The satellite-linked personal PC would give her a clearer view of the main grounds from the

Lawrence satellites. Pulling her PDA free from the utility belt, she powered it on and checked her inbox for the files she had ordered on Caroline Carrington.

She had received part of them the day before, but the Breed contacts in New York had promised her more sometime today. There were no files listed, but there were two messages from Callan and one from Merinus. They weren't marked priority, which meant they were personal.

She didn't open them.

She knew her brother and his wife. If there was an order in one of his messages that he was afraid she would ignore, then Merinus would know about it, and Merinus would add her own gentle pressure that Dawn see his side.

Merinus had softened Callan within the first years of their marriage. The savage killer, the Council-trained assassin that Callan had been, had bent beneath the gentle weight of Merinus's love. And it was a good thing, Dawn reflected. But when it had happened, Callan had suddenly begun directing his attention to Dawn. To seeing things she didn't want him to see. To trying to make up for things that had never been his fault.

"Your mate has finally left his balcony," Moira sighed in regret and relief. "He should really wear a shirt this early in the morning, Dawn."

Dawn sent her a muttered growl. "Don't look at his chest."

Moira chuckled.

"We have a heli-jet incoming," Noble reported. "Lawrence Industries. Were we expecting more guests today?"

Dawn quickly pulled the information up on her laptop.

"All guests present and accounted for," she informed him before hitting the security button and pushing the PDA back into its protective pocket. "Moira, you're with me. Noble, Styx, converge on the jet and get me visual. Dash, are you available?"

"Stand down, the jet is expected." Dash spoke quietly into the link. "Styx, Noble, resume radio silence and stealth protocol. Dawn, in my room."

Dawn stiffened, her eyes narrowing at the resignation in his tone. She flipped the mic up, disconnecting voice ability into the link while maintaining the connection to the group.

She stalked to her bedroom, jerked her door open and started toward the opposite hall. And saw Seth slipping into the bedroom he had taken Caroline into the night before. She paused in the hall, glaring at the door, a growl rumbling in her throat as she fisted her hands at her sides.

From her ear, privacy protocol beeped its summons. Absently she lifted her fingers and pressed against the back of the ear clip as she flipped the mic down.

"I'm waiting on you, Dawn," Dash said quietly.

Her eyes narrowed as she turned and moved quickly to Dash's suite.

The door opened as she neared it, and Dash stood back from the entrance, watching her quietly. He was dressed in jeans and a silk shirt, and he pulled the link clip from his ear as she moved inside.

He was alone. Evidently Cassie and Elizabeth either hadn't awoken yet or were busy elsewhere.

"Why the heli?" She rounded on him as he closed the door and turned to face her. "And why wasn't I informed?"

He ran his hands over his short, black hair and breathed out roughly. "The heli is here to transport Miss Carrington back to her home. Seth is sending her off the island."

Dawn's lips curled in satisfaction. Seth might be in the witch's room, but he wasn't touching her. She knew he wasn't. If she'd thought differently, there would have been no way to control the feral rage she could already feel brewing inside her.

"Sanctuary's heli is being prepped on its pad as well. You're to gather your gear and return to home base. You'll be sent out on another mission the moment you arrive."

The smile slid from her face as she focused that anger simmering inside her on the powerful Wolf Breed.

"I won't be leaving."

She watched as Dash crossed his arms over his chest and stared back at her broodingly. "You were given an order, Dawn," he stated flatly. "I'm command here. It's your place to obey it."

"You don't have the right to give that order." She kept her voice calm, confident. "My mate is here. Mating heat has been established. You can't order me to do anything that requires leaving Seth's presence."

She knew her Breed Law where the Bureau was concerned, and she knew Dash did as well. They couldn't make her leave. Only Seth could make her leave.

She watched the subtle, almost hidden curl of Dash's lips.

He knew that, and she wondered at the point behind making such a useless order.

"I made a deal with Seth last night," he stated then. "He would send Miss Carrington home, and I would send you back to Sanctuary. This is a very delicate time, Seth needs his wits about him, as do the Breeds protecting him."

Dawn lifted her head as she felt her chest clench at the knowledge that Seth would make such a deal.

"Why would he do that?" she asked then, a frown pulling at her brow as she tried to hold back the pain of knowing that Seth would attempt to do such a thing.

Dash shook his head. "Ten years of mating heat, Dawn, that he managed to kick. Ten years without his mate. Without ease. I suspect he doesn't want to revisit that hell."

"But it would be worse now," she said softly. "And I'm here. He's not alone."

Dash stared back at her calmly, compassionately. "Are you aware that ten years ago, Jonas and Callan showed Seth portions of the lab tapes that Callan found when they searched Dayan's home?"

Dawn stepped back warily. If her chest had been tight before, there was a band of pure agony clenching around it now.

She licked her dry lips and fought to pull her eyes from Dash's. She could see it in his eyes: the truth, the knowledge that Seth had seen her, as an animal. A creature snarling, spitting, screaming. Abandoned by the God she had screamed out to.

She shook her head slowly. "Callan wouldn't do that." Her brother would never—he couldn't—do something so vile to her as to allow her mate, the only man whose eyes she could bear looking into for long, to see the horror of what she knew had happened. What she knew, but couldn't remember.

"I talked to Callan this morning," he told her. "He's more worried for you now than he was then, Dawn. He was desperate to give you time to find your confidence, to get past what Dayan had done through the years that you should have been free. He thought he was saving you."

"No!" Her hands came up as she shook her head, blinked. "No. He didn't do this to me." Her cry was a ragged, feral sound.

Oh God, Seth had seen those images. The images the Council had placed in the files that Callan had managed to steal before their escape.

Her lips parted as she forced herself to breathe, forced herself to get control of the pain beating down on her. God, when would it end? When would the pain and the betrayals stop?

Her mate had a lover. Had considered marrying another woman, having children with her. Her brother had betrayed her by showing her mate her worst nightmare, her greatest humiliation, and her mate didn't want her. Even now. Even after the pleasure they had shared the night before, he wanted her to leave.

"Those days were bad for the Breeds, Dawn," Dash continued. "For Callan. He was fighting to keep his family safe, his pregnant mate secure, and trying to hold back the supremacist societies rising against him. And you were almost broken by Dayan. Callan had only learned what happened with Dayan's death the year before. He was grief-stricken, guilty that he hadn't protected you. He had to protect you. It was his place to do that as your pride leader."

"Stop!" She pointed her finger back at him, and couldn't look him in the eye. He knew. He knew what Seth had seen, he had probably seen it himself.

"Did you think I didn't know what was on those tapes?" she growled furiously. "Did you think Dayan didn't show them to me? Often?" She sneered at the memory of them. "He had no right. Callan had no right to do that to me."

"He had every right," Dash said gently. "As your brother and your protector."

"I'm sick of his fucking protection and I don't need yours," she yelled out at him. She didn't cry, she didn't beg. Her voice rose in anger and in determination as her gaze met his. "You have no right to make deals with my mate and you have no right to conspire with Callan to keep me from him."

"And you have no right to destroy a good man's life with something you can't go through with, Dawn. You've seen the images. Fine, you know what's in them. You still wake up Sanctuary with your screams when you dream of it, and you still haven't remembered the events that those discs are made of. You've run from Seth for ten years; now you expect him to fall in with your wishes, despite his belief that the first time he takes you, he's going to throw you back into that hell. Aren't you asking too much of him? He's a strong man, but I don't think he's that strong. I couldn't be that strong."

Dawn straightened her shoulders and refused to break his gaze. Her soul cringed at the words falling from his lips and she could feel something breaking inside her heart. Because of what others had done to her, her mate couldn't bear to take her?

"This is none of your business." She felt as though she would crumble to the ground with the effort it took to force those words past her lips. "You can't order me from here. If Seth wants me gone, then he can lodge a complaint with the Breed Cabinet and go through the proper channels to get rid of me."

She forced herself to walk calmly, sedately across the room, past Dash and to the door.

"Dawn, Seth is going to hurt you," he said behind her, his voice heavy with that knowledge. "Mating heat isn't controllable. When he takes you, he may not be able to stop if the past rises against you and sends you back to those memories. And then I'll have to kill him. I won't be able to stop myself. You're family. Don't do this to your entire team. To yourself or to your mate."

Her lips twisted bitterly as she turned back to him. "What makes you think that I don't want to remember what they did to me?" she asked him heavily. "That I don't want to be a mate to Seth? What makes you think that for ten years my heart hasn't broken a little more every day without him? And what gives you or Callan the right to make these decisions for me?"

She stared back at him, seeing in his eyes the lack of confidence they all had in her. All these years she had fought, strengthened herself, forced herself to fight past her fears of just being in a room with another man, for this? So no one could even give her her due and see that in so many ways she had succeeded.

"I'm not a child. I'm not the daughter that you still bloody Breeds over flirting with, nor am I still the broken little girl Dayan created. And as God is my witness, I don't know if I can ever forgive either of you for interfering in my life this way. Not you, Callan or Seth. I don't need any of you to make my life decisions for me." She snarled, the anger beginning to burn, not flame. It was burning. It was a hot, bitter coal in the pit of her stomach that sent pain tearing through her entire being. "Fuck off, Commander Sinclair," she gritted out. "And tell Pride Leader Lyons and Director Wyatt they can both do the same. Because if I leave here, I won't be returning to Sanctuary ever."

She jerked the door opened and stepped out of the room before slamming it behind her and moving quickly along the hallways to make her way from the house.

Turning toward the main hall, she saw Caroline's door open and Seth step out of it. He was pale, sweating, and the woman's scent hung on the air around him like a stink that sickened her gut.

She stopped in front of him, staring back at his harsh face, into his brutally stark gaze.

"You're a coward," she whispered. "Even more so than I ever was."

She didn't give him time to answer, but brushed past him, making certain she didn't touch him, that she didn't tempt the feral fury brewing inside her by allowing that woman's scent on her own body.

She left the house and joined her team to ensure her mate's protection. The mate that didn't want her.

◆   ◆   ◆

Cassie stepped from her bedroom and turned her eyes to her father as he pulled the sat phone from his belt and, she knew, prepared to call Callan.

"Stay out of it." The words slipped past her lips as she watched him, watched him frown back at her darkly.

She could feel Dawn's pain like a lash of psychic energy whipping around the island. It was so great, burning so bright, it seared at the edges of her mind.

"Cassie—"

"Dad, Callan can't protect her any longer. Dawn's awakening. You can't make her go back to sleep or you'll kill her."

He closed the phone slowly.

She rubbed at her arms as she stared around the room. The fairies were so few now. Or the ghosts, as others called them. They were so dim, and the one that had carried her through the most hellish years of her life was rarely present at all.

But there was one. The small, huddled shape of a child. The child Dawn had left behind so long ago. Ghosts were the energy of those lost souls that had left their mortal bodies. Cassie knew she also saw the forms of other beings. Parts of people and Breeds who were lost or left behind, denied by the living beings that should shelter them.

It was that part of Dawn that followed her like a bleak little shadow, begging for shelter, begging to come out of the cold nightmares that held it.

"She promised me," that little being whispered. *"She promised me, and now she ignores me. You have to make her see. She has to keep her promise or we're all lost."* That child that Dawn refused was dying. And if the child died, then Dawn would be no more than a shadow of what she was now.

"Cassie, she's not as strong as the others." Dash sighed. "You know that as well as I do."

Sometimes her father understood her. He always accepted her and trusted her. Tears filled her eyes as she felt the conflicting urges rising inside her. The good and the bad, she called it. The wolf and the wicked coyote. And he loved both.

She turned back to him as a tear fell. "You have to let her fight this battle. If you don't, she's dead to us." She looked at the fog that made up the child. "And if that happens, then one day I'll be lost as well." She turned back to him, her lips trembling as her own nightmares rose within her mind. But she knew her demons, met them each night and remembered them each time she woke. "If she doesn't remember, then more than just the child she refuses to remember will die."

She watched as he slowly slid the small phone back into its clip then opened his arms to her. She ran to them, ran to the security, the safety and protection he had given her, without question, most all of her life. He was her rock. Her father. More a father than any man who could share her blood, and she knew he had seen and sensed the terror inside her.

As his arms closed around her protectively, she let another tear fall, for Dawn. She wished Dawn could know this security as well.

· CHAPTER 8 ·

That night, Dawn dropped her clothes to the floor and collapsed into her bed before curling into a tight ball. Her womb was twisting inside her belly, convulsing as fire poured through her veins and the taste of the mating hormone filled her senses with dark arousal.

She lay atop the sheets, the temperature control in the room turned down to the fifties, and still she was sweating. Sweating and exhausted. So weary from lack of sleep, from fighting the mating heat and herself, that she was praying for sleep. For once in her life the nightmares weren't as frightening as lying here night after night, awake, and needing Seth with a bitter intensity that she was suddenly afraid would pour free.

She had stayed far away from him as much as possible throughout the day. She stared blindly into the darkness of her room, her eyes dry, the tears locked inside her. She couldn't force herself to be around him, even to breathe in the scent of him that she needed so desperately. Just the scent of him.

She locked her arms around her stomach and tensed against a wave of gnawing pain. She couldn't look him in the eye, because he had seen—

She swallowed tightly against the sickness rising inside her.

She didn't want him to see her, she didn't want to see that knowledge in his eyes again. Because she had seen those discs, she knew, frame by frame, the images they contained. And he had been the one person she was certain, to her soul certain, hadn't seen them.

And she had been so wrong.

She rolled over on the bed and stared up at the ceiling, feeling the need that tore through her like a hungry beast. The arousal, the aching desperation for his touch. It hadn't changed for her. She hadn't lost the need as he had; this was just another night, another torment to add to the others.

How could Callan betray her this way?

She pushed her fingers through her hair as waves of red-hot mortification and confusion whipped through her mind. She had depended on Callan that first year, she knew that. After Dayan's death. After Callan killed him. She had let him protect her, let him draw her beneath his wing and help her find her way.

She shouldn't have done that, she saw now. She shouldn't have placed that burden on Callan's shoulders.

You're weak, Dawn. Look how weak you are. So weak you couldn't endure what the rest of us learned how to live with. Look at that, Dawn.

The girl on those discs fought. Feral. Enraged. And she prayed. She prayed, and Dayan had laughed at it, laughed because he told her God didn't care. He had proved it by taking her mind and leaving the animal to fight.

And Dawn felt no more for the memory of the images he had showed her than she did for any other image she had ever viewed of any other Breed. She felt regret, compassion for that child. And she felt humiliated, dirty, because Seth had seen it. He had seen her pray, and he had seen that God had turned the other way.

She blew out a weary breath and closed her eyes. She had to sleep. She couldn't afford to leave Seth's protection to a broken, exhausted woman. Just a few hours. She set her mental clock, her inner defenses, to awaken her in time to keep the dreams from slipping into her head like the malevolent creatures they were.

Not that she ever remembered the dreams. But she couldn't let that animal free again. The one that awoke Sanctuary with feral, enraged feline screams. God help her if Seth ever had to see that, because she didn't think she could bear that humiliation.

Sleep. She forced herself into the sheltering darkness, shut down her thoughts and made herself rest. As she had done so many times before.

◆　◆　◆

An imperative, though slight, knock sounded at the bedroom door. It was muffled, but it didn't stop. Seth snapped his lips together as he rolled from the mattress and padded in his sock feet through the bedroom and into the sitting room.

He didn't have to pause to dress, because he was still damned well dressed. Slacks, shirt and socks. He wasn't about to take his clothes off and feel the sensuous slide of the silk sheets against his flesh and remember how much softer Dawn's flesh had been.

Hell no, he wasn't going to try to sleep. He was going to stare at the damned ceiling all night long. Again.

He jerked the door open, then paused in shock at the sight of Cassie. Her face was paper white, all those curls hanging around her and flowing to the waist of the long, white gown and robe she wore.

"Seth." Her voice sent chills up his spine. "You have to do something, Seth. She's waking up." Her eyes were huge, neon blue in a face parchment white.

"Dawn." His gaze jerked to her door. He knew she hadn't left her room. "What do you mean, Cassie?"

A tear fell from her eye. "She's waking up, Seth. You have to go to her. Now. You can't let her wake up alone. Please, Seth. Please."

He clenched his fists at his side then ran his fingers through his hair.

"Cassie," he groaned in frustration. "Dammit, I can't go to her."

"Seth. Don't you love her anymore?"

Love her? He had never stopped loving her.

"This isn't about love, Cassie."

"But it is, Seth. If you love her, you'll be there when she begins to wake up. You have to, Seth. You have to, or she's lost to us forever."

The chills that went up his spine turned to daggers of fear. He didn't know what the hell she was talking about, but he had heard enough about her over the years that he couldn't ignore it.

He grimaced painfully, then stepped back into his room and closed and locked his door, before striding to the door that connected to Dawn's room. And, of course, it was unlocked. She could lock the hall door, but she just had to leave this one unlocked.

He stepped into the dark room, not certain what to expect, but he wasn't expecting what met his eyes. She lay on her bed, stiff and still, her breathing harsh and heavy as small, terrified mewls left her lips. She was sweating heavily, her body jerking.

And something broke inside him, because he knew where she was, he knew what dreams had stolen her and why Cassie was so concerned now.

"Dawn," he whispered her name as he moved to the side of the bed and sat down warily.

He didn't want to frighten her, didn't want to make the nightmares worse. But God damn it if he could stand to see her this way.

"Dawn, baby, wake up." He reached out and realized his hand was shaking as he touched her hair then and had to clench his hands to keep from shaking her.

"Oh God. Oh God. Oh please God . . . save me . . . save me . . ." The words whispered from her lips; desperate, guttural, tight, pain-filled sighs, a breath of sound, nothing more.

"Dawn! Wake up!" he snapped, raising his voice, suddenly terrified.

Her eyes flew open. She stared at the ceiling, her breathing harsh, her pupils dilated and she jerked as though attempting to free herself.

It hurt him to watch her try to breathe, hurt him to see her gasping for air. He reached out and gripped her shoulders, unable to stop, breaking apart inside at the fear on her face, and pulled her to his chest.

"Dawn, please, baby. Please wake up." He held her head to his chest, his head bent over hers, and he wanted to cry. He wanted to kill. He wanted to spill the blood of the bastards who had dared to hurt her this way.

"I'm okay." Her voice was ragged, tearing past her throat in rough growls as her hands jerked up and gripped his forearms.

"Get away from me." She shuddered, shook as though freezing. "I'm okay."

But he wasn't. He buried his face in her hair and held on to her. He couldn't let her go. God help him. The feel of her against him, in his arms, against his chest—that was all he wanted. Right now, just this.

"Did I scream?" Panic filled her voice now as she began to shake harder. "Please, did I scream?"

Seth shook his head. "No. No, Dawn, you didn't scream."

No scream could have been as tragic, as desperate as those frightened mewls, that desperate, whispered prayer that had fallen from her lips.

"I'm okay then." She shook off the nightmare with an ease that left him in shock. Her muscles lost their tension, and she relaxed in his embrace, breathing out softly. "Don't let me go yet."

Let her go? Coyotes couldn't pry his arms away from her right now.

"I've dreamed of this." She sighed against his chest, her nails kneading at the material of his shirt as she shifted from fear to sensuality.

Seth gritted his teeth, and he tried to unlock his arms from around her. He tried to let her go. She was awake now, she would be okay, surely to God she would.

He had never known torture like he knew it now. He remembered once, when he had been captured during a mission in his years in the military. One time, and the bastards had spent two days torturing him. That was nothing compared to this. The pain of holding her, the arousal building in his body like a fever, and feeling her slide against him.

"It's another dream, isn't it?" she whispered. "I like these dreams. They don't hurt." Her lips touched his flesh where the shirt parted and he swore flames sizzled against the sweat he could feel building there.

"Let me dream a little longer." She pulled at the material of his shirt. "I hate it when you go away. When the dream just fades, right before I know what it's supposed to feel like."

He closed his eyes, his palms flat against the light, thin T-shirt she wore to sleep in. He could feel her flesh through it, damp, heated, her muscles relaxing beneath the fingers that pressed against her.

"Dawn," he whispered against her hair. "This isn't a good idea."

"It's just a dream." Her teeth scraped over his chest, those sharp little canines pausing to bite.

And he let her. He let out a hard, desperate groan as her lips moved up his chest to his neck. She licked and his heart almost burst from the pleasure. Then those sharp little canines raked over the flesh at the base of his neck, and she bit down.

"Shit!" His hand jerked to the back of her head and he had every intention of pulling her back.

Instead, glutton that he was, he pushed her closer and tilted his head for her, let her have her way. Let her tongue lick and stroke as heat seemed to sink clear to the vein that throbbed beneath her lips. He would have let her tear his throat out if she wanted to, he realized.

"I like this dream." She moved in his arms, her lips still at his neck, moved and pressed into him until he was leaning against the headboard and she was straddling his thighs.

He was a strong man, he had always told himself. He did the things he had to do whether he liked doing them or not. He understood his responsibilities, and he fulfilled them to the best of his ability. And he knew, he knew Dawn couldn't handle the sexuality that fucking heat bred inside him.

But was he moving away from her? Or was he touching her, helping her to slide down until the blazing heat of her pussy was riding the hard ridge of his cock with nothing but her panties and his slacks to separate them.

And he was dying from the pleasure of it. The feel of her lips against his neck, the feel of his hands on her bare flesh. And he had to have more. If he didn't have more, he was going to die.

If it was another dream, then she didn't want to know. Dawn knew she couldn't be dreaming; she knew she was awake, knew Seth was holding her, knew that she was grinding herself against the thick length of his erection, and she couldn't stop. Even though she knew he didn't want this. He had come to her though. She had awoken and he was there. She had come out of a pain-filled darkness and he had been waiting on her, holding her, his arms wrapping around her and chasing the horror away.

"I like this dream," she whispered.

"This dream is going to kill both of us." His voice was strained, and she almost smiled, but her tongue was thick in her mouth, the hormone filling it spilling from the small glands. And she needed to share.

She lifted her head from his neck, from the bite she had given him, and pulled his head down to her. He was so big, so hard and broad. In his arms she felt cocooned, protected against the darkness.

"Kiss me, Seth." She stared up at him, drugged, drowsy with the need. "Burn with me. Don't make me burn alone this time. Don't leave me again."

And she burned worse. He could see it in her, feel it in her.

"Sweet heaven, you'll destroy us both."

A man could only be so strong. He couldn't deny the sweet taste of her, and he couldn't deny her need. He could have denied his own. He could have fought it, he could have pushed himself from her, but he couldn't deny her hunger.

His lips covered hers, his tongue parting them, and he sank into bliss.

The hormone was like a narcotic, but her lips, her lips were silk and satin, and the stroke of her tongue against his was ecstasy itself.

He couldn't help but lift against her, to grip her hips and press her into the desperately hard length of his cock. He wanted inside her. He wanted to peel the clothes from both of them and let her take him just like this. Pull her down and impale her on the impossibly hard flesh as he took her with a kiss just like this. Hungry and searching, a melding of lips and tongues and a single breath that they fed to each other.

He felt his shirt slide off his shoulders to catch at his elbows, because he wasn't letting go of her ass. Hell. Fuck. His hands were clenched around the cheeks of her ass, teaching her how to move against him, how to make him insane with lust.

He was teaching her how to destroy him.

"I want you naked, Seth. Just like my dreams. Naked against me."

No. No. Hell no. He was not getting naked with her. He wasn't going to let this happen.

Her hands, silken, heated, pulled his belt free as he bucked against her. The snap loosened and she was easing back, wiggling against the grip his hands had on her, pressing into it as he felt his zipper slide free.

And was he doing a damned thing to save himself? He was a

fool. Mindless. A mindless fool, and he deserved anything that slapped into him at this point.

"Can I touch you, Seth?" Her breath whispered over his lips and fed his lusts.

"Dawn, bad idea." He was fighting to breathe, drawing in her breath and dying in pleasure.

"I dream of touching you, Seth." Her voice was the sexiest sound to ever brush across his senses.

"I'm not letting go." His fingers flexed against the curves he held captive.

"Do you like my ass, Seth?" the temptress whispered as he nipped at her lips before she leaned away from him.

He opened his eyes and knew he should have left them closed. There she was, her hair mussed and wild around her sensual features. And her hands were moving, gripping the hem of her T-shirt and pulling it up. Up.

"Ah hell, Dawn." He was staring at her breasts, her nipples stiff and reaching out to him.

His hands clenched on her ass again and he bared his teeth in torment as she lowered her hands and released his poker-hot, iron-hard dick from its confinement.

He was a dead man, that was what he was. He might as well blow his own head off rather than wait for an assassin to do it for him. Because her hands, butter-fucking-soft hands, were wrapped around his cock, stroking it between their combined bodies, sending his senses exploding with pleasure. So much pleasure. Sweet God in heaven, he had never known pleasure like this.

"Seth?" the temptress whispered.

"What, baby?" He had to grit his teeth. "What? Anything. Dawn, sweetheart, don't stop."

He opened his eyes and there were those sweet, cherry red nipples again. And he liked cherries. No, he loved cherries, and the ripest, sweetest ones in the world were right there for him to taste.

His head lowered. His lips opened, and a second later he was drawing succulent, heated flesh into his mouth. He was sucking her nipple like a man starved for the taste of a woman, lifting her against him and drawing as much of that sweet breast into his mouth as he could consume.

"Yes. Seth." She arched into him. She wiggled that tight,

sweet ass into the palms of his hands, and right there, he wondered if he would die with the pleasure of it.

Her hands were on his cock, her nipple in his mouth. He was drunk, drugged, dying with the feel of her.

"Seth. It's so good." She lifted, she moved. She undulated against him, and a second later he froze. Stock still, his head falling back to stare at her as he felt the head of his cock meet blazing, slick, wet flesh.

And then he saw it in her eyes, like a shock of cold, icy water. He watched her eyes dilate, watched the realization and the haunted fear begin to build in her gaze.

He swallowed tightly, his hands gripped her tighter, and then he lifted her, slowly, so fucking slowly and with agonized regret, away from the painfully erect flesh of his cock.

"No." She clutched at his arms. "What are you doing?"

Seth shook his head; hell, his entire body was shuddering as he pulled her away from him.

"Don't stop."

He sat her on the bed jumped from the mattress and forced the unruly flesh back into his pants as her gasping breaths sounded behind him.

"How can you do this?" Furious, hurt, the question that broke from her lips had him turned, shrugging his shirt over his shoulders as the bite at his neck burned like wildfire.

"I won't take you in fear, Dawn," he growled furiously. "I won't take you while you're staring at me with fear in your eyes. I can't fucking do it."

Dawn blinked in shock as he turned on his heel and stalked out of her bedroom, back to his own room. She came from the bed in a furious burst of energy, anger and lust zipping through her veins in equal parts as she jerked her T-shirt from the floor, pulled it over her head and stomped after him.

"How dare you!" she snarled, catching up with him in the sitting room. "Damn you, Seth . . ."

She stopped, the scent of blood whipping through her system as Seth suddenly turned, tackled her and threw her across the floor.

Bullets slammed into the walls. The ping ping ping of silenced, automatic gunfire nearly without sound until a mirror shattered, raining glass around them.

"Are you hit?" she screamed. "Seth. Seth."

She tried to roll him off her, terror lending strength to her muscles as she smelled the blood, so much blood.

"Seth!"

"Dammit, Dawn, stay still. I'm fine." He grabbed her wrist and dragged her to the door before she could regain her feet, threw them into the hall.

Bullets slammed into the door behind them.

Then they were on their feet, moving swiftly through the hall as Dash's door jerked open.

"I need a link." Dawn slid into the room with Dash, scrambling to the side bar where she knew Dash's link lay, while he rushed for another.

"Report. We have gunfire in the main room. I repeat, gunfire slamming into the main room. Report."

Her unit reported in instantly. All present and rushing to locate the source.

"Weapon is silenced. Gunfire came from the north through the balcony doors. Suspect night vision and long distance," she ordered fiercely as she caught a wrap Elizabeth threw at her as Cassie moved silently from her room.

Dash was checking the locks and the blinds on the balcony doors to the room and arming himself quickly.

"Cassie, I need clothes," she snapped before turning to Dash. "I need your secondary weapons and utility belt."

"I have them." Elizabeth was pulling them from a bag she had carried from the bedroom, and Cassie rushed from her own room with clothes and shoes.

Dawn grabbed the clothes, rushed into the bedroom and within seconds had dragged them on and tied the hiking boots Cassie had brought her on her feet. The shoes fit perfectly; the jeans and top were a little snug.

She jerked the utility belt on, secured the weapon and rushed back to the sitting room as she secured the link back on her head.

And she came to a full stop.

"No!" Terror gripped her in blinding waves. "You lied to me."

He was hit. She watched as Elizabeth tried to staunch the blood running in rivulets down his arm.

Seth's head jerked up, and she realized he had been listening to the reports coming through another link. He held a weapon in his hand, one of the heavy handguns Dash carried that were equipped with laser bursts.

She moved to him quickly, ignoring the silent, warning look he was giving her. As though she had no right to be angry with him.

"We have bigger problems." His jaw clenched furiously.

"Bigger problems than you bleeding to death in front of me?" she snapped.

"Much bigger." He rose to his feet as Elizabeth tied off the bandage. "It wasn't just my blood you smelled in there. We have a body. One of my board members, and one of the few who supported me."

· C H A P T E R   9 ·

Dawn crouched by the body and lifted her gaze to watch Dash's expression as he surveyed the dead board member as well.

"Seth has contacted the authorities on the mainland," she murmured. "They're on their way in."

Dash nodded slowly, his amber eyes narrowed as he stared at the blood that stained the carpet and the expression of blank shock on the dead man's eyes.

His name was Andrew Breyer. He had a wife and two children who were currently being comforted by Elizabeth and Cassie in another room. He was fifty-two years old, robust and in good health, and he had three holes made by a high-powered, silenced rifle buried in his chest, dead center to his heart.

"He's close to Seth's height, though wider, a bit thicker in the middle," Dash murmured. "There's no doubt the shooter was after Seth."

Dawn swallowed tightly. That shooter had managed to lay a gouge along Seth's shoulder before he had thrown them both to the floor.

She stared around the sitting room, feeling the bile gather in her stomach and in her throat. The shades were drawn across the balcony doors now, the windows closed tight, but Dawn knew that if an assassin could get his hands on a silenced high-powered rifle then one with penetrating night vision could have easily picked Seth out through something so paltry as shades.

"There are storm shutters at the side of all the windows and doors." She rubbed her hand over her face and stared around the room again. "He won't leave his suite; we can secure it. That would ensure his safety here."

"Did your team find the shooter's nest?" He lifted his head, his gaze penetrating, icy.

Dawn shook her head tightly. "It couldn't have come from the island, Dash. My team has checked everywhere. The angle of the gunfire, the complete stealth. I suspect one of the tour ships that leave the mainland and pass by. The shooter had to be there. There's just no way to achieve the same angle in a smaller craft."

"There are plenty of trees, plenty of cover around the house," he pointed out.

Dawn nodded. "That's true, but neither Styx nor Noble can find a hint of the scent. And you can silence a weapon, but you can't cover its scent, especially once it's fired. It would have been there, somewhere. The entire team has canvassed the area and there's nothing. I've called Callan and asked for reinforcements. We're going to have to have another team out here. We don't have enough agents."

He stared at her silently for long moments. She was only second command, but she was in charge under his supervision. Calling in more agents was her prerogative, but she knew if he felt they weren't needed, they would be called back.

Finally, he nodded. "You're right. We need two full teams to cover this. Amazingly, none of the other board members or their families are requesting transportation off the island. Rabid curiosity." He shook his head. "God save me from it."

Dawn shook her head and moved back from the corpse to get a better look at the middle-aged board member. She had met him the night before, wandering the gardens alone. And now he was here, dead.

Lowering herself, body flat, she ignored Dash's curious gaze as she inhaled the scents closer to the floor.

Thankfully Seth was in the hall with the other board members. If he had been closer, her senses would have been so swamped with him that she could have never sifted through the scents here.

She wanted to turn the body over, wanted to do her own investigation. She was hampered by the authorities, who had demanded preservation of the scene. As though Breeds didn't know how to conduct an investigation. Prints had already been dusted for; ultraviolet had already swept the room, and a collection of fibers, hairs and other assorted evidentiary items had been collected.

Her eyes narrowed as her gaze was caught by something lying close beside the hand that was tucked partially beneath the victim's body. She could barely make out the tiniest hint of a piece of paper.

"I have something here, Dash. Paper. It's under the body."

Dash growled at the inconvenience of the position. They couldn't touch the body in any way and risk the authorities' ire in this matter. The situation was too tricky.

Dawn adjusted the latex gloves on her hands and waited until Dash could move in beside her. He flattened himself to the floor and peered at the area Dawn was pointing to.

"Merc, get the forceps from my bag," Dash murmured.

A second later the surgical steel forceps were in his hand and Dash flashed her a smile. "Never know when you might have to extract something in our line of work."

Then he was wedging the forceps beneath the body and slowly pulling the paper free. They were lucky; the dead man wasn't gripping the paper. It had fallen from his hand as he fell, and it was marred by only a spot or two of blood, sheltered as it had been between the arm and the body.

"Here we go," he muttered, taking it from the metal grips and slowly unfolding it.

Dawn read it, then looked back at Dash in concern.

Tell Seth now! the note read.

"Someone is paranoid," Dash said softly. "Hard copy rather than e-message. I'd suspect Breyer found this note in his room rather than having it passed to him."

Tell Seth now. Tell Seth what? Dawn rose to her feet beside Dash as he had the note stored in an evidence bag, then tucked it easily into the inside, hidden pocket of his military-style shirt.

"Dash, Callan just contacted. He'll have four additional

agents flying in within the hour." Merc's leonine features were harsh, the dark, gold brown eyes flat and cold. "Satellite also pinpoints a large vessel anchored within line of sight of this room, for four hours prior to the shooting. It pulled anchor and moved out just after the shots fired at Seth and Dawn. We have no reports of the vessel docking at any of the nearby harbors, and all indications are it was stealth equipped. It wasn't on our radar."

"Not a tour ship but close to it," Dawn snapped, furious. "Son of a bitch, how were they able to stealth equip such a large vessel?"

"They couldn't, unless it was military," Mercury rasped. "We almost missed it with the satellites, and identification of it is going to be impossible."

"Council." Dawn pushed her fingers roughly through her hair as fear began to brew in her stomach. The Genetics Council still had ties to the military in every section of the world.

"Why would the Council target Seth?" she growled, looking back at Dash. "He isn't the only one funding Sanctuary. Why him and not others?"

Dash's eyes were narrowed as he stared around the room.

"Merc, Dane Vanderale is in residence. See if you can convince him to get his people to loan us one of the Vanderale sats. If we combine it with the Lawrence sat we're using, then we can possibly keep this from happening again."

"They'll find a way onto the island next," Dawn muttered. "This didn't work, so they'll be pissed. They'll come in closer."

"And when they do, we'll have them." Dash's smile was cold. Hard. "I want this suite secured, doors and windows shielded at all times. And you're off the team now." He turned to Dawn as she blinked back at him, shock and anger slicing through her.

"Not because of performance, Dawn," he snarled quietly. "I want you close to Seth at all times. I want your attention on him, your focus on him. Besides the fact you're now in full heat and that compromises your focus, I know if you're with him his chances of surviving this increase. You're at his back, watching every breath he takes. Is that understood?"

She swallowed tightly. He was right. Her focus was compromised and she knew it. Already she could feel her insides shaking, her need for Seth's touch, his smell beginning to undermine her strength.

She nodded tightly before she sighed in agreement and looked around the room again, searching for Seth. She was furious with him. He had not only lied to her about being hit, but once dressed and armed he had joined the team to search for the shooter. And he had ignored her objections, only staring at her with those cold, steel gray eyes before turning away and doing as he pleased.

"Civilian authorities are flying in," Moira reported through the comm link. "We have two official helis with six heat contacts inside."

"Direct them to the private heli-pads," Dash ordered through the link. "Sanctuary is due in approximately eight hours. Contain and secure until reinforcements arrive."

"Contained and secured." Noble came through. "We have visual, four points. No other air traffic, and all water traffic is being redirected for the next three hours only."

Dash blew out a hard breath and stared back at Dawn. "Time to dance, Cougar. Let me do the talking; you smile and be pretty."

She stared at him in surprise. "Excuse me?"

"Civilian forces are fascinated with the female Breeds. Hopefully, these will be too. Let's not show how slick our women are if we can get by with it."

Dawn's lips almost twitched in amusement. Even the Council had never known what they had created when they stepped into creating the female Breeds. The females' delicate builds, at times preternatural beauty, and air of delicacy had been a disappointment in the labs. The females were naturally cunning though, in ways the males weren't. Instinct had perfected that ability.

So few of the females had survived though. The males numbered in the hundreds, the females only a few dozen. But those who had survived were more dangerous than even the male Breeds wanted to admit. And were filled with such fury, such hatred, that even Sanctuary worried about their survival.

Like Dawn, the torture the females had endured had scarred them psychologically in ways the males hadn't been. It had created killers that even the Breed Cabinet didn't understand, in ways that the females never shared with any but their own kind.

Like the Lionesses Dawn had commanded at Sanctuary. They had formed groups. They hunted in groups and they killed with deadly efficiency.

Women were supposed to be the gentler sex, but the Council

had ensured that all the gentleness was raped, maimed and tortured out of their females before they ever reached maturity.

It was another secret the Breed community kept closely guarded. They kept their females as tightly within the compound as possible, protected them when they no longer needed protection, and fought to preserve the belief in the civilian population that their females were no more dangerous than any civilian-trained female.

There were times it was laughable. Because the females that had come from those labs were more feral than any human woman Dawn had ever encountered.

She played her role. She stood back, watched the men and few women investigating and used shy looks and a soft voice. She fooled the men, but she knew the women suspected. Instinct to instinct, she felt that connection and let it pass.

Her demeanor and unthreatening air allowed her and Dash to negotiate for information and concessions. What they wouldn't give Dash, they were more willing to agree to with her.

As she worked, she was aware of Seth watching her, his eyes narrowed on her and the scent of his arousal and his jealousy flowing around her. He didn't like seeing her in the midst of these men, working their ignorance and their superiority. And that was too damned bad. Because this was his life. If it wasn't, she would have left Dash to deal with the species-superior bastards who stank of their prejudice and their hatred.

They didn't care why Breyer had been murdered. As one of the detectives stated, "Play with fire and someone will try to burn you."

Seth was playing with the Breeds, and evidently that was reason enough to die in the eyes of these men.

By the time the body had been bagged, the evidence collected and the statements taken, the sun was rising over the island and the guests were wandering slowly to their beds.

Dawn stood beneath the shelter just past the heli-pad the authorities had used to land, and she watched their heli-jets lift slowly into the air, bank and head back to the mainland with the body and Breyer's family.

"They've been corrupted by the Council." Mercury stepped from the darker shadows of the small radar and control room used to bring the jets in.

Dawn nodded slowly. She had sensed it more strongly in the

head investigator. Whoever had planned this already had their cards in place and was waiting for that winning hand.

Mercury leaned against the doorway of the electronic room, his gaze narrowed on the rising sun, the savagely hewn, lionlike features tight with disgust. "Makes a Breed want to go hunting."

Dawn watched him carefully, seeing the glitter of death in his dark eyes. "You've been around Jonas too long." She sighed.

And he grinned with a flash of savage, sharp canines. "Maybe Jonas has been around me too long."

Shaking her head, Dawn moved from the heli-pad and strode across the cement walk that led back to the main estate grounds. She was careful to stay in the shadows or within the lush patches of vegetation that afforded cool comfort beneath the heated rays of the sun.

She watched the area closely, her senses reaching out—sight, smell, instinct. She sensed something, but couldn't put her finger on it, couldn't get a scent or hear anything to place with it.

She paused next to one of the low-branched sheltering trees and watched closely, cautiously. Was it the heat making her feel off balance? Making her feel as though she were too easy to see and someone or something was curious? Perhaps dangerous?

She narrowed her gaze and swept it over the areas where an assassin or sharpshooter could be hiding with a line of sight. She couldn't sense anything, couldn't feel anything moving but the breeze.

But she could feel the heat. She could feel the swollen folds between her thighs, her clit throbbing, her juices building once again around the sensitive little bud.

Her nipples were so tight and hard they were painful beneath the soft cotton of her tank top. They rasped against her bra and sent a shiver racing over her flesh at the remembered feel of Seth's mouth devouring them.

She shook her head and moved quickly back to the house, keeping low and within shelter, watching her back even though she wasn't certain there was anything there. And all the while her flesh ached for Seth's touch, for the man she was certain didn't really want her, despite the lust tearing through him.

He had never loved her, she thought sadly. Otherwise, the heat wouldn't have receded from him, and he could have never taken another woman.

She shook her head at another pang of betrayal and couldn't

manage even to work up the anger against it. But as she stepped into the house, she couldn't help the sense of complete and total isolation that swept through her. Her mate wasn't really her mate, and the brother she had loved so dearly had betrayed her in ways she couldn't comprehend.

She could understand Seth's reaction to the renewed heat, and even his inability to love her. But Callan—she couldn't accept what Callan and Jonas had done. And accepting that Seth had seen that disc and walked away had been one of the hardest things she had ever done.

He had walked away when he should have fought for her. She would have fought for him. Through hell or high water, Coyotes or a brigade of Council soldiers, she would have fought for him. Just as she was fighting for him now.

She was unaware of the fragile, broken sound of pain that left her lips at that thought. But there was someone that heard the sound as it drifted along the breeze. Eyes narrowed, lips tightened.

◆　◆　◆

As she moved into the house, he lowered the gun sight and blew out a silent breath, too soft for even the earth itself to feel.

If he wasn't watching, waiting, if he wasn't the shadow drifting around the Lawrence Estate, he would have shaken his head at the sound of the broken child. It was a sound he had heard many times, and it still had the power to effect him.

As he watched, a lone figure stepped out from an upper room. Dressed in snug jeans, her cropped shirt conforming to full young breasts, her flat belly glistening in the morning light as long, pitch black curls whipped in the wind.

Her scent carried to him, and his eyes narrowed. She was and yet she wasn't. The fabled half-breed, sought after by every Council scientist in existence and rumored to be psychic. The bounty on her head was horrifically high. A man could live three lifetimes on the money to be had in securing this one, tiny young woman.

And she was tiny. Fragile in appearance, but he sensed the strength in her, the steel core of determination and stubborn resolve that filled her.

And he felt something more. He felt the dark sensual side of his nature as it gave a curious, heated stretch.

And she was staring right at him. Dark brows were creased into a frown, her lips parting as something akin to fear flashed across her expression.

And a muted cry slipped past her lips. One of fear.

A second later, Dash Sinclair whipped past the doorway, his large body blocking sight of her as he swept her against his chest, sheltered her and rushed her back into the house.

He tilted his head and watched curiously. There were many players here, many targets with bounties on their heads higher than the income of some nations. All in one place.

He smiled, a tight, hard smile that kept his canines hidden, kept the sun from flashing against them. He sniffed the breeze and closed his eyes at the smell of sweetness, of innocence only subtly marred by feminine fear.

That girl had every right to feel fear. She was marked as no other Breed in existence was marked. Sought after, searched for, the bounty paid only if she was delivered alive and with her virginity intact.

She was a weakness he was surprised other Breeds hadn't already disposed of. Of course it was said her father, Dash Sinclair, protected her ruthlessly.

Interesting. Very interesting, he thought. And intriguing.

He couldn't afford to be intrigued at the moment.

He placed his eye against the site of his weapon once again and resumed his scan. His target was here; he just had to find him.

◆   ◆   ◆

Dawn stepped back into the house and tried to shake off the vague, discomfited feeling she couldn't make sense of. Only to have it return tenfold as the refrigerator door closed and Jason Phelps grinned at her from across the room.

"Things are getting bloody around here." He snapped open the top of a beer. "Uncle Brian, one of Seth's board members, is having an aneurysm over old man Breyer's death. Can't figure out what the hell he was doing in Lawrence's suite."

Dawn's eyes narrowed at the certainty that he was fishing for information from the dumb little female Breed. Her hand rested on the grip of her weapon within its holster.

"I'm sure we'll find out," she told him. "If you'll excuse me."

"Why don't you like me?" He lifted the beer and took a long drink.

Dawn watched his throat convulse as he swallowed, and she had to shake away the need to see blood there. The heat was affecting her mind, there was no doubt. She had never felt so bloodthirsty, so close to violence.

"I don't dislike you, Mr. Phelps." She disliked most men. It was a part of her, as natural now as the color of her hair and eyes. It couldn't be changed, only temporarily hidden.

"I wish you liked me." He shook his head as a charming male pout crossed his lips. But it was his eyes she watched, not that there was anything different about his eyes. A little bloodshot, a little amused.

He stank of too much drink, and little else.

"I don't know you." She smiled tightly. "If you'll excuse me, I need to return upstairs. I still have things to do today."

"Yeah, none of us got much sleep last night." The tentative friendliness in his voice and demeanor didn't sway her in the least.

"Hopefully we will this morning." She nodded again and left the room before he could delay her any longer. But her hand stayed on her weapon, and her senses stayed alert. Until she hit the upper floor and scented Seth's lust.

• C H A P T E R   1 0 •

Cassie stared at Seth Lawrence as he stood talking to her father, her senses gathering the information she needed, processing it as she tried not to watch the pitiful shadow of the child hiding in the corner of the room. That ghost of what was dying inside Dawn. If the child was lost then Dawn would be lost as well.

She was still shaking from whatever she had sensed outside, just before Seth's arrival. She had been drawn to the balcony, some sense, some awareness pulling her outside though she knew better than to go there. She wasn't a stupid little girl, and she wasn't ignorant of the danger to her life at every moment.

But something had been out there. Something she was certain she couldn't miss. But she had felt . . . scared. Not in danger, but frightened on a level she didn't understand. So frightened a cry had come unbidden from her lips and drawn her father's attention.

She gave herself a mental shake and focused on Seth again. He hadn't taken Dawn. She had marked him. The mark was prominently displayed at the bottom of his neck, the little wound clearly Breed-made. The scent of the marking filled the room, the scent of Seth and Dawn, though the two hadn't mingled yet to form that unique smell that combined the two mates and changed them forever.

She frowned at that knowledge. Dawn would start remembering soon. Cassie wasn't certain why the memories would start emerging here, or why it was so important that Seth made love to her before it began, but she knew it was imperative.

The child whimpered again from the corner of the room. A sound of loneliness and pain that had Cassie whimpering. She glanced to the corner. The fragile image was huddled in on itself, weak, lost. Terrifying in the complete isolation that surrounded it.

When the memories began returning, if Dawn didn't wake up and accept the child she had forgotten, then she would never heal. And she would never be able to save Seth.

"Too bad no one will be there when Dawn wakes up." She looked at Seth, angry at him now, knowing the risk he was taking. But if she told him, if she explained, then it wouldn't be Seth's choice. And she couldn't do that to Dawn. Callan had betrayed her in showing Seth those discs; she had heard Dawn's rage and pain when Dash told her of it. She wouldn't betray Dawn further by guilting Seth into the other woman's arms.

She had warned him; there was nothing more she could do.

"What do you mean, Cassie?" he asked her then, his eyes narrowing on her.

She frowned back at him. "I can't tell you everything, Seth. I'm only eighteen and I'm not a damned seer." The uncharacteristic anger shocked Seth as well as her father. It shocked her. "But it's too damned bad, if you ask me, that you can't see what's right in front of your face. And if you're not man enough to see it, then I wouldn't point it out to you even if I did know."

She turned away from them and moved quickly to her own bedroom, aware of her mother following her, those maternal instincts reaching out to her daughter. But she didn't want her mother, she didn't want her father. For some strange reason, she wanted to return to the balcony.

Seth watched her flounce back into her room as Elizabeth followed, and he turned to Dash. Dash was staring back at the door, his jaw clenched as a growl rumbled in his throat. Seth could see the frustration brewing in the Wolf Breed and felt a flare of male sympathy. Cassie was a gorgeous young woman and her unique Breed traits made her both an asset and a weakness to the Breed community.

"What's going on?" he asked the other man.

Dash shook his head, his expression concerned. "She went out on the balcony earlier after I warned her not to. She never ignores those warnings, until now. I heard her cry out and jerked her inside. She's been acting strange ever since."

Strange with Cassie could be terrifying to others, Seth thought. The girl was strange in and of herself.

He pushed his fingers through his hair and shook his head. Hell, he could barely think right now. Exhaustion and arousal were weighing down on him, and his control was shaky as hell.

"My suite should be clean by now." He sighed. "I'm going to catch a few hours' sleep. We've delayed meetings until tomorrow, but tonight's party is still scheduled and I'll need some rest to face the questions there from the board members."

"I've taken Dawn off the protective detail." Dash surprised him with the announcement.

Seth tightened his jaw. "She's leaving?" It would be for the best, for both of them.

"No, she's not. She won't be on detail, she'll be on your ass. She sleeps in your room, eats where you eat, goes where you go. She's your shadow."

Every cell in Seth's body screamed hallelujah, while his mind seemed blank in shock. His shadow? There wasn't a chance in hell he could keep his hands off her if he allowed that.

Dawn, at his beck and call? At his back every second? In his bed and close enough to touch anytime he needed to touch her, anytime he wanted to pull her against him?

"No," he snapped.

He'd spend every moment of his time buried inside her and begging her to let him touch her just a little bit more. Hell, he'd kill them both with his lust if he had a chance. And God help his soul if he managed to trigger the memories inside her.

That was his nightmare. That was the demon that rode his back even when he had her in his arms.

"Fine." Dash shrugged, his gaze hard, determined. "But you can be the one to throw her out of the room. She has her orders, and besides that, she's your mate. She's a danger to herself if she's anywhere but at your side. Don't underestimate that part of her that's claimed you, Seth. The woman might be hesitant, but trust me, the animal that shares her soul won't let her do any-thing else. Hurting the woman won't change it, but you could end up destroying someone that so far has managed to survive despite others' attempts to destroy her. Tread warily, my friend. I'd hate to see you fuck up here."

"And I'm getting damned tired of these riddles and half warn-ings," Seth growled. "There's not a damned one of you facing what I have to face. Do you have any fucking idea how much that woman means to me, Dash? Do you think I walked away because it was what I wanted to do? That I left her alone because I didn't crave her with everything in my soul and not just with my body?"

"I don't know," Dash said quietly, glancing to the door that opened into the hall. "Maybe it's something she needed to know though."

Seth swung around to the doorway, and something in his chest, his heart, melted, burned. She was staring at him, her lips parted, innocent, so fucking innocent her eyes were shining with it as she stared back at him. She looked like a woman in love, filled with hope, terrified to believe that anything could be hers, let alone the man she was staring at.

He knew that look, he knew it, because sometimes he felt it within himself. The hope that she could be his, one day, some-day in the future, the prayer that the woman inside her could fill those parts of his life that were so empty.

He snapped his teeth together, furious at being manipulated as he had been. Dash would have known she was on her way up, known she would be there to hear every word. And there he stood, his soul bared to her, and every measure he had taken to protect her lying at his feet in the dust.

"Son of a bitch," he muttered.

He was too damned tired for this. Breed mating heat and the symptoms of age delay served him well during board meetings and all-night negotiations against younger, up-and-coming ty-coons, but it wasn't doing a damned thing to aid his control and his strength where one tiny Breed female was concerned.

As he watched, the look slowly eased from her face and it became smooth, her expression curiously bland. Shaking his head at the look, he strode to the door, gripped her arm and pulled her with him.

"At least I'll know you're not out there hip deep in fucking bullets and looking for blood to spill," he snarled.

As she had been for ten years. Oh yeah, he'd kept up with her, and the resulting nightmares had left his guts cramped with terror.

"But I dodge bullets and spill blood so well," she pointed out with wide-eyed, obviously false innocence and a flash of bitterness.

"No doubt." His mouth thinned with displeasure. "And I guess you think that's going to work for me if I take you to my bed?" He pushed her into the sitting room, dragged her past the newly cleaned carpet and into the bedroom, where he secured the doors and turned to face her. "Do you think for one damned minute I'll tolerate you running around the world being shot at? Risking your life and mine?"

"You act like I enjoy it." Where had the bitterness in her eyes come from? He had never seen that. He had seen mocking amusement, anger, but never regret and bitterness like this.

"Don't you? Dammit, Dawn, every Breed in Sanctuary is terrified of you."

"Of course they are." She rolled her eyes mockingly then. "I practice on them. They never know when a roof will fall in on them or when they'll get caught in a trap I laid for them." She shrugged. "I'm sneaky like that. It comes from being so short."

Short his ass.

"You're like fucking dynamite. A little bit goes a long way."

Amusement replaced the bitterness. For a second, just a second, her eyes sparkled with it, before they dimmed and she became solemn once again.

"Look, I get that you're not all about this mating thing with me." Desperate levity filled her expression. The smart-ass was making a comeback because the woman couldn't bear to be hurt again. "And I can handle it, really. But I'd at least like to see you keep breathing. Even if you do have a habit of fucking other women when I'm not around."

"Dammit, it wasn't like that." He reached out for her, then jerked his hands back, clenching them. "I didn't think there was a chance for us, Dawn. If I had, for even a second, things would have been different."

"And of course you didn't think to ask me." She lifted her shoulders as though it didn't matter, when he knew it did. "Just as you never ask me now. You just keep playing the martyred male, Seth. It hangs so well on you."

He was hurting her and he knew it. She could feel and smell his regret, his hesitancy in taking her. They were going to have to talk, he knew it, and he hated it. Because he knew it was the last barrier to accepting all of it. Hell, he'd already accepted it; he just needed her to know, to understand. It hadn't been a lack of love—it had been an excess of love.

"Tell you what." She cocked that shapely hip again, propped her hand on it and arched a brow. "You just contemplate this to hell and back, and I'll go shower. I smell like blood and sweat, and frankly, I don't sleep so well when I stink."

Oh yes, the smart-ass was back. Dawn was pissed off and she didn't hide it really well. His lips almost twitched. He would never have to worry about whether or not she was angry with him—he would know it by her flippant speech and total disregard for his male pride. Or what pride he would have left, because once he had her, he knew he would be on her ass 24/7, eager for more.

He watched, slowly shaking his head as she turned and stalked to the bathroom, the door slamming behind her.

No one will be there when Dawn wakes up. Cassie had said those words, and now Seth knew why the need to refute them had risen in his head. Because he intended to be right there, beside her, holding her, no matter what she awoke to.

She had come to him so many times, and he had turned her away. He had stayed away when he should have fought for her. He had left her alone when she needed to be held.

And now he had no choice but to go to her, and he prayed she didn't reject him. He prayed because, suddenly, life looked very bleak without her.

◆   ◆   ◆

Dawn adjusted the shower to a temperature as hot as she could stand and, naked, stepped beneath the stinging spray of three separate shower heads.

For pity's sake, who needed three shower heads in one shower? It defied explanation. Just as the emotions rising inside her defied explanation. She felt like crying. She wanted to lay her head against the shower wall and sob, but Dawn hardly ever cried. Not when she was hurt, not when she was angry, not when friends died or when they walked away.

She hadn't fallen to the floor with the screams welling inside her when she learned her mate wasn't her mate, and she didn't let the need hovering inside her now escape.

Because she wanted to pray. And if Dawn didn't cry, she certainly didn't pray. Why pray to a God that had deserted her? That hadn't heard her screams as a child, and hadn't heeded her tears? She believed in His existence, but unlike other Breeds, she didn't believe He agreed with theirs.

She shook her head and washed her hair quickly before tipping her head back to rinse the soap from her hair. As her head lifted, her eyes jerked open, and her lips parted on a gasp.

The shower door was open and Seth was stepping into the spray of water. Powerful muscles rippled beneath his flesh, and standing out from his body, thickly veined, the crest dark and furiously engorged, his cock demanded her attention.

A light mat of hair covered his chest and arrowed down his abs. It sprinkled over his arms, thighs and legs, and as she watched he slowly soaked the cloth he held in his hand and soaped it with a bar of sweet-smelling soap that he held in his hand.

"Ten years ago," he said, "I started collecting soaps for you. There were about half a dozen before I was led to believe that you didn't want me, that you wouldn't want me. But somehow, the habit held. There are over two dozen now. Several are quite unique, one-of-a-kind scents just awaiting your approval before the soap makers I found create more of what you enjoy."

Her lips parted in surprise as he carefully set the creamy bar on an inset shelf.

"This one I found in Morocco." He stepped forward and laid the cloth at her neck before beginning to wash her. "There's just the lightest touch of sandalwood, though it's often used just for men. Once I described you, the soap maker thought perhaps a scent that denotes male and female would be appropriate. A combination of us both."

Dawn almost swayed as she stared up at his face, fascinated by this information, by the gentleness and the heat in his expression.

"The scent is simply Dawn," he said softly. "The soap maker said it would hold the scent of a new day. Fresh and renewed, and touched by fire."

And that was how it smelled. Not flowery or strong or even musky. Just clean and warm as it frothed with thick, rich bubbles.

"I think I like this one," he told her, his voice harsh despite its gentleness. "It does smell like you, Dawn. Like both of us, combined."

She stood, shell-shocked, as he soaped her from neck to ankle. The thick, scented lather clung to her skin and filled the steamy interior of the shower with the scent of a new day and a heated male. Like the smell of Seth last night, his need flowing from him, wrapping around her and heating her all the way through her pores.

He washed her stomach with slow, sensual strokes. He parted her thighs and her breath caught in her throat as he washed her there. Washed her thoroughly, then cupped water and rinsed her with all the anticipation and reverence of a boy opening a Christmas present.

"What are you doing?" she finally managed to whisper, uncertain how to respond, or what she should do.

"I'm seducing you, Dawn." He leaned forward and kissed her thighs, pausing to inhale the scent of her as she felt the juices slowly building on the sensitive folds of her sex. "Every woman should be seduced her first time with a lover. Gentled. Eased. Pleasured."

She shook her head at the sight of the water running through his hair, where her hands should be.

"But it's not the first time," she forced herself to remind him. "I'm not a virgin, Seth. You know I'm not."

He had seen the discs, he had seen what they did to her. Not just once. More than once before her escape with Callan.

He touched his lips to the top of her mound then, and she shivered with the pleasure before his head lifted and he stared up at her, his gaze dominant, possessive.

"You're wrong, Dawn," he said then. "You are a virgin. Sweetly innocent, untouched by a lover's hands. All your pleasure is mine, isn't it? Your passion for me, your need for me. You are a virgin, sweetheart, more than you'll ever know."

She blinked back at him in confusion as he rose, towering over her, to turn her. The spray from the front shower washed the soap from her body as he began to lather her back. And that was even more sensual. She couldn't see him; she could only feel him. Feel the suds gathering on her, caressing her even as his hands caressed her, stroking her flesh, delicately massaging her muscles.

"Once, I was in Russia," he murmured at her ear. "It was colder than I could ever imagine cold, and there I was, standing on the balcony of my hotel looking out at this pristine, gorgeous snow-covered forest. And I imagined you there, sharing that with me. The next morning I went out and found a soap maker. And I requested that scent for you. The scent of the forest at evening, of those first rays of the moon striking the snow. When I use that soap on you, I'm going to be buried inside you. So you can feel the heat that snow holds trapped. Deep within the earth, burning and waiting for spring. That's what I'm going to be, Dawn, that fire burning inside you as I bathe you with the scent of snow."

Dawn felt the little cry leave her throat and her knees went weak. The next instant his arm was around her waist, holding her steady as that diabolical washrag began to wash her rear.

"And this is the most gorgeous ass in the world," he growled. "I almost started collecting panties for you, but somehow that just struck me as obsessive, don't you think?"

She shook her head.

"Good, then you won't be surprised when I pull out the few pairs I collected for you, no more than a few dozen, and ask you to wear them for me. Silk and satin and lace so delicate it's no more than a whisper against your flesh. I'll come just thinking of you wearing those panties beneath those mission pants you wear. They have ribbons too. And little bows. And some don't have a crotch. I could slip right inside you, and not have to worry about tearing them from you first."

She couldn't breathe. She was sweating despite the water pouring over her and wondered if she was going to melt right there in the shower.

Curling tendrils of white heat were traveling through her body, and she could feel her flesh prickling with the most amazing pleasure. As though his words were stroking her skin, traveling over her entire body rather than stroking that damnable washrag over her ass, over and over again.

He dipped into the cleft between the cheeks, cleaned her there, and then she felt the water rinsing her. Rinsing as he stroked, as he cupped the cheeks of her rear and hummed his appreciation in a kiss on each curve.

"I love your ass, Dawn." His voice was rough, filled with hunger. "I swear I'm going to come in my pants every time I watch you walk. I watch these sweet muscles bunch and move, and all I can think about is clenching them while you ride me."

She couldn't swallow, she couldn't moan. Her legs were shaking as she felt the weakness in them, and when his tongue licked over the inner curve of one cheek, she knew she was going to sink to the floor of the shower.

"Steady there, sweetheart." He gripped her hips and held her still. "Stand right there for me. I'm dying to touch you. To taste you. My mouth is watering for your kiss the same way it's watering for the taste of your sweet pussy. I want both. I want to suck that pretty tongue in my mouth and I want to drive you crazy while I suck your sweet clit into my mouth."

She was going to—do *something*. She had read about this feeling, but she hadn't read about it being so strong it clenched her womb, sent agonizing streams of pleasure tearing through it as her clit throbbed with a feeling of near rapture.

She had never, never known pleasure like this. There was nothing to compare it to. No way to know what she should do or what she should say.

"I want to touch you." Her voice was whisper thin and pleading. If she was touching him then he couldn't be stealing parts of her soul a little piece at a time with his words, his touch.

"Not tonight, Dawn." He rose behind her and she felt his erection, so thick and hot at her lower back. Powerful, throbbing like her clit was throbbing, and her mouth began to water. It began to water and the hormone that filled the glands of her tongue began to flow free.

The taste of heat filled her senses. The scent of him wrapped around her, and as she felt the water shut off, felt him pull her back against him, the woman and the animal merged to stretch, to rub, to prepare herself for possession by her mate.

‧ C H A P T E R   I I ‧

She purred. Seth heard the sound and felt the head of his cock flex and throb before pumping a fierce blast of semen against her back.

He thought he was going to lose it right there. She had purred for him. Rumor was that the female Breeds didn't purr. The males could, especially during sensual, sexual activities, but not the females.

His female did. She stretched in his arms, her pert little ass tucked against his thighs, and a low, soft rumble vibrated either in her throat or beneath those pretty, swollen breasts, he couldn't be certain which.

It wasn't a constant rumble, about the duration of a sigh, but it went through his bloodstream like wildfire. His Cougar purred. His fierce, determined, explosive little mate had purred for him.

His teeth clenched as he opened the door of the shower, keeping one arm securely around her, and jerked the towel from the warming bar on the shower door. It was soft and warm, perfect to dry her. Just as the scented oil he had laid out by the bed was perfect to stroke her. If he could find the control to do it. If he could wait just a little bit longer to possess her, then he would try it out as well.

He had oils to match the soaps. What was obsessive if not that? God in heaven what had made him think he could ever live his life without this woman?

"Let me dry you." He turned her in his arms, gazing down at the drowsy, sensual features as she stared back at him in feminine confusion.

"Why are you doing this?" She was watching him as though the answer were important to her. As though the fact that he was doing it astounded her.

"Because I've dreamed of it." His lips quirked into an unwilling smile. "Dawn, I've fantasized about it. Even after the hormones from the mating heat disappeared, I still stood in the shower and jacked off thinking about it."

"Even when you were with the others?" A sparkle of anger lit the depths of her eyes.

Seth drew the towel down her back, over her rear, and stared back at her somberly. "Even then, Dawn. And even then, there was no satisfaction. There was only the emptiness that gnawed at me, no matter where I went or what I did."

He should have fought for her, he thought again. He should have told Jonas and Callan to go to hell rather than letting them play upon his own fears. That had been his weakness. She was so small and delicate, and he was so much larger that he had already feared hurting her. Once he'd seen those images, the soul-deep knowledge of the damage he could do to her had slammed into his brain.

"I dreamed of you too," she whispered, and the sound of her voice broke his heart. All the loneliness, all the agonizing nights of arousal and heartache that he had felt now echoed in her voice. "I dreamed you came to me."

"And I've come to you." He dried her slowly before quickly whisking the towel over his own body.

When he lifted her in his arms, his chest actually ached. She gasped in surprise, her hands catching at his shoulders as though no one had ever carried her. And he didn't doubt no one had. He doubted Dawn had ever been spoiled with either affection or pleasures.

"What are you doing?" Her voice was thin, faint, as he carried her to the bed.

"Seducing my mate." He put his knee on the mattress and lowered her to it. "Are you willing to be seduced, mate?"

Her face seemed to transform. It softened, grew more sensual as her eyes slitted with seductive awareness.

"You really want to seduce me?" There was innocent wonder in her voice, a woman's surprise and pleasure. A lover's sensuality.

"More than I want to draw my next breath," he revealed, and he knew it was the truth. Nothing mattered—not riches or fame, not breathing or living—other than seducing this woman.

He had lived his life, gone through each adventure, each trial and success, for one purpose. For this purpose. For this moment when everything he had was focused on pleasuring his woman.

He moved over her, watching as she reclined on the bed, alluring and naturally sensual, her leg bending, her knee rubbing against his hip as he braced his arms on the bed beside her and leaned in to taste paradise.

To taste her kiss.

Magic and flames, pure energy and electricity—that was Dawn's kiss, and it sank into his soul with the force of a tidal wave. He tasted the mating hormone that flowed from the glands of her tongue and murmured his appreciation for the sweet spiciness. But it was her lips, the curl of her tongue against his, the feel of her hands, her nails sliding over his arms that entranced him.

He wanted to feel those sharp little nails on his shoulders, his back, digging in and raking him in her pleasure.

Seth pulled back from the kiss as he heard a moan whisper from her throat. He licked at her lips and let her chase his tongue with hers. He nibbled at the lower curve and felt her tongue rub against his upper lip. It was sexy and sensuous, wickedly seductive. It wasn't the devouring, desperate greed of their past kisses. This was slow and sweet, his eyes locked with hers and that confused innocence filling her face. The rapt, absorbed pleasure, the uncertainty that he would complete it.

"Let me know," he whispered against her perfect, passion-swollen lips. "Tell me, Dawn, if I frighten you."

She frowned back at him. "Why would I be frightened?"

Why indeed.

He kissed the tip of her nose and felt her stretch beneath him, the inside of her thigh rubbing against his leg, her pebble-hard nipples burning his chest.

He could feel the need to bury himself inside her building in his balls, but stronger, moving deeper inside him was the need to simply love her. To give her the pleasure, the caresses, the building need and loving adoration he had always fantasized about.

Seth had never loved another woman. He had fucked them, he had played with them, but until now, until Dawn, he had never loved.

Dawn couldn't believe the pleasure coursing through her senses as Seth kissed her nose, then moved his lips to her jaw, to the sensitive flesh of her neck.

The glands beneath her tongue had eased, the hormone that filled them now filling him instead. He had taken it, suckling it from her, using his lips, his tongue, the warmth of his mouth to take it all. To consume it, to leave her free of the torrential effects that came from having it fill her senses.

And still he touched her so gently. His lips moved over her neck as she panted for air; his hands bunched on the bed beside her, holding his weight above her as he pleasured her with his lips. Just his lips.

He sipped from her flesh, then from her nipples. He drew the tight, hard points into his mouth and ignored her desperate cry as he suckled them into the heated depths of his mouth.

"Seth. Oh, Seth. It's so good." It was a pleasure she didn't know if she could endure. She could feel each tug of his mouth as it sent echoing sensations to her clit. Her juices spilled from her vagina, gathered on the folds of her pussy and tormented her clit with the moisture.

She opened her eyes, staring at where his lips covered the tip of her breast and watched the perspiration as it ran in slow rivulets down the side of his face.

The heat. It was burning in him and she knew the destructive power of it. But he was slow, easy, licking at her nipple and groaning as her hands caressed his shoulders, his back.

"Ah yes, Dawn," he rasped as his lips slid down the slope of her breast to her stomach. "Touch me, sweetheart. I dream of your touch. Your hands on my flesh. So soft, so sweet."

His lips moved lower. Lower.

Dawn held her breath and watched, watched as he kissed and licked his way down her stomach. His tongue dipped into the indentation of her belly button, then went lower.

She held her breath, her thighs falling apart as his broad

shoulders wedged between them and he hesitated. He hovered over the wet folds between her legs, his breathing harsh, heavy. A drop of sweat rolled down the side of his face, dripped to the sensitive mound, and she gasped.

His gaze jerked up.

Dawn watched as he licked his lips, lips swollen with need, his eyes nearly black with lust as his arms strained on the bed beside her.

"I've dreamed of this, Seth," she moaned, dying to know the feeling, to experience his lips there. "You always stop. Right here. You always stop."

"I can't stop." His eyes drifted closed, dark lashes lying on his cheeks for a moment before they opened again. "God help us both, Dawn. I can't stop now." And his head lowered.

The first swipe of his tongue through the drenched slit had her arching and crying out his name. The second teasing little lick had her hands in his hair, trying to hold him to her. After the third she lost her mind.

He settled between her thighs and slid his hands beneath her rear, clenching his fingers in the curves and lifting her to his mouth.

Lips, tongue, suckling kisses and desperate licking strokes had her writhing beneath his lips. This wasn't pleasure. This was torture. It was agony and ecstasy all rolled into one and she didn't want it to ever end. She would die if it ended. It was building in her womb, in her veins, it was whipping over her nerve endings, every one, every cell of her body, and sending them into a cataclysm of sensation.

She twisted beneath the teasing flicks of his tongue. She screamed when he plunged it inside the clenching depths of her pussy. When his lips surrounded her clit and suckled with deep, groaning pulls, she exploded.

Dawn had never orgasmed. She had never known this building, this desperate flight, this explosion that tore through the core of her body and flashed through her soul. It shook her, inside and out, had her muscles jerking, her torso lifting and her nails scouring his back as he held her there, his lips milking her, taking her places she had never imagined she would go.

Seth was burning. Not the burning he had known in the past. Not the burning he had known since her kiss. He was on fire. Flames were licking at his balls, semen seeped from the tip of his cock, and he swore the internal heat would melt him before he could get inside her.

It was the most exquisite, most painful pleasure he had known in his life.

Ten years. He had waited ten years for this. To feel her juices against his tongue, to bring her to climax with his mouth. To hear her screams in his ears and to feel her nails scratching his shoulders. And damn her, could she scratch. He arched into the little pain, growled against her pussy and licked again. And again. He consumed her release, the sweet taste of her pleasure, and when she dropped back to the bed, moaning at the slow echoes of renewed pleasure, he came to his knees and lifted her to him.

He wouldn't move over her. He couldn't take her like that. He couldn't risk the memories in either of them. Instead, he pulled her over him as he lay back and stared into her dazed eyes.

"Ride me, Dawn," he groaned, so desperate to feel her enveloping his cock that he was willing to beg. "Come on, sweetheart, take me inside you."

He gripped her hips as she straddled his thighs, watched as her fingers, so delicate and graceful, gripped the shaft and led it to the fluttering entrance of her pussy.

He was on the point of praying. She had to hurry. She had to do this or he swore his heart was going to explode from the pleasure.

He had to grit his teeth as she ran the thick head between the pouting lips of her sex; then she tucked it at the opening and he stilled. He forced every muscle in his body to freeze as he watched her face, the intensity of her arousal, the dazed, desperate pleasure in her eyes and her flushed features.

"It's not a dream," she moaned as he felt her press against the thick head and begin to impale herself. "It's not a dream."

It wasn't a dream. This time, he was here. Dawn stared down at him as he held her. If he didn't hold her, she would melt against him like butter, flow over him and sink right into his pores. And she would always be a part of him. She could never lose him if she was as deep inside him as he would soon be inside her.

She felt the pinching tightness, watched his face as it twisted with pleasure, and knew, if it hurt, if somehow it hurt bad, it wouldn't matter. To see this look on his face, she would give more than her body, she would give her life.

But it wasn't pain. Not the pain that tears and rends. It was a pleasure-pain. Agony and ecstasy as she fought to breathe, following the movements of his hands, feeling her juices ease his way, saturating their flesh as she worked herself on the stiff stalk of flesh.

His cock throbbed. The heavy veins pounded against the inner walls of her pussy and caressed in another way. The thick head opened her, the shaft stroked her. Inch by inch she impaled herself on rapture and cried out with the beauty of it. The pleasure of it. The feeling of something finally coming together. Something, someone finally belonging to her.

By time the full length was lodged inside, they were both gasping for air. Sweat covered their bodies and the fire raging between them was burning them to cinders.

"Seth, help me!" Her fists clenched against his chest as the hard cry tore from her throat. "Please." She clenched around him, felt the muscles of her vagina contract and more of her moisture ease between them. "I don't know . . ." She arched, cried out. "I don't know what to do."

But he did. His hands pulled her to him, one cupped her head and drew her lips to his, and he began to move. She was screaming into his kiss, her tongue tangling with his, his thrusting into her mouth, mimicking the hard, desperate lunges between her thighs.

"Dawn, ah God—" He bit at her lips as his cock pushed inside her pussy, stretched her, caressed nerve endings so sensitive she swore each ecstatic thrust was going to destroy her.

She tore her lips from his and lowered them to his neck. She had to breathe. She had to. Because she could feel the burn building again, as it had when his lips suckled at her clit, but this time worse. She could feel it growing in her womb, building and spreading throughout her body.

She was coming apart. The pleasure was unraveling her soul and she didn't know how to stop it. Her hips writhed as he fucked her. He fucked her hard, deep, each thrust gaining in momentum until she felt herself erupting into a cascade of flames.

She couldn't scream this time. She couldn't scream so she bit. Her teeth buried in his shoulder and she tightened to the point of breaking. Certain her body couldn't maintain such pleasure, it couldn't survive. She couldn't survive.

But she did. Suddenly, bone and muscle melted into him,

and the explosion that took her then was mindless. The ecstasy poured her into him even as he poured into her. Deep, heated spurts of semen pulsed inside her as the muscles of her vagina clamped, rippled, sucked at the hard flesh and left him crying out her name as she finally collapsed against him.

When Seth finally managed to pull his mind back into his body, he found his arms clenched around Dawn, holding her to him as she licked his shoulder lazily and he realized— A rough chuckle left his throat. "You bit me again."

"Hmmm." She licked over the wound.

"Makes three times." He had to smother a yawn before kissing her shoulder.

They were plastered against each other, damp with perspiration and fading pleasure. Seth was still buried inside her, and she was still hot and tight around him, the muscles of her pussy flexing lazily around the still-erect flesh.

She was like a sleepy little cat against him. As he stroked her back, he heard that faint little purr again. Just for a second, as though it had slipped past some unconscious barrier.

"I like that," he whispered drowsily.

"Like what?"

"That little purr." He rubbed his chin against her hair and placed a kiss at the tip of her ear. "I love the sound of it."

She was silent, still, for long seconds. "I've never done that before," she whispered, as though the fact she had done it was somehow frightening. "It makes me weird. I've never heard of the other female Breeds doing it."

"Who cares what they do. I love to hear you purr. It sounds sensual and lazy. Satisfied." And all his. He had her first, and if God was willing, he would provide many, many more purrs in the future.

He stroked his hands down her back, rubbed slowly at those pert little ass cheeks and moved her slowly along the length of his still-hard cock.

He could wait for more. He was aroused, thick and hard and buried inside her. But he could wait. Right now, he wanted to touch her. He wanted to feel her flexing against him, feel the catches in her breath and the little ripples of response each time he moved against her.

"I'm not satisfied." She stretched slowly, her hips lifting in an undulating little movement before sliding down again, consuming his cock with a heated, tight grip.

"Not even a little bit?" He smiled as he felt her lips curve as she kissed his shoulder.

"Just a little bit. Just for a few seconds." She lifted and braced her hands against his chest. "And you're so very ready, Seth. We could play some more."

Her eyes gleamed with heat and the lightest sparkle of amusement.

"You want to play, do you?" He skimmed his hands from her hips to the full mounds of her breasts.

Her nipples were diamond-hard points, her breasts flushed and lifting and lowering heavily as her breathing began to grow deeper.

Lower, where her body cradled his, deep inside the snug depths of her pussy, he could feel her response gathering again. The heated flesh was gripping him more tightly, becoming slicker, if possible, and tempting him to madness.

"Come here," he whispered. "Kiss me, Dawn. Deep and sweet, like only you can."

He watched the joy that suffused her gaze, even as pleasure washed through her body. He drew her down for the kiss, feeling her sink onto him, around him, inside him.

Sweet heaven, how would he ever survive without this again? How could he ever live without knowing her kiss, her touch?

He watched as she lifted above him long moments later, her eyes slitted, heat burning in the rich, golden brown depths. She was the most sensual, erotic sight he had ever seen in his life.

Nothing had ever prepared him for the beauty moving above him, following his direction as his hands clasped her hips and he taught her how to destroy his senses with a slow downward glide, a shift of her hips, the tightening of her thighs.

She growled as he tilted her back, directed her hands to brace behind her on his thighs and used his thumb with slow, sure movements on the tight, hardened bud of her clitoris.

"Hell, I love it when you growl like that." He watched his cock slide inside her, then she lifted, revealing her sweet juices as they clung to his heavy flesh.

"I don't growl," she panted, then she made the sound again. Soft, a rumble that was more than a purr. A sound of complete pleasure.

She tossed her head, the silken strands of her golden hair feathering around her face and neck as her back arched and he felt her tightening on him.

Seth increased the movements of his hips, plunging into her, his own breathing rasping from his lungs then. He pulled her forward, took her lips in a kiss and felt her melt around him.

She was crying out against his lips, calling his name, and the sound sent him exploding into his own release. Hard, forceful spurts of semen blasted from his cock, filling her. The pleasure tore through his body, burned up his spine and left him fighting to breathe long, long moments later.

Seth knew he should get up. He should lift her from him, clean them both and tuck her in against him, but he didn't want to move. He didn't want to move her. He wanted to hold her, just like this, where he was a part of her. Where he was connected to her in a way that filled his soul.

Ten years he had fought the mating heat. Ten years and he had given up on Dawn ever coming to him. Now she was here, and he swore, no matter what it took, he would hold her here.

❖   ❖   ❖

Dawn slept. She slept harder than she could remember sleeping in her entire life. Sheltered in Seth's strong arms, tucked close against his chest, she felt safe. Secure. She could sleep now, knowing he would hold back the night. And she slept deeper. So deep that the protective layers she had built in her mind to hold the past at bay weakened. Relaxed.

Suddenly, she wasn't in Seth's arms any longer, but standing amid the glare of bright lights and a cold that chilled her to her bones.

I'm frightened.

She turned and stared at the child that uttered the words. She was almost insubstantial. Almost a ghost. She was huddled in the corner of the cage, naked, her long hair covering most of her body, her brown eyes stark and blind with pain.

It wasn't just a child. Dawn knew who it was. It was her. The child she had forced herself to forget, forced herself to bury as deeply as possible.

As she stared at her, she felt betrayed. A betrayal that cut deeper than Callan showing Seth those images. It cut deeper than any betrayal she could remember, and she couldn't place its source. Refused to search for the source of that pain.

She shook her head. She wasn't here. It was just a dream. That was all. She was with Seth. He was holding her. Even as the nightmare images coalesced, she could feel his arms around her, the warmth of them, the safety, even though she could no longer see him.

Dawn looked around and felt terror chill her soul again. She was no longer someplace safe. She was no longer seeing shadows or darkened shapes. She didn't sense an enclosure, she felt it. She saw it.

The underground labs of the New Mexico facility that Callan had rescued them from. But this wasn't the rubble left after the escape and the explosions. This was the lab, fully functional, the monitors beeping, the computer screens showing the cages and cells. And the cages. The cages that held the children when they were unruly or when they were insane from the pain of the experiments conducted on their young bodies.

"I don't want to be here," she whispered, feeling the words lock in her throat.

"Don't bother praying," the child whispered. "If you pray, they get mean. And He doesn't listen anyway. You know He doesn't."

"Then don't pray," she warned her, furious. "Keep your damn mouth shut."

Dawn was angry with the child and she wasn't certain why.

Why would the kid want to pray? Why call out to a God that didn't listen, that didn't protect the Breeds? He hadn't created them, why should He care if they lived or died? If they survived or lived without nightmares?

The little Breed female laid her head against the bars of the cage, dejection and hopelessness surrounding her as Dawn felt her chest clench with pain. She moved closer. She wanted to comfort her, even though she knew there was no comfort she could give. She was a step closer when the girl's eyes opened again.

"Did you see his eyes?" she whispered. "I looked as he hurt me. At his eyes. Just at his eyes. I want to remember them forever so you can rip his throat out. Remember his eyes. Remember, Dawn, we're going to kill him dead. We're going to tear out his throat and bathe in his blood. We swore it. Remember that, we swore it." Agonizing pain, a brutal, animalistic growl of rage and helplessness, filled the room as the words slammed into her.

Dawn jerked back. She remembered that vow. As that knowledge tore through her brain, light and color, the ground beneath her and the world around her, shifted in a dizzying array.

Suddenly, she was being restrained, cruel hands gripping her arms and legs as she fought and bucked. Her eyes jerked around, staring at the dark shapes. They wore black masks, black shirts. They were hiding themselves, but she could see their eyes. She could see them and she could smell them and she was going to kill them.

She bared her teeth and snarled, enraged, the animal inside her tearing at her mind with vicious claws as it sought escape.

"I smell you," she screamed. "I smell you. I see your eyes. You'll die. I'll kill you."

She was screaming at one. Just one. As he moved between thighs that were restrained by steel. His lips curled into a smile as he worked his pants loose. And she stared into his eyes.

"I'll kill you." Demented, enraged, a haze of bloodred fury filled her senses as he came over her and she knew the pain he would bring to her. Not just to her body, but to the soul they said Breeds didn't have.

"You'll have to find me first."

A second later she began to pray. Fear filled her, dark and oily, sliding over her senses as she felt that first touch.

"Oh God. God save me . . . God save me . . ."

"God doesn't care." His smile was cold, triumphant. "When are you going to accept that? God doesn't care about what isn't His. You're not His. You're ours—"

She came awake. Her eyes jerked open, staring into the enraged, agonized gaze of the man she loved more than her own life.

"Wake up, damn you!" He shook her shoulders, his face tight, savagely hewn, his eyes tormented as she stared back at him.

Her body was stiff, the fragmented memories of the dream almost, just almost, receded. She could almost remember. She could still taste her own fear, hear her own prayers and the answer she had been given.

And as she stared into Seth's eyes, she knew he had heard. He knew. He would have heard her prayers. She knew she prayed in her sleep, where she refused to pray while awake. She didn't pray, because she knew He didn't listen.

But Seth did. He had heard her and he had brought her back from the dream. He had kept her from her screaming. He had kept her from feeling the pain. She knew that in a distant part of her consciousness. She might not remember the dream, but she knew the pain she always awoke to. Until now.

"Hold me." Her voice was harsh, desperate. "Don't make me be alone."

But he was already gathering her closer, the muscles in his powerful arms flexing around her as those prayers, a child's prayers, echoed in her head.

"You'll never be alone again," he whispered at her ear. "Don't you know, Dawn? God sent me to you. Tell me what to do, baby, just tell me what to do."

"Just hold me."

She wasn't shuddering, she wasn't praying. She held on to him like a lifeline and felt a coil of dread begin to unravel in her soul. Because she remembered the eyes, and she knew, knew, somewhere at some time, she had seen those eyes again.

◆   ◆   ◆

Seth stared into the dimness of the room and felt Dawn slip slowly back into sleep. He still rubbed her back in slow, easy circles as he held her tight to his chest, his heart racing furiously.

Terror had clenched his heart when she had jerked out of his arms, her arms and legs slamming to the bed as though jerked in place by some unseen force. And then she had begun praying.

Distantly, he remembered hearing the rumor that Dawn never prayed. She never attended the religious services provided for Sanctuary, and refused to be in the pastor's presence. She was one of the few that claimed God hadn't made Breeds and He hadn't adopted them.

But she prayed in her dreams. In a child's broken voice, hoarse with pain, she prayed in her dreams. *God save me . . .*

And he knew what she had pleaded to be saved from. She had prayed to God as they raped her, and they hadn't stopped. They had hurt her, over and over again. She had been taught in those labs that she didn't have a soul. That she was created by man, not by God. That God had no interest in Breeds. A child suffering through what she had suffered through, how could she help but believe it was the truth?

His little Cougar Breed believed God had abandoned her. And then everyone else had as well. Callan had left her to Dayan's insanity and then Seth had left her to the mating heat. Dawn had known only betrayal, only pain.

And yet here she lay in his arms, relaxed, sleeping deeply.

Seth had demanded monthly reports on Dawn after he left her. For years, he had called Jonas personally, making certain she had everything she needed, providing what he could to make her safer, more comfortable. And through those years he had gained some information on her.

He knew she often woke the estate with her screams, until the past few years. He knew most nights she didn't sleep at all. She dozed through the day, sometimes she napped in the forest. She made few friends, she trained religiously, and the male Breeds within the compound lived almost in fear of her. Jonas hadn't mentioned why. Dawn had been amused at the accusation, her gaze glittering with laughter.

He saw glimpses of a prankster in her, a smart-ass if ever one had been born. A strong, stubborn, determined woman, far different than that shadow of a broken child that he had glimpsed ten years before when his chauffeur had mauled her breasts and called her a Council plaything.

And now here she lay in his arms, more a lover than any other woman who had ever touched his body.

But still plagued by the shadows of a past that she refused to remember, and the God she believed had deserted her.

He sighed tiredly and kissed her brow, a smile, both of sadness and of thanksgiving, curving his lips as she purred for him again. A slow little rumble as she tucked herself tighter against him, her thigh sliding between his, her little fingers flexing against his flesh.

She was his. Now he had a find a way to save her.

"Sleep, baby," he whispered as she muttered against his chest and tried to turn. "Right here, Dawn. I have you safe."

She relaxed against him once more, her breathing light and slow, and a few moments later another little purr. And how he loved those purrs.

How he loved his Cougar Breed.

· CHAPTER 13 ·

The house came awake several hours later. The tragedy of the other night wasn't forgotten, and the guests were filled with snide questions and brittle remarks concerning the deceased.

It seemed there were few people who had truly liked Andrew Breyer aside from Seth, Dane Vanderale and Ryan Desalvo. The other guests, while outwardly shocked, some even appearing grief-stricken, were gluttonously excited over the fact that someone had actually died.

Dawn could feel the excitement humming among the guests, which totaled nearly a hundred. Hell of a board meeting getaway, she thought as she followed Seth and watched how effortlessly he played the perfect host.

The evening's festivities were yet another party. Despite her objections, the band that had been hired for the event had flown in that afternoon and set up in the huge ballroom at one side of the house. The many French doors lining the room were thrown open and crystal chandeliers cast a golden glow over everything.

Drinks flowed freely, a buffet had been arranged for those whose hunger hadn't been assuaged by the outdoor barbecue earlier, and many of the couples were dancing slowly in the center of the floor set aside just for that.

Dawn stood beside Seth, aware of his hand at the small of her back as he once again talked with the CEO of Foreman Motors regarding the vehicles they supplied Sanctuary. Timothy Foreman was also on the board of directors of Lawrence Industries and, Dawn knew, one of those who had been voicing concern over the gifts that the company was making to the Breeds.

Dressed in yet another black uniform, she was aware of the looks the other women were suddenly giving her as Seth made no secret of the fact that they were now a couple.

Dash's orders to stay on his ass not withstanding, Seth seemed to want her at his side as well.

She restrained the sudden need to fidget as the Foreman daughter looked her over once again, a moue of distaste on her lips.

Dawn stared back at her, lifting her brow mockingly. Patience Foreman didn't stink of corruption, merely a small degree of selfishness. Her pale blue eyes were curious, a bit arrogant and definitely disapproving as her gaze flicked over Dawn's clothing again.

"Would you like one?" She indicated her uniform. "I hear it's all the rage with the teenagers this year."

Unfortunately, that was the truth.

Patience's look was one of supreme offense. "Not hardly. I would have thought Seth had enough money to actually buy you some clothes."

"Why would he?" Dawn blinked back at her. "I make enough money hunting that I can buy my own."

Patience's eyes widened in shock as Dawn felt Seth's hand press warningly against her back. She smiled back at him placidly, catching the twinkle of amusement in his eyes.

"Patience is such a girly girl," Mrs. Foreman said proudly. "She's never had so much as a speck of dirt on her."

Dawn gazed sympathetically at Patience. "I'm so sorry. I promise I won't tell anyone."

If she wasn't mistaken, Timothy Foreman's cough was completely faked and the clearing of Seth's throat was more a muttered laugh than anything else.

Surprisingly, Patience's lips twitched in amusement. "I would appreciate that," she replied drolly. "And I'll be certain not to tell anyone your taste in clothes leaves much to be desired."

"Yeah, I'd hate for anyone to find that out," Dawn replied. "It could be embarrassing in my line of work."

At that moment the comm link at her ear beeped demandingly. Dawn reach up and activated it before turning away and flipping down the mic hidden in her hair. "I'm here."

"Additional agents have arrived," Noble reported. "We have four incoming. Your presence is requested in Dash's suite."

Dawn let her gaze rove around the room. Catching Styx's eye, she indicated that he should take position at Seth's back. With a quick nod Styx moved across the room, his powerful, bold presence receiving more than a few appreciative female looks.

"I'll be right back." She turned to Seth as he leaned closer to her, his gray eyes concerned now. "Styx will keep you company." She shot him a grin as he grimaced at that information.

"If you'll excuse me." She nodded to the Foremans politely.

She left the group quickly, made her way through the house and then to the upper floor. The place should have come with a map, she thought as she moved past the other guests then took the stairs quickly before maneuvering through the hallways to Dash's suite.

She gave the door a quick knock, then waited until it opened. She knew the moment she saw Dash's expression, the compassion and sympathy in his eyes, that she wasn't going to like what was awaiting her.

She stepped inside anyway, aware of the door closing behind her as she faced the two men she had hoped to avoid, preferably indefinitely.

"Well, what an honor," she drawled mockingly. "Pride Leader Lyons and his henchman, Director Wyatt. To what do we owe the pleasure? Or were you just looking for a really cool party to attend?"

"Dawn," Dash said warningly, his voice darker, more commanding.

"Oh yeah, that whole respect thing." She shrugged her shoulders as she shoved her hands into the back pockets of her uniform pants. "Sorry 'bout that, Dash. I must be low on sleep or something." Or tolerance. Forgiveness. Or maybe it was understanding she was low on. Understanding how her brother, the man she had depended upon totally, could have betrayed her as he had.

She watched the wariness that flashed in his beautiful golden eyes, the regret and the anger. In Wyatt, she saw only cold silver eyes staring back at her from a savagely remorseless expression.

"I'm busy right now," she told them both. "So if you just wanted to say hi, consider it said and I'll go back to the party. It's really great. My uniform is all the rage."

She swallowed back the pain, the incredible fury at the knowledge that these two men had stood with Seth in that office in Sanctuary. That they had shown him that disc, the images of the child that she had been, the animal those labs had turned her into.

Callan grimaced, his canines flashing as he pushed his hands through his hair and glanced at Dash. There was a flash of retribution in his eyes.

Seeing him dressed in a silk business suit, his heavily muscled body flexing dangerously beneath it, Dawn knew she should be wary. Callan was normally a patient pride leader, but he didn't tolerate disrespect at all. And that was too damned bad tonight.

"Dash, you aren't needed right now." Callan flicked his gaze to the Wolf Breed. "I'll take care of this."

Dash crossed his arms over his chest and stared back at Callan. "I'm her commander here, Callan, that supersedes your authority over her outside Sanctuary," Dash pointed out to him.

"Then I'm telling you to leave," Jonas growled. "I am your superior."

Dash laughed at that. "If you want to try me, Jonas, we can go head-to-head right here, I'm all for it. But it's not something you want to do."

"And all this flexing of male Breed muscle is really swoon worthy," Dawn injected sweetly. "But completely juvenile. Can I get back to the party now? Seth promised me a dance, you know."

"We're going to talk," Callan snapped. "Now."

"We have nothing to discuss, Pride Leader Lyons," she informed him coldly. "The time for talking to me is, oh, I'd say about ten years past."

As she stared back at her brother, she found herself, amazingly, wanting to cry. There was a difference between battling tears and wishing one could shed tears. In this case, Dawn wished she could shed the tears and maybe, in the process, ease the agony filling her as she stared back at him.

Jonas didn't matter; he was just a prick and everyone knew it. A calculating, manipulating, game-playing son of a Council member. That was what everyone knew him to be, so there was no foul there. A Breed could expect him to do something so utterly evil. But Callan. Callan, who she thought loved her, she couldn't make sense of at all.

"Dash shouldn't have told you," Callan sighed, shaking his head. "Not yet."

"Really?" She blinked as though in amazement, when she wanted to scream at him in fury. "Perhaps he should have told me sooner, Callan. Then maybe, just maybe, my mate wouldn't have gotten over me. Maybe he wouldn't have slept with other women instead of me." Her voice rose before she snapped her teeth together in fury. "Oh, how calm and regretful you were before I came here," she whispered. "Telling me that my mate, my fucking mate, slept with other women. That he would marry another. That he *deserved* a life outside me." She was shaking now. She jerked her hands from her pockets, and before she could stop it her finger was pointing at him accusingly. "You nearly cost me everything I hold dear with your bloody interference."

"Or did I save your sanity at a time when you could ill afford to divide your strength between a mate demanding your presence in his bed, and the strength you needed to deal with what Dayan did to attempt to destroy you?" he asked. "Tell me honestly you could have slept with him, Dawn, and I'll accept your judgment of my actions."

She hated that tone of voice. The grieving resonance, the pain in his eyes as he stared at her. The way his fists clenched at his side.

She remembered the day he had found those discs. How he had drawn her into a room alone, closed the door on the others and laid them slowly on the table as she stared at them in horror.

A tear had slid down his cheek. A single tear as he asked in a voice savage with raw emotion why she hadn't come to him.

Dawn shook her head now, as she had then. "I don't know. No more than I knew when I came here how I would respond. But since that question has been answered to everyone's satisfaction now, perhaps it could have been then."

"You were still waking us with your screams almost nightly," he snarled. "You couldn't bear to be in the same room with the man without shaking in fear, and you ask how I could do such a thing to you? How could I not?"

"Because it wasn't your call," she snarled right back at him. "He was my mate. He wasn't a ravening monster that had no self-control. You should have trusted him. And you should have given me the chance." Her fists clenched as the rage threatened to engulf her. "You took my choice, Callan. And that was wrong. You took my mate when I ached for him, when I needed him. And you took my choice." Just as it had been taken so many times before.

"That smirking son of a bitch. He was so arrogantly cocky, strutting around Sanctuary as though he owned the place and watching you like a hungry dog. You were too fragile. He had no control then, Dawn. He had nothing but his hunger and his certainty that what he wanted should be his."

"If that were true, then he wouldn't have given a damn what you wanted," she yelled back. "You let your guilt nearly destroy me, Callan. You didn't want me with Seth, because if I left, then you couldn't make up for the years that *I*, myself and no one else, allowed Dayan to destroy me."

The room was silent as she finished. She stared back into Callan's tormented gaze before she turned her attention to a silent Jonas.

He stared back as expressionlessly, as coldly and unmovingly, as an iceberg. She respected him, but she didn't particularly like him. There were very few who did.

"I wanted to protect you, Dawn." Callan exhaled roughly. "I still want to protect you, but not to the extent that I would have held you back from your mate if I thought for a second that being with him wouldn't have traumatized you worse at the time. I did what I felt I had to do."

His golden eyes swirled with emotion. Anger and regret and power. Callan carried his power easily. His shoulders didn't bend from it, and he never flinched from what he had to do. Callan was never weak, and he never faltered. And she knew he didn't regret that long-ago decision he had made. Nothing she said, nothing she felt, would ever change that about him.

"You and Jonas make a good pair," she finally whispered sadly. "You don't care about the individual Breed you're making the decisions for, all you care about is your own idea of what you believe is right for them."

"That's not true," Callan snarled furiously.

"But it is true," she refuted calmly, yet she felt broken inside. She felt as though she had lost something imperative to her life, and in a way she knew she had. She had lost the brother she knew she could depend on—no matter what, she had believed Callan would be there for her. And she had been wrong.

"I nearly left Sanctuary that first year without Seth," she told him. "I nearly ran, because I couldn't bear smelling the scent of him each time he came to Sanctuary and believing he didn't want me enough to so much as seek me out and say hello." She shook her head painfully. "You and Jonas decided my life for me, and you nearly decided my death. If Seth had married another, if he had impregnated that cow who'd been trying to trap him into marriage, then it would have destroyed me as nothing else. Is that what you wanted for me?"

"I wanted you whole," he bit out, pushing his hands through his long hair as he glared at Dash again. "That's all I ever wanted for you, Dawn."

"I'm whole now," she assured him flippantly. "You can fly back to Sanctuary with a clear conscience. Been nice seeing you. Tell Merinus hi."

"Don't be a smart-ass," he growled. "It's not pleasant."

"Oh, you think it's not pleasant?" She rounded her eyes and stared back at him incredulously. "Wow, Callan, should I bow and ask your forgiveness now? I guess you just might have to accept it for the time being, because attacking you isn't an option. Merinus might hurt me."

Jonas shifted then. A smooth flow of muscle, not a tensing, but a warning. She turned back to him and smiled coldly.

"I want to be around when you find your mate," she snarled.

His brow lifted. "I doubt she would give me the trouble it would appear you give those who love you, Dawn."

"I bet she digs a very deep hole and does all she can to hide from you," she retorted insultingly. "And I couldn't blame her. Her life will be nothing but a series of attempts to avoid your calculations. Tell me, Jonas, how did keeping me away from Seth benefit you? It must have, or you would have never done it. Did it keep the money flowing in? Was Seth more charitable when he believed he was protecting his woman than you thought he would have been if he had had her?"

Her fists clenched at her sides as the pain drove spikes of

fury into her brain. She knew Jonas. She knew how calculating he could be. One person's pain wouldn't be a blip on his radar when it came to the welfare of the Breed society as a whole.

"It was my decision, Dawn. Not Jonas's," Callan stated firmly.

She stared back at her brother. She had always admired his strength, his integrity, his determination to see not just the Breeds as a race survive, but each individual Breed survive whole and intact. Until her.

"Why, Callan?" she whispered. "Why would you do that to me?"

Before he could answer, Dawn tensed at the scent of her mate outside the door. A second later the door opened behind her and Seth stepped inside.

"Come to join the party?" She turned to him with a bright smile and a clenching of her stomach. The arousal was there, but so was the pain. "Come on in. It's just getting fun."

He didn't say a word. He moved to her, his broad palms cupping her shoulders as she turned, drawing her back against his chest. She felt his heartbeat, his warmth. His scent and his strength wrapped around her, and her breath hitched with the renewed pain that fed into her soul.

"Callan." She felt Seth nod behind her as Callan glared at Seth, the gold of his eyes flickering with anger.

"You weren't invited to the meeting, Mr. Lawrence," Jonas said, his voice dark, controlled.

"My house." Seth shrugged before Dawn could snarl back at the Breed director. "I didn't need an invitation."

Dawn breathed in, her gaze still locked with Callan's as she moved slowly out of Seth's embrace. She would face them all on her own terms. She didn't need a protector, she needed a partner.

"We were discussing old times," she told him brightly, crossing her arms over her chest as she watched his hands slide into his trouser pockets. "You know, all those nasty little images they used to run you off without telling me about it." She met his eyes, and it hurt. There was somber acceptance there.

"I had a right to know, Dawn," he told her. "Callan wasn't wrong in allowing me to see the hell they put you through. I was wrong to stay away."

She flinched. Suddenly, for a second, those images were more than just the images of a Breed being tortured. They were *her.*

For a second, the protective shield she had placed between herself and the past slipped, and she was sucked into a rage, a horror, an overriding shame so deep, so agonizing, she had to turn her back on them to hold back a cry.

Just as quickly it was gone, but not before she heard the muttered curse and enraged growl that came from Callan's throat. In the past, it had been his arms that had sheltered her when she felt broken; now, it was her mate's arms. They wrapped around her, strengthened the control she was fighting for and returned the strength to her limbs. How had that happened? Those feelings, so intense, slicing away at her entire being? How had they slipped through?

"I'd die for you," Seth whispered at her ear. "And so would he."

She shook her head; she knew that. That painful realization was all that had kept her from breaking the day she learned Callan had betrayed her.

She straightened and turned back to Callan.

All the pent-up rage brewing inside her broke free. Years of knowledge, of hatred, of the aching pain that drove her to run until she felt as though she would drop. All the needs, the fears, the pain exploded in her brain until it was all she could do to hold on to the animal clawing at her emotions.

"All these years I thought there was one man's eyes that I could stare into who hadn't seen those horrible discs. One man who didn't know how I begged to a God that didn't care." Callan's eyes widened in shock as the throttled scream tore from her throat. "You let him see. You let him see me become an animal. You let him see how little we mattered in the eyes of the god that didn't create us and damned sure didn't adopt us. Damn you to hell, Callan. You had no right."

And she couldn't stand here and hurt like this. She couldn't accept what he had done, not yet, maybe not ever. And the animalistic fury rising inside her couldn't be given a chance to escape. Never again.

"Dawn, that's enough." Seth's voice was steady, controlled, when she felt anything but controlled.

"Yeah, it is enough." She jerked the door open and moved quickly from the room. She walked, she didn't run—but everything inside her was screaming to run. To push herself, to put distance between herself and the pain.

"You will not turn your back on me like this." Callan grabbed the sleeve of her uniform, pulled her around and stared down at her in snarling fury.

Angry, he was a dangerous sight to behold. His amber eyes glowed almost red; his lips had pulled back to reveal the fearsome canines, strong and sharp, as a feral snarl twisted his lips.

"Why not?" she hissed back. "You turned yours on me when you dared to betray me this way. When you showed another man what they did to me. Not just my mate, Callan, but anyone." She was shaking, she could feel—something. Something worse than rage, something worse than betrayal, building inside her. "They raped me. They forced me to act like an animal and you let him see it. Hell, why not just send it to those fucking documentary bastards to use and then the world can see it too? Hell yeah, why not? Why fucking care at this point?"

She tore away from him and moved quickly down the hall. She needed to run. She needed to hunt. Those options were closed to her though. As she made her way back to Seth's room, she knew she couldn't leave the house. She couldn't lose herself in the shadowed vegetation that ringed the island, because Seth would come looking for her. He would come looking for her, even though his life was in danger and an assassin was just waiting to get his sights on him.

· CHAPTER 14 ·

Seth caught Callan's arm as the other man tensed to rush after Dawn. He had seen what he knew Callan didn't want to face. The woman emerging inside her, the one fighting with the past and the child she tried to keep buried.

Quickly, Seth moved in front of Callan and ignored the powerful hand that latched on to his throat, the sharp canines that flashed in lethal warning.

"She's not yours to protect now," he told the other man softly, staring back at him in determination.

Callan wasn't a man he wanted to fight, but he would. The Breeds were damned strong, they had been engineered for strength, for endurance, but Seth had found there were more than a few advantages to the mating heat hormone. In the past ten years, he too had grown stronger, his muscles more adaptable, gaining in strength and endurance.

A decade ago he would have been no match for the pride leader, now, he'd at least give him a hell of a fight.

"She'll always be mine to protect," Callan snarled, jerking his hand back as he cast a frustrated glance down the hall. "She'll run now. She'll try to hunt. Her senses are compromised and she'll only end up hurt if that fucking assassin is out there."

"She won't leave the house, Callan."

"And you know this how?"

"Because I'm her mate. She knows I'll follow her. You hurt her, and she doesn't understand why," he told the other man. "I do. But you won't make her accept it this way. Let her realize it on her own. You're too much a part of her life for her to turn away from you permanently. Unless you push her."

"Understand, do you?" Callan's teeth snapped together furiously. "You're just as fucking arrogant now as you were then, you cocky little bastard."

"And you're just as much the frustrated father trying to make up for things that were no fault of yours," he shot back. "And now I know where Dawn got her smart-assed tendencies. She's not a child, and I'm not the big bad seducer trying to break her heart. I'm the last person you have to protect her from."

He didn't give the Lion Breed a chance to answer but turned and moved quickly along the hallway, following his mate. The pride leader was stepping close to a line in the sand that Seth hadn't even been aware existed. A line he had come perilously close to crossing only once before, ten years earlier the day Callan had accused him of attempting to buy Dawn.

Son-of-a-bitch Breeds had more pride and sheer balls than anyone Seth had ever met, and he was getting flat tired of their habit of poking their noses into his and Dawn's lives.

Callan had let her suffer when Seth could have been there, when he could have tried to ease her pain, tried to be the mate she needed. His guilt and his fears for her had overcome everything else. And Seth understood why, but enough was enough.

He stalked to his bedroom, where he knew Dawn was waiting. She wouldn't endanger his life, and she knew he would follow her. He would always follow her now, no matter where she went.

He stepped into the sitting room and watched as she flung her utility belt to the couch. He'd heard the comment Patience Foreman had made regarding Dawn's clothes. He wondered how she would react to the deliveries being made in the morning. The clothes he had always dreamed of dressing her in. Silks and satins, the colors of the earth and of dawn.

"I don't want to talk about it." She turned back to him, her body vibrating with the anger and the hurt rolling through her.

Seth closed the door and locked it before crossing his arms and leaning back against it, remaining silent.

The dim light from the lamp he had left on earlier cast a soft shadow around her, but nothing could dim the fire glowing in her eyes.

"I mean it," she snarled, and the little feminine hiss of fury had the effect of arousing him further rather than warning him off.

She turned her back on him. Slender, stiff hands propped on her hips as she paced off the other side of the room, glancing back at him with a furious curl on her lip. For some reason, Breeds always thought that flash of canine would intimidate. He wondered what she would think if she knew that the sight of her canines just made his dick hard.

"Don't you have a party to attend?" she sneered. "Go right ahead and take care of business, Seth. I'll sit right here where I can't embarrass you with my uniform and my lack of class."

He almost snorted at that one. Instead he just tilted his head and watched her. She needed to get the anger out first and he'd be damned if he'd let her do it by fighting with him.

A furious growl left her throat before she clamped her lips shut and turned her back on him. A second later the tension left her shoulders enough that they seemed to slump dejectedly. And that broke his heart. He hurt for her, with her. His little Dawn. She didn't understand Callan's love for her any more than she understood how to handle the emotions that only built between her and Seth.

He forced himself to stand where he was, to let her work through that initial fire.

"Dayan made me watch those discs," she finally whispered, and Seth flinched at the raw pain in her voice. "For years. Years and years, over and over again. He made me watch them. I never remembered what they did to me, but I remember watching those discs."

Dayan had been insane. Seth thanked God he was dead; it saved him the trouble of fighting Callan for the right to strike the killing blow.

"After the escape, I went to sleep. Callan said I slept for days. When I woke up, I didn't remember any of it. I remembered the labs, I remembered the beatings and the training and the pain. But I didn't remember the rapes clearly." Her voice was at a near whisper, confusion filling her tone. "How do you just forget something that molded you?" She turned back to him then, and the aching pain and loss on her face tore at his soul.

"Sometimes, God gives us strength, Dawn, where we only perceive weakness."

She sneered at that. "God didn't create me, Seth. Don't pull that on me. He had nothing to do with this."

He shook his head at that. "You can't convince me of that, Dawn. Would you like to know why?"

"I guess you're just going to tell me whether I want you to or not," she bit out resentfully.

"Man can't create a soul, Dawn, only God can. And you can't live without your soul. You know that as well as I do. If what you're saying is true, then the Breeds would be no more than the automatons the Council dreamed of creating, rather than free and fighting to live and to love."

With those words he moved toward her. She stared back at him, denial and furious pain resonating in her eyes. Those beautiful eyes. Not the amber of Callan's, but the color of sweet honey touched by fire. And they broke his heart with the shadows that filled them, even as the heat that seemed always present now simmered his blood.

She was a part of his soul now, and he wondered if she even realized how much a part of him that she was, that they were of each other. Earlier, as morning filled the sky and only the dimmest light pierced the bedroom, he had felt it. Felt it as she moved over him, as she purred for him.

"I wanted to come to you without those images between us," she whispered hoarsely, refusing to shed the tears he knew lay trapped within her. "I wanted you to touch me without remembering that, without seeing another man touching me."

The shame that curled inside her nearly brought her to her knees now. She had no idea what to do with the emotions ripping through her, the need for something that she couldn't identify, and a sudden terror that the shadows she could feel pressing against her mind were memories she didn't want to see.

"And do you think that's what I saw, Dawn?" he asked her gently, his hands settling on her shoulders before running lightly down her arms. "I didn't see another man touching you. I saw a monster attempting to destroy something so pure and so innocent that it defies my ability to describe it. And I saw its in-ability to do so. Because the soul of that child was too strong, and too well protected by the being that gave that soul to her. You're pure. As innocent as a baby's breath, and, whether you believe it or not, sweetheart, protected by the most powerful being in the universe."

Dawn shook her head. She couldn't believe that. Not again. Not ever again. Because if she dared, then she might trust again, and if she trusted in His help then she might as well trust in a coyote's.

"Yeah, real pure and innocent," she sneered instead. "So pure that you ran the second you saw it. Just took Callan's word for the fact that I was too weak to be a mate. Too damaged to be your woman."

"He loves you, Dawn. Like a brother. Like a father. Like the man who failed to protect you when he knew you needed him the most, and he was determined not to fail again. Will you pun-ish both of you by refusing to forgive him for it?"

She jerked away from Seth, tossing him a resentful glare as she moved jerkily to the bar and pulled a water from the mini-fridge there. More as an excuse for time than out of any real thirst.

As she drank, she fought the logic he was using against her, as well as the heat beginning to build within her. She wanted to fight that logic. She wanted to fight Seth, Callan and Jonas. She wanted to tell them all to fuck off, to leave her the hell alone. And she couldn't. She couldn't because she loved both Callan and Seth too much.

"I should have had a choice," she whispered as she capped the water and set it on the bar.

She hunched her shoulders against the pain driving inside her like a bitter blade. "Someone should have given me the choice." The choice to accept her mate, to grow strong beside him rather than without him.

"Yes, we should have."

He surprised her with his answer. It didn't surprise her that he followed her, that he cupped her cheek and stared down at her, his gray eyes cloudy, darkening with emotion and with acceptance.

"You deserved the chance to choose for yourself, and I'll take that blame on my shoulders Dawn. Callan shouldn't have to. I was the one who walked away when I knew better. I walked away because I was terrified of putting fear in your eyes, and I knew I was too damned weak to bear to see it there."

And she was weak. Too weak to listen to this. Too hurt and too unsettled by the emotions and the edge of panic she could feel rising inside her.

"Do you see fear?" she snapped back at him.

His lips quirked, sadly, wryly. "I don't see fear, Dawn."

She reached up, speared her fingers in his hair, gripped the silken strands and pulled his lips to hers.

"Prove it."

She licked his lips then pushed her tongue past them as they parted—to argue or to kiss, she didn't know, and she didn't care. The mating hormone had been spilling into her system for hours, burning through her, lashing at the control she prided herself on.

She didn't have to have control now. She didn't have to wait or suffer in silence. This was her mate, and she was tired of waiting.

"Fuck!" Seth's head jerked back, but she knew the heat was in him too. She had smelled it on him, she could taste it in his kiss.

"Yes, fuck," she hissed. "Right here. Right now."

She jerked his belt loose as he stared at her in surprise, and a second later had the zipper lowered. Before he could form the words she saw hovering on his lips, she had his cock free and she was on her knees.

She had been dying to taste him. For years she had dreamed of tasting him, of taking him with her mouth and her tongue, laving the mating hormone over the stiff flesh of his erection just to see the result.

"Oh hell, Dawn." A strangled groan left his throat as she gripped the hardened shaft with both hands and her head lowered to consume the throbbing tip with her mouth.

Desperate fingers drove into her hair then. Seth's fingers. They grabbed handfuls of hair and clenched, just enough. Just enough to prick at her scalp, but not enough to cause pain or fear. Just enough to make certain she didn't release him.

She had no intention of releasing him. The taste of male lust and strength filled her mouth now, and she found she was a hungry woman. She might very well have found her favorite treat.

Treat nothing, this was a smorgasbord. A banquet of male flesh rising stiff and hot for her pleasure alone. Heavily veined, throbbing with desire, the thick crest dark and spilling precious drops of pre-cum, it filled her mouth, her senses and her desperate heart.

He was hers. She had waited ten years. Ten years to feel his touch and know his passion, and she would be damned if she would let him go now.

"Dawn, we need to talk." Seth's breathing was hard, sawing from his lungs as he groaned the words.

But he didn't move his hands. He didn't let go of her hair and he didn't stop thrusting against her lips. They didn't need to talk. They needed to touch. They needed to still this fire raging between them and burning through her defenses.

As she felt his cock head throb against her tongue, she tucked under the sensitive flesh beneath it and rolled her tongue against it before drawing back. Slowly, so slowly, staring up at him, seeing the glitter in his eyes, and knowing, feeling the certainty that he belonged to her.

He would never again lose the hormone that filled his blood now. He would never again walk away from her into the arms of another woman. He would never want to, even if he could. He was hers. It was there in his eyes, in his expression, in the muttered groans of pleasure and the hard hands in her hair.

He was her mate.

Seth couldn't believe what he was seeing, what he was feeling. Dawn's mouth wrapped around the crest of his dick, sucking it into the hot cavern of her mouth, stroking it with her tongue.

The inexperienced caresses were hotter than anything he had ever known. Her pleasure in it, seeing it in her eyes, hearing it in her mewling little moans, was almost too much to bear. Because those moans were vibrating on his too-sensitive flesh, stabbing into his balls and nearly destroying his self-control.

There he stood in his fucking sitting room, his pants and underwear around his thighs, and her absorbed, passionate expression filling his gaze. Dark gold eyes gleamed in the dim light of the room; her face was flushed, her lips becoming swollen as he slowly fucked the hard flesh past her lips.

"I won't last." It was all he could do to breathe.

Heat was curling up his spine, building at the base of his neck. He could feel the warning tremors of his nearing release clenching his testicles. If he didn't come soon, he wondered if he would die.

She moaned for him again. Half purr, half feminine hum of satisfaction and pleasure.

She was still dressed, for God's sake, as was he. He wanted her naked. He wanted to watch her naked breasts rising and falling, see her nipples stiff and flushed. And he wanted to see her pussy. Wanted to see it slick and hot with her need, ready to take him as he worked every inch of his cock inside her.

"God, your mouth is hot," he panted, unable to hold the words back as that heat, the sucking of her mouth and her sweet lips drove him insane with lust. "So sweet and hot, Dawn."

He clenched his hands in her hair again, kneaded her scalp, felt the sweat dampen his back. She'd always done that to him, even before the mating heat began. Just being close to her, smelling the sweat scent of her, and he would sweat. Ache. She made him crazy for her then and she made him even crazier for her now.

There was nothing he wouldn't do to touch her. No one he wouldn't kill just to ensure that he held her in his life forever.

"Dawn." He groaned her name, clenching his teeth as she licked and sucked and made him crazy with the need to come. "Let me have you."

Her answering moan was definitely a denial.

"Sweetheart, I'm going to come." Any second now. And instead of trying to pull away from her, what the hell was he doing? Holding her still, fucking her mouth, feeling the come building in his balls and threatening to explode.

"Dawn, for pity's sake." He clenched his teeth and fought to hold back.

The pleasure was incredible. It lashed at his senses, burned through his system, and before he could find a chance to catch his breath, it exploded out of control.

His body tightened to near breaking point, his head fell back, and before he knew it he was pumping hot, furious streams of his semen into her mouth.

Where she consumed him. She moaned and licked and drew every drop from his body for her consumption.

He had held back for so long. He had fought the rising force of lust, need, love and hunger for so many years that he found himself unable to fight it any longer.

Somehow, Seth managed to pull free of her sucking mouth, his cock still furiously hard, raging, desperate for more. He lifted her to her feet and tore at her pants, so violently aroused he didn't bother with her boots. He pushed her pants to her ankles, turned her, and there, with her pretty butt lifted for his viewing pleasure, he slid his hand between her thighs.

"You're wet, Dawn," he bit out, finding the sweet, heated syrup that ran from her body.

"Go figure." She panted, pushing into his hand, moaning as his fingers slid over her clit.

She needed this. Dawn had never needed anything as desperately as she needed Seth to fill her right now. She was burning, on fire from the taste of his lust and her own needs. They singed her flesh, stroked her nerve endings and clenched her womb in hard blows.

"Smart-ass." He leaned over her and bit her ear, and Dawn nearly came in his hand.

She ground herself into his hold, panting for breath as her head tipped back against his chest and a cry fell from her lips as he pulled his fingers from her.

A second later, the thick, pulsing head of his cock parted the sensitive lips and tucked against the clenching opening of her sex.

"What are you waiting on?" she cried out, pushing her legs farther apart as she felt his knees bend behind her. "Next year?"

"Smart-ass," he groaned again.

"So spank me. Later." She rolled her hips and growled. A heavy, feline sound of need that almost had the power to shock her.

"Spank you now." His hand landed at the side of her rear as his hips pushed forward and she once again felt the heavy, heated stretching of her vagina.

Her breath caught in her throat, then she gasped as his hand fell again. Firm little pats, not really a spanking, a burning caress that tore through her senses and had her vagina clutching and milking him just inside her.

She needed him deep inside her. Needed him to fill her. Now.

"Dawn, baby." His voice was hoarse, almost broken with his hunger.

"Do it," she snarled. "Damn you, fill me."

He filled her. Slowly. Too slowly.

"Is this what you want, baby?" He worked another inch in as she cried out with the burning pleasure-pain of the impalement.

"Is this what you want, Dawn?" He penetrated further. "I have more, darling. Do you need more?"

"More." She tried to scream the demand, but it was taking every breath to stay conscious as the pleasure whipped through her senses like a demented tornado.

"How much more? A little more?"

He was teasing her, destroying her. But with each word from his lips she heard him sinking further into the inferno as well. Burning with her as control began to dissolve.

The next thrust had him filling her. A ragged feline scream tore from her as she slammed back against him, ground against his pelvis as her hands bit into the leather of the bar stool in front of her.

"Seth, I need you." She pressed her forehead into the padded edge of the bar and moaned in desperation. "Please, Seth, like I've never needed you."

His hands clenched on her hips, his fingers holding her tight before he groaned behind her, and began to move.

He didn't take her easy this time. Not as he had that morning where every touch was a seduction. This wasn't seduction, this was a claiming and Dawn knew it. The woman understood it, and deep within her the animal that was as much a part of her as her scent, her flesh, stretched and snarled in agonizing pleasure.

Seth's flesh slapped against hers as he fucked her. The sound of damp skin meeting damp skin, of lust and hunger, meeting lust and hunger, filled the room. Her growling moans and his deep male grunts.

Each thrust caressed hidden nerve endings, sent flares of torturous rapture whipping through her. Her womb clenched and her pussy flexed against the thrusting shaft. She was crying out, the crescendo rising inside her, flames shooting outward, inward, burning her, until in a single, fiery blaze, she exploded beneath him.

She felt the muscles of her vagina clamp down, ripple in hard, desperate pulses, and a second later Seth slammed deep, tightened further, and the fierce, heated pulse of his semen releasing inside her sent her spiraling higher, into another orgasm that almost ripped away consciousness.

She jerked in his arms, bucked against him, milked his seed

from his body and, when they were both drained, collapsed against the bar stool and the bar that faced it.

Behind her, Seth was fighting for breath, and she wished him luck, because she didn't think she would ever find her own.

"You make me crazy." He nipped her ear before groaning and forcing himself back.

Dawn whimpered as his cock slid free of her, stroking her again, making her wonder if she could possibly stand more.

"Come on, little wildcat." He wrapped his arm around her and forced her to straighten up. "Shower. Bed."

"Bed, shower," she mumbled, leaning against him for strength.

"In your dreams," he chuckled as he led her to the bathroom despite her weak protests. There was just no way she could put any strength into anything yet.

"You're mean to me," she said with a pout as they stepped into the opulent bathroom and he sat her on the padded stool beside the shower stall.

"You won't think that when you smell the soap I bought for you in Paris. The city of love, sweetheart. Let's see what we have here."

Her interest perked. She did so love the soaps Seth had been collecting for her.

She peeked up at him through the fan of her lashes as he opened the drawer beneath the sink and pulled a small bar free. Already the scent of it had her sighing at the thought of the pleasure to come.

"You're going to bathe me?" She watched as he unwrapped the bar.

A wicked, erotic, totally male smile shaped his lips. "In ways you could never imagine, Dawn. You just can't imagine."

She hadn't imagined. But it wasn't long before she was coming for him again, her nails biting into his shoulders, the water spraying around them and the smell of love filling the air.

CHAPTER 15

The next morning Seth had no choice but to attend the meetings that had been scheduled for the the two-week-long house party. Too much had happened, and the other board members were growing distressed and angry now.

The subtle rumblings of dissent against the Breed presence were growing louder, and many of the board members felt that Breyer had been killed because of that presence.

Only Dash, Seth, Callan and Dawn knew better. Because they had the note Breyer had carried with him. *Tell Seth now!*

But tell Seth what? Dawn and Dash had gone through the Breyers' suite; they had questioned the family and searched every article of clothing and every drawer, looking for an indication of the information Breyer had possessed. There was nothing to be found.

There was an investigator to deal with though. As Seth continued the meetings, Dawn and Dash waited next to the heli-pad for the investigator's heli-jet to land.

Detective Bryan Ison, as Dawn remembered.

"Give me your impression of Ison," Dash ordered as they waited for the landing.

"Council." She shrugged.

It was easy to tell those in law enforcement who erred on the side of the Genetics Council and their lackeys, the pure blood and supreme race groups they funded.

Dash grunted, and as Dawn glanced at him, she saw the scowl that marked his face.

"He's going to attempt to blame the murder on Breed presence rather than an attempt against Seth. Should we apprehend a suspect, he'll demand custody and somehow they'll slip away, as they always do in these situations."

"The detective called ahead," he told her.

Dawn glanced back at him curiously. "I wouldn't have expected that."

"He wants to question our enforcers."

Dawn stilled. "He wants to lay the blame on one of our enforcers. Did he mention which one?"

He crossed his arms over his chest and his scowl deepened. "He mentioned Merc."

Dawn's eyes widened in surprise, then narrowed as sudden understanding hit her. Mercury Warrant was an anomaly among the Breeds. The man could frighten little children on the street if they weren't so damned curious about his almost lionlike features. The thinner lips, the broader nose, incredibly high cheekbones and tilted eyes. His leonine mane fell to his shoulders, and his canines were stronger and more pronounced than most Breeds'. He looked dangerous; he was dangerous, if pushed far enough. Mercury was also known to be one of the most contrary, stubborn and determined Breeds Dawn knew.

Mercury only killed when there was no other choice. He defended. He would wound, concuss, roar at in fury and terrify the enemy, but he was the Breed that could have been voted least likely to kill.

The world was unaware of that. This investigator had no idea what he was facing if he went up against Mercury. Mercury liked head games. He enjoyed terrifying the enemy and he enjoyed confounding them.

"Just what we need, a pansy-assed Council ass-kisser trying to pin this on Mercury."

"He's petitioned the Bureau to question him," Dash informed her.

"And Jonas is here, which means he's not in his office taking stupid memos."

"And the investigator knows that both Jonas and Callan are present. He's trying to go over my head."

"Callan won't allow it." She shook her head quickly.

The laughing snort that came from Dash's mouth had her lips twitching.

"Hell, I wish he would," he muttered. "Maybe I could dance one dance with my wife while I was here instead of playing referee between Jonas and Sanctuary's enforcers. They don't always get along well."

"Does anyone get along with Jonas?" Dawn frowned at the thought. She couldn't think of anyone.

"His flavor of the night?" Dash had the same questioning look on his face.

"Last I heard, his flavors had run out." She snickered. "That lawyer he appeared so enamored of walked out of his office and shot him the finger on her way."

Dash laughed at that one, then shook his head. "Callan and Jonas should have appraised Merc of what's going on by now. Hopefully, we can stall Ison, or distract him."

The heli-jet eased overhead and hovered for a long second before settling down on the landing pad. The bronze tone of the vehicle reflected the afternoon sun, and as the door swung open, the investigator and his sleek, blond-haired assistant stepped from the craft.

"Great," Dash muttered. "Two for one. Can we get any luckier? Head on back to the meeting rooms," he told her. "Seth will be out soon, and I don't want to risk a repeat of the other night. Keep him in the house, if possible."

Dawn nodded quickly before turning and heading back inside the mansion. Keeping Seth in the house wouldn't be the problem. Keeping him out of Investigator Ison's face would be the problem. Once he learned the law enforcement agents had arrived, he would be right there, in the thick of things.

Backing down wasn't in Seth's nature, nor was giving up. Yet he had done both, when he thought being with her would harm her. Though it pissed her off, it also sent a warm surge of emotion rushing through her.

That emotion was tinged with a hint of worry though. Seth, for all his romance and seductive gentleness, had yet to tell her he loved her. He had yet to even hint at understanding the permanency of the mating heat or to discuss a future with her. It was as though all intentions and thoughts of that future didn't exist within the relationship they were building in his bedroom.

Breeds had been taught that relationships and marriage weren't for them. But Dawn had to admit to a kernel of hope that it wasn't true. Why she did so, she couldn't explain to herself. They had been taught that God wasn't for them either, and hadn't He turned his back on her just as the scientists knew He would?

She needed to eradicate that hunger for more than just the mating. Wiping it out of her heart was the biggest favor she could do herself.

Or so she almost convinced herself until Seth walked out of that meeting room.

He was talking to Dane Vanderale, both men's expressions somber and intent as they spoke. Seth had a light scowl on his face, but when his eyes met hers, the cloudy depths lighting with the barest hint of a smile as he continued to listen to Dane, Dawn knew her own heart was lost.

She felt it thump violently in her chest, felt the heat blazing through her veins as mating heat began to ratchet inside her. And she knew that just having his body was never going to be enough for her.

She needed all of him. She needed it to the point that it was a physical pain thrumming at the center of her being.

She needed his love.

"Ah, and here's our lovely Dawn." Dane's eyes twinkled as a smile curved at his lips. "I must say, Seth, you've managed to capture the interest of the most intriguing woman currently inhabiting this island."

Dawn didn't blush, she barely blinked at Vanderale's obvious flirting. Dane was a man-whore if Dawn had ever met one. A personable one, a charming and generous one, but a manwhore all the same.

"Stop flirting with Dawn, Dane," Seth drawled as he moved across the hall to where Dawn stood against the banister that ran the length of the upper landing.

The warmth of his hard body surrounded her; the hand that clasped her hip pulled her to him as she continued to watch Dane.

There was something different about him, something she had never been able to put her finger on exactly.

"Dawn's easy to flirt with." Strong teeth flashed in a curiously feline smile. "She's taken. I don't have to worry about her."

"She's also getting tired of being discussed as though she weren't here," she informed both men.

Dane chuckled, then Dawn sensed him tensing. He didn't change expression, his body didn't shift or tighten. It was an animal awareness of danger that reached out to her.

Her gaze slid to his side as she watched Marion Carrington, Caroline's father, move to face Seth.

It was obvious Caroline had gotten her looks from someone other than her sire. Marion was broad, fit for a man in his fifties. His complexion was ruddy, his watery blue eyes narrowed in anger, and it was obvious that anger was directed at Seth.

"My heli-jet will be collecting me this evening," he snapped. "You can consider my final vote on this measure a nay. I won't countenance wasting Lawrence resources in such a matter." He flicked an insulting look at Dawn.

"And you know my stand on it, Marion. We can negotiate this, or I can call in the codicil on the shares. That's your choice. My father made certain none of you could overrule me when it was important, not just to Lawrence Industries, but to the family as well."

Marion Carrington flushed a darker hue. His body was fairly vibrating with rage. "You need two other votes to carry that codicil, Seth."

Seth inclined his head slowly. "I do, and I have faith they'll come through."

"I think we all know he already has one of those votes." Dane spoke up then. "The negotiation points are important, as Vanderale would like to share in the future profits I'm certain will come in from the ventures. Business is no place to allow personal conflicts to arise, Carrington. Your company, Carrier Resources, could pull in its own stake once Sanctuary and Haven begin pulling in their contracts. That's rather like cutting your nose to spite your face, my friend."

Haven was the Wolf Breed compound in Colorado. Both Haven and Sanctuary were working to establish themselves as viable corporations in their own rights. They had a talent. A talent that went for ridiculous amounts of money within the world: personal, business, electronic and military security. The future growth of their services, as well as their reputations, could make billions for not just the respective communities, but also for their backers.

Carrington wasn't impressed.

"Mark my words, Seth." His finger pointed imperiously toward Seth. "You'll regret this, even more than you will otherwise. I'll block you. Codicil or not, you won't do this."

Seth straightened arrogantly, staring down his aristocratic nose, his eyes narrowing dangerously.

"That codicil holds other clauses as well, Carrington. I suggest you and your lawyer go over them closely before you threaten me further. My father may have been ill-advised in his backing of the Council before we learned what it was. But we know now, and he ensured, when he sold the shares to the company and before his death, that nothing interfered with what I needed to do to protect his family and future grandchildren. Don't underestimate my determination to do just that." No one could underestimate the determination and the steel will behind his voice.

Children. Dawn refrained from placing her hand against her stomach. The hormonal treatments she had been receiving for years would block any pregnancy . . . perhaps.

She focused on Carrington instead and scented the indecision and the banked fury brewing inside him. He was greedy, but the anger he felt over the dissolution of Seth's and his daughter's relationship was more than apparent and it was swaying his decision to back Seth.

The frustration was evident in Carrington's eyes, and in his face. His gaze flicked to Dawn then, and she saw hatred. Pure, malicious hatred. This man would have known what the Council was, who and what he was backing. And he despised the benefits now going to the Breeds, the creations he felt should have willingly given their blood and their dignity to the monsters that created them.

She hated him right back. But she didn't have to like him, and she didn't have to deal with him. Seth did. And as long as she was standing at Seth's side, Carrington would never back down.

"Excuse me, gentlemen, and I'll let you talk." She ignored the tightening of Seth's hand at her hip and moved away without rushing, without showing regret. Though she regretted.

She regretted losing the warmth of his body, the stroke of his heat along her flesh. It eased the need building inside her and calmed the animal that fed her hunger.

Seth watched as she walked away, her back straight, her shoulders stiff as she moved toward the hall. She would be close; he knew she wouldn't go far. But that didn't ease the need to touch her, to hold her.

He turned back to Carrington, staring at him coldly.

"Insult her again, and I'll force the sale of your shares," he kept his voice low, though he didn't give a damn who heard what he had to say.

He watched the sweat pop out on Carrington's forehead, a clear indication that the other man was becoming increasingly concerned. Let him worry. Let him twist in his bed at night worrying about future profits. Seth twisted mentally every fucking night, remembering what the Council had done to Dawn, remembering and hating the bastards for every second of pain they had put her through as a child.

"This has nothing to do with business," Carrington snapped. "Weren't you the one that warned me to keep it separate?"

Seth stepped closer. "Do you have a soul, Carrington?" He growled. "Let's see if you have one. Go back into that room." He pointed to the meeting room. "Reload those discs and watch them. Watch them and know they're the truth. Imagine the lash of those whips on your own flesh as a child. A fucking baby, too young to defend yourself. And imagine the discs you didn't see in there. The ones where they raped children to death." He clenched his fists at his sides to keep from using them on the other man. "Imagine your child, your precious Caroline, staring back at a camera in death, as every atrocity that could be committed against her young body was committed." Rage was burning inside him.

Before Seth could stop himself, before he could contain the brutal talon-sharp fury tearing at his mind, he gripped the sides of Carrington's jacket and jerked him close, nose to nose, and let him see the murderous emotions burning inside him.

"Do you have a soul, you spineless little fucker, or are you just as fucking demented as those bastards you helped fund for all those years?"

Carrington lost all color in his face. He stared back at Seth, horrified.

"They didn't show you those babies they raped, did they,

Carrington?" he snarled brutally. "All those years they sent reports to those certain few who fully backed them, they never showed those poor, pitiful, bloodstained bodies. But you know what? Those that survived? Some of them were made available to the monsters that backed them. Were you one of them?"

Carrington was shaking his head, slowly, almost shocked. "That was propaganda," he wheezed. "The Breeds, they lied."

Seth threw him back. "Is that how you salve your conscience?" he bit out, then stared at the incredulous expressions of the board members watching the scene. "Is that what the Council and their fucking puppets cutting my throat with you are telling you? Propaganda? Let me tell you propaganda. Let me tell you how they fucking destroyed babies." His expression contorted, the images of what they had done to his Dawn, his woman, flashing through his mind. "How many of you paid for the privilege of helping? By God, let me find out one of you, just one of you, did, and I'll destroy you. Pray to God, get on your knees and beg him not to let me find out any of you were involved so deeply, or I promise you, hell hath no fury like that which I'll visit on you. Every last fucking one of you who dared."

"They proved those discs were false." Carrington was still shaking his head. "The Breeds did that themselves. They proved it. The Breeds don't disprove it. They refuse to address it."

"Tell you what, let some bastard rape your daughter until she's mindless with the pain. Until her blood is flowing from her body and her eyes turn glassy, and see how many of your good buddies you want to see it, Carrington." His chest was tight, his rage thundering through him. "Any of you. Those who survived, do you think they want you to see their pain? Do you think they care at this point what men like you believe? Those who supported those fucking monsters? Fuck you. Every damned one of you. Negotiations are off. My lawyers will contact yours next week. I don't negotiate with pedophiles or those who defend them. Get the fuck off my island."

He turned and stalked from the group, his body vibrating with a killing rage as Dawn stepped from the hall and stood watching him, her eyes dark with pain, her face pale. And concerned.

She glanced back at the board members, and for a moment, just a moment, he thought tears glittered in her eyes before she blinked them back.

"Seth, wait." Dane was behind him. He caught Seth's arm and pulled him to a stop as Seth reached Dawn.

"Back off, Dane." He jerked his arm out of the other man's grip and turned again.

"Let me talk to them now, Seth," Dane hissed softly. "Listen to me, you have them scared now, let me pull them in. We'd have no fight if we strike now."

"Listen to him, Seth." Dawn dug her heels in, her voice soft but resonating with pain. "Don't go to war unless you have to."

He paused, his body vibrating with the need for just that. War. All but a few of those board members had personally supported the Genetics Council over the years. A few he knew would never turn against them, but if they could get a majority, if they pulled in the right vote, then those few would have no choice but to follow them.

"I won't back down." He felt murderous. He wanted to tear the bastards apart, he wanted to go back, he wanted to wipe out every fucking scientist and soldier who had dared to touch Dawn or any other child in their care.

"Let me mediate this point," Dane urged him again. "Let me work them now that you have them running scared. This, my friend, is what I'm good at."

Seth nodded sharply. "No negotiations, Dane. Negotiating is over. I want the full concessions that I asked for. Period. Or they can get fucked."

With that, he pulled Dawn closer and moved her toward their room. He didn't want them to look at her, he didn't want them to see her or to breathe her air. They were an insult to her presence, an insult to every child breathing, Breed or not.

Dawn was his. His woman. His breath. He hadn't realized that until she came to him. He hadn't realized how long he had waited, how hard he had hoped that she would come to him. He'd be damned if he would back down an inch now. Dawn and her people weren't the only ones depending on him. The children he would have with her needed him to stand for them now. If he didn't, who would stand for them later?

Dane watched Seth and his mate disappear around the corner of the hall. He pushed his fingers through his hair and glanced back at the board members watching him in concern as he appeared undecided.

Appeared, as he wasn't in the least undecided. He had expected this to happen, he had planned for it. Anyone with an ear to the ground where the Breeds were concerned knew that Dawn was Seth's mate. Especially anyone with Dane's senses. Breed senses, senses made stronger by the human blood that flowed through his veins.

Dane was the worst sort of predator. He preyed on the emotional weaknesses of his enemies. Their greed. Their lust for power. He preyed upon it, helped to weaken it, then built it back as he needed it. He needed these men in place, but not at the risk of destroying the Breeds they benefited.

Exhaling roughly, he played the part of concerned businessman and reluctant mediator. That role he knew very well.

Rye, Ryan Desalvo, his bodyguard and friend, met him halfway.

Dane lowered his head to Rye's ear. "Bring the discs."

He felt Rye tense. "Seth will cut your heart out."

"And dine on it for dinner, I'm certain," Dane drawled. "Bring the discs."

They had brought the discs as insurance, just in case. Just in case this happened. Just in case the votes needed didn't appear forthcoming. Because the majority of those men didn't know the true scope of the atrocities the Council had committed, and they clung to the hope that it was indeed Breed propaganda that claimed it had happened.

As in so many events in the past, those of evil and malicious intent twisted the truth to suit their own purposes. The discs and images of the true scope of cruelties committed against Breed females were hidden, for the most part, within the Breed strongholds. But Seth was an enterprising chap. He'd found many of them. And they were needed now.

Lawrence Industries and Vanderale Industries were the Breeds' major supporters. If they fell, so many others would fall as well.

As Rye moved along the hallway, turned and headed for their rooms, Dane moved back to the board members.

"He's surely not serious," said Brian Phelps, owner and CEO of a large import/export business that Lawrence had taken under their wing and refinanced. Phelps had been given a seat on the board, while the import/export business had become a part of Lawrence Industries at a drastically reduced amount.

"I believe he may be," Dane admitted with a sigh. "Let's reconvene, gentlemen, and see what we can do to draw Seth back to the table." He glanced back in the direction Seth had gone as though worried, when in fact he was damned near gleeful that Seth had finally pushed the board members to resolve this. Now they would learn who their allies were and who was backed by the Council.

Seth had been serious, and the members of the board had seen it. Seth rarely became upset; he never walked away from negotiations, preferring to fight them out instead. Dane remembered the year of hell that he had worked to get on this board. Drawing Seth in had been nearly impossible. The other man had made him sweat, and it hadn't been pleasant.

"Let him enact the codicil," Theodore Valere, the member that worried Dane the most, inserted arrogantly, and too smugly.

Valere owned the majority of Spain's pharmaceutical companies; unfortunately, he had made the supreme mistake of allowing his brother a large share of those companies. The brother had sold them to Aaron Lawrence when Valere refused to bail him out of a rather large gambling debt.

Hence the reason Valere was on the board to begin with. He couldn't take the shares back; all he could do was give his input or vote on how the majority profits of Lawrence Industries were used. And then only if Aaron or Seth were willing to negotiate. The codicil to the major shareholder agreement was completely legal and enforceable.

"Theodore, if Seth enacts that codicil, we could all be shitting with our thumbs up our arses the next time we've a problem facing our own companies."

"It's not as though it will affect Vanderale. Lawrence Industries is no more than a pet project of yours, Dane, admit it," Carrington snapped. "The holding Lawrence bought from you was in no way attached to Vanderale."

"Father can be a shade possessive of his holdings." Dane sighed as though he were the reckless playboy he was perceived to be. "He's going to expect results from me here, and he does have a soft spot for the Breeds. Disappointing him here would not be in my best interests."

Or those of the others. The world was no longer such a small place and Vanderale Industries had always had its sights toward that. It had a finger in many pies, just as Lawrence Industries did. Many of those pies were now staring back at Dane, sweating, uncertain if they should stand their ground or allow Seth's measures to continue to back the Breeds.

Backing Sanctuary and Haven was a smart business decision, as Dane well knew. Callan Lyons and the Wolf Breed leader, Wolf Gunnar, were excellent leaders and strategists. They would lead the Breeds into a future that would one day see them not just secure, but completely profitable and self-supporting.

"Ah, here's Rye," Dane murmured then and glanced back at the board members. Yes, the members of Seth's board of directors were about to receive a very rude awakening. "A few discs I've managed to attain myself from some very greedy Council soldiers. Should we go view them?" He extended his arm to the meeting room as the others watched him with almost fearful curiosity.

Valere was quiet, but in his black eyes Dane glimpsed the evil that he could smell hovering over the man like decayed flesh.

Theodore Valere came from Spanish aristocracy. His family could trace their roots back to the Middle Ages. Hurrah, hurrah. Dane's father had traced the Valere family roots as well and found a history of depravity and petty cruelties. The past three generations of Valere money had filled the Genetics Council coffers.

The Council had ruled the Breeds with an iron hand, destroying their creations despite the billions, perhaps trillions, of dollars that had gone into giving them life. The miracles they had created were ignored. The scientists didn't see them as miracles; they saw them as tools and as expendable creatures.

The discs Dane had acquired had been authenticated by the world's foremost authorities on video and audio production, enhancement and duplication. There was no doubt each event, each bloodcurdling scream, each demented plea for mercy was real.

The blood that filled the labs, the cold faces of scientists and soldiers alike, the complete inhumanity of the experiments, all in the name of science, were events that even the staunchest stomach couldn't bear.

And the girls. The faces of young female Breeds, were those that were hardest to bear. Dane stood by the viewer and stared back at the board members, his eyes hard, the sounds of agonized wails echoing in his head, as they always did, even in his nightmares.

All but Valere turned away. He stared at the images, a heavy frown on his face as he watched, a glimmer of pleasure in his eyes. And Dane swore, before much longer, he would have the proof he needed. When he did, Valere would die.

Dane wasn't bound by Breed Law. He didn't have to turn his evidence over to the Breed Ruling Cabinet, law enforcement agencies or senators. All he had to do was assure his own conscience. Once that last shred of doubt was assuaged, then Valere blood would spill.

As Breed blood had spilled.

Over and over again.

⋅ C H A P T E R   1 6 ⋅

"I should start flying every last one of them to the mainland," Seth growled as they entered the suite, his body tight, humming with anger as he released her arm and moved to the bar.

Dawn watched him, her chest heavy, her heart aching as though someone had cut into it with a dull knife as she watched him pour a drink and breathe out heavily.

"Board members are like death and taxes. Can't get rid of them." Dawn quoted him. He'd made that comment years before at one of the parties he had attended at Sanctuary.

He glowered at her, but his shoulders seemed to relax marginally.

"Bastards," he finally muttered before sipping at a whiskey and turning back to stare at her.

The look in his eyes fired her blood immediately. It made her think of soap made in Paris and the wild scent of his lust clinging to her body.

"The board members aren't the only problem we have," she told him, hating the necessity of making the situation worse. At least in his eyes. "Investigator Ison arrived just before I met up with you in the hall. Dash and Callan are with him, but they're wanting to question Merc about the death of your board member."

The whiskey glass was set on the bar carefully. "They're trying to pin Breyer's death on a Breed then?"

"That's what we suspect. Mercury would make an excellent target. Flash his picture across the television screens of the world and parents would fear not just for their children but for themselves. I think they're wanting to turn this on us."

Seth closed his eyes and pinched the bridge of his nose. He was tired, she thought. Neither of them had slept much the night before, or this morning. The mating heat had taken them in its grip, and every ounce of energy had been given to it.

The thought of those hours had her thighs weakening and her sex clenching in need.

"Where is Investigator Ison?" He sneered.

"We had the library secured before his arrival. Dash is hoping that he and Callan can distract him or somehow divert the direction of his investigation."

His jaw clenched. "Let's go. I'll be damned if I'll sit here on my ass and watch them try to pin Breyer's death on an innocent man. Has Dash run a background check on him yet?"

Dawn nodded. "We've found preliminary evidence of an association to several Council contacts, though those contacts aren't verified. At this point it would be only speculation in the eyes of the law."

"All I need." Suddenly he looked taller, broader, harder. He looked like a man that most people would be frightened to push much further.

And Dawn had to admit to feeling a curl of trepidation. Not personal concern, but rather that gut feeling that should Seth lose the control she could now glimpse as a core of steel inside him, then death would result.

"Do you have his file on that handy-dandy PDA of yours?" He nodded to the electronic device.

Dawn pulled it free of her utility belt, activated it and pulled up Investigator Ison's file before handing it back to Seth.

He took it, his eyes narrowed on the screen as he scrolled through the information. His jaw was rigid, his nostrils flaring as he read the file.

"His brother married the sister of a suspected Council soldier," he murmured. "Past military career, possibility of Council and/or lab involvement." He looked over at her. "And Dash is letting this son of a bitch live?"

Dawn shrugged. "Breed Law goes both ways. It's for the protection of the Breeds as well as those who aren't, Seth. Until we have proof of involvement after the enactment of Breed Law, there's nothing we can do other than make their names public knowledge."

He rubbed at his jaw, his broad hands and long male fingers stroking over the beard-darkened flesh as she inhaled slowly.

She wanted him. She wanted him inside her.

His eyes lifted from the PDA, darkened.

"Are you wearing those panties I gave you this morning?" His voice was suddenly deep, dark with lust.

The panties were nothing but lace. The softest, most delicate lace Dawn had ever felt. The thong was a perfect fit, the shimmery fabric cupping her mound and lying over it like a cloud. She had never worn anything so wickedly sexy in her life.

She felt her face flush. "Yeah. I'm wearing them." She cleared her throat. "Those panties are decadent, Seth."

"Are they wet?" Still holding the PDA, he moved closer, his expression suddenly more sensual, his gaze as wicked as the panties. "Have you dampened all that soft lace yet?"

Her face flamed, because of course she had. Just looking at him made her wet.

"You're insane," she breathed out roughly, taking the PDA from him and securing it quickly in the leather case attached to her utility belt.

His eyes moved down her body, his gaze locking on her thighs. "I want to lick all that sweet soft flesh. You know your pussy is softer than the lace, Dawn?" His hands settled on her shoulders and smoothed down her back as he pulled her close, his eyes meeting hers then. "Does your tongue ache, baby? Do you need my kiss?"

His head lowered, his lips teasing at hers then.

"If you kiss me, we'll never make it out of here." Her lashes drifted over her eyes as his tongue stroked over her lips.

She wanted his kiss. She wanted those teasing licks to stop and she wanted his lips moving over hers. Not to ease the hormone swelling the glands beneath her tongue, but because she *felt* him when he kissed her. She felt connected to him, a part of him.

"I ache for your kiss," he whispered against her lips then. "The feel of it, the warmth of it. The way you make those feathery little sounds when my tongue touches yours."

Her lips parted. She needed him. Needed the touch of his tongue against hers, the feel of his kiss making her mad with hunger. So insane to feel all of him, to touch all of him, that nothing else mattered. She wasn't afraid of the shadows that had begun forming within her memories when he held her. Shadows that she knew were filled with pain and horror and the screams of the girl she never wanted to have to remember.

As his tongue stroked over her lips, the link at her ear beeped imperatively.

Dawn moaned in denial, her hands tightening on Seth's powerful forearms as she fought to ignore it. It beeped again, then again on the secured private channel. It had to be Dash or Callan. Only they would contact her privately, and it would have to have something to do with the investigators downstairs.

She didn't want to deal with them. She wanted to stay right here, in Seth's arms, and feel the kiss he was teasing her with.

Seth pulled back, his grin slow and knowing as he jerked her hand to the small activator at the back of her ear.

"Dawn here," she snapped as she flipped the mic down.

This better be important.

"How did I get this link, is your first question." Obviously disguised, a voice that sent chills down her spine whispered the statement. "Which of your very well-trained enforcers did I take down, little girl?"

Dawn felt the flash of sickening knowledge, a realization she didn't want to sense, didn't want to hear.

"Who is this?" She could feel the bile rising in her throat.

"Ah, Dawn, sweet thing. You don't remember your first? First cut is the deepest, sweetie. I made that first cut, and now I'll make the last. Remember that, Dawn, I promised you that. That you'd always be there for me. You're my fuck toy, little girl. Always mine."

She was going to be sick. So sick.

She was instinct, pure instinct and training. She rushed to the laptop and activated the locator program for the island. All the Breed links had a locator, a beacon that allowed her to track them. That locator beacon was coordinated with one inset in the Breed patch they wore on their uniforms. If the link was separated from the Breed, then she'd find it.

It was a security measure, in case a Breed became separated

from the link, or the worst happened and the enemy managed to acquire the link.

"Are you searching for me, Dawn? Come get me, baby. You were the best fuck I ever had and I'll be your last fuck."

She was going to throw up. That voice echoed in her head, over and over.

Scream for me, little cat. Little girl.

She tore the link from her head. She wasn't listening. She couldn't listen. She hit a command to coordinate locator beacons and watched as each began to line up.

All but one.

"Moira," she whispered, horrified, terrified as she stared at the screen while typing in the electronic emergency access to all links but Moira's.

Moira was well trained. She was one of the Lionesses Dawn herself had helped train. How had she failed the other woman? How had she not taught her to avoid this?

This was her fault. Somehow, it was her fault. She had trained Moira. The delicate Breed had come to Sanctuary almost broken, and she learned to laugh. But she was down now and Dawn had failed to protect her.

She heard Seth curse. A vile, enraged curse that had her jerking her gaze to his and horror flashing through her mind. He was listening. Listening to every vicious, dirty word coming out of the link.

"Here," she hissed, pointing to the steady blink of the locator light. "Southern tip, within the vegetation."

She sent the order to the links; the electronic signal would display as directions on the PDAs they would have pulled the second the emergency signal went to their links.

She turned to him then, quickly, some instinct, some knowledge warning her. She was unable to catch him as he threw the link and stormed from the bedroom, a weapon she hadn't even known he had close clenched in his hand.

"No. No." She shook her head, frantic as she grabbed the link from the floor, attached it to her ear and ran after him.

She had to catch up with him. He couldn't do this, not without her. Nothing could happen to Seth. How would she live? How the hell was she supposed to face the night without him? What would keep the nightmares away and surround her with warmth if anything happened to Seth?

Her finger was hovering over the main channel activator when a low laugh came over it.

"Is your lover on his way? I'm waiting for him, Dawn. And this time, he'll be the one that dies. You belong to me, little girl."

She deactived, hit the reset and cleared the channels teamwide before reactivating to a channel now blocked to the compromised link.

"Alert. All agents alert. Seth is moving out of the house. I repeat, he's on the run to the link location. Converge and cover. I want him back in this house. Styx, locate Moira . . ."

"Located. Tranqed and out of it but alive. Dash and Callan are moving for Lawrence at the back entrance. I repeat, she's tranqed, and it's powerful from the smell of it."

Dawn was taking the steps two at a time before hitting the foyer, sliding and righting herself in a second to rush to the back of the house, following Seth's scent.

"Well hell, guess they're all moving out tae-gether, lass."

"No. Dash. Get him in this house. Get him back here now." Panic was setting in on her. There was an assassin out there, waiting on Seth, and he had found a way to draw him out.

"Dawn, hold position." Dash's voice came over the link. "We have Seth covered. That's an order. Hold position."

"No. No," she yelled into the link, rushing for the kitchen. "Get him back in here."

"Dawn, you can't cage him," Callan came back. "Let him fight this battle."

"No." She was moving from the house, finding cover and following. "Don't do this, Callan. Don't you risk him this way. Don't you do this." She was begging him. She could hear the plea in her voice, the demand.

He came back, his voice cold. "He's your mate, Dawn, not your possession. Return to position and await orders."

She was shaking, fury and fear filling her at the sound of Callan's voice. Why would he do this? Why would he allow her mate to risk his life this way?

Her breathing was harsh, her heart racing out of control as she reached the back door. Surely he wouldn't deliberately draw Seth into danger. He wouldn't let her mate walk into an ambush, would he? Could he? Did he hate Seth to that extent?

She shook her head. He was arrogant, he was powerful, but he wasn't a cold-blooded killer. He was a man, and so was Seth.

What the hell, was this a fucking male bonding moment or something?

They had a head start, and though she knew the location of the link, she had no idea which direction they had taken. Keeping low, her heart thumping in her chest, fear clogging her senses, she sprinted from cover to cover until she hit the tree line. Once there, Dawn let the animal clawing inside her free.

That instinctive, predatory half of herself that she kept reined so closely gave a small, hissing growl as she crouched in the shadows. Her head lifted, her nostrils flaring, searching for the scent of her mate.

She could still hear the sound of that voice. Evil. Vicious. It echoed in her head. *Little girl. Fight me, little cat . . .*

She shook her head. She wouldn't remember. She wouldn't let herself. She had pushed that child out of existence years ago and she would be damned if she would let her back in now.

She let herself recede. That human part of her brain slipped to the side and allowed instinct to take over. She had trained for this. She had worked her ass off for ten years, pitting herself against the best trackers, the best assassins Sanctuary housed.

She was a predator. She could track, she could kill. She would be there with her mate, by his side. If he was stupid enough to race into danger, then he could damned well accept her being with him.

She moved through the underbrush, her senses humming, Seth's scent clear in her head as she searched for it on the breeze. Every particle of her being narrowed to one thing, to one stone-cold purpose: the protection of her mate. The man who brought her to life. Who touched her without shame, who bought her soaps that smelled of emotion and panties as soft as a lover's sigh.

She moved in the direction of the link, her senses probing out in either direction, searching for the scents she needed. Seth's scent. The scent of a weapon, of danger and of evil.

Her gun was held close to her leg, a knife within easy access, one tucked into each boot, another at her opposite thigh.

As a large frond waved in the breeze, she slid with it, her shadow merging with the shadow of the leaf, hiding her from an assassin's eyes. The electronics built into her uniform would camouflage her from heat-seeking sights or electronic detection. Only eyes could see her, and her training combined with the animal half of her being ensured no human eyes or Breed's picked her up.

As she moved through the dim shadows of the thick vegetation and trees, a scent whispered past her. The scent of rage barely contained, a man's fury, a lover's determination to protect.

Seth's scent. Her head lifted, the smell of him rolling through her senses a second before another sharper, bitter smell hit her nostrils. And it was closer.

She whirled around, a snarl leaving her lips as a hard, sharp pain tore through her shoulder.

Her gaze jerked to the dart buried in her flesh, and for a second a memory flashed across her mind. The prick of a needle, the drugs racing through her system, ensuring that her body was weak but her senses alive. The drugs the Council used during their experiments to impair the Breed senses, to make them easier to control.

A second later she was flying through the air, a shadow picking her up, tossing her to the ground as a snarl left her lips and she stared into those eyes.

Eyes the child she thought forever vanquished inside her recognized.

An enraged feline hiss tore from her lips as she gripped the weapon at her side, dragged it weakly from its holster, lifted it and fired. She held her finger on the trigger, her senses thrown off by the tranq, her eyesight dazed, her reactions jerky, uncoordinated as she fired the shot through the silence of the lush jungle-like surroundings.

A foot connected with the gun, kicking it from her hand and numbing her fingers as a rough laugh seemed to echo inside her head.

"Fight me, little cat," he laughed as he jerked her to him then straddled her smaller body.

The pain of his touch exploded through her senses. Agony unlike anything she could remember. A thousand daggers ripping at her flesh as he pawed at her.

She couldn't separate the scents or the sounds within her head. She couldn't pull in his scent. But she could see his eyes. Eyes she knew.

Oh God . . .

She cut off the prayer, her fingers flexing, scrambling for the knife at her thigh before hard hands gripped her wrist, nearly breaking it before jerking it with the other over her head.

She writhed beneath him. The pain was agonizing. It burned and blistered, peeled the skin from her bones and left her fighting to scream.

"You forgot who you belonged to, didn't you, Dawn?" A smile curved beneath the black face mask he wore. A snug-fitting, light material. Just as they had worn in the labs on those discs. Hiding the face of evil.

She hissed, trying to buck beneath him, fighting against the strength in his arms as he ripped her shirt open.

Beneath, the full uniform bra hid her breasts. The material held her breasts confined, stretched over them, under them, covering her entire chest area.

"Remember who you belong to, bitch."

She tried to curse him, to scream her rage as he twisted her nipple painfully.

The feel of that flashed through her brain and the memories threatened to break free. Desperation tore through her, clawed at her brain and fought to pour adrenaline into her system.

She was stronger than this. The paralyzing effect rushing through her body was fear, nothing more. She had been trained to fight past the tranqs, to function as long as possible. She had learned how to avoid capture, to escape the enemy and to fight back, all while drugged. She had learned how to do it. She could do it now. She had to, because she knew the alternative would destroy her. Her and Seth.

With one last surge of strength her legs came up, hooked around his neck and dragged him backward as she twisted. When she felt him break the hold she had on him easily, she tried to scramble away. His hands clawed at her hips a second later, at the snug waist of her pants, in an attempt to jerk them off her hips.

He was not going to rape her. Pain was radiating through every cell of her body at his touch, and agony pierced the tranquilizer. That pain diluted its effects and gave her the strength to send out a snarling cry. An animal's scream of rage that every Breed on the island would pick up.

"Bitch." A fist connected with her head. "Fucking whore."

Shards of paralyzing pain pierced her at the blow. It dimmed her gaze, sent sickness roiling in her stomach and stole the strength from her limbs as he jerked her to her back once again.

"Let's see if we can't show the world who you belong to." He lifted her knife, the blade gleaming above her. "I'll mark you until no other would consider touching you. All mine, little girl."

He was going to cut her. Scar her. Mark her.

A shot fired. Her attacker jerked, cursed and threw himself back.

The weight was gone as quickly as it had come. The agonizing pain of the male touch receded, to be replaced by the pain of the blow to her head.

She shook her head, whimpering as she felt unconsciousness trying to take hold of her. She couldn't pass out. The enemy was here. He was here and her mate was in danger. She had to fight.

She tried to cry out, tried to find the strength to locate her link and call for help. She had to get to Seth.

"Seth." She heard his name slip past her lips, a whisper of the scream that ached to be voiced.

Every part of her body hurt. She could feel the agony in her wrist, in the back of her head. Her ankle felt numb, yet glowing with pain.

A mewling moan left her lips and she hated that sound. She sounded like a child again, like a worthless animal whimpering in pain.

She tried to drag herself to her knees, to get to her feet, but she collapsed in the dirt again, her nails digging into it as she fought to hold on to reality, to consciousness.

She had to find her mate.

She could hear more screams, enraged roars and a male battle cry that would have frozen her senses if she'd had enough of them left to freeze.

She shook her head as she fought to clear the haze from her mind.

That lion's roar sounded again. But it was the human scream of rage that sent chills down her spine. There was gunfire, and the answering call of Breed roars—Lion, Jaguar and Wolf. They spun within her head as she tried to pull herself to her knees.

She wavered, the earth spinning around her, before her eyesight darkened and she collapsed to the ground. The last sound she heard was that of her name, fury and agonized pain echoing in her mate's voice.

He was alive. He lived.

She closed her eyes and let the darkness have her.

"Dawn!" Seth slid to the ground, his hands moving over her quickly, checking for broken bones, for blood. From her neck, down her back to her legs.

He turned her carefully and felt the breath leave his body on an enraged cry. Her shirt was torn open; scratches marred her upper chest and collarbone.

He was aware of the Breeds surrounding them, two teams, their backs to Seth, Dash and Callan as they quickly checked her for injuries.

"I want fucking secured access into the house. Find that damned shooter, Styx, or I'm going to peel your bones," Callan was yelling into the communications link as Seth checked Dawn's wrist.

It was swelling but not broken. Her ankle was twisted. Scratches marred her arms, upper chest and stomach, but there were no wounds. There was a lump on the back of her head. The bastard had hit her.

The son of a bitch had let them listen as he attacked her. Let them know he had her. Seth had heard the note of possession in his voice, the demented lust, and knew a terror unlike anything he had ever known.

"I told you she was going to follow," Dash reminded him and Callan both. "Where do the two of you get the idea your women are going to sit and twiddle their thumbs when you're in danger?"

Seth cast him a furious look as he quickly pulled Dawn's shirt over her breasts and secured several buttons.

"Is that fucking route cleared?" Callan was snapping into the link before turning blazing eyes on Seth. "Pick her up. They'll surround the four of us and pull us into the house."

Seth picked her up gently, his teeth clenching with the pain streaking through his soul at the limpness of her body. Defenseless. God, how was he ever going to erase the mark on his soul that he had put her here? That he had let this happen.

"Seth, stay low." Dash put his hand on his shoulder as he moved to rise. "The others need to be above us. We'll move carefully to the clearing, then they'll surround us entirely. We have a shooter in the trees."

He nodded, unable to unlock his teeth, to relax his jaw enough

to speak. If he did, he would howl in fury. He would never contain the rage burning inside him.

He stayed low, keeping his head below shoulder level of the
Breeds surrounding them. He understood as they made their way
through the natural cover. The Breeds surrounding them were
unmated. Those within their protective circle were mates. The
Breeds were so protective of their women that the mated males
were also extremely careful of their own safety. The women's
survival, he had learned, depended on those matings. Should a
mate be lost, then his partner would suffer and the consequences
of that loss could be devastating.

"Our Breed doctor is flying in," Callan snapped. "Elizabeth
put the call into Sanctuary immediately. The heli-jet will be en
route within minutes, ETA less than two hours."

"She's stable." Seth was finally able to speak as he ran at a
near crouch. "Bruising, scratches and some swelling; nothing's
broken. He hit her in the back of the head, possible concussion."

"We'll keep her stable till Doc Morrey gets here." They
eased to the clearing leading to the house.

"Jonas is perched at the top of the house with his rifle," Callan
informed them. "We move in hard and fast to the house. Keep
moving. God forbid one of you go down, stay down, don't move
until we can drag you out," he ordered the unmated Breeds.

Jonas's voice came over the link. "Move out. You have a clear
field."

They made it across the clearing, the Breeds rushing them
into the back of the house as the guests gathered around,
shocked, concerned, ignored by Seth as he ran to the back stairs
and up to the second floor and his suite.

She needed to be in their bed. Wrapped in the scent of their
bodies. She had to know she was safe.

God help him, how could she ever feel safe in his care again?

· C H A P T E R 1 7 ·

Consciousness didn't return in a rush. It came slowly, the sound of voices rising from the mists of her own screams and the brutal dark eyes staring down at her.

When she felt the prick on her arm, the knowledge that a needle had pierced her flesh, awareness flooded into her brain. Her hand shot out, her fingers clenching around a slender neck, tightening.

Her eyes jerked open, but her senses were still dazed, her vision hazy.

"Dawn. Let the doctor go." A hard hand slid over her wrist, not gripping, just touching.

Seth's touch.

She blinked, letting her fingers loosen slowly as she felt her hand cradled in his and her vision slowly cleared to see Dr. Morrey standing over her.

Ely's face was pale, her dark eyes worried as she drew back the hand and the hypo-syringe she was using.

"What is it?" Dawn questioned the injection groggily.

"Just something to clear your head." Ely coughed slightly, a hand lifting to her neck as she massaged the reddened skin. "I didn't expect you to have the strength to react so quickly."

Dawn blinked drowsily, feeling the effects of the tranquilizer still in her system as her gaze sought Seth's. He was sitting on the side of the bed next to her, his eyes dark, anger and concern swirling in the cloudy depths.

"Did anyone get him?" she asked.

Seth shook his head, his jaw tightening. "He got away."

"Moira?" She was almost afraid to ask about the Irish Lioness.

"Unharmed. Groggy but coming out of it quickly."

Dawn turned her head to stare at Dash where he stood at the other side of the bed. Callan stood beside him, silent, his golden eyes flaming with the intensity of his fury.

"Good." She turned away.

"Dawn, don't turn from me," Callan growled.

She turned her gaze back. "I have put my body in front of your mate's to protect her," she whispered hoarsely. "You led mine into danger and ordered me back." She remembered that, distinctly, clearly. "What happened to you, Callan? Once, long ago, you would have never betrayed me."

It hurt, that knowledge. Knowing that he had done the one thing guaranteed to force Seth out of her life ten years ago had been bad enough. But now, this time, he had led Seth into danger.

"Callan doesn't control me, Dawn. Don't ever imagine that's possible." Seth's voice was hard now, cold. "And the next time you put your ass out there like that I'll paddle it."

She turned back to him, her responses still slow as she frowned. "I'm trained to."

"And you think I'm not?" His lips tightened dangerously. "You don't protect me. Understand that now. You will never place yourself between me and danger, or you'll not sit on your ass for a week after I get finished."

A frown jerked between her brows. He was daring to threaten to spank her?

"I'm gonna shoot you," she mumbled.

Callan snorted, and Dawn wanted to grin at the sound of amusement she heard in it. But she couldn't grin. She had to blink against the flash of horror that snapped inside her mind. The feel of shackles at her wrists, her ankles. Cold steel holding her down. She jerked before managing to control the reaction.

"Are you okay?" Ely, ever observant, checked her pulse, her hands carefully covered by the thin gloves she had specially coated to examine Breed mates.

Her touch brought no pain, only a sense of discomfort.

"I'm fine." She shrugged the doctor off. "Go aggravate Moira and leave me alone."

Ely grinned at the order.

Brutal eyes flashed in front of Dawn's memory then. Hazel brown, filled with smug satisfaction, with horrible pleasure, as thin lips smiled. A smile of triumph behind a black mask.

"We're tracking the tranq we found next to your body," Dash told her drawing her back. "The attacker took the one he used on Moira, but whoever shot at him frightened him away before he could retrieve the one he used on you. We're hoping we can trace him with it."

"What shooter?" She wanted to shake her head, but she was afraid to. Afraid any shift in her body would bring another flash of horror.

"Someone shot at your attacker. Someone positioned in the trees, we suspect. We haven't found a sign of him, or his scent. We hoped you had."

Dawn blinked back at Dash. "There was another unknown out there?" she asked faintly. "That's not possible."

"All guests were accounted for when we got back to the house," Dash continued. "There were none missing. All our men were accounted for and none of them took the shot. We were rushing to your location when it was fired."

"He was going to cut me." The edge of the blade over her face flashed before her mind. "Mark me."

"We heard." The ice in Seth's voice was frightening to hear. She had never heard him so cold, so killingly furious.

"We heard everything on the link," Callan told her, and his voice was just as dangerous, just as lethal. "When the shot fired, he disappeared."

"Scents?" She frowned. Surely one of them had smelled something.

"Covered. A combination of subtle alterations that we haven't been able to pick up on the guests. We haven't placed the underlying scent yet," Callan told her.

"Capzasin." She licked her dry lips slowly. "I could smell it on him, but it was wearing off even then. I recognized the underlying scent."

She had to clench her teeth to hold back the fear that wanted to grow inside her then, the panic. Ten years of training and still, it nearly escaped.

"Who?" Seth's single word echoed with the need for blood.

She stared up at him miserably, wishing she could hold back the words, wishing she could hide what she knew.

"Dawn?" Dash's voice was lower, commanding. "What did you recognize?"

She turned back to him. Better to see his eyes rather than Seth's.

"The labs," she whispered, her gaze flicking to Callan. "The eyes, the voice, the underlying scent. It was the soldier . . ." She inhaled roughly and jerked her gaze from them, her jaw tightening.

"No." Callan's growl rumbled from his throat. "He's dead. They're all dead, Dawn."

She shook her head. "He's not dead."

She knew he wasn't dead. He had touched her, held her down; she had seen his eyes and his smile and she had known. And beneath the sense-numbing scent of Capzasin had been the scent of a unique rot, an evil she didn't want to remember.

"You remember the labs?" Dash asked then.

"I remember him." But the memories were returning and she knew it. She could feel them moving inside her, gripping her soul with sharp talons and raking across it.

The pain was almost enough to steal her breath. She refused to look at Seth, refused to let him see fear in her eyes again.

"Dawn, it's not possible," Callan snapped. "I made certain of it."

She inhaled roughly and turned back to him. "I saw those tapes, over and over, for years," she whispered. "Dayan made me watch them, Callan. For hours on end. I know his voice. I remember his eyes and I remember his scent. Like a rotting soul mixed with the scent of the man. I remember it." Her eyes locked with his and she flinched at the pain she read there. "He managed to escape, or he wasn't there when the labs blew. But it was him."

Callan's fists clenched as he glanced over at Seth. Dawn refused to follow his gaze, refused to let Seth see what she was feeling, the panic beginning to ride inside her, the fear that rolled in her stomach and had the bile gathering at the back of her throat.

"I'm sorry," Callan suddenly whispered, his face smoothing out, his expression becoming cold, remote. "I failed you again, didn't I?"

Dawn sighed. "You're not Superman, Callan. What happened then or now isn't your fault."

She ignored Seth's muttered curse and Ely's worried gaze as she pushed herself from the pillows. Her wrist was wrapped, her ankle tender, and her head throbbed as though gremlins were ripping holes in her brain.

"Ely, I have a headache." She sighed tiredly. "Do you have a fix?"

"An injection," she answered. "You have a concussion. I still have yet to treat it."

"Then treat it before those pickaxes burrowing in my brain do some real damage." She lifted her hand and gingerly felt the knot at the back of her head.

"Dawn, talk to me," Callan bit out. "You have to be wrong about this."

Dawn closed her eyes as Ely prepared the injection. She wasn't wrong. She wanted to be. They had no idea how much she wanted to be wrong, but every sense had been tuned into her surroundings then. The animal she had learned to control had taken in everything.

"He's older now," she mused. "Not as strong, but just as arrogant, and just as cocky. And perhaps more insane than ever. He was possessive. You heard that?"

"He's playing with you," Callan snarled. "It's not the same man."

"Yeah, it was." She steeled herself as Ely placed the syringe against her arm and injected the medicine into her system.

She felt distant, separated from what she knew and what she felt.

"He wore gloves and camouflage clothing," she told them. "A black mask. The clothes were treated to shield his scent, and the smell of Capzasin was wearing off. His voice was a little huskier, but it has a distinctive sound of lust." She almost, just almost, flinched as the voice from the past echoed around her. "The eyes were the same, but there was more madness in them, as though he's slipped over an edge that he was teetering on before."

"You don't fully remember the labs," Seth rasped from where he stood beside her. "You said you didn't remember."

She swallowed tightly. She felt numb, the numb that comes before realization.

"You should have recognized the voice, Callan. You just don't want to. I don't blame you that he's out there. You can't kill them all." She shrugged as though it didn't matter.

The pain was easing in her head, the pressure against her scalp receding as Ely's drugs began to reduce the headache and the swelling in her brain.

Her fists clenched in the comforter beneath her as she felt those shackles against her flesh again, felt her own blood dampening her skin.

This was going to be bad, she thought. Could she control the pain and the fear that would swamp her when those memories returned?

She touched her forehead and fought them back. All it took was control. She was weak right now; she knew how weak she became when she was concussed, how hard it was to keep from drowning beneath the fogging memories that wanted to roll over her.

"He has my knife." She could feel the weight missing against her thigh.

Callan cursed as he turned away and paced across the room. Dash watched her silently, and she could feel Seth at her side, the rage barely contained as he fought the information.

"We've searched every inch of this island," Dash finally said. "We've found nothing. Whoever he is, he's hiding himself well."

"We'll clear the island," Seth retorted. "Get the guests out of here and see what he does."

"No." Dawn would have shaken her head, but her brain still felt a little edgy.

"Don't tell me no, Dawn," he snapped furiously. "I won't risk your life this way."

"And I won't risk yours," she said calmly.

She felt too calm. She knew what was coming though. It wouldn't take long before the fallout began.

"We're clearing the island."

"Then we'll transport you to Sanctuary and have you locked in a bunker for your own protection."

"You don't want to try that," he warned her quietly, though his voice rasped with shocked fury.

She turned to look at him then. She loved him. She loved him until she felt as though her heart would burst with it.

"We play this out here." She eased to the side of the bed. "I need a shower, if no one cares. I need to wash the stink off me. Dash, have our shooter, Byron, flown in. He's the best eyes we have, even better than Jonas. I want him on the top of the house."

"He's here," Callan snarled.

The anger in the room was going to smother her. It was weighing down on her like a heavy, wet blanket as the testosterone pouring through the three men nearly overwhelmed her.

"Moira's to go back out tonight. I want her with Styx. Tell him his chocolate will become nonexistent if he babies her. I want her back up to peak. I'll meet with the team in a few hours . . ."

"You're no longer lead, Dawn," Dash reminded her calmly.

"Get over yourself, Dash," she grunted as she reached the bathroom door. "I trained for this. He's my mate. If you don't like it, then go growl at Elizabeth, because I don't want to hear it."

"Elizabeth growls back," he muttered as she closed the door behind her and leaned back against it.

The shaking was starting now. The tremors were working through her muscles and she had to swallow tightly before turning on the hot water and pouring the basin full of a scented liquid soap. Its scent was strong, hopefully enough to mask the smell of fear from Dash and Callan. Because she was scared. More scared than she had been since Dayan's death.

The past was returning with a vengeance and she didn't know if she could bear it.

◆   ◆   ◆

Seth stared at the closed door, then at the Breeds that watched it as well.

"She's terrified," he said softly.

Callan sighed heavily as he raked his hands through his hair and gave him a brutally fierce look. "I've not smelled fear like that rolling off her since we were in the labs. And it makes me crazy. Son of a bitch. Those bastards nearly destroyed her there." He stalked across the bedroom. "There was nothing we could do. No way to help her. And there's no way to help her now."

"Yes, there is," Dash said. "We find him and slice his throat for him. It's that simple."

"Her blood pressure is also elevated and the hormonal readings on her blood work are off the charts," Ely said as she moved from the small desk where she had set up the analysis equipment she had brought with her. "If she follows the pattern as she does with the nightmares, she'll head out at dark to hunt."

"The hell she will." Seth wasn't having it. He glared at the doctor, then Dash and Callan. "She does not leave this house."

"Then it's your job to keep her in it." Dash shrugged, his expression savage though his eyes glimmered with an edge of humor. "Try taking her to the exercise room you have in the basement. Let her work it off there; otherwise the adrenaline will make her crazy. Dawn's survived, Seth, admirably, by remaking herself. Don't try to change who and what she is now. Let her fight it out, even if she has to fight with you."

"She'll have to fight," Callan injected. "She has to let the rage out or it festers into the worst of the nightmares."

"I'll handle Dawn. I want that shooter and the bastard that attacked her found," Seth snapped, angry with both the situation and the men who gave their advice so easily.

They wanted to continue to pamper her, and, Seth admitted, he wanted nothing more in this world than to protect her himself. But Dawn wouldn't be protected. She was ten years past the ability to allow anyone to stand between her and danger.

It didn't mean he wouldn't try.

And she had been in that bathroom alone long enough.

"I want a progress report before nightfall," he ordered coldly, moving to the bathroom. "And I want that bastard found, Dash. I want him found and I want his blood."

He jerked open the bathroom door and stepped inside, closing and locking the door carefully behind him.

Steam rolled from the shower, but Dawn wasn't standing beneath the spray. Seth took just enough time to toe his shoes off before he jerked open the door to the large shower and felt his heart break with grief and pain.

Dawn wasn't crying. Dawn never cried. How many times had he heard that over the years? Tears did not roll down her cheeks—instead they sliced through her soul. She lifted her head and stared back at him, the eyes golden brown, and filled with pain, as she stared up at him from where she sat, her legs pulled up to her bare breasts, her back against the shower wall, the water falling around her.

"You're ruining your clothes." Her arms tightened around her legs as he pulled her between his upraised knees, enclosing her in the shelter of his arms.

"I'll buy more." Seth kissed the top of her head as she rested her cheek against his chest.

The was a long silence then, nothing but the sound of the water flowing around them as he rubbed at her back, her shoulders.

Seth had never felt more helpless in his life than he did now. He had no idea how to help her, how to ease her pain, and that sent additional fury pounding through his brain. He wanted to smooth those shadows from her eyes, wrap her in safety and protection and never see fear in her face ever again.

"I wish you had stayed in the house," he finally sighed, his inadequacies rising inside him.

What was he, that he couldn't even protect the woman that meant more than life to him?

A small sound escaped her. Caught between a laugh and a dry sob, that sound tore at his heart.

"You're not made of steel."

"Neither are you, Dawn." He rubbed his cheek against her hair, his eyes closing at the smell of Paris with Love, that unique scent that had its matching vial of shampoo and conditioner. He would have to call the soap maker and request more of that scent. It seemed to suit her.

"You're my mate, Seth," she whispered. "You're more to me even than that. I've trained to protect, not to hide in a dark room and be protected. What happened was my fault. I let my fury overwhelm me. I didn't take the proper precautions or he wouldn't have taken me down so easily."

"He used a tranquilizer, Dawn." Disbelief filled his voice. "You're not immune to it, and you sure as hell can't avoid that damned dart once it's fired at you."

"Actually, you can," she breathed out wearily. "I should have heard it, sensed it. I have before. I'm trained to know."

Seth closed his eyes at the confusion in her voice, the sense of helplessness and failure she felt.

Dash said she had remade herself. She hadn't. The potential

for the strong, valiant woman she was had always been inside her; otherwise she would have never survived the life she had been forced to live in those labs.

As the water saturated his clothes, ran off them both in heavy streams, Seth saw what Dash and Callan hadn't.

"Next time, we'll work together," he promised her, knowing he would never take the chance of leaving her behind again.

It wasn't a lack of trust in her abilities. She would have never survived that attack if she wasn't strong and well trained. He had heard the battle she waged with her attacker; the strength in the man's voice, and his shock when she overpowered him.

He had seen the proof of it on the ground around her—the struggle to survive—and he had been too far away from her to defend her. He had left her, when he knew he should have realized she would never wait on him.

Pure rage had governed him though. She had remained calm when the bastard first made contact. She had found the Breed he had attacked, sent her help, begun coordinating the search when Seth picked up the comm link and heard the vile, smug laughter in that voice. The lust and possessiveness, the certainty that he would destroy the woman as he had nearly destroyed the child.

"Next time, we'll let the team do their job and stay in place." She leaned against him tiredly, curled against his chest, her naked body warmed by the heat of the water, and by his body. "I can't lose you like that, Seth. Don't make me lose you like that."

The utter loneliness, the helpless emotion in her voice, tore at his soul. If she walked away from him, it would destroy him. God help him, if she were to die. Could he live through the pain? He didn't think he could.

He lowered his hand until his fingers were tilting her chin, lifting her face to his.

"You won't lose me," he whispered, staring into the shadowed eyes, his chest clenching at the fear she was fighting so hard to hide.

He had known this would happen. Had known the memories would begin returning once he had her in his bed. How was he supposed to protect her from those?

"I can kick ass." She stared back at him somberly. "I trained, Seth. I know what I'm doing. I kept him from hurting me."

She kept him from raping her. He heard her unspoken words.

"I watched your training vids," he revealed. "I know you can kick ass, Dawn. You kick righteous ass, babe."

And she did. She was small and light, but she could turn the most hardened Breed Enforcers into pretzels as she moved around them.

"You watch too many vids of me," she whispered. "Don't watch vids, Seth. Watch me."

"No more vids."

He lowered his head. He couldn't resist her lips. She had been biting at them; they were red and luscious and he wanted to soothe them. He rubbed his lips against hers, licked at them.

"Shower sex again?" She smiled against his lips.

He stared into her eyes. "I'm hungry for you. Now, Dawn."

Her hand lifted and speared through the wet strands of his hair as she pulled his mouth back to hers.

"Here I am," she murmured against his lips. "All yours, Seth. I'm all yours."

The fear was burning in her stomach, nearly as hot as the arousal, tearing at her control and the memories she had contained for so many years. Dawn didn't want to face them. She didn't want to face the pain and the horror, the helplessness she knew she would have felt.

She didn't want to feel that, ever again. She just wanted to feel this. Seth's hands as they roamed over her wet body, sliding and heating, stealing her mind from the fears and the shifting shadows of pain and turning it to pleasure instead.

Kissing Seth was like kissing sunlight. The same heat, the same blinding acceptance and wash of joy moved through her as it did when the sunlight touched her face.

In the past days, experiencing passion in his arms had opened a world for her that she had never known existed. A world she never wanted to lose.

"You're still dressed." She dragged her lips back from his long enough to pull at the sodden shirt.

Curled against him as she was, she could feel every inch of his chest along the side of her body, every beat of his heart.

He ignored her little protest. His hands cupped her head as

he drew it back once more, his lips covering hers, his tongue pressing into her mouth to tangle with hers.

As he rubbed against the swollen glands beneath her tongue, Dawn felt the hormone that built there flowing free. He lapped it up. A low, throbbing growl left his lips as he teased her tongue to his mouth, then suckled at it. Sweetly, seductively, stealing the hormone and letting it course through his body as she came to her knees, turning to him, desperate to give him more.

She needed to bind him to her, if only in this way. Any way. That instinctive, animal part of her fought to make certain there was no part of Seth Lawrence that didn't belong to her. Make certain he could never again forget the strength of his hunger for her and touch another woman.

He was hers. She was his. She was so totally his that at times she wondered if she could survive without him now.

"Don't think, Dawn." He pulled back from the kiss, only to run his lips down her neck as his hands cupped her breasts.

They were so sensitive. The mounds were hard and swollen, desperate for his touch. Her nipples were pebble hard, extending toward him, aching for his mouth.

Dawn shook her head, her hands pulling at his shirt as his lips covered one of the hard, too-sensitive peaks and drew it into his mouth.

Instant, ecstatic pleasure tore through her. She felt his tongue flaying the hardened flesh, his mouth suckling her. Deep. The pressure a pleasure-pain, as a half mewl, half purr escaped her throat.

Her fingers tightened in his hair as her womb clenched, spasmed. Between her thighs she could feel the moisture gathering, easing from her pussy to coat the swollen folds that parted in anticipation of his touch.

"Touch me." She needed his touch. She needed his hands stroking all of her, his fingers delving into her.

And she needed to touch him.

Dawn knelt between his thighs, between his knees, feeling his lips pulling at her nipples, his tongue raking across them, and she let herself fly.

She couldn't think when she was in his arms, she could only feel.

"Purring for me?" He dragged his lips back, his breathing

harsh as his hands gripped her hips and he forced her to her feet. "Grab the metal rings, Dawn. Hold on tight."

The metal rings were two towel holders hanging out of the way of the water. Her hands latched onto them as he turned her, then rose before her.

He stripped quickly. The sodden clothes were tossed to the corner of the shower and his erection stood out from his body, flushed dark, the veins pulsing beneath the flesh.

Bronze flesh rippled over hard muscle as he moved to her again, his lips tasting hers, his tongue stroking over hers, tasting the last remnants of the heat spilling from her tongue.

His hands caressed as he tasted, skimming down her sides, over her hips, parting her thighs.

"I want to taste you." He reached up and readjusted the fall of water until it cascaded around them rather than over them. "I want my tongue inside you, licking all your sweet cream. Feeling it on my tongue, against my lips."

She nearly lost her breath at the look of sensuality on his face. Her hands tightened on the rings as he slowly went to his knees once again.

He lifted one of her legs, placed it gently over his shoulder, then bent his head to her.

"Seth—" She cried out his name, her head falling back as her hips tilted forward, giving him access to her flesh, feeling his tongue stroking, slowly, so slowly around the hard nubbin of her clit.

His thumbs parted the folds and his lips covered the pulsing knot of nerves so he could suckle it, making her insane with need. Powerful flashes of sensation raced through her nervous system. Tiny implosions centered in her womb had her jerking, reaching, begging for release.

"I could taste you all day." His voice was hard, lustful. "Every day. The sweetest flesh in the world." His lips caught a flushed pussy lip, sucked it into his mouth, licked over it.

The bare flesh had no protection. There were no curls between his touch and her flesh. There was only the heat tearing through it.

Then one hand cupped her rear, the other looped beneath her leg and dragged it to his other shoulder. He was supporting her, his hands on her ass, holding her to him, and he began to devour her.

Hard, hungry thrusts of his tongue speared into her vagina as he lapped. Lapped and moaned and caressed flesh, so needy, so hungry for touch that it rippled and milked his tongue.

She tightened on the thrusting flesh, her thighs framing his face as she writhed into the delicate fucking. She was pierced by flames. Flames that whipped through her body, clenched her muscles and left her reaching, climbing, desperate for release.

Then he licked up, circled her clit, surrounded it with his lips and sucked, sending her spinning, racing into ecstasy as she wailed his name, certain she would never recover from the pleasure tearing through her.

But he didn't give her time to recover. He came to his feet, her legs sliding down his arms until he was wrapping them around his waist.

"Hold on tight." His voice was hard, his expression heavy with lust as he gripped his cock and fitted it against the hungry opening between her thighs. "Hold on to me, Dawn. I'm going to fuck us both into oblivion."

He eased inside her.

Dawn's head thrashed back and forth. "Harder. Take me, Seth. Take me hard."

He stretched her open slowly, inch by inch, the muscles in his upper body straining, his neck corded at the force of control needed to take her so slowly.

"Please." Her hands tightened on the rings as he bucked against her once. One inch driven in hard, and it wasn't enough.

She couldn't breathe. She couldn't beg. Pleasure was attacking her from all ends, wrapping around her as she felt him throbbing inside her.

Dawn tightened her legs around his hips, tilted her hips and tried to take him deeper. Seth held her steady, his gray eyes nearly black, locked on hers.

"I want to feel every clench, every flexing little ripple over my dick," he growled. "I want to feel you take me, Dawn. Inch by inch." And there were a lot of inches to take.

By the time he penetrated her fully, Dawn was a writhing mass of nerve endings, jerking in his grip as she fought for release. She couldn't speak, words wouldn't escape, only the little mewling cries that Seth seemed to love so much.

The pleasure was almost agony. It was building inside her, tightening her womb. As his pelvis rubbed against her clit, he drove her higher. As he pulled back then worked his way inside her again, a frustrated, tormented growl left her throat.

Her head lowered to his neck, her teeth raked the little wound she had left there before. She sucked it, feeling him tense, curse, but his movements grew stronger, the thrusts harder.

She felt him moving inside her, more than filling her, stretching her, burning her, and the pleasure of it was building until it whipped through her, exploded in mindless rapture and had her arching tight against him. She tightened, her pussy flexing on his cock as he gave a hard groan, pushed in hard and fast, once, twice, then buried deep as his semen began to spurt inside her. The deep, heated pulses of pleasure extended her orgasm, sent another hard shudder through her body.

She was awash in pleasure. Taken past ecstasy. She hung in his grip, his head bent to her shoulder as both of them fought for breath, and felt as though she had become a part of his skin.

And she never wanted him to let her go. She wanted to spend eternity, right here, with the steamy water surrounding them, and Seth buried inside her.

I love you. She mouthed the words against the wound she had reopened, where shoulder and neck met, where her lips pressed a kiss to the reddened area and she closed her eyes tight. She loved him until her heart was breaking with it, and she still had no idea if his response to her was love, lust or the mating heat.

◆   ◆   ◆

The next day, there were still no answers to solve the mystery of Seth's heart, or of her attacker. The morning sped by; Seth's meetings took up most of the morning and early afternoon before lunch. Later, Seth needed a shower. With her, of course. The playfulness he displayed eased the fear shadowing her, and Dawn let herself live, just for the moment.

She blocked the memories as much as possible and hid her awareness of the shadows creeping closer in her mind.

The knock at the suite door came as they were dressing early that evening. The investigator for the death of Andrew Breyer needed to speak to Seth immediately. He was due back on the mainland and he needed to complete his statements.

Styx was less than polite as he relayed that information to Seth. "He's goin' tae piss me righ' off," he snapped, his brogue thick. "Get his arse off the island afore I slice his dandy li'l throat."

The investigator was still pushing at Mercury, and from all accounts, Mercury might have pushed back a time or two by targeting the female investigator and keeping her off balance with hungry eyes and little growls. But there was no arrest, because there was no evidence. Hopefully, the investigation Dash and Callan were conducting on the side would find more answers.

That was her hope as she moved to the closet and began to dress for the upcoming party they would attend directly after Seth's meeting with the investigator.

As Dawn pulled another uniform from the small closet she was using now, Seth took it from her hands, tossed it back in without hanging it up, then pulled her to his closet.

"Those were my clothes. Am I going naked today?" She was wearing another pair of the panties he had given her. Violet silk thongs as soft as air. At the back between the rise of her buttocks was a single little bow that he seemed to be fond of.

"No, but I'm tired of those uniforms." He pulled her into the huge walk-in closet, where she stopped in surprise. One side was women's clothes, all in her size.

"How did you do this?"

A grin tugged at his lips. "I'm smart that way. Now, find something pretty. We have another of those damned parties in an hour or so anyway and I want to dance with my woman."

My woman. The words shouldn't have sent a thrill racing up her spine, but they did.

"Come on, Dawn, you know what pretty clothes are. I've seen you wearing them at Sanctuary functions and you look damned good in them."

She loved pretty clothes; she just didn't have many. Not because she couldn't afford them, but because she had no place to wear them. No one she wanted to impress, and impressing herself had always seemed a waste of time, especially when all she did was train to fight.

She moved to the rack of clothes. Dresses of every sort hung in a long line. Then jeans and blouses, T-shirts and sporty tops. What wasn't here probably hadn't been invented yet or wasn't worth having.

Beneath the clothes were rows upon rows of shoes in protective clear boxes. And they were all her size.

"You're trying to spoil me," she murmured, keeping her back to him to hide her reaction to the gift.

"I'm still seducing you." He kissed her shoulder, a smile curling his lips as he pressed them to her flesh.

"Hmm, so what are you after other than what you've had already?" She turned to him, her brow arching as he stared down at her, that sexy little half grin tilting his lips, his gray eyes swirling with whatever emotions he kept within himself.

Didn't he know he already had all of her?

"You—" He touched her nose with his index finger "—have no clue. Now, see how fast you can make me drool with one of those dresses. I'm betting I can hold out all of ten seconds."

"Think you can make it ten seconds, do you?" She fingered a bronze "almost there" dress. So soft and buttery she was certain she'd barely feel it against her flesh. It was short, the back low, the straps strappy, the bodice obviously snug, and low as well.

Seth looked at the dress and swallowed tightly. "Five seconds?" he said faintly.

Her lips twitched. "I'll get dressed."

She pulled the dress from the rack and bent to pick up the strappy high heels that went with it.

"You have matching panties," he said hoarsely. "They have a bow at the back too."

He did like those bows.

Dawn gave a low, light laugh, surprised at how lighthearted the sound was. For a moment, a few short moments, she'd forgotten the events of the day before and allowed herself to be free. Just free.

As Seth pulled his evening clothes from the closet, Dawn retreated to the bathroom with her clothes. It didn't take her long to dress. Her hair was to her shoulders now, layered about her head so it lay naturally and easily around her face. She added a slight curl to the ends, then applied a minimum amount of makeup.

She changed panties. She wore the bronze. The bow at the back was tiny, flirty. If she moved just right, the impression of it would show through the dress.

And the dress was a dream. Light as air, it flowed over her. Snug and flattering, it shimmered over her body to just below her thighs. The strappy sandals added to her height, and as she stared in the full-length mirror, she let a rueful smile tip her lips.

She loved girly clothes. She loved dressing up, but there had been no fun in it with no one to see her efforts but herself. No, that wasn't true, there had been no fun in it without the chance of seeing Seth.

She brushed at the long fringe of hair that fell over her forehead, a narrow ribbon of it brushing past the side of her eyes, then applied a light gloss to her lips before reentering the bedroom.

Seth was lacing his dress shoes. He glanced up, then froze. His expression shifted from curious to downright wickedly lustful as his gray eyes darkened.

"You didn't last five seconds," she informed him as she posed before him, one hip cocked, propping her hand on it and letting him look his fill.

She felt beautiful when he stared at her like that. She felt awake, aware, and all female.

"God have mercy on mortal men," he finally breathed out roughly as he came to his feet.

His white silk dress shirt emphasized his broad shoulders. The black slacks cinched at his flat abs and made his ass look like a female fantasy come to life.

He breathed out roughly, shook his dark head, then moved to the dresser across the room. When he returned, he was carrying a gold chain, close to half an inch thick and gleaming with a soft sheen.

"Seth, you can't keep buying me things." She stared at the chain until he laid it around her neck and attached the clasp.

It lay just at her collarbone, and as she turned to the mirror, she saw how the rich luster picked up the light tan of her skin.

"And these." The gold hoops were simple in design, but as they came together with the dress, Dawn realized she looked classy. That understated elegance she had always admired in other women was now a part of her.

She touched the chain as his hands settled on her shoulders and his eyes met hers in the mirror. They gleamed with possessiveness, with hunger and something more. Something she could hope was love.

"I want to see you in emeralds." He bent his head and kissed her shoulder, his fingers playing with the thin strap next to his lips. "Nothing but emeralds. A necklace of them, with a tiny gold bow as a clasp. And dew drops of emeralds falling from your pretty ears." He nipped her earlobe.

"Yeah, those would go great with my uniform." She frowned in the mirror. The woman looking back at her was too familiar, somehow, too easy to get used to.

"You don't have to go back to Sanctuary, Dawn." His fingers tightened on her shoulders. "You could stay, with me."

In his concrete jungle. Where cement and iron covered the earth and the smell of the land was obliterated by the smell of toxic fumes, industrial waste and those who would no more know how to survive in the mountains than a babe.

But, as she stared back at him, she realized that unless she could adapt to his world, then she would face her world without him.

"You don't have to decide right now." He stepped back, his expression becoming bland, cool. "We can talk about it later."

She stared at the gold chain, already warming from her flesh, shimmering against her flesh, and realized that Seth had given her more than a piece of jewelry.

"I don't want to leave." The concrete jungle couldn't defeat her, but being without Seth could.

His expression stilled; the clouds raging in his eyes calmed. He gave her a small nod, as though he were hesitant to push that declaration, then picked up the small purse that matched her dress. The one she hadn't known she had.

"You have a weapon, a comm link and a dagger inside," he told her, his lips quirking in amusement. "I made certain your accessories would fit."

"Seth?" She took the purse but couldn't break away from his gaze, not yet.

"Yes, Dawn?" He touched her cheek with the tips of his fingers, the caress striking her heart with a weakening blow.

Her lips trembled, the words there, ready to spill between them as fear held her back. What if she said them and he didn't return them? If he rejected her and it was just the heat holding them together, the certain knowledge of it would destroy her.

"You're beautiful," he finally whispered. "So beautiful you steal my breath."

She nodded slowly and inhaled slowly, deeply. Later. She would face this battle later. When she was stronger. When she didn't feel off balance, when she didn't feel the heavy panic weighting her stomach.

"Shall we go see about making certain Investigator Ison has

the information he needs?" He extended his elbow out to her. "I'd like to get rid of him so we can have fun later."

"You have more soap?" She arched a brow.

"Even better," he drawled. "I have massage oil."

As he escorted her from the bedroom and down the hallway, his hand low on her back, feeling the softness of her flesh, Seth knew the situation was getting radically out of control.

He knew what she needed. Knew she needed to hear the words from him, the commitment he had felt in his heart for ten years now, and he couldn't give those words to her. Not yet. Not until they caught that fucking assassin.

Hell, he should never have let her be dragged into this. He should have knocked her out and put her right back on that damned heli-jet the moment she stepped foot on his island.

Instead, what had he done? He had promised to let her fight by his side. His side? The bastard with some maniac assassin's sights on him. He was so weak, so crazy fucking in love with her that he hadn't been able to bear the look in her eyes when he held her in that shower the day before.

Yeah, she had trained. She had managed to save herself. And he was certain she was just as deadly as any other Breed out there. But she was barely fucking five-foot-four in her stocking feet, if she weighed a hundred pounds soaking wet he would have to have the scales checked, and the thought of her receiving so much as a single bruise defending him made him see bloody red.

He was so wrapped around those delicate fingers he was a lost cause, and he was man enough to admit that it scared the hell out of him. Added to that was the certainty that soon, very soon, the memories of those labs were going to return.

Would she even want him then? Would she remember the playful passion, the soul-deep kisses and incredible pleasure, with a sense of hunger or a mind filled with fear?

He knew he was terrified it was the fear she would feel.

As they stepped into the library and faced a frustrated Investigator Ison, Seth pushed the emotional problems to the back of his mind and concentrated now on the business of besting a council that would see his woman destroyed.

He faced Investigator Ison as he had his board members earlier. Coldly. Silently. He sat at the head of the long table, Dawn at his side, his fingers playing absently with hers, and stared the man down, let him fumble his way through the fact that he didn't have jack shit.

Five minutes into the questioning, Ison began to stutter and sweat. Seth had perfected the look. Cold. Hard. Brutal and all-knowing. Oh yeah, he knew quite a bit about Ison now. Things the other man couldn't imagine, and Seth promised himself that once things were settled in his own life, then he would take care to make certain Ison paid for several of the dark, violent acts he had committed against Breeds over the years.

Seth wondered if Jonas had the information Seth had managed to acquire, and then assumed he didn't. Because if he did, the other man would be dead. It was that simple. He would have disappeared as others had, and the Sanctuary heli-jet would have once again flown a little too close to the mouth of a live volcano. Jonas could often be amazingly efficient.

Within half an hour, he'd read and signed the statement the investigator had prepared from his notes then slid it back across the table, his eyes meeting the investigator's again.

There was a glint of promised retribution in the other man's gaze and Seth smiled. *Come after me, you little bastard. I dare you.*

He sat back in his chair, his hand catching Dawn's again as she watched him with a placid, almost amused expression.

When the library door closed behind Ison, Seth turned back to her.

"Keep your weapons close," he murmured. "He's up to something."

Dawn glanced at the door as he watched her; when she turned back, her eyes were flat, hard. "Of course he is. He's a Council puppet. He stinks of it." She shrugged. "And I always keep my weapons close."

Yes, she did. And that, Seth found, was both a comfort and an ache of regret. Dawn shouldn't have to worry about keeping her weapons close.

⋆ CHAPTER 19 ⋆

It was the parties that were making her nervous, Dawn realized several hours later as she stood next to Seth while he socialized with Dane, Rye and another of Seth's allies on the board, Craig Bartel, and his wife, Lillian.

Lillian was taller, with the lush womanly figure and breasts Dawn knew men lusted after. She was dressed in a loose, flowing evening gown of smoky grays and ice blues that complemented her eyes and cool blond hair.

Her husband was a bit more portly, but he had a friendly smile and warm hazel eyes when he wasn't arguing with Seth over some ball team they both seemed to have a stake in.

What, did these men own the known world? The twelve board members were practically the Who's Who on the National Registry of Arrogant Billionaires or something. And Seth was in his element.

She listened to him argue the team's stats, the players' weaknesses and strengths, and realized he did it with the same daring and confidence that he had used when relating financial figures and company information during the board meetings.

"They could talk about that ball team all night." Lillian Bartel smiled as she caught Dawn's eyes. "And he promised me a dance tonight."

Dawn glanced at Seth. "He wasn't the only one that promised."

She turned and looked out at the dance floor, watching with a smile as Dash, Elizabeth and their daughter, Cassie, stepped into the ballroom.

Every male eye in the room turned, and the scent of male lust flowed in the soft breeze that wafted in through the open French doors.

Dash scowled over at his wife, Elizabeth, who merely smiled in return.

Cassie was a vision. All that long black hair rippled and curled around her face and to her waist. Strands were pulled back from the sides to the crown of her head and secured with a gleaming gold comb that cascaded with strands of diamonds on golden chains. The gold and diamonds gleamed beneath the chandeliers within the midnight darkness of Cassie's hair.

Her evening gown was black, the Empire waist doing nothing to detract from the fragile delicacy of her lithe body.

"She's a little freak. It's so sad," Lillian whispered, and Dawn tensed at the words. "Such a beautiful little girl to be so worthless."

Dawn turned back to the older woman. "Excuse me?"

"Don't you know? She's one of those little Breeds running around here. A mixed Breed even. What do they call those?" She frowned at the thought. "Ah, yes. A mongrel."

Dawn curled her fingers into the silken material of her purse.

"There's another tramping around here somewhere." Lillian shuddered. "Be careful, I heard she had her eye on Seth. She's already forced his lover off the island. You'll be next, no doubt."

She needed to dress up more often, Dawn thought. Evidently a nice dress, a little makeup, and no one paid attention to anything but the boobs on display or, in the women's case, the jewelry on display.

"Tramping around here, is she?" She arched her brow, careful to keep the other woman from seeing the canines that were aching to bite her.

"Squalling like a cat in heat." Lillian grimaced as she kept her voice too low for Seth or her husband to hear. "Craig doesn't want to understand how horrible it is that Seth is dirtying himself with that trash. When we get home, I'll set him straight though."

"Of course," Dawn murmured.

How she hated women like this. She hated their vindictiveness, their judgmental attitudes and their lack of compassion.

"You know she's merely after his money." Lillian sighed. "How sad. Caroline would have made such a perfect match for Seth."

Dawn nearly saw red. She promised herself she would control the anger flowing through her. This was Seth's world, just a very small slice of it.

"Excuse me," she said before turning to Seth and drawing his attention. "Dash and Elizabeth have just arrived with Cassie." She nodded to the couple. "I think we should go help him."

Craig Bartel chuckled. "She's a beautiful little girl. Dash and Elizabeth should be very proud of her. I hear she was accepted into Harvard last year?"

"A law degree." Seth nodded. "She's taking her classes via remote link and doing wonderfully. And Dawn's right, we should go help Dash."

Because there were several unattached men moving in on the young woman and Dash looked murderous, despite his wife's glare.

"If you'll excuse us then." Seth nodded to the couple, and at the last moment Dawn flashed Lillian a smile. It was all teeth.

The other woman gasped, then paled, her eyes widening as the full implications of what she had just revealed to Dawn flashed across her face.

"That was very naughty," Seth murmured in her ear. "I might have to spank you later."

"What did I do?" She widened her eyes as she flicked him a look before turning her attention back to the room.

"Whatever you were leading Lillian in over," he said softly. "What did she say?"

There was more than curiosity, and the amusement was blatantly fake.

"Girl stuff." She shrugged.

She glanced over her shoulder. The middle of her back itched, and she could feel the hairs at the back of her neck lifting in primal warning.

"Dawn." His voice was warning. He wanted answers; he wasn't a man that was used to being denied either.

"Seth, I'm a big girl, I can take care of myself." But she couldn't find the source of unease pulling at her. She could feel it, like a lost word on the tip of her tongue.

She looked around again, ignoring Jason Phelps as he tried to get her attention, just as she ignored several other men who tried to catch her eye.

"Dawn, I'm a bigger boy and I'm going to spank your ass if you keep up the silent act."

Her lips twitched. "I'll be sure to pretend I don't like it. I'd hate to spoil all your fun."

Sizzling, heated lust filled the air then. It swirled around her, flowing from Seth and seeming to sink inside her flesh as his fingers pressed a little tighter against her lower back.

She could still remember his voice, the scent of his need, the expression on his face when he told her she didn't have to return to Sanctuary. As though a part of him had been as hesitant as she was to tip the balance of the tenuous relationship developing between them.

She could feel something else moving within her though. A welling panic that wasn't pushed aside as easily as it had once been. A feeling of danger that she couldn't put her finger on.

"Dash, you're growling."

Dawn looked up at Dash, to realize he was doing just that as Cassie stepped out on the dance floor with one of the young men who had attended the house party with his parents.

"He's twenty-five," Dash snarled. "He drinks too much and he drives too fast. I read his file and he has no business dancing with her."

Elizabeth snorted and rolled her eyes.

"He's a good boy feeling his oats," Seth countered. "I've known Benjamin since he was a child. She's in safe hands."

"As long as she doesn't get in a car with him," Dash snapped.

"It's a small island, Dash," Seth chuckled. "We don't keep cars, only a few ATVs."

As they talked, Dawn turned and watched the crowd again. She could still feel it, those eyes watching her, malevolent, filled with an evil promise.

She had felt those eyes before. Cowering in a cage, terrified. She was hungry and she was weak. The labs were too cold again. They did that when they wanted to punish the young Breeds. Put them in separate cages, naked, hungry, and let the air grow cold.

She could feel the cold around her. It settled in her bones and she had to force her teeth not to rattle. And she knew the eyes were watching. Watching all of them. The mirrors across the room weren't mirrors, they were the eyes from hell.

She shuddered at the thought, blinking desperately as she tried to push it back. She didn't want to remember the labs. She didn't want to remember that scared, frightened child, and she sure as hell didn't want to remember the horror of it.

She stared past the guests to the open French doors and the night beyond. She should be there, she thought. Watching for danger, sliding through the shadows, stalking the bastard that waited for her. She could feel the animal side of her wakening, stretching, preparing for battle.

"Dawn. Is everything okay?" She flinched as Elizabeth whispered the words close to her ear.

Dawn turned and met her friend's concerned blue eyes. Elizabeth, like all Breed mates, seemed frozen in time. She hadn't aged a day since Dash had mated with her, though she took the effort to fake a few lines here and there in her otherwise creamy, clear complexion.

"I'm fine." She knew her smile was tight. "Why?"

"You were growling, sweetheart, and it wasn't a sound I thought you would want Seth to hear."

In other words, it was primal, angry. A warning to the enemy that she was coming, that he couldn't avoid her. Her nails bit into her purse, the feel of her gun beneath them a comfort.

"Dawn, what's out there?" Elizabeth asked as she turned back to the room, staring over the crowd, then back to the doors.

"The past," she said softly, hoping she was right. "Just the past."

She turned back to Elizabeth and inhaled deeply, aware of Seth turning to her, as though he had sensed her uneasiness, or the evil stalking them.

"You owe me a dance," she told him, trying to tamp back the panic.

It was the effect of the memories moving in, she told herself. She had never felt this way, in ten years of training and missions, she had never known such primal, instinctive fear.

"And Dash owes me one," Elizabeth drawled. "Maybe I can help take his mind off the fact that his little girl is growing up."

Dash glowered helplessly back at her. He had the look of a man fighting that realization to its last breath.

"You know, dancing with you could be dangerous," Seth told Dawn as he led her onto the ballroom floor and took her in his arms.

"Really?" She questioned him lightly. "Is that bow tempting you?"

He breathed out heavily as they began to move around the floor.

"I want to see you in nothing but the damned bow," he growled. "It's driving me crazy."

Dawn felt a surge of heat rise inside her at the sound of his voice, the scent of his need. It hadn't changed; every time was just as intense, just as searing, as the one before it.

As his arms tightened around her, moving her against him, Dawn pressed her head against his chest and tried to assure herself that everything would be fine. It was going to work out, she promised herself. They would find the assassin and Seth would be okay.

"You're worrying too much." He kissed the top of her head, the hand that pressed against her back holding her closer as they circled the dance floor. "Everything's going to be fine, Dawn."

"Of course it is." She lifted her head and smiled, but inside she felt as though she were walking a tightrope.

"Come here. Let me hold you closer." The deep murmur of his voice sent a shiver racing down her back. "You're trembling, sweetheart. Are you cold?"

"Considering I'm barely wearing clothes?" She smiled at that. "I have a serious draft where there's usually no draft, Seth."

The heat intensified as a muttered groan left his throat. "You're trying to kill me."

The feel of his erection against her lower stomach, the scent of his need and the strength of his arms around her assured her Seth had little thought for anything but that draft and that bow beneath her dress.

"There's a serious arising where there's usually no arising in public too," he growled, causing a hint of laughter to escape her.

She laughed with Seth. She could go years without laughing at Sanctuary. There had always seemed to be a veil between her and happiness. It always seemed to hover around her, but never touch her, until now.

Something inside her seemed freer, less contained, but she was terribly afraid that the loosening of emotion inside her was also the reason the memories were returning. Why the panic was building inside her.

She could still feel that amplified sense of being watched, being touched by evil. Her shoulders were tight with it, her skin crawled with it.

She looked out over the dance floor again, trying to make sense of it. They were far enough from the open doors that they couldn't be seen—that couldn't be it. No one appeared to be watching, except Jason Phelps. He looked as inebriated as ever, a smile on his face.

He looked like a weasel. And she didn't like weasels.

Seth could feel the tension slowly building in the woman he held, and it made him want to hold her tighter. Because he knew. He had known what was coming the first time he took her to his bed.

She had held the memories back because she had never let go of that amazing control enough to give them a chance to slip free. There was no control in the passion they shared though. Not for him, and not for her.

It was like wildfire.

That, added to the stress of the mission she was involved in and the assassin no doubt still lying in wait, was too much for her.

He hadn't just walked out of her life ten years before. He had consulted the best psychologists and psychiatrists in the world and discussed the situation. He'd needed to know what he was facing if he ignored Callan's and Jonas's request that he walk away from her.

He had stayed away because those professionals had warned him that under the right circumstances, those memories would definitely return.

As he held her close, their bodies swaying to the music, the heat of arousal, tenderness and some undefined something that had existed since their first touch wrapped around them.

He let his fingers press against her lower back, hoping to

ease some of the tension. He pressed his lips to her shoulder and felt that little purr he loved so well.

He almost grinned as he thought of the smile Dawn had given Lillian Bartel. Whatever the other woman had said to her might not have set well with her, but she knew how to be a lady.

Not that Seth didn't intend to find out exactly what Lillian had said. The woman could be a bitch; everyone who knew her was aware of that.

Her husband, Craig, was a good man, enamored of his wife and accepting of her faults, but aware. He made apologies where they were needed and reined her in when he had to. She would learn, though, not to snipe at Dawn—he wouldn't have it.

"This is nice," she sighed, finally relaxing against him marginally as they seemed to exist in their own little world.

He was conscious of the other couples around them, many of them watching him. They were used to seeing him with Caroline. They had come to accept that Caroline would be around permanently. They were surprised, and in some cases shocked, to see him with the little bodyguard.

And he didn't give a damn. Hell, he had known things wouldn't work out with him and Caroline. This only confirmed it publicly.

As he looked around, he did grin. Dash and Elizabeth were across the room, and Dash appeared to be surrounded by female fury.

Elizabeth was glaring at him, and Cassie looked mortified.

"I think we should go rescue Dash," he murmured, turning her until she could see the small group across the room.

"Hmm, I can smell Dash's anger from here." She stepped back, taking his hand as they started off the dance floor.

"Hey, Dawn. It's my turn to dance." A hand gripped her arm from behind, tried to pull her from Seth, and something inside her snapped.

She turned back with a snarl, barely holding back her violent reaction as she jerked her arm from the grasp, her flesh feeling blistered, dirty.

"Whoa!" Jason Phelps fell back, a look of surprise on his face as Seth quickly pulled her back against his hard body.

Other dancers were pausing now, watching, avid curiosity in their gazes.

"Don't touch me again." She leveled furious eyes on him,

the animal inside her reacting with a ferocity she couldn't understand. She could smell his blood, beating hard and fast in his veins, and she wanted to see it spilling to the floor.

"Dawn." There was an edge of warning in Seth's voice and it pissed her off.

"If you want him to have a dance, then you dance with him," she hissed, pulling away from him and casting him an accusing glare.

He knew the mating heat. He knew the symptoms of it by now. A mated female couldn't tolerate another male's touch during those first weeks and months of the bonding.

Betrayal flashed through her as he watched her with a frown, and what she perceived as an edge of censure in his gaze.

"Excuse me," she bit out between gritted teeth. "I think I'll find a drink."

"Hey, come on, gorgeous, I just wanted a dance." Jason laughed. "I thought we were friends." A male pout pursed his lips and it sickened her.

The mating heat was destroying her. Her nerves were strung as tight as a banjo string, and the animal inside her was clawing for freedom, almost a separate entity, attempting control.

"I don't have friends," she told him with deadly softness, making certain her voice carried no farther as rumor-greedy eyes tried to listen to the exchange. "I warned you of that before. Remember it."

With one last furious look at Seth, she turned and moved across the ballroom as she motioned to Styx to cover Seth's back. She couldn't do it right now. Her emotions, her sense of balance were so compromised she felt almost outside her own flesh. As though her spirit were gliding alongside her body rather than within it. And before her inner eye Jason Phelps's face flashed back at her. Shock, surprise But how could he be surprised? He would know . . .

She stopped and shook her head before turning slowly and staring back at him.

He couldn't know about the mating heat, and he wouldn't know about the reaction female mates had to touch from males other than their mates. A reaction the males were supposed to experience as well, but with female touch only.

Seth knew.

That's why her reactions were so extreme, almost violent.

He knew, and he had still attempted to curb her response as though—what? She was going to spill Breed secrets in the middle of his ballroom floor?

She shifted her gaze to Seth. Suddenly, the need for him swept over her. Her juices flooded her pussy, instantly dampened her panties and had her forcing back a growl as she turned once more and stalked to where Dash and his family stood.

"Dawn, get a handle on it," Dash muttered as she stopped beside Cassie.

"Yeah," Cassie murmured. "Make certain you're the one that gets a handle on it. It's not their responsibility to do so."

Dawn blinked at Cassie. She was watching the dance floor, her eyes restless, her cheeks flushed. The scents coming from the other girl were contradictory. Fear and confusion, anticipation.

"Elizabeth." Dash's voice was warning, the voice of a man begging his wife to do something with his teenage progeny, since he sure as hell didn't know what to do with her.

"Dawn, you've walked into a family feud," Elizabeth sighed as Dawn watched Seth finish his discussion with Jason Phelps before heading back to her.

Her eyes narrowed on him, and she didn't understand why she was so furious.

"Don't worry, Elizabeth, I think it's something in the water," she snorted. "All the men are acting weird around this place."

Cassie smothered a laugh, and when her blue eyes turned to Dawn, there was a sense of thankfulness in them. Her father was obviously stressing over all the male attention she was receiving, and responding to the scents of his daughter's confusion and awakened womanhood. It had to be hard on him. Every day that Cassie lived was a miracle to them. She had a price on her head set by the Council scientists, a price that would fund a small nation.

"Dash." Seth nodded at the other man as his fingers loosely circled Dawn's wrist. "If you'll excuse us, Dawn and I have a bit more circulating to do before the evening is over."

She glared at him as he gave her a hard look. "Circulating?" she asked sweetly. "Is that another word for flirting with the pretty boys you invited? What, Seth, I didn't perform as expected?"

He stopped, his expression surprised, angry as he stared down at her.

Dawn grimaced, knowing she had gone too far. Knowing and not certain why. "I'm sorry," she whispered, shaking her head. "I don't know—"

"Don't." He shook his head wearily then. "No apologies needed, Dawn. We'll just say good night to a few friends and then go to bed." He reached out and touched her cheek. "Whatever's wrong, we'll work it out there. All right?"

She wanted to cry. She knew there should be tears, but her eyes were dry, painful from the need to shed the poison that seemed to be consuming her.

"I'm losing my mind, Seth," she whispered. "I can feel it."

"No, sweetheart, not your mind." He sighed, his gaze heavy and filled with regret. "Just your control. And, sometimes, that's almost worse."

· CHAPTER 20 ·

The party waned in the early hours of the morning, and the house took on a heavy silence, almost as though it were waiting for some unforeseen event.

Or he was.

Seth lay beside his woman, his mate. That term should have been uncomfortable, yet it wasn't.

She lay against his chest sleeping deeply, her breath light and easy against his chest as he held her and stared at the ceiling above her.

The dreams were there, he knew. He'd eased her from several of them, stroking her back gently until she lapsed into a more comfortable sleep.

He felt the heavy tension of the house in his heart, his soul. As though he were waiting on that final boom. For the storm to strike and wipe away everything that had come before it.

The cougar was an incredibly strong, adaptable creature. It roamed the high places, the deserts and forgotten cliffs, the forests and boundaries that man tried to impose. It survived on its own rules, and Dawn had done the same.

She was as graceful as the cougar, as adaptable, as incredibly beautiful and dangerous as the creature she had been created from.

But even with that strength, he didn't know if she could survive what he feared he had been the catalyst for.

He stroked her hair as she shifted restlessly in her sleep, a muttered growl, a sound that lifted the hairs on the back of his neck, coming from her throat.

Seth closed his eyes and fought the agony building inside him. He admitted he was terrified for her to remember that past, terrified of what it would do to the woman and to the future he could have with her.

He'd had her now. He'd stroked that incredibly body, felt her passion and her hunger and carried the primal mark she had never given to another man. He didn't want to live his life without the woman who had given him those gifts. Hell, he couldn't imagine life without her now. He hadn't even realized how much she was a part of him until she stepped into his life and took her place in his soul. As though it had been waiting on her, and opened for her with an ease that amazed him.

"Oh God . . . Oh God . . ." The words whispered from her as he grimaced tightly and pulled her closer to him, stroking her back, his lips touching her forehead.

He couldn't stop what was coming and he knew it, but his prayer echoed hers as she whispered the words.

She never called for God while awake. She never prayed; she avoided it with clear intensity. Because God hadn't answered her prayers as a child. He hadn't saved her from the rapes or the horror.

She didn't see her rescue as salvation, because Dayan had moved so easily into position and begun his own campaign to destroy her. She didn't see Dayan's death as a salvation or as an answer to her childhood prayers.

She didn't see the strength inside herself, that strength that went clear to her soul, as a gift from God. She believed the scientists and soldiers in those labs were right. That God didn't create her, and He didn't claim her. She believed she was without grace.

Grief welled inside him. It tightened his throat and his chest, and left him aching with a depth he hadn't previously believed possible. He ached to the core of his being, a pain he feared would never ease or find relief unless Dawn did.

". . . Save me . . ." The words whispered past her lips, and he knew, in a second, she would wake up.

He could feel her gathering for it, pushing herself back to consciousness to escape those shattered memories and the child determined to find acknowledgment.

She came awake with a hard jerk as he let his eyes close. He didn't want her to feel shame, didn't want her to have to fight back her emotions because she knew he watched. She shouldn't have to see the knowledge in his eyes, the memories she fought in his gaze.

Because he knew what they had done to her as clearly as she did. Dayan had forced her to watch the disc, and Seth had forced himself to watch those images in that office where Jonas and Callan had turned their backs on them.

He felt her rise, felt her move from their bed and slowly dress in the uniform she kept lying on the padded stool.

She wouldn't leave the house; he was confident of that. She needed to run, to hunt, but she wouldn't leave his security, his protection, long enough to do so.

The knowledge that she restrained herself for him in such a way was a grim reminder of the life she had led and the discipline she imposed on herself.

He lay still and listened to her finish dressing then leave the bedroom. She left the door open into the sitting room. A second later he heard her muted conversation with the Breed guard outside the door, then the door closed and he was alone.

He waited. She would need time. A little bit of time before he followed her. A chance to breathe and to find her balance. He understood the nightmares well.

He gave her half an hour. She wasn't getting any more than that. The fact that he was able to lie there, to force himself to patience, was a testament to his control, not his patience.

Seth rose from the bed and breathed a weary sigh before dressing himself. He chose jeans and a T-shirt and tied leather running shoes on his feet before leaving the bedroom.

The guard came to attention as he opened the door, his amber eyes somber as Seth stepped outside.

Mercury's expression was grim as Seth watched him for a long, silent moment.

"Where did she go?" he finally asked.

Mercury ran a broad hand around the back of his neck, rubbing at it in indecision.

"I won't ask again," he stated. He would simply go looking for her himself.

"Exercise room," Mercury finally growled. "Let her work it out, Lawrence. She doesn't need you down there."

Seth tightened his jaw as anger lashed inside him.

"So who does she need down there with her, Mercury?" He asked sarcastically. "The ghosts she carries with her and nothing more?"

Mercury grunted at that. "The Breed whose gonna get his ass kicked. You don't want to play that role tonight."

Because the rage building in her was growing, and Seth knew it. It was lashing at her emotions and her control, and the only way Dawn knew how to fight it was by lashing out at something else.

"If you warn her that I'm headed down there, then I'll kick your ass," Seth told him, ignoring the Breed's look of disbelief. "She doesn't just need a fight, Mercury, she needs me as well. Deal with that however you need to, but keep your mouth shut."

He didn't wait on a reply but started down the hall, heading for the basement level where the gym room was housed. One wide section had been partitioned off for hand-to-hand combat practice. It was an exercise Seth often participated in with the bodyguards Sanctuary provided for him.

The house was silent, shadowed and dim. Even the household staff was in bed by now, having cleaned up quickly after the party and prepared the rooms for the next day.

Pushing open the door into the basement level, he could hear the sounds of combat coming from behind the netted screens at the other side of the room.

Shadows twisted behind the partition, blocked and struck as feral growls erupted and the sound of a male grunt could be heard.

A slender shadow jumped, two graceful feet aimed for the head but struck the shoulder as a purely catlike twist-and-drop was performed while the larger figure was pushed back, but not down.

Seth stood, his heart in his throat as he watched the maneuvers. He could see the size of the Breed she was sparring with and guess at his identity. Stygian—he hadn't taken a last name. A dark Wolf Breed created from the DNA of the black wolf. Blue eyes and coffee-colored skin. He was massive, six and a half feet tall, with shoulders a football player dreamed of having.

He struck out as the too-small form advanced again, locked his arms around her neck as a feline scream erupted.

"Does it hurt?" Stygian growled as he suddenly pushed her away. "You're mated, little Cougar. You think I'm gonna stand here and let you beat on me to keep from touching you?"

"Bring it on, asshole." She was panting, crouched, waiting for him.

A dark chuckle filled the room as they began a slow, intricate dance around the area. Thrust and parry, a slender shape striking where the larger would least expect it.

A powerful kick to his knee and she was ducking, twisting, kicking out at the opposite knee from behind before executing a quick roll and jumping to her feet several feet away.

Stygian swayed, but he didn't go down.

"Next time I catch you, I'm taking you down, little girl," he laughed.

Little girl. The soldiers had called her little girl.

Feline rage erupted and the next time Dawn struck, she managed to sweep Stygian's feet out from under him.

To give the Wolf Breed credit, once again he didn't go down, but bounced against the netting and cursed before righting himself.

"Almost had you," Dawn snapped as the weave and advance between them began again.

"You live in a dreamworld," Stygian grunted. "You weren't even close."

Back and forth, she moved to strike and he countered. Long seconds later he caught her again, her smaller frame swallowed by his. As Seth ran, sprinting across the room and rushing into the partitioned section, the only sounds in the room were those feline screams of rage and pain. Stygian quickly pushed her away from him and retreated, his blue eyes flickering with flames of warning, and Seth stopped, prepared to launch himself at the Breed if he touched her, just laid a single finger on her one more time.

Dawn turned to him. Her face was wet with sweat, her eyes were red, haunted, tormented, as she snarled at him in aggressive fury.

"Stygian, you can leave now," Seth snapped.

He had never seen Dawn like this. She was primal, fierce, ferocious.

"Get the hell out of here, Lawrence," Stygian retorted rather than doing as he was ordered. "This is no place for you."

Dawn turned and snarled at Stygian then, her canines flashing, her pale face white beneath the harsh lights.

Stygian's jaw bunched, and something akin to pity flashed in his eyes.

There was something desperate, desolate about the sound that came from her throat. All the pent-up rage and horror rushing through her was in that sound. The memories she didn't want to allow freedom, the child she couldn't face.

"Let him stay." Dawn whipped around as Seth moved closer, a step closer. Her lips were pulled back in a primitive grimace of warning.

Stygian watched him, his eyes those of a predator, his expression savage. Seth wondered if he was seeing the true color of the man's eyes now. Stygian liked his contacts. Colored contacts. He liked shocking, surprising, throwing others off balance. Especially those who weren't Breeds.

"This is my fight, Stygian." Seth faced his mate, feeling the power that filled his own muscles, his mind. Mating heat was a pain in the ass, but in this, it had made him stronger, faster. The decrease in aging kept him at his peak, and since the full mating had begun the adrenaline coursing through him had only amplified it.

Stygian shook his head. "She's going to kick your ass."

Seth smiled as he watched anticipation rise inside Dawn. She couldn't be weakened by the pain if he touched her. She wouldn't lose that delicate edge that the agony of another's touch stole from her.

He smiled back at her. A slow, sensual curve to his lips as he suddenly realized it had been coming to this. As the memories fought Dawn's instinctive animalism, the situation had demanded this confrontation. The animal wouldn't let her give herself totally to him unless he took it. There could be only one alpha male, and to accept him, that part of her needed to know he was stronger, faster, that he could take her down and force her submission if he needed to.

"I can take you," she growled, her voice raspy and so sensually exciting his dick immediately responded by growing harder than ever before.

"Can you now?" he drawled. "Shall we put that to the test, sweetheart? Do you think you're the only one who trains? The only one who fights?"

Oh, he had fought. He had trained beneath the best the Breeds had to offer for years. Stygian knew it; he knew Seth was more than a match for Dawn, but he thought Seth would let her win. Let her beat on him out of pity and love.

Stygian had another think coming.

He would never strike her. He would never hurt her. But there were other ways to bring her down.

He was only barely aware of Stygian retreating to the opposite exit as he and Dawn began to circle each other, to prepare for the strengths and weaknesses they would detect in each other.

As they did, Seth felt his mind settle. The turmoil that had been rising inside it in the past few days hardened to resolve.

"The next time you need to fight, you won't go to another man," he promised her.

She growled. "The next time I need to fight, you'll run with your tail tucked between your legs."

Seth chuckled, seeing her response to the amusement. Her eyes narrowed and the rumbling growls in her chest grew more warning, harder, more dangerous.

And the battle began.

She was damned good. Seth hadn't realized how good she was, how strong, how coordinated. She twisted and turned and fought to kick, scratch, wound.

And he laughed at her. He forced himself to laugh at her. He dragged the sound from his chest and wondered if she knew how much it tore at his soul to do it. He pushed her, chided her, assured her she couldn't win.

He blocked most of the moves, took the ones he couldn't block, and each time he got his hands on her he restrained her. He held her against his chest, or pushed her into the padded wall. He held her for long seconds.

"Fight me, Dawn." Holding her broke his heart; hearing those feral screams tore at his soul.

He released her, jumped back and ducked as she kicked off from the wall and flew over his head.

She executed another of those feline twists and landed in a crouch.

"Is this how you deal with it?" He finally struck, as realization slapped him as hard as one of her fists did and she flew by him again. "Is this what you do, Dawn? You fight because you can't cry?"

She froze, crouched, a black shadow, her face paper white, her eyes flames of agony, the whites red, the need to drain that fury and that pain welling just beyond them.

God, the tears that were trapped inside her.

"You fight to get rid of the pain. You hurt yourself, you let others bruise you, and you deliver as much pain as you can, don't you, Dawn?" he whispered into the silence of the room, watching her, knowing he would see a shift of muscle before she moved. And he would feel it, he would know it was coming.

He watched the eyes, locked on his, the pupils dilated until her gaze was nearly black as sweat poured from her hair and her face.

"Does it take the pain away?" He shifted to the side, moving slowly, almost casually. "Does it make the memories subside?"

She flinched and everything inside his soul was torn to shreds. Because he knew that was exactly what she did.

"You don't know—"

"What I'm talking about?" He finished for her.

"You don't." She struck.

The words weren't out of her mouth before she moved. Seth barely avoided her claws or those lethal feet before he hooked his arm around her waist and slammed her into the mat beneath them.

Feral, inflamed, her scream echoed through the training room and through his soul as he held her down.

"Is this what fighting others won't give you?" he yelled over the snarls. "Is this it, Dawn? They won't force you to remember? Because you can't let it go yourself."

And he knew it was the truth. Callan had put out the order years ago. When sparring, Dawn was not to be held down, no matter the circumstance, for more than a three-second count. There were no excuses allowed; ignoring that order called the wrath of their pride leader down, and none of the Breeds in Sanctuary wanted to tangle with Callan.

He wasn't pride leader by election, but by strength.

And he wasn't Seth's pride leader.

Seth tightened his legs on her thighs, held her wrists with one hand, a hard hand pressed between her shoulders, flattening her to the mat.

"Is this what you are, Dawn?" he yelled, furious himself now, livid that she had to beat herself to exhaustion to still the memories, to still the pain raging inside her. "Are you an animal? Is that what God gave Callan the strength to rescue you for? So you could hide? So you could deny what you are by pushing it back forever?"

God forgive him.

The scream that came from her throat must have echoed through the house.

"Listen to yourself," he roared. "Feel yourself, Dawn. What are you? Are you the animal the Council wanted? They fucking won, didn't they?" He wanted to shake her. He wanted to hold her and still the pain in both of them, and his tears fell because hers wouldn't.

"Answer me, damn you." He twisted his fingers in her hair and held her head still, her cheek pressed into the mat as he stared down at her.

He could hear the feet pounding on the stairs leading to the room, the door slamming into the wall as others rushed to them.

"Get out of here!" He lifted his head, rage scouring his voice as Callan, Jonas, Elizabeth and Dash stood in the entrance, watching in shock.

"Let her go!" Callan's voice was more animal than man. "Let her go or I'll kill you."

Dawn's scream had them all flinching. Elizabeth's eyes welled with tears as she buried her face in Dash's chest and they turned, pulling back.

"You turned your back on her," Seth charged, holding Dawn as pure animal screams left her throat now. "You didn't even watch those fucking images you showed me, you turned your fucking back on her then and you can do it now."

Dawn bucked, fought, her muscles tightened to the breaking point as she screamed again.

"Let her fucking go!" Callan jumped to race to them before Jonas caught him. Jonas, then Dash, pushed their pride leader to the wall as he snarled and struggled against them.

"You son of a bitch, let her go!" Callan's rage was a terrible sight, nearly as terrible as the sound of Dawn's feral screams rising.

"You sons of bitches, let her go!"

He was the new Breed. He was young. Dawn knew his voice, knew he was strong and had been free before they brought him to the labs. She knew he fought for them, took the lashes for them and screamed out in rage each time they took her from the cage.

And this time, they brought him to the lab. They chained him to the wall and he fought the chains. Fought them until blood welled beneath the steel as it welled beneath the restraints that held her.

She was screaming. Held to the metal table, the soldiers laughing around her as one moved into position.

"You bastards! I'll fucking kill you!" Feral, primal rage filled the room as she felt that first touch. And the animal, it rose inside her. Her screams tore from her throat, her prayers . . . If she prayed, they hurt her worse, she knew they hurt her worse, just for praying. But the animal, the animal wouldn't listen . . .

"Oh God . . . Oh God . . . Save me! Save me!"

They froze. Seth's gaze jerked back to Dawn as he heard the wail, a child's cry filled with such agony, such brutal, soul-searing pain that it sliced into him with a wound he knew would never heal.

"Save me!" she screamed again. Jerking. Crying. Sobs ripping from her throat. "Oh God! Save me!"

The strength went out of her. Seth moved to her side carefully, trying to pull her into his arms.

She shuddered and fought, curling into herself, a fetal position of agony as her arms wrapped around her stomach and the woman's cries tore free.

This wasn't the animal. This was the woman, the child, the fury and pain that couldn't be contained tearing through her as the memories rushed inside her.

Seth couldn't bear it. He jerked her to him, curled himself around her and bent his head over hers. To cry with her. He couldn't hold back his own tears.

God help him, she was his. His heart and soul and everything he had known or loved in his entire life. She was steel and satin, lace and courage. And she was so much a part of him that when she latched on to him, he could only hold her tighter.

"*He* wouldn't save me!" she screamed out, agony resonating through her voice. "*He* didn't save me. Oh God. Oh God, why didn't you save me!"

Her tears were soaking through his T-shirt, burning into his heart. Scars, of such brutality that he had never imagined feeling them, ripped at his being as he rocked her. He fought to hold her.

"*He* saved you, Dawn," he whispered. "He brought Callan to you. Callan rescued you. Callan slew Dayan and freed you. Then Callan brought you to me. God brought you strength, Dawn. He saved you."

"I prayed," she sobbed. "I prayed like that stupid book I hid told me to pray. I prayed and I begged and I read and *He* didn't make it stop. It didn't stop!"

They had still hurt her. The Bible had promised her God's protection, and Dawn hadn't seen the protection God had given her.

"Did Callan hurt you?" He could barely speak for his own tears. "Callan could have been sent to any lab, but he was sent to yours. He defied the safeguards they had in place and he destroyed the monsters, Dawn. God sent him to you. And God sent me to you. And you to me. And God helped you hide those memories. *He* gave you escape. *He* heard you, baby. He heard you."

She collapsed against him. The sobs were tearing from her throat now, shaking her body, and he knew, he knew as certainly as anything in his life, as certainly as he knew that God had indeed watched over her, that those memories were pouring back.

And all he could do was hold her.

The demons were long dead, but for this moment they were as fresh and as clear as yesterday. Right now, as he held her to his chest and fought to shelter her with his strength, Dawn could do nothing but remember. And shed the tears . . .

He carried her to their bedroom.

Dawn was aware that they were alone. The Breeds that patrolled the house were noticeably absent, and Callan, Jonas, Dash and Elizabeth didn't follow them.

They held back as she cried. Broken sobs that should have been silenced long before this, and the tears that still soaked Seth's shirt.

She remembered. The memories were bleak and ugly, filled with pain and hopelessness, just as the images had been. But that wasn't why she cried. She cried because as the memories flowed over her, so had realization.

She hadn't been deserted. Not by God, and not by herself. She had hid from them. She had hid from the child she had been because she had sworn, vowed to herself and to God that she would kill the bastard that had tried to destroy her. She had sworn it to every child that died by his hand during their stay there, and she had sworn it to herself.

But she hadn't killed him. His blood hadn't soaked her hands. She hadn't tasted her own vengeance, and that was part of what she couldn't face. That and the fear that she was lost, never a part of the true circle of life. Neither human nor animal in the eyes of a supreme being.

"I'm sorry," the half sob came as she tried to unclench her hands from his neck, tried to ease the desperate hold she had on him.

"Apologize to me for your pain, Dawn, and I really will spank you," he snapped. "As God is my witness, if you take another helping of guilt on your slender shoulders then you'll destroy my heart."

She could do more than scent his pain now, she could feel it. His pain that she had suffered, his willingness to do anything, no matter the cost, to ease her. His complete, unquestioned dedication to her.

Her true mate.

Something inside her had shattered as he held her down, as he yelled at her, as he forced her to remember, to realize what she didn't want to remember or to accept. She had smelled his pain, felt it blending with her own, tearing through her, breaking down the walls she had erected so long ago.

Those memories lived inside her. Knowing what had happened hadn't helped her to know why she hid from it. Now she knew.

She knew, and knowing didn't change anything. She had no identity to place to her rapist. There was no way to taste vengeance or to fulfill the promise she had made to God as a child.

If he would save her, she would kill. If he would just make the pain go away, she would shed that bastard's blood and make certain he never raped another child, Breed or human.

She had failed, God hadn't.

"I didn't keep my promises," she told Seth as he stepped past Mercury and into their sitting room.

She scented the other Breed's compassion, and rather than shaming her, she felt thankfulness. The Breeds as a species, as a race, or however the world defined them, were worthy. God had given them a soul, no matter what the scientists believed. He had adopted them.

"I swore I'd kill him," she whispered. "I didn't."

"Callan did it for you, Dawn." He carried her into the bedroom, then to the bed. "You were a child. No one could expect you to do it all."

He sat on the bed, still holding her, his arms so strong. He was so strong, so warm and so important to her very existence.

"I swore," she whispered again.

"And He forgave," he told her gently, his hand moving to tip her head back.

And then she saw the destruction of his tears. His expression was ravaged, heavy with grief, his gray eyes nearly black with emotions as he cupped her face in his palm.

"I love you," he whispered, and her heart stilled in her chest. "I have loved you since the day I saw you, and the depth of that love can never do anything but deepen, Dawn. Whether you stay with me, or you walk away, I need you to know that. You define my soul."

She blinked back at him, swallowing tightly.

"The mating heat . . ."

"Didn't start until we touched," he told her. "I loved you before I touched you. When I saw you, I felt my heart beat and I swear to you, I felt it beating for you."

She stared up at him, feeling all the fears begin to lift, all the fears that he would reject her, even now, after the mating heat, after every touch he had used to show her how important she was to him.

"I wanted you then," she whispered. "You left me alone, Seth." Another tear fell. Another weight rose from her soul. "Callan was wrong. I didn't want you to leave me."

His lashes drifted closed as a pain-filled grimace twisted his expression. "It wasn't time. You know it wasn't time, sweetheart. As much as I loved you, you needed your distance, and you needed your strength."

"And you had others," she bit the words out. "You were going to leave me forever, Seth."

His head shook, his gaze became rueful. "I forced myself to let go of you, or I would have withered away, Dawn. And that's not your fault, it's mine. But no matter what I wanted to convince myself of, Caroline was on her way out. She knew it, and I did as well."

"She didn't look on her way out." Feminine fear, Dawn knew what it was, the fear of losing what she knew had to be hers.

"She wasn't sleeping in my bed," he reminded her. "And she

wouldn't have been. No other woman has slept in this bed, Dawn."

And that she knew was the truth. There was no scent of feminine lust permeating the room, no taint of another woman's hunger for his body.

"I didn't want to remember," she finally said. "I knew what had happened. It wasn't the memory of the rapes I was scared to face."

"It was the memory of feeling deserted." His thumb brushed over her trembling lips. "Of having no hope, no promises to believe in. And the memory of betraying the vows to yourself."

She nodded. "I hadn't kept the promises I made to Him. Why should He keep the promises I read of? Each time it was over, I swore the next time I'd kill. And I never did."

But the promises had been made. Another realization she had hid from herself for so many years. The agony had stopped, and eventually, freedom had come. And then, there had been Seth.

"Come here." He lifted her until she stood between his thighs, shaking, trembling as her body realized how incredibly tired it was.

There was no adrenaline rushing through her, no anger or fury spurring her to fight against the darkness she always felt inside her.

And now she was tired.

The sun was rising; she could feel it in her blood, heating her despite the weariness as Seth slowly undressed her.

He didn't caress her as a lover would. He caressed her as a mate. Loving, soothing kisses where she was bruised. A murmur of regret at a scratch to her flesh.

He had no idea that this was the least damaged she had ever been in a fight with Stygian. He rarely gave quarter, and he taunted her in the bargain. But it had never drawn free the primal fury that Seth had drawn from her.

Because no other Breed had been allowed to restrain her; Callan forbade it. Seth didn't kowtow to Callan, and he didn't fear him. He had staked his claim there in that room, on a mat that dampened with her sweat and her tears. And he had given her the gift of making her whole.

Dawn wasn't a fool, and she knew Seth wasn't either. There would be other nights when she would cry, because when she awoke from the nightmares, the memory of them would be there. But she knew he would be there to hold her. He would shelter her, and her tears would be welcome.

"I need you," she finally whispered as he stood and stripped his sweaty shirt from his body.

"You need a shower, then you need to rest." He finished undressing and turned to lead her to the shower.

"No, Seth. I need you." She dug her heels in, staring back at him, the confidence of a lover, the woman that belonged in his soul rising within her. "The shower can wait. I need your touch."

Dawn leaned forward and touched him. She licked over his chest, let her teeth rake over it.

His muscles jerked beneath the touch as a hard hiss left his lips.

She liked that sound. Male frustration, and male pleasure. Seth's pleasure.

She pulled her wrist free of his fingers and let her fingers rake through the curls that covered his chest. The lighter brown almost blended with the deeply tanned flesh and fascinated her.

Breeds didn't have body hair below their necks. Some Breeds could grow a beard and mustache, but it was extremely rare. Hair grew quickly, and brows and lashes were natural, but there was no crisp, silken chest hair on the males. No covering growth between the thighs.

Seth's body hair continually drew her touch. It was light, sexy, soft and warm. She leaned forward and rubbed her cheek against it, feeling the purr that came to her throat when she meant only to give a whispery moan of pleasure.

Her hands pulled at his belt, the metal buttons of his jeans as she felt him toe his way out of his running shoes. She pushed the denim over his hips, carefully lowered it over the thick length of his cock.

The hard flesh stood out from his body, throbbing, flushed, heavy with need.

She dragged the material down his muscular thighs then let him deal with the rest of it. She had what she wanted. That gorgeous cock, full to bursting, a small bead of pre-cum dampening the tip.

She went to her knees, ignoring his strangled groan as her lips covered the flushed crest.

She needed the taste of him in her mouth. His pleasure racing inside her.

She drew his cock head nearly to her throat, sucked and licked as her hands, both hands, cupped around the shaft and stroked.

The muscles in his abdomen stood out clearly, his thighs bunched powerfully.

"Dawn, I won't last long with this," he groaned. "Come here, sweetheart." He threaded his fingers through her hair and tried to lift her. "Let me love you."

A growl met the tug on her hair, a light raking of her teeth.

"You're spanked." The hard retort was a sound of extreme pleasure.

Promises, promises, she thought without lifting her lips to speak the words. Maybe one of these days he would actually get around to making good on it.

She swirled her tongue over the pulsing crest, licked and purred. God, he tasted so good. He tasted like life, like a miracle, like love. And she needed all of it to warm the places in her soul that had been cold for so long. To ease the shock of the revelations inside her and, quite simply, because he made her hot.

He made her horny.

He made her want to knead his flesh in pure joy.

Instead she sucked. She sucked and licked and heard his groans, his growls, his muttered oaths and, finally, felt and tasted the hard, deep spurts of his semen filling her.

She eased back, stared up at the glitter of lust gone mad in his gaze and licked her lips slowly. Satisfyingly. Because he tasted so damned good she knew she would need more, often.

"My turn." He lifted her.

Dawn didn't protest it; it would have done her no good to, because her body was burning for his touch now. She had erogenous zones where there weren't supposed to be erogenous zones.

As he laid her back against the soft spread, the caress of the material on her back made her arch. But when his hands gripped her thighs and parted them, the pleasure was like a tidal wave, consuming her and sucking her into a vast ocean of sensation.

She was lost within it as his head lowered to the heat of her pussy and his tongue worked slowly through the ultrasensitive slit.

He set fires in her that she knew would never be completely sated. They could be banked, nothing more.

Her hands slid into his hair, she twisted beneath him, arched and cried out in ecstasy as his lips surrounded her clit and sucked her to climax. Then he pulled her to him as he went to his back, dragging her over him and pulling her head down for his kiss.

His cock pierced her pussy as her tongue slid into his mouth. He sucked the hormone gathering in her tongue from her as she sucked him into the heat and snug depths of her sex.

They moaned together, moved in a dance as ancient as time, and they loved.

Dawn had never felt sensations as she felt them now. As though by confronting the worst that her past had to offer, she could now accept her present with a joy she had never known before. And she did more than accept it now; she demanded it.

She straightened until she rose above him, her body consuming his as his hands held her hips in a viselike grip. Sweat beaded his forehead, his chest. A small rivulet rolled down his abs to where their bodies met, and that just turned her on. It made a purring little growl leave her throat as she shifted her hips, stroking him internally with the flexing of her muscles.

"I love your body." She ran her hands up his hard pecs, slid them over his shoulders as he watched her from hooded eyes. "Every hard inch, inside and out." She shifted her hips again and watched his teeth clench.

"You're being bad," he groaned. "Driving me crazy is very bad, Dawn."

"Yes. And one of these days, you're going to spank me for it." She smiled down at him. "Promises, promises."

His eyes narrowed on her. As his muscles bunched as though to move, Dawn moved instead. She lifted, her breath catching as his erection slid against the sensitive flesh, stroked and heated her. She lifted until he barely penetrated her, barely heated her before lowering herself slowly, steadily, and taking all he had to give her once again.

She shook her head, feeling her womb clench and convulse as he stretched her, burned her. The pleasure-pain of each impalement was almost enough to make her orgasm instantly. She was dying from the pleasure; it raced over her, stroked her flesh even where he didn't touch her, and left her gasping, crying for more.

She felt as though she were burning within the center of a flame of pure sensation, pure emotion. Twisting within spirals of rapture and needing it to last forever.

"Seth. It's like the sun," she cried out, feeling the heat gathering and burning inside her. "You're inside me like the sun."

"Fuck! Damn. Dawn, sweetheart, *you're* the fucking sun." He was straining beneath her, his muscles tight, vibrating and trembling with the need to hold back.

Dawn was fighting to hold back too. She wanted more pleasure. Hours of it. She wanted to hold it inside her forever and feel this, just this. Oh God, she wanted to feel held like this, loved and pleasured, just like this, for eternity.

"Seth." She cried his name because she couldn't find a center other than him.

Her head was spinning with the pleasure. Her vision dark, dazed. She was moving faster, harder, and it was never enough. It wasn't enough to still that fire, to throw her past the boundaries of her body and into an ecstasy that defied description, defied need, hunger or desire. A fire that poured into her soul.

She twisted; she held on to his hard biceps, thrust and rolled her hips and screamed out her frustration.

With a shattered cry Seth lifted her, flipped her to her back as he rolled behind her, lifted her hips and slammed into her.

The thrust impaled her deep and hard, every thick, iron-hard inch boring into her in one deep lunge that had her back arching and pleasure rocketing through her.

It wasn't just one thrust. It was another. And another. His hips slammed into her, the sounds those of flesh smacking flesh, his male groans and her cries of building pleasure.

Until it exploded. Until he thrust into her and triggered an orgasm that obliterated her mind, sent fire exploding and rushing along nerve endings, through her bloodstream, into her veins.

Her pores opened and drew ecstasy into them, until she was the burning center of a flame that turned into a rushing conflagration.

She heard Seth cry out behind her, felt her muscles lock on his cock, stroke and milk it until he bucked against her and spilled more heat into her. Hard jets of liquid heat that filled her womb, rushed through her, exploded inside her again and left her mindless. Pleasure. It wasn't just pleasure rushing through her, it was the center of ecstasy.

Seth collapsed over her.

He was always careful to keep his weight from her, to never

take her as she had been forced in those labs, to never make her feel restrained, held down.

But as she drained his seed from his body, she drained the strength from his muscles as well. He fell over her, barely catching enough of his weight to keep from crushing her.

She still held his cock in a grip impossible to break. He jerked, shuddered, bit off a curse and finally let a strangled groan or two leave his throat. Because nothing in his life had ever prepared him for Dawn's orgasms.

Her pussy tightened around his cock until it wasn't possible to move. The muscles flexed and stroked and milked the hard shaft until there was no holding back his release. His cum pumped into her, spurt after spurt, stealing the breath from his lungs and leaving him helpless in her grip until her own pleasure eased.

And she did like to hold on to her pleasure. It rippled endlessly through her pussy and stroked endlessly over flesh so sensitive that the added stimulation was ecstasy and agony combined.

When the contractions eased enough to allow him to slide free, he found himself reluctant to. His lips were pressed to her shoulder, his breaths sawing from his lungs.

He just needed to catch his breath, then he could pull free and shift from her.

"I wish I could hold you inside me." A little shudder worked from her body, a gasp left her throat. "Forever."

Her voice was pure sensation, a dark caress over senses destroyed by the power of his release and the effect she always had on him.

She would do this to him, no matter their age, no matter how weak or how tired he ever became. Her pleasure would always spur his, always leave him helpless to do anything but feel, touch, taste and experience the never-ending pleasure that only she could give him.

Finally, he found enough breath inside him to drag his body off hers and pull her against his chest.

"We need a shower," he sighed. "I even had the soap laid out."

A weak laugh left her lips. "How many soaps do you have, Seth?"

He frowned. How many did he have?

"I don't know. How many trips did I make in ten years?"

He felt her thinking. She would know, if she could think. Hell, he couldn't find the energy for a fucking thought in his head.

"A lot," she said finally and yawned, shifting and turning, finding her place against his chest.

She had a particular position she liked to go to sleep in, one that left him wrapped around her and her wrapped inside the curve of his body. Hell, he loved that position.

"A lot of soaps then." He smirked into the predawn shadows of the room. "If a scent made me think of you, I found a soap maker. Ireland in all seasons. Scotland during a highland summer beside a clear running stream. I thought of you there. I even bought the land. Paris, the countryside alive with spring. There was even this little town, somewhere in Egypt, where the scent of the desert sands met a private oasis. Damn, I got hard thinking of you there."

A light laugh against his chest. "You had a soap made for me every time you got hard?"

"Hell, not enough rooms in this house to store that much soap." He grinned. "Nah, I had to be someplace I thought you'd like. A scent I wanted to share with you. An emotion I wanted you to know." The grin turned rueful. "I wanted to share it all with you, and that was the only way I knew how to do it."

"You never gave me the soaps though," she pointed out.

"Because I wanted to bathe you with them myself," he sighed, his hands running over her body. "I wanted to seduce you with scents and touch. Hell, Dawn, I wanted a reason to make myself believe I could have you. If I had the soaps, maybe you'd be curious about the scents. If you liked the silks and lace of the panties, maybe, just maybe," his voice thickened, "you'd model them for them."

"So you could seduce me?" Her voice was soft, and in it, he heard her joy.

"So I could seduce you. Forever." He pressed her head against his chest.

"I love you, Seth. Until there's no tomorrow, no beginning or end, I love you."

And for a second his eyes closed, because the emotion that swamped him nearly undid him.

"And I love you, sweetheart. Until I'd wither away and die without you."

And there, curled into each other, as dawn lifted across the sky, they slept. The ragged survivors of a tempest.

◆   ◆   ◆

Cassie stared into the darkness of her bedroom.

The child was gone. It had slowly faded away hours before, but it had done so with such a look of hope that she had shed a tear and whispered a prayer that Dawn had finally let her in.

Every Breed in the house had heard Dawn's screams. Cassie's parents still hadn't returned to their room after rushing to the basement, but Cassie knew it wasn't because Dawn was in pain any longer. Dawn had awoken, just as the new day was rising.

She rose from her bed and stared down at the evening gown she still wore. They hadn't been back in the room long before Dawn's screams had pulled her parents away.

Her mother had been brushing Cassie's hair. Sometimes her parents took turns brushing her hair, as they had when she was a little girl, despite the fact that she often protested it.

Her father couldn't seem to accept that she was growing up. And her mother, Cassie often thought, saw her daughter's maturity with a sense of fear.

She moved from her bedroom to the sitting room, pausing in front of the doors, pulled there as though by an unseen force she couldn't understand.

She didn't dare walk outside.

She gripped the handle and breathed in deeply, the fear building inside her.

She knew her own death was coming. Not how it would happen, or where, but she knew there was no avoiding it. If it happened here, then her father wouldn't be nearby. Her mother wouldn't see it. They would be safer.

She had known she would die here. She had dreamed it. The visions that followed her, the ghostly forms that had drifted away from her over the past months, had warned her of it. They had told her that this was her destiny, that only here, and only with her blood, would the future become what it should be.

She didn't want to die. She was only eighteen; there was so much that she wanted to see, wanted to experience. She wanted to dance and laugh. She wanted to know the truth of the shadowed vision of a man she saw in her dreams. Hear his laughter in life rather than just in sleep.

She wanted to watch her baby brother grow, and she wanted to be a woman, rather than the woman-child she knew she was.

But here, she had been warned. Here, her blood would be spilled by the one that held the wavering form of a child bound in the past. He would set into motion the future for the Breeds, for Dawn, and lay yet another piece of the puzzle that would eventually form a strong, able Breed community.

She would die by that man's hand. And far better that she die alone, with none but her killer to see her fear.

She turned the door handle and slowly opened the door.

The sun was rising, casting a million shades of muted colors across the sky. Everything lay in shadow, and the shadows welcomed her as she moved onto the balcony. A clear target. And she knew someone had taken sight. She could feel it. Right there, the center of her forehead.

She stared out into the thick covering of trees and ached. She ached for so many things, so many thoughts and dreams and a life she would never have. Because she was unique, her father said. The truth was, because she was a freak.

And whoever watched her knew. He knew what she was, and he knew she couldn't be allowed to live, didn't he? They wouldn't want to take her in; in the Council's hands she would be a lever against the Breeds, a shift in the balance of power. And at present, there were so few who wanted anything to shift. War was always profitable. Even a silent war such as was being waged on the Breeds.

No, whoever was out there didn't want to take her in. But his sights were on her, gun sights, steady. Clear. She stared into them, and with a mocking smile, mouthed the words, *I dare you!*

From his nest, he leveled the sights on the perfect face, right between those beautiful blue eyes, and imagined caressing her.

She was dressed in an evening gown, black, and it flowed around her like the night.

He read her lips and his own quirked into a smile. His finger didn't move for the trigger. Instead his eyes stayed on her, stroked over pale, luminescent flesh, and he drew in the scent of innocence. Pure innocence tinged with fear.

I dare you, she had mouthed.

He smiled at the challenge. One day, she just might dare him too far, but he doubted it would be a bullet he'd penetrate her with.

CHAPTER 22

The next afternoon, Dawn sat at the long table that held the meetings of the board of directors of Lawrence Industries and watched as each of them signed the agreements Seth had laid out for them.

With the agreement to finance Sanctuary and Haven were agreements Lawrence Industries made to individual companies. A promise to restructure here, to strengthen there. Each board member was also the vice president of one of the sections that came together beneath the control and guidance of Lawrence Industries. Former owners or CEOs who had lost control because of bad management, buyouts or other varied reasons.

Because they had backed Seth, Seth in turn would reach out and support them more fully as well. Concessions they had been bargaining for were given, some in part, some completely, until all but one had been satisfied.

All but Valere.

"You're going to regret this, Seth," he bit out as he glared at them from the end of the table. "Lawrence and Vanderale Industries will pay for backing creatures such as that." His gaze flicked to Dawn.

Dane leaned back in his chair, lit the thin cigar he invariably kept close, smiled and lifted his hand as he beckoned to Valere. "Do your worst, chap," he dared him. "Better jokers than you have tried."

It was regrettable that Valere had fought the plan to ensure the Breed society and the funding of Sanctuary for the next five years. The five-year forecast had been drawn out to allow the Breeds the time needed to complete the training that would allow them to move into the private security and law enforcement arenas with far fewer problems.

At present, their social skills frankly sucked when it came to political maneuverings in a job setting or working with others, except in a clearly laid-out team. Move a Breed into an investigative team in any major city at the moment, and there would be more bloodshed within the ranks than there was on the streets.

Five years would allow them time to complete the honing of that training, as well as the programs already being put in place to make use of the Breeds' exceptional genetics and their training in other areas.

When the five years ended, the Breeds should be in a position that funding would no longer be necessary, and the profits from the agreements made with both Sanctuary and Haven, the Wolf Breed compound in Colorado, would begin trickling in. Slowly for the first few years, but within another five, those who'd initially signed onto the deal would be very rich indeed. The board members of both Lawrence Industries and Vanderale would be rich many times over from the profits gained from the Breed corporation.

Capitalism was alive and free, and it thrived. The Breeds were poised to become a very profitable, very wealthy industry in and of itself, because of Callan Lyons and the Breed Cabinet's foresight.

Dawn was still amazed as she stood in the meeting room that afternoon and listened to the measures agreed upon, the work Seth had been doing for the Breed community over the past ten years.

He had apparently worked tirelessly on their behalf, fighting to overthrow the legacy his father had begun by funding the Genetics Council. It was a legacy he reminded his board members of several times.

That they had sat back and gotten fat from profits made by those who suffered a hell the board members couldn't imagine.

That the profits they had gained from their agreements with the Council had been paid in blood, in the rape, murder and torture of innocent children and adults.

From what Dawn had glimpsed, he hadn't had to fight very hard. They were signing the measures before he had begun the hardest selling points of his argument. All but Valere, who stank of the Council and something more.

Dawn watched him closely, and he knew he was being watched. His hooded gaze was cold, malicious, as it moved over her. But it wasn't the right gaze. He wasn't the one who had raped and attempted to destroy a child's mind. At least not hers. She was certain, so certain she had to force her hand from her weapon, that this man had been neck deep in the rot that infected the Genetics Council.

When the others pushed their signed agreements to the middle of the table, Valere's face flushed with fury.

"Don't do this, Theodore," Seth warned him quietly. "You can't block anything we're doing. You're only hurting your own companies. Because, trust me, I will drop every one of them once you walk from this room. Imagine what that will do to the Valere family holdings."

Seth's voice was hard, harder than Dawn could ever remember hearing it.

"You've let this little Breed tramp corrupt you, Seth." Valere ignored the gasps of shock and outrage at his words as he indicated Dawn. "She dresses in your wealth and your jewels, but we all know the animal she is. Screw her, toss her out, then return to us with your senses and fortune intact."

Lightning fast and dangerous, fluid, like a vengeful wind, Dane was out of his chair and across the short distance two chairs from his own. He jerked Valere's head back, a wicked knife in his hand before anyone knew he had it, and laid at the other man's throat.

Death glittered in Dane's dark gold eyes, tightened his features and strengthened the savagery in his expression.

Valere's eyes bulged from his head as a thin line of blood oozed from the shallow cut beneath the blade.

"Mate, you don't want to go there," Dane warned him carefully as Dawn rose slowly to her feet.

The Breeds providing security for the meeting were tense, their hands on their weapons, fury flaring in their eyes.

"Enough," she said calmly, causing Seth to pause and glare back at her.

"You have no say in this," he snapped.

Her gaze met Valere's and she saw smug, vindictive hatred there.

"When he returns to the mainland, we don't want him to have reason to fuel any fires during the press conference he'll be making. Better to escort him nicely from the house than to beat him to a bloody pulp. Besides . . ." She smiled back at Valere as rage flickered in his eyes. "You might splatter blood on the silk your wealth dressed me in. And it is so hard to get bloodstains out."

She smoothed a hand over the maroon skirt she wore before adjusting the gold chain at her neck, just above the white silk of her sleeveless blouse.

They were her clothes. Well, except for the panties. She had brought a few nice things with her from Sanctuary. Just in case.

Seth's lips almost twitched. Dane eased the dagger back.

"A true lady shows herself in not just her actions but in her compassion," Craig Bartel said then, his tone drawing her gaze, his rueful smile an apology for his wife's words the night before.

"Compassion?" She lifted a brow as Valere rose from his chair. "I have very little compassion for pedophiles and murderers."

"Compassion perhaps for your fellow board members," Bartel suggested. "My wife can tell you, I become ill at the sight of sliced arteries. It's a particularly distasteful sight. So I'll claim your compassion for myself."

"Stop flirting, Bartel," Seth grunted, the tension easing from him as Mercury and Stygian moved close to Theodore Valere, their eyes hard.

"Don't bruise him when you toss him off my island," Seth requested. "Dawn's right. He needs to be presentable for the press conference he will no doubt hold. Just as I'll be presentable for mine a few days later. When I announce my engagement to Ms. Daniels, as well as my regret that the Valere family would prefer to fund the Council than to aid the survival of the Breeds."

If rage had simmered in Valere's eyes before, it burned in them now. Seth had just blocked him, and he knew it. They all knew it.

Valere's jaw tightened as he straightened his silk jacket with a jerk and stomped to the door. There was no parting shot, no "fuck off" or "fuck you." The door didn't even slam, as Stygian managed to catch it and close it quietly as he and Styx followed the other man.

The other board members watched quietly.

"Is there anyone else who would like to follow him?" Seth asked softly, his tone dangerous. "We all know he most likely never broke from the Council. Do any of you have the same problems?"

"We signed the agreement, Seth," Brian Phelps sighed. "Hell, I don't know what Valere was doing then or now, but I didn't know what we were funding. And now, knowing . . ." He shook his head, sincerity evident in his scent and his expression. "Knowing doesn't help my nightmares at night, I'll tell you that much right now. I'll be letting my nephew know the changes and they'll be implemented upon our return."

"Jason will fight it." Bartel spoke up then, glancing at Brian. "He's always fought Lawrence support to the Breeds. I think it dips too far into his inheritance to suit him."

Phelps grunted at that. "Little bastard." There was obvious affection in his voice. "He's the only heir I have left. I'm stuck with him."

"Adopt," Dane suggested mockingly, rising to his feet, the sweet scent of his cigar curling around the room, teasing the senses.

Phelps shook his head with a smile, his reluctance to defend his nephew apparent. "He has his good points."

"The ladies like him," another member piped up. "Perhaps you could marry him off to an heiress."

Now that the tension of negotiations was over, Dawn glimpsed another side to Seth's board of directors, joking, teasing, bashing like little boys around a campfire.

Seth moved back to her, chuckling a bit.

"So, we have an engagement to celebrate?" Dane drawled as Seth's arm curled around Dawn's back. "Funny, I don't see a ring, my friend. Surely you were prepared?"

Seth grinned as he stared down at her. "She keeps me off balance, Dane. But trust me, she'll have a very special ring soon."

Dawn felt pleasure warm her; she knew the flush that flooded her cheeks was as much from joy as from the appreciation directed her way by the board members.

"And now we have a party to get ready for." Dane drew on the cigar, his gaze on Dawn, the brown of his eyes hiding secrets and amusement. "Will you save me a dance, beautiful?"

"All her dances are taken," Seth assured him.

"He's a greedy bastard," Dane laughed. "Ah well, the lovely Cassie should be present. She likes me."

"Yeah, for an old man," Bartel snorted with laughter as Dane cast him a mock glare. "What are you? All of thirty?"

Dane grinned. "Look that old, do I?"

They all laughed.

"Gentlemen, if you'll excuse me, my fiancée and I are going to have lunch in our suite and we'll join you and your families in a few hours for the party. Thank you again, and we'll all look forward to the profits Sanctuary and Haven will bring in soon."

"You're such a businessman," Dawn sighed as he pulled her to the door.

"There are definitely perks," Seth laughed, his look heated enough, male enough, that she flushed as the others laughed again.

They filed from the meeting room as Seth curved his arm around her waist and they headed to their suite. She loved the way he touched her, how he allowed her to touch him. Needed her to touch him.

"Valere is going to be a problem," she told him as they turned toward the suite. "He speaks out often against the Breeds' role in the private sectors of law enforcement and security. Once he leaves the island, he's going to find another way to hurt Lawrence Industries."

Seth was silent for long moments before he spoke. "He and his father were very strong supporters of the Council. Though they covered it well. Finding proof of their activities to nearly impossible. They were the ones who originally pulled my father in. I swore while my father was alive, Roni would never learn that he had known all along what was happening in those labs. And he supported them anyway. Once I took over, after his accident, and learned the truth, I could barely stand to be in his presence."

Seth remembered watching the news flash of his half-sister, Roni Andrews, when the press had attacked her in her hometown of Sandyhook, Kentucky. Wild-eyed, terrified, she had been a younger version of the maid Aaron Lawrence had seduced and fallen in love with years before. She had disappeared, and all the

Lawrence money hadn't been able to find her. Until that news flash. Until Aaron learned his daughter was the lover of a Breed. And he had been terrified. He had lost his son because of his involvement with the Council. He didn't want to lose his daughter.

And he hadn't. In the six years Aaron had lived after that, he had grown close to Roni. Before he died, she had called him dad. And Aaron Lawrence had died a happy man. He'd seen his first grandchild. Felt his daughter's love. And he knew Seth would never tell her the horrible secret he carried.

"She knew," Dawn said softly, glancing up at him as they neared the suite. "Within days of his arrival Taber had the information, and Roni found it. He can't hide much from her. She knew the worst of him, Seth, and she loved him anyway, because he was out of it. Because he was trying to be a father."

Something, Dawn admitted, she hadn't understood, but she had accepted Roni's decision. The other woman found it hard to hate. She had her husband, her mate, Taber. And the happiness they found together had helped her forgive. Taber had helped it as well by encouraging it. The love the two shared went both ways.

"She never told me." He nodded to Styx as the Breed opened the suite door when they neared it.

There was now a Breed posted at the door and two on the balcony outside his bedroom. Styx was confirming their positions outside as they stepped into the house.

"Dawn." Styx's heavy brogue had her turning back. "We've had verification of an unauthorized transmission from the house while the two o' you were in the meeting. Jonas is tracking it but he's requesting that you remain indoors at all times."

Dawn tensed. She nodded shortly and watched as Styx turned and closed the door behind them.

"Whoever it is won't give up," she murmured as she turned back to him. "It's not over, Seth."

"And they'll be caught." He shrugged as he slid the jacket from his shoulders and paced across the sitting room. "Men like this make mistakes eventually, Dawn. They've tried half a dozen times already and failed each one. They'll slip up here."

"Or put a bullet in you?" She whispered her worst fear.

"It won't be the first bullet I've taken." He shrugged again as he turned to her. "I don't intend to cash out now, sweetheart.

Not after all this. I'm careful, and I have a damned good security force. We'll let them do their work."

She nodded, slipping off the high heels she wore and moving to him as he sat on the loveseat facing her.

She moved into his lap, curling against his chest, feeling him surround her again. She lived for this.

Seth chuckled against her hair and she let a smile curl her lips.

"We killed ourselves this morning," he reminded her as her lips found his neck.

Dawn licked delicately, tasting his flesh and feeling her juices preparing her. The heat was easing; it wasn't as destructive to the senses, but the need for him was still there, a part of her soul. That would never change, she knew that. His touch, his presence, was integral to her happiness, her survival.

"Maybe I can wait until tonight," she purred. "But only because I'm really hungry, and I know lunch is coming soon."

"How do you know that?" He tilted his neck, allowing her tongue to run over it, her teeth to nip.

"I smell it," she drawled, moving from his lap before he could catch her.

She paced across the room, wrapped her arms around her breasts and turned back to him. She was still nervous, unbalanced. The feeling had returned that morning. That vague sense of panic that rolled through her, that left her grasping for a reason for it.

The memories weren't easy to deal with, but she had spent years under Dayan's cruelty, watching those discs, over and over again, seeing them in her dreams even if she didn't feel the pain of them. The memories were no surprise to her. They cut at her. There was no escaping that.

"What's wrong, Dawn?" He leaned forward and watched her intently. "Are there more memories returning?"

She shook her head. She could see the concern in his eyes, the flicker of inner rage that the memories existed to begin with.

"I thought this feeling of panic would go away." She tried to laugh, but knew the sound fell far short of the mark. "It hasn't. I want to slide into bed with you and hide until it's over. Until there's no threat, no reason to fear for you."

"We'd spend our lives beneath the covers," he told her somberly. "Neither of us can do that, you know that."

Of course she did. She had known that all along, but it didn't make it any easier. It didn't ease the fear welling inside her.

Seth sighed heavily as he rose to his feet and moved to her. "We're going to be okay."

"You suddenly have a crystal ball?" She sniped as his hands settled on her shoulders. "You don't know that, Seth."

"No, I don't know that, Dawn." Frustration flashed in his eyes. "I know we can only do the best we can. I'm careful. I can't, and I won't, do more than that."

She shot him a glare as she moved from his embrace. "I'm not asking you to." She rubbed at her arms, fighting the chill that seemed to move over her body. "Something feels off. It feels wrong, and I can't put my finger on it. I hate that, and I hate not knowing what to do to combat it."

"Your training didn't cover emotions, huh? Damn, go figure."

"I'm the smart-ass in this relationship, Seth." She smirked. "Don't take my place there and I won't take yours in the board-room."

There was a bark of laughter before he moved, caught her up in his arms and planted a long, luscious kiss on her lips.

"My little smart-ass," he murmured against her lips. "You're definitely the expert there. But I still know how to spank."

"That threat is getting old."

He chuckled again as a knock came to the door.

"Lunch, children," Styx called out. "Ye may be missin' the cho'olate dessert though. Seems they ha' forgotten it."

The door opened and the tray wheeled in. There was a smear of chocolate at the corner of Styx's lips.

"They forgot it, huh?" she asked as Seth released her.

Styx smiled. " 'Tis a shame it is. Such forgetful staff ye seem to ha', Seth."

Seth snorted. "Wipe the evidence off your mouth, Breed, before lying to me about dessert."

Styx did so with amazing panache. He winked at Dawn. "I may ha' saved yours," he admitted. "But 'twas a hard decision to be makin'."

The chocolate fiend. She shook her head as he left the room again.

"Lunch." Hunger was definitely driving Seth this afternoon, and not just a hunger for her body. "Board meetings make me hungry."

And panic killed her appetite. Still she moved to the small table at the other side of the room with him and took her plates. Only one dessert was present. Chocolate truffle cake, Styx's favorite of course, and wine.

She ate, but the feeling only grew. She tried to joke, to tease, to allow Seth to soothe that ragged feeling of impending doom, but it didn't totally abate.

Later, as they dressed for the party, she flirted and she tried to seduce. She almost succeeded before Seth drew back and stared at her soberly. "We have to face whatever's coming," he told her then. "Hiding from it won't save us, Dawn. It only makes the fear worse."

She stood there in the expensive evening gown he'd bought her, with his jewels gracing her, his touch warming her, and Dawn found she was terrified. She found that, unconsciously, she was praying.

God protect him. Because she knew that losing him would destroy her.

"We stay close together," she whispered.

"Always," he promised.

"We don't leave the house."

"We stay right inside, away from all opened doors and windows." He crossed his heart before turning and moving to his dresser.

When he returned, he shocked her by going to his knees, taking her hand and sliding a ring on her finger.

"And you'll marry me when this is over," he told her.

The ring was obviously old, obviously horrendously expensive. The diamond wasn't huge, but it was by far one of the clearest, most perfect specimens she had ever seen. Surrounding it were several dark, swirled tiger's-eye stones, new insets.

"The ring was my mother's, my grandmother's, and my great-grandmother's. Lawrence wives wear the diamond, always. But tradition stands that a new stone replaces those surrounding it with each successive bride. And I chose tiger's eyes. Because they remind me of your eyes, your strength and your heritage. This ring has been waiting for you for nearly ten years. You're my life, Dawn. Will you share it with me, since you own it?"

And she cried again. A tear slipped from her eye and her lips trembled. "Always," she whispered. "Oh God, Seth, I'll always love you."

· C H A P T E R   2 3 ·

That party was well under way when Seth and Dawn stepped into the ballroom. He led her across the floor to the small, raised dais, where the band had set up, and stepped up to the microphone as the Breeds assigned to his protection moved closer.

All eyes turned to them. The board members and their families had expected an announcement during the house party, but Dawn knew that this wasn't the announcement they were expecting.

"Ladies and gentlemen. Friends." His lips quirked as he looked out on the crowd. "I want to thank you all for being here, for your patience during the board meetings, and for once again filling Lawrence Island with your laughter and your presence."

It seemed as though the whole room held its collective breath as Seth held Dawn's hand and stared out at them.

Dawn watched the room as well. She could feel herself looking for something that she couldn't put her finger on. A reason for the panic that tightened her stomach and her heart.

"I would like you to join me in celebrating the most momentous occasion in my life now," he continued, his big body moving closer to hers as he stared out at the crowd. "Today, Miss

Dawn Daniels has consented to be my wife." He lifted her hand to display the ring she wore as Dawn felt her heart melt.

His voice was rough, rasping. His eyes as they stared at her were cloudy and dark with emotion, his expression tight with it. She stared back at him, and despite that edge of waiting, of almost fear rising inside her, she smiled and accepted the kiss he placed against her lips.

Who knew tough man Seth Lawrence could be so romantic. That he would have a stone reset in a family ring only months after meeting her. That he would buy soaps around the world so he could share the unique scents that reminded him of her, or that he would pick up silks, satins and lace in panties as delicate as a dream for her to wear.

And now he stood in front of his friends and closest business associates and claimed her as his heart. He didn't see her as a Breed, he saw her merely as his woman, and that knowledge brought a lump to her throat and the betraying emotional tears to her eyes.

"To Seth and Dawn." Craig Bartel lifted his glass in a toast as all the others followed.

"To Seth and Dawn," they all called out while glasses were handed to her and Seth to toast the event as well.

It was magical, a dream come true. Dawn felt like Cinderella after Prince Charming slipped the shoe on her delicate foot and declared her his woman for all time. She felt as though she had finally found a place where she mattered, where she belonged. No, she thought as she stared into his eyes. She knew she had. Right here, she had found the one place in the world where Dawn Daniels was a woman rather than a creature or an animal.

They toasted once more amid laughter and congratulations before the band struck up a tune and Seth led her to the dance floor once again. He pulled her into his arms, smiling down at her as he swept her around the room, the other guests moving back and giving them this first dance to themselves.

Dawn would have felt self-conscious, even days ago, at having so many eyes on her. Tonight, she felt the panic build even as a sense of euphoria and happiness nearly overcame her.

Maybe that was the problem, she thought. She wasn't used to happiness such as this. She was used to being content, not ecstatic and definitely not floating with the joy that seemed to strike her at the oddest moments now.

Like now, while they danced in front of several dozen of Seth's closest friends, all eyes turned to them, and happiness was singing through her veins.

His body moved against hers, one arm around her, the other gripping her hand as the dark chocolate silk of her evening gown flowed around her, curled around his legs, and caressed both of them when they turned.

"Caught ya," he whispered in her ear as a smile of pure joy curved at her lips.

"Oh yeah?"

"Oh yeah." He nipped at her ear. "And I'm going to keep you."

She prayed. She realized that in the past two days she had been doing that a lot. Praying fervently that God wouldn't take this dream from her, now that it was so close, right there in her grasp.

Her hand tightened at his shoulder and she wished she had managed to keep them in that damned room. She needed him now. Needed him near her, moving over her. She needed him loving her, whispering his need in her ear and stroking her into oblivion.

As the dance drew to a close, Seth moved back, his hand still clasping hers, turned to the crowd and slowly bowed before turning to Dawn.

With an impish smile, she curtsied, long and low, the skirt of her gown swirling around her as she held the position for long moments before straightening again amid the applause and Seth's wicked wink.

Dawn realized she must be smiling like a loon. She couldn't seem to control the curve of her lips for the happiness that bubbled in her veins like ecstasy. It fought with the panic, determined to win this battle, to hold itself inside her mind, where it was rarely allowed to materialize.

"Miss Daniels. Seth." Craig Bartel approached, his fingers curled around his wife Lillian's wrist as they stopped before Seth and Dawn.

Lillian Bartel was not happy to be there. Dawn could scent her hesitancy, her anger at her husband and her embarrassment.

"Seth." Craig extended his hand. "Let me tell you, I admired you before, but seeing the beauty you've found to love, I must say I admire you even more."

"Thank you, Craig." He shook the other man's hand and glanced at Lillian.

"Miss Daniels, your beauty is only overshadowed by your compassion." He turned to Dawn and tugged his wife forward. "My wife and I would both like to extend our congratulations."

Lillian Bartel drew in a hard breath. "And my apologies," Lillian forced past her stiff lips. "What I said last night was uncalled for, and undeserved. I'm sorry, Miss Daniels. Sometimes, as my husband tells me, my mouth forgets there's a brain driving it."

Dawn tilted her head to the side and stared at the other woman. Seth was stiff beside her, unaware of what the other woman had said, but aware that it must have been extremely insulting for Craig to force this apology from his wife.

And it was sincere. Whatever Bartel had said to the other woman, it must have been taken to heart, because Lillian meant the apology, and not for the first time, Dawn thanked the Breed senses that allowed her to pick up on that sincerity.

"We'll consider the words unsaid," Dawn finally told her softly.

Lillian stared at her in surprise, and Dawn realized that she had prepared herself for the worst. An insult as well, or perhaps more.

"Craig was right," she said. "Your beauty is only overshadowed by your compassion. Thank you." She extended her hands, and preparing herself for the contact of another's touch, Dawn accepted it.

She was surprised, no, she was shocked when the feeling only produced mild discomfort. It was a bit stronger when Craig shook her hand as well, but the pain she should have felt wasn't present.

That could mean only one of two things. The mating heat was easing or she had conceived. She wasn't certain which. She didn't feel pregnant, but then again, how the hell would she know what it felt like?

"You have the most incredible look on your face," Seth murmured as the Bartels moved away. "You're making me hard."

"You stay hard," she purred. She really did love that about him.

He grunted at the comment, but there was laughter in his eyes, a smile pulling at the corner of his lips. As she smiled back at him, a peculiar feeling swept over her. Not so much panic, or even fear. As though the panic had hardened inside her and turned silently feral.

Her head lifted, her gaze swept over the dance floor, and her senses seemed to come alive in a way they never had before.

She couldn't see anything out of the ordinary, couldn't smell anything that could explain the sudden feeling, and she felt like growling in fury at the odd warning traveling through her system.

This was why she had been so adept at tricking the Breeds she trained with. This feeling. It warned her when something was coming, warned her when danger approached, whether it be Breed, human or inanimate. This extra sense, this animal knowledge and instinctive self-preservation.

"Dawn?" Seth's hand settled at her nape and rubbed at the tense muscles there. "Is everything okay?"

"Fine," she answered absently, continuing to search.

As her gaze swept over the entrance to the ballroom, Dash and Elizabeth stepped inside with their daughter.

Dawn's gaze stopped abruptly at the sight of Cassie. Her makeup was expertly applied and appeared barely there. But it was there. It was masking her pale face, but nothing could mask the other girl's wide, haunted eyes. Just as nothing could hide Dash's and Elizabeth's tension.

"We should talk to Dash and Elizabeth," she murmured to him, feeling the instincts inside her latching on to the small family.

Dash was dressed in an evening suit, Elizabeth in a gorgeous gray silk gown that smoothed over her breasts and hips and gave her a seductive appearance.

Cassie wore black once more, a shimmery fabric that gleamed and glowed as she moved. Thin straps extended from the snug bodice, and the material displayed her curved figure without appearing too seductive or alluring. The dress was like Cassie herself, understated and shielding the secrets it covered.

Seth nodded, took her hand and led her to the fairly private table they had taken across the room.

Cassie wasn't dancing. Her father's stern, forbidding expression kept the admirers held back for the moment. As Dawn and Seth neared the table, Dash rose, resplendent in black evening clothes, his black hair pulled back at his nape, his brown eyes glittering in anger.

"You look gorgeous, Dawn," he murmured as he shook Seth's hand.

"And you look ready to explode," she pointed out. "Is everything okay?"

She carried her weapon and her link in her bag, and she knew Dash hadn't tried to contact her before coming down. The link would have vibrated and warned her of his attempt to do so.

"It will be." Dash nodded. "Elizabeth and Cassie and I will be leaving first thing in the morning. We need to get back to Sanctuary."

Not just to their home. Dash wouldn't consider the brief stop at the Breed compound to collect his son as getting back there.

Dawn's eyes flickered to Elizabeth's concerned gaze and Cassie's averted one.

"Is anything wrong?" She turned back to Dash. "What's happened?"

"*I* happened," Cassie drawled then, her soft voice stiff, bordering on angry. "I don't obey so well anymore. Perhaps there's been an error in my training program."

Dash's eyes flashed with pain as Elizabeth's lips compressed.

"She won't stay off that fucking balcony," Dash muttered. "She was out there this morning when we returned to the suite, shaking like a leaf."

"*She* was thinking and attempting to make sense of things." Cassie shrugged. "And it was a little chilly."

Her father cast her a fuming look as Dawn glanced at her in surprise. Cassie never disobeyed her father's orders when it came to her safety. She well knew what awaited her if all protection failed and the Council managed to get their hands on her.

"Cassie?" Dawn questioned her softly, staring back at her quietly.

They had been friends. Cassie was always invading her space when the dreams were rising hard inside her in the past. With her spooky little riddles, her compassion and the knowledge that others' pain hurt her as well, Cassie had never been one to deliberately make things harder on those around her. Especially her parents.

"I'm fine, Dawn." She rolled her eyes, but Dawn could feel the tension in the other girl. There was also a certainty that

Cassie had no intention of discussing it. It was in her eyes, in her closed expression.

As Cassie turned back to Dash, he merely shook his head; the frustration he was feeling was clearly evident in his expression.

"If you need anything, just let us know." Seth nodded then. "We'll circulate a bit more and then perhaps return to our suite for drinks. I'd like to talk to you before you leave."

Dash nodded again before moving back to his seat, his hand finding his wife's naturally as Seth and Dawn moved away from the table.

"What's going on?" Seth asked her quietly, his gaze sharp, picking up, she knew, on the tension rising inside her now.

"I don't know." She shook her head. "But whatever is going to happen, it's going to happen tonight, Seth." She knew that as well as she knew her love for Seth.

It burned clear to her soul.

Seth paused, his hand dropping hers to allow his arm to curve around her back and pull her to him.

"We'll get through it," he promised her.

"I can only pray." And for the first time in ten years she was doing just that. She was praying hard, praying with everything inside her. Because losing him now wasn't something she could consider. Losing him now would kill her.

She stayed at Seth's side through the hours they chatted, danced and celebrated not just the end of the board meetings and an agreement in Seth's favor, but also the engagement that she had dreamed of.

They were watched closely. Some gazes were angry, some surprised, others genuinely happy for them. As they moved about the room, Dawn instinctively used a set of silent signals to the other Breeds there, keeping them carefully around Seth and close enough to stop a bullet if they had to.

Breed physiology could survive wounds that the human body couldn't. They were more resilient, better able to endure as well as heal from life-threatening wounds. They weren't just stronger and faster, they were created for abuse and trained within it.

That training had killed more Breeds than lived now. More than a century of the scientists' work had created bodies and internal organs that could continue to fight under circumstances that would leave a normal human dead hours before. It was the reason they were created. To endure and to succeed despite all odds.

"Seth." Brian Phelps moved toward them, a smile on his face despite the concern in his hazel eyes. "Congratulations again. She's a beautiful woman." He nodded to Seth and handed Dawn a glass of champagne before taking one for himself.

"She is indeed, Brian." Seth smiled.

"I just received a report from one of my people in Los Angeles," Brian told him. "Valere landed and immediately called a press conference. It's a few more hours before it's due to air. I'd hoped he wouldn't do it."

Seth shook his head as Dawn felt, scented, his regret.

Seth finally shrugged. "He can't hurt the deal, Brian. And it's not the first news conference he's called to try to put pressure on the board to force our decisions his way. It won't work now any more than it worked in the past."

Brian nodded his thinning gray head, but his expression was lined with worry. "It makes me wonder if the rumors of his family's involvement with the Council are true," he finally sighed. "As God is my witness, I didn't know the true scope of what we were funding, Seth. Research and development, they called it. The reports I received didn't mention anything about children, or adults, being created."

It was, Dawn suspected, no more than that truth. The Council reports to many of the companies funding them had been in terms of "weapons" developed; the testing of those weapons, the units built or destroyed for lack of efficiency.

A lack of efficiency. More clearly defined, the inability to endure the horrors of their "training." And the scientists' excuses?

Callan had nearly lost his sanity during the Senate hearings just after they revealed themselves. The Council scientists' reasons for their cruelties, expressing their utter lack of humanity, had been brief. The Breeds were weapons that could be tortured for information. Better they understood the torture before embarking on their missions.

Their unique physiology and DNA required the various tests that were performed against them. Tests such as autopsies performed while the Breed screamed in agony. Beatings inflicted while electrodes measured pain, strength and neural synapses. It went on and on, the horror of it often too much to grasp, even for a Breed reliving it through those hearings.

"Lawrence Industries went over the records of its board members carefully, Brian," Seth reminded him. "We're aware of the reports that were sent out, just as we're aware of the evidence that proved the knowledge of those we forced off the board ten years before."

Brian nodded, then his lips quirked. "Have you regretted allowing Vanderale to take the place of one of those board members?" he asked. "He's definitely a unique personality, Seth. Not always a comfortable one, but unique all the same."

"That's the most tactful description I think I've heard of him." Seth chuckled as Dawn's gaze began to move around them once again. "Normally, the language gets much more colorful."

"Not to mention threatening," Brian admitted. "I think I threatened to rip his throat out for him during a meeting last month."

Dawn jerked her gaze back to the portly, charming board member in surprise. This little man had threatened Dane Vanderale? Dane wasn't a man that even Dawn wanted to meet in a fight.

"I was a little irked," he informed her with a deep chuckle. "Dane has that effect."

She smiled at that, her lips parting to speak, when she felt him. She *smelled* him. That touch of evil was so deep, so invasive she felt pummeled by it.

She stiffened, aware of the growl the rumbled in her throat, of Seth stiffening and Brian watching her with narrowed eyes.

He was here. The one from her dreams. She could feel him watching her now and she realized she had felt him the entire time she had been on the island.

She had known him, but the block within her memories had hid the knowledge from her. The smell of liquor and smug satisfaction. Of malicious pleasure and depraved lusts.

"Dawn," Seth murmured at her side, forcing her into a position where he could protect her, rather than the other way around.

She searched the room. He was in the room. That brief whiff of his evil had been enough to assure her of that. She turned, scanning the crowd, knowing, fearing the worse.

He wasn't outside. He was here, in the room. He wouldn't be unarmed; he would know better than to ever go unarmed. As the scent reached her again, she tensed further, the various layers of smell sorting through her mind as she tried to identify him.

She had smelled him before, though there had been other scents around him at the time. Scents guaranteed to throw off the Breed senses. Liquor and drugs, they temporarily affected the body's chemistry, and their basic scent hid him. Her memories had returned though, and with them the memory of his scent beneath the liquor and drugs.

Her eyes were restless, her mind working, ignoring Seth's demand for an explanation as it began coming to her, slowly. So slowly.

The soldier who raped her had used drugs to maintain an erection. Even then. He had been young, in his early twenties, she had sensed that much about him. He drugged himself for the added pleasure as well as the added length of time it afforded him to torture the children he enjoyed.

He still raped. She could smell the scent of that depravity, the subtle smell of the pain he had inflicted that still clung to his body now that he wasn't attempting to disguise his scent.

"He's here," she murmured.

"Who's here?" Seth's hand was in the pocket of his jacket, his fingers curled over a weapon she had watched him place there earlier.

"*He* is," she whispered again.

There was a long, strained silence as Dawn searched the faces her gaze touched upon.

"That's not possible." Rage burned in his voice now.

"It's possible," she told him quietly, ignoring Brian Phelps, knowing she couldn't worry about him now. Wherever his wife was within this crowd, she would have to worry about him.

"Where?" Seth snapped out, motioning several Breeds closer.

Dawn was aware of his every move, just as she was suddenly aware of every guest within the room. She could feel their heartbeats, smell their emotions. Many were so oblivious, but there was one. One that was waiting, watching.

His scent hit her again, her eyes widening, her lips parting as the fear nearly overwhelmed her. Her gaze jerked to Dash's table, her heart nearly stopping in her throat as it returned to the room.

And then she found him.

Her heart slammed in her throat. He had worn contacts when she had seen him before. Colored contacts to shield the hue of his eyes. He hadn't bothered tonight. And he wasn't drinking tonight.

The smell of liquor was still a part of him, but his system wasn't affected by it. He wouldn't be slow, he wouldn't hesitate to use the young woman who danced in his arms.

Dawn took a step, intending to rush across the room, to jerk Cassie from his grip. The sight of that bastard's hand at Cassie's waist sent rage tearing through her.

At that moment, his head lifted. His eyes were filled with triumph, and before Dawn could move, before she could gasp, Jason Phelps swung Cassie around, jerked a gun from his jacket and had it at her temple.

He smiled then. The curl of his mouth so familiar, so hated that Dawn snarled as guests gasped, screamed and rushed out of the way.

And through it all Cassie stood still and silent, unsurprised as Jason gripped her neck and held her in front of him, her back against his chest, her heart blocking that shot. The muzzle of his weapon at her temple, the fingers adding just the right amount of pressure to the trigger to ensure that a head shot would take her life as well. His throat was blocked by her head, no way to take him out there. He had thought of all the angles. And now he was playing his hand.

CHAPTER 24

Dawn heard Seth curse. She felt Brian's shock, his pain. This was his nephew, his heir. He was also the scourge of the Breed labs. A figure so horrifying that the female Breeds in the New Mexico labs had cowered at the thought of him.

He had been smarter in those days. He'd kept his face covered by the snug, black mask he and his fellow rapists had worn. *Just in case,* he had always laughed. *Smell me, good little breed. Kill me if you can.*

"Jason, what the hell are you doing?" Brian moved for his nephew, only to be jerked back by Seth and pushed to one of the Breeds that stood protectively around Seth.

The other man was pale, staring at his only heir with horror and outrage. As though he couldn't believe his own blood could do such a thing. As though he were fighting to convince himself this wasn't some horrible nightmare.

Dawn could have assured him it was no nightmare. The monster that stood in the middle of the ballroom, Cassie as a shield in front of him, was very, very real.

Jason smiled as he noted the Breeds' position around Seth, a gleam of triumph in his eyes. He had done what no Council soldier had managed in the eleven years since the news broke

of the Breeds' existence. He had their most prized possession.
The female that both Felines and Wolves cherished. The light,
the wonder, of Cassie Sinclair.

"It's not Cassie you want, Phelps," Seth bit out. "You came
for me. Well, here I am."

"It never was you I was after, Lawrence," he sneered with a
laugh. "Six tries and all of them failures? My little cat beside
you can tell you, I never miss."

No, he didn't. He had killed Breeds. Trained, wary Breeds
who knew to watch for him on missions. He never missed. He
always had a plan and he had never failed. She should have
guessed. She should have known that Seth wasn't the target. But
how could he have guessed Cassie would be here?

The decision was made at the last moment. No one had a
clue that Cassie and her mother would arrive with Dash.

She stared back at Phelps, trying to read the intent on his
gloating face, seeing his sense of triumph. Why? Because he
had gained more than he had ever imagined he could?

As she watched him, she was aware of his gaze turning to
her, his eyes stroking her as though with a lover's caress. Her
flesh crawled.

"You acquired a name," he drawled, that gaze so hated, so
despised it had followed her for twenty years. "Dawn. How re-
freshing. Does he whisper your name when he's fucking you?"
He nodded to Seth. "Or do you even fuck? Did I mark you for
life, little girl?"

Dawn stared at him silently, looking for a weakness, a way
past Cassie's fragile body to the larger one behind her.

Phelps was careful. Cassie covered all his weakest spots and
she knew it. Knew it and was doing nothing to fight it. It didn't
make sense. She knew if he escaped this island with her, then her
life would effectively be over. Hers, her parents' and the entire
Breed community's as well.

"Jason, you've lost your mind," Brian called out. "Let that
child go."

Jason laughed. "This child, as you call her." His fingers
stroked Cassie's neck. "She's worth more than all of you combined. Do you have any idea how much the Council will pay for
her?" His expression hardened. "Which is where she belongs.
She's an animal, as the rest of them are. No more than tools and
pets. Isn't that right, Dawn?"

His gaze was oily, reeking of evil, just as his scent did.

Dawn lifted her head, her hands clutching her purse, her finger on the trigger of the powerful handgun it contained.

She let a gloating smile curl her lips. "We escaped though, didn't we? We survived."

A frown tugged at his brow as anger flashed in his eyes. His hand tightened on Cassie's throat as a wolf's snarl filled the room.

The absolute rage that filled that wolf's growl was a testament to a father's love for his child. Dash was enraged, barely controlled, the scent of his fury filling the air as Dawn kept her attention on Phelps.

Jason wouldn't make it out of the ballroom. It wouldn't be allowed. Jonas was amazingly efficient and Dawn knew the order that had gone out concerning Cassie. Every attempt would be made to save her, but if she were ever taken in such a way, then ensuring the Council didn't acquire her was imperative. She would be killed before it was allowed to happen.

Dash knew it. Dawn knew it. Every Breed there knew that getting her out of Jason Phelps's hands was the only way to ensure her survival. There would be no rescue attempts later, there would only be a funeral and more death. More blood spilled.

Jason laughed. "You should have kept her at home, Sinclair. I still haven't figured out what possessed you to bring such a valuable little jewel out of hiding." He lowered his head and licked Cassie's cheek. The caress was disgusting, insulting.

"Then Cassie was the goal all along?" Seth asked him, his voice icy with the promise of death.

Jason chuckled. "Actually, no. Cassie is a side benefit. A twofer, you might call it. No, Lawrence, I wanted what belonged to me. And there was this nasty little rumor Caroline so enjoyed telling of the little Breed's name you whispered in your sleep. Little Dawn. My little girl."

You'll always be my little girl, his voice whispered through her mind, his vow each time he dirtied her body.

"You look shocked, Lawrence," he said tauntingly. "Haven't you figured it out yet? She was mine in those labs, and I want her back. That was the object all along; it just took me a while to arrange things to my satisfaction once she arrived."

"You won't take either of them, Jason," he snapped. "Give it up now, while you're still alive."

Jason smiled, an evil, malicious twist of his lips. His fingers caressed the smooth line of Cassie's throat with just enough pressure to cause her to part her lips to draw in more air.

Rumbled growls and enraged, throttled snarls filled the room as the guests were pushed behind the line of Breeds now facing Phelps.

He was surrounded, and yet so confident. Dawn knew if he managed to actually escape the ballroom then his success would be almost guaranteed.

"Are you going to let me take her out of here without you, Dawn?" he asked then. "We can do this one of two ways. You can come and be my pet." He stroked Cassie's throat. "Or I can make her my pet for a while. You know how the scientists enjoy watching me work. Do you think she'll survive it?"

Cassie would survive, but her mind would be damaged forever, and Dawn knew it. She knew it, but as she met Cassie's gaze, she saw only acceptance. Acceptance and regret as she glanced at her parents.

I love you. She mouthed the words to them as a sob escaped Elizabeth.

"Come on, Dawn." Jason's voice took a teasing tone. "Tell me you don't dream of me taking you. You've missed me, little cat, you know you have."

The scent of horror filled the room. Finally, finally the cream of the world's financial crop was seeing the evil that filled the Council and its soldiers. The complete disregard for life. Adult's or child's.

Noble, one of the Breeds on the security detail, shifted in front of her carefully, hiding her from Jason's sight for the few precious seconds she needed to jerk her link from her purse and attach it to her ear.

A shot fired and he fell. The smell of blood filled the room, pouring from the chest wound as Noble pressed his own hand to his chest and fought to hold the blood inside his body. The other Breeds didn't move, but the air of savagery that filled the room was nearly stifling now.

"Move between me and what's mine again...," Jason sneered, before turning to her. "Now come here, little cat."

Dawn slid away from Seth quickly, feeling his rage as she did so, as Stygian moved between them and the Breeds surrounded him. They would restrain him if they had to, but Seth was smarter than that. He watched her with tormented eyes, but she saw the determination in his face. He would never stand still if she tried to leave the room with Phelps.

She glided several feet away, then stopped.

"Dawn, we can't get a bead on him. Cassie's head is in the way," Jonas spoke through the link. "You have to get him to shift."

She moved again, several more feet, but though he turned with her, he kept Cassie in a fully protective position in front of him.

"You've lost your edge," she told him calmly. "Against me, as well as Seth. You showed yourself too soon, Jason. That was a miscalculation on your part."

He made a tsking sound. "I like your voice better when you're screaming and begging God to save you." He grinned. "Did he ever save you, Dawn?"

She arched her brow and spread her arms. "I'm free."

"You were for a time," he agreed. "And now Daddy is here to collect you." He chuckled at his own joke.

And Dawn smiled as she shook her head. "You'll never get out of here alive, Jason."

"Everything's in place, Dawn," he assured her. "I'm smart, remember? I trained your animal asses and I can take you out whenever I want to. As many of you as I want."

Dawn let her gaze drift to Cassie. She was staring at her parents, tears washing over her face as Elizabeth's broken voice whispered her name.

"Let Cassie go." She bargained then, stepping close as Seth snarled Dawn's name. "And we'll go."

Jason laughed at that, as she had known he would. "Not going to happen," he promised her. "She's payday. You're my reward. I'm going to strap you down, pump you full of those nifty little drugs the scientists wouldn't let you have before, and I'm going to fuck you until you're screaming in pleasure. Fuck you and tape it and send it to your fiancé." He smiled tauntingly at Seth. "He can see how a real man tames your particular Breed."

"He doesn't need drugs to make me scream in pleasure, Jason," Dawn pointed out as the Breeds closed in around Seth.

"Dawn, damn you, stop," Seth hissed. She heard him, but Jason didn't. He was laughing at her, but there was fury in the sound.

The black fury toward this man had settled inside her, hardening into a knot of resolve in her soul. She had made a vow, one that had meant so much to her that she'd had to forget it to live. She had vowed, to herself and to God, that she would wash her hands in this man's blood.

"Don't talk like a nasty whore, little girl," he snapped back at her. "I'll teach you better once I have you alone. You'll bow for me. You'll go to your knees and beg for me."

Dawn widened her eyes. "What a little fantasy world you live in. Shall I tell you my fantasy?"

The link crackled at her ear. "Be careful, Dawn. We can't lose Cassie to a madman's bullet," Jonas warned her.

He wouldn't kill Cassie. Jason knew what she was worth alive, with her virginity intact. Whatever plans the Council had for her involved that innocence. But Dawn knew well how they used innocence against the female Breeds.

The guests were watching the scene that played out before them in horror. Cassie had made an impression on all of them, with her laughter and wry sense of humor, her teasing jokes and her habit of drawing out even the shiest of the group.

They had known she was a Breed, but there had been no one who had been able to resist her appeal. They watched her now, as Dawn did, their hearts in their throats.

"Let her go, Jason," she warned him again. Softly. "Number one, you'll never make it out of here alive with her."

He smiled. "I could blow her brains out right now, be out that door and gone before any of you could recover from the shock."

Elizabeth's muffled sob tore through her.

Dawn shook her head. "We're too well trained. The second she dropped, you'd be dead."

◆　◆　◆

He watched, his finger caressing the trigger, a growl threatening to give away his location as Breeds raced for a position to get a bead on the man holding the dark-haired girl.

He was in the perfect position. High enough to see everything going on through the ceiling-high windows, his sights trained on the back of Jason Phelps's neck. He could take the shot, he should take the shot, but the risk held him back.

If he did it, at this angle, the bullet would tear through the

spine at the back of the neck, releasing Phelps's grip on the gun
as he fell. But there was a 90 percent chance that when the bullet tore out of the front of the neck, it would tear a slice through
Cassie Sinclair's scalp.

It wouldn't kill her. Maybe.

He grimaced, tested the wind again, and prayed it held. He
was high enough to hide his scent from the Breeds below for the
time being, except, perhaps, one. The one several branches below him trying to get the same bead that he had.

Hell, why did the bastard have to grab that particular female? The one guaranteed to weaken him, to make him caress
the trigger rather than shoot.

Dawn would have been a regrettable casualty, but his fascination with her wouldn't have held him back as this one did.

He lowered his eye to the sights and adjusted again. He
couldn't let this one young woman change the course of the battle between the Council and the Breeds.

If Phelps escaped with her, Dash Sinclair would move heaven
and earth to take her back. He would slice through suspected
Council members like a swath of overriding fury, and the Breeds
that followed him would wash in the blood he shed.

The Breeds would forget political maneuvering and show
the world the savagery they were capable of. That couldn't be
allowed.

He inhaled slowly, forced back the tension that would have
gathered inside him and lined up the shot. Just one small shift
was all he needed.

◆　　◆　　◆

"Dawn, we just need a small shift," Jonas spoke softly through
the link. "We have sight, we just need more room. You have to
maneuver him."

She glanced around the room. Callan was there as well,
Jonas's words causing him to tense and bounce on his feet. She
knew what he would do. He would place his own life in the path
of a bullet to force Jason to move that needed quarter of an inch.

He was their pride leader. His safety and the safety of his
family was uppermost. She couldn't allow him to make that
move.

"Let her go, Jason." She moved closer, lowered her voice,

watched him carefully. "You can get out of here with me. You can never escape with Cassie. They will kill her first. Cut your losses."

"So you can kill me the moment we step into the night?" He laughed. "It's not going to happen, little girl."

Cassie was pale, her eyes large, the tears shimmering on her face. There was no way to get a message to the girl, though Dawn knew, she knew, Cassie's training was better than this. Cassie should have already disabled him, should have already made a way for Jonas to get a shot. Unless she knew something, sensed none of them did.

"You were easy, Dawn," Jason chided then. "The minute you thought your precious Seth was in danger, you came running. You should have run right back to Sanctuary instead."

She let a ghost of a smile touch her lips. "But if I had, I would have never remembered you, would I?" she pointed out and watched his eyes widen with surprise, almost in fear.

"You remember all of it?"

"I remember all of it, Jason," she assured him. "Years' worth." She forced herself to laugh lightly. "And you didn't even faze me. You're barely a hiccup on my little radar now."

He frowned heavily, his finger flexing on the trigger of the gun held to Cassie's temple.

The girl's lips were trembling, her expression stark, but not with fear. Rather with pain as she watched her parents.

The bond between Cassie and her parents was absolute. It had been forged in steel, her mother's connection to the Wolf Breed naturally including the child that had brought them together. Seeing her pain, seeing the same knowledge Dawn saw in Cassie, would be killing Dash and Elizabeth. The knowledge that their daughter was meeting death without a fight.

"I'll become your radar." He chuckled. "Now get your ass over here with us. We're going home, baby. Where we can play all by ourselves."

All by themselves. Dawn moved slowly across the room, praying the others stayed in place. She just had to get beside him, get in place and then she could jerk Cassie that needed distance to save her from a bullet to her brain.

"To the left, Dawn," Jonas directed her. "That will turn him where we need him."

She moved to the left, still going forward, pretending to skirt around a couple huddled together as they watched Phelps.

"There's a good little kitty. Come to Daddy, little girl."

❖   ❖   ❖

The bastard moved.

He leveled his eyes on the sight, readjusted and recalculated the odds.

The shot would still strike the girl, but not as deep. He could only pray the wind stayed calm and the players before him stayed in place.

❖   ❖   ❖

"Dawn, a little more to the left," Jonas ordered quietly.

She moved more to the left, always advancing, one slow, hesitant step at a time, as Phelps followed her with his gleeful eyes.

❖   ❖   ❖

He smiled. Yeah, that was better. Just a little more.

❖   ❖   ❖

Dawn could feel her heartbeat, slow, steady. There was no panic, there was no fear. She knew this maneuver. She had trained with it, perfected it. Any hostage situation or variable imagined and she had gone through it. She needed to get close enough, to get in position. She would have to move swiftly, but Breed reflexes were faster than human, and for all his strength and experience at killing Breeds, the Council soldiers still hadn't yet figured out that the Breeds trained now to adjust to the knowledge the Council had on them.

They didn't fight as they'd been trained. They didn't react as they'd been trained.

She could feel Seth behind her; she sensed Callan a bit to her side. Both men were tensed and prepared to jump.

Just a little more, she thought. Be patient. Let me fight my own battles.

Callan's protection was absolute and she knew it. He would easily sacrifice himself to save one of the female Breeds under his care. Just as Wolf Gunnar would do, as Dash would do.

They had their own mates, their own children, but the value they placed on all females and their protection would push them to extreme lengths.

She was several feet from Jason now. Frustration was lining his face.

"If you don't hurry, bitch, I'm going to hurt her," he warned. "I might not kill her, but I can spill her blood easy and get away with it."

Yes, he could. But Dawn didn't hurry. She stepped carefully, cautiously.

"I said now." The gun shifted from Cassie's temple toward Dawn and a roar sounded.

"No!" Dawn screamed as she tried to jump for Callan.

Horror flashed through her brain as the gun aimed and fired, the bullet slamming into Callan. And he kept coming.

As though it were a dream, slow motion, time slowing almost to a stop. Jason Phelps's head exploded as Cassie jerked, blood spraying from the side of her head. She toppled forward, hand outstretched, her beautiful eyes closing.

Dawn felt that child's life flash before her eyes. The little girl that bargained for chocolate, her smile flashing, her blue eyes gleaming with laughter. The child that saw "fairies," ghosts Cassie had told her about not long ago. Shimmering forms of lives long past who came to her, whispered secrets to her.

She had watched Cassie grow. Sanctuary had been the haven Dash had brought his family to when he needed additional protection for them.

Before Dawn's eyes Cassie had grown from a child to a young woman, always laughing despite her feelings that she would never fit in, that she would never be accepted because of her dual genetics.

And Callan. She stared at the blood pouring from his chest, his golden hair fanned out around him, his aristocratic, beloved features still and pale as Breeds rushed for him and Dash bellowed in white hot rage as he rushed for his daughter.

And it was Dawn's fault.

"No. Oh God, no!" She froze; she didn't know where to run, what to do.

Screams were echoing in her head, orders barked furiously into the link about an unknown shooter, location and trajectory.

And all Dawn could see was Cassie and Callan. So motionless, so pale. Their wounds those that few Breeds had survived. Callan's to his chest, Cassie's to the head.

God in Heaven. An enraged roar tore through her as Seth's arms surrounded her, jerking her to his body as the pain struck in blinding waves through her head.

She jerked from him, fury pumping through her as she fell on the body of the bastard that had hurt so many. Callan's pale face filled her vision. The image of Cassie, broken, taken from them, filling her head as her hands sank into warm, rich blood and her head tipped back, her roar shaking her body.

Oh God. All because of her. They were gone because of her.

"I have you, sweetheart." Seth's rough voice was in her ear as he dragged her back from Phelps's cooling body. "I have you. I have you, Dawn."

She collapsed in his arms, sobbing, holding on to him because she couldn't hold on to herself anymore. She screamed Callan's name as Breeds tried to staunch the bleeding, as she heard the words *losing him* ricochet in her mind.

No! They couldn't lose him. They couldn't. She hadn't told him she was sorry. She hadn't told him she understood why he had tried to protect her from Seth. He hadn't hugged her. He hadn't growled at her with that playful half-warning growl that assured her everything was fine between them.

She was losing her brother. Her pride leader. She was losing him, and the agony that lanced through her had her holding tight to Seth. Begging him, begging God, because she didn't know how to endure this guilt.

Callan and Cassie had died because of her.

◆   ◆   ◆

His rifle secured on his back, he jumped from the trees soundlessly, ducked and ran. He could hear the screams from inside the house. The Cougar screaming her pride leader's name.

Fuck, that wasn't supposed to happen. Callan Lyons had thrown himself at Phelps just in time to take a bullet. His own bullet had slammed into Phelps less than a breath later, the bullet tearing through his neck as someone else struck Phelps's head, taking Cassie Sinclair down as well.

Regrettable. Damned fucking regrettable, and he was pissed off over it. But there was no time to stick around and make certain his aim had been true and his own calculations perfect. He had tried to save the girl. A first for him; he had never tried to watch out for casualties before, especially those who deliberately stood in the way.

Cassie Sinclair was better trained than that. She had a fucking suicide wish, and allowing her to follow through on it made him want to shake the shit out of her.

He sprinted across the mansion grounds, a shadow racing around the shadows racing to the house. The Breeds were pouring in from all quarters because their pride leader was down.

He could hear the reports on the link he had managed to acquire and disable the tracking receiver on. He had heard the orders for the Breeds to converge on the ballroom.

"Callan's down," someone had yelled into the link. "Son of a bitch, the bastard got him. I repeat, our pride leader is down. He's down." There was a heavy silence then. "Oh God, we're losing him . . . We're losing him . . ."

Fuck! This mission hadn't gone at all as planned.

CHAPTER 25

The sixth-floor ICU and surgery had been cleared ahead of the Sanctuary heli-jets landing on the helipads on the roof of the hospital.

Feline Breed doctor, surgeon and Council-trained scientist Elyiana Morrey was already prepped and waiting with her Wolf Breed counterpart. They had three Breeds arriving. Pride Leader Lyons; an enforcer, Noble Chavin; and the young Wolf-Coyote Breed, Cassandra Sinclair.

Wolf Gunnar and his mate were on their way in, as were teams of Wolf Breed Enforcers, several of which had arrived due to proximity to the hospital.

The Breed community was converging en masse, protection and security paramount as the pride leader's family was flown in. His mate and his son. Possibly the heir to the mighty kingdom his father had built.

Initial reports weren't good. The chest shot was severe, resulting in massive bleeding. They had already lost him once. The great Callan Lyons could be lost to them all before he ever reached surgery.

Waiting with Dr. Morrey were several human surgeons.

In a nearby operating room there were three more awaiting
Noble, working beneath her assistant. She cast them all a hard
glare.

"If we lose Lyons, for any reason, the four of you will die before we leave this operating room." She nodded to the Breeds
that had been forced to scrub up and placed in the room, their
rifles held ready. "Don't fuck with me, gentlemen. You're the
best the Council had in this area, and killing you will not affect
me. Killing your wives and seeing your daughters tortured will
be my pleasure. Understand that well."

And they did. They had created the monster they were facing. These four. Each of them had had a hand in her genetics
and in her training. They were the best of the best, and in their
eyes she saw their fear and their determination to succeed.

"If Lyons dies, they die. It's your job to then seek out their
families, and on their bodies you will practice every torturous
method of pain the Council ever taught you," she ordered the
enforcers.

They stared back at the scientists, their gazes flat, hard. All
Lion Breeds. All a part of Sanctuary. Their loyalty and their
love for their pride leader was absolute.

"The threats aren't needed, Ely." Only one had the nerve to
speak so comfortably with her.

Her smile was hard as she heard the announcement that her
pride leader was within seconds of the surgery. "Pray you're
right, Montaya." She flashed her canines and growled. "Because
liking you above the others won't save you. It won't save you,
your wife or your daughters. Gentlemen, don't fail."

The nurse quickly tied off her mask as the surgery doors
burst open, Jonas at the head of the gurney, and Ely felt tears
flood her throat, felt pain rush through her body as she glimpsed
the wound.

Dear God. She had given an order to kill so many. The damage
was severe, the chances so slim. She turned her eyes to Montaya,
and rather than anger or rage at the knowledge of the additional
blood that would spill if Callan died, she saw only compassion
and determination.

She jumped to the gurney as he did, moving quickly, working with him as she had so many times before to save the
Breeds that had been brought into the labs. They knew wounds.

They knew the Breed physiology. If anyone could save this man, they could.

✦   ✦   ✦

Seth clasped Dawn to him as they rushed into the waiting room filled with Breed Enforcers, leaders and Callan Lyons's family.

Merinus sat with her son, David. Even at eleven the child sat straight and tall, his eyes dry, his body perfectly balanced between patience and curiosity about his surroundings.

Merinus.

Dawn fought back her sobs as Merinus turned to her, her lips trembling, her eyes welling with tears as she fought to blink them back.

"I'm sorry." Dawn knelt in front of her. "I'm so sorry."

The tears were falling from her eyes again.

Dressed in jeans and one of Callan's T-shirts, the pride leader's wife looked ravaged.

Merinus shook her head as a tear fell. "It's not your fault, Dawn. He wasn't going to let Phelps touch you, ever again. That was his decision. Not yours." Her voice was husky, filled with tears.

"I'm tellin' you all, Dad's going to be okay." David breathed out wearily as though he had repeated this many times. "You'll see. He's tough."

Merinus's hands shook as she brought them to her mouth and turned away from her child. Unlike David, they knew the extent of Callan's injuries.

"Merinus." Wolf Gunnar and his mate, Hope, stepped forward then. "Dawn." He stared down at her, his savage features and dark eyes filled with compassion. "Our enforcers are in place, both here and at Sanctuary. Everything's secured until Callan can take the reins once again."

Merinus nodded, tried to speak and couldn't.

Callan. She whispered his name. She prayed and fought to curl into herself to bear the pain. How would she live if he was gone? How would she go on and raise their son as he expected her to? How could she bear it if she lost him, and he hadn't even known of the child she was carrying now?

She touched the tears on Dawn's face and tried to tighten her lips against her sobs. This sweet child that Callan loved as he loved his own. The one that awoke him with her nightmares and left him helpless with his rage because he couldn't heal her above all others.

She loved Dawn herself as a sister, a dear, dear friend. But Callan's love ran deeper. Nearly as deep as a father's love and just as binding. He couldn't have borne that bastard laying a single finger on her, for any reason.

"Dad's gonna be okay," David snapped again. He was so sensitive. He could feel the helplessness, the fears running through the room.

Merinus shook her head. She had to believe that. She had to. If she didn't, she might well lose her mind.

As the thought raced through her, a commotion in the hall began. Gasps, curses, Breeds rushing to make way for something, someone.

Merinus jerked to her feet and pulled her son next to her, uncertain what this new threat was. As it materialized in front of the door, shock raced through her.

It couldn't be.

She reached out, then pressed her hand to her lips as his gaze found hers. Beside him, another man and a slender woman were consulting with a doctor, but it was the first male that held her rapt attention.

It was Callan, and yet it wasn't. The same imposing features. The same mane of hair falling to his shoulders, the same golden, piercing eyes as he found her.

It couldn't be. It couldn't be who she thought it was. Who she knew it was.

"That's Grandpa." David suddenly piped up. "He smells like Dad and Jonas. And that's my uncle Dane. I told you he smelled like Dad."

And David had told Callan many times that Dane Vanderale smelled like him. The problem was, no Breed but David had detected that scent. The Breed's gaze slid to David, fierce, filled with pride before returning to Merinus.

"How's my son?"

His son. Merinus stared back at him, as much in shock as every Breed standing in the room.

This was the first Breed to have ever been created. The fabled first Leo and the mate he had stolen from the Council lab he had been created within nearly a century before.

He was rumored to be more than a hundred and twenty years old, yet he looked in his prime, only a few years older than her beloved Callan.

He could have been Callan's brother rather than his father, and now Merinus knew why Leo Vanderale was so rarely in the public eye. So rare that no one had detected the disguise he obviously used in public, yet hadn't bothered to use here.

The photos Merinus had seen of him showed a much darker-haired Leo. Eyes more dark brown than golden amber shot with darker hues. The lines on his face in those photos weren't present now, and the powerful, corded body was very much downplayed in public with what must have been an exceptional eye for clothes and artificial enhancements.

The Leo's mate, the scientist that had been rumored to be a genius in the genetic workings of the Breeds at the time, still retained a glow of youth. And, like her husband, had drastically altered her appearance at the public events she had attended and in the photos she'd had taken over the past years.

Straight, long dark hair, gray eyes, pert features and clear, unblemished skin. This wasn't the woman whose hair was shot with gray, whose face was lined to make her appear two decades older than she looked.

They had preserved their secrecy throughout the decades. There had never been so much as a hint that Leo Vanderale could be a Breed, nor that his son could be the first fully grown breed-human hybrid.

Her eyes flashed to Dane Vanderale. He barely looked thirty, but he had to be older. There was proof that Elizabeth Forteniare had conceived before she and the first Leo had escaped confinement in the labs so long ago. There were rumors that the child had survived birth. Dane had to be that child, and no one had ever known.

"So much shock." His voice was well modulated, just a hint of a foreign accent present in his voice. "Did you think I wouldn't arrive when my son lies so close to death?"

The first Leo. He was the first Leo and he had been so close for so long. Dane Vanderale stood, strong and sure beside him, and Merinus saw the resemblance then. The same proud features, piercing eyes. The same cocky, arrogant assurance.

Breeds stared at the vision as though staring upon a deity they hadn't believed existed.

The first Leo. Alive. So close. And the father of the Breed that had made a way for his people, a place on earth that none had been able to steal.

"You took your time," she whispered.

And he grimaced. Pain and longing filled his eyes as the small woman beside him turned to him. He lowered his head, listened and nodded before motioning Dane toward her.

"My wife, Elizabeth." His lips quirked. "A strong name, I believe." He glanced at Dash and a tearful Elizabeth. "She'll oversee Callan's surgery and go then to Cassie. Cassie is stable, I'm told, the shot was a surface wound, but the bruising to the brain is a concern."

Merinus shook her head, shock still racing through her.

"She's his . . ."

"Mother?" he asked. "Yes. Elizabeth's ovum was extracted before our escape. Several, actually. She was the Council's foremost authority on Breed genetics and physiology. He's her son. She won't lose him."

"But she couldn't come to him," she cried. "Ten years they searched for you. Ten years they begged you to come out of hiding. His parents. David's grandparents, and you didn't give a fuck?"

"I gave enough of a fuck to care about whether the world knew our secrets and our weaknesses," he growled, flashing his canines. Like Callan. Warning her back. Arrogant and certain of his power. "I gave enough of a fuck that I helped weed out your spies before I made my decision to reveal myself. Blame me if you must. But those secrets were more important than my personal needs or Callan's. Let alone that arrogant by-blow Wyatt." He sneered the name, though not with hatred, but with a challenging, brooding tone.

He looked like Callan, but Merinus knew to her soul which son carried his temperament.

"My son, Dane." He indicated the man who had followed the Leo's mate to surgery. "He's been my eyes and my ears."

Dawn stood beside Seth, staring at the Leo. She couldn't believe it. It wasn't possible.

Seth was holding her upright. She couldn't have kept herself balanced on her own. The Breeds that filled the room were in as much shock as she was.

Around the Leo were more Breeds. They were unfamiliar,

harder, colder. They looked like the creatures the Council had created. The killers they had dreamed of.

"My security force." He indicated the dozen armed Breeds. "And now my sons." He stared around the room, inhaling slowly and nodding as though pleased. "And David's right. His father will be fine. He's too damned stubborn to be otherwise."

CHAPTER 26

Two days later, dressed in jeans and a T-shirt, Dawn stepped silently into Callan's ICU room and stared at the man who had saved her.

Seth was at her side, as he had been for the past two days. She gripped his hand and moved to the bed, staring down at the monitors that beeped and flashed and created a subtle buzz that flayed her nerves.

"He would hate being here," she whispered on a sob. "It's like the labs. He hates hospitals."

She moved her hands to the metal rail on the bed. He looked as strong and as sure as he always had. Pale. Tired. But strong.

She knew the Leo and his wife had spent countless hours in here with him. The powerful first Feline Breed, along with his other son, Dane, had given their own blood to transfuse Callan. Ely had sworn the combination of it had helped stabilize Callan as nothing else could have. Elizabeth Vanderale, the Leo's mate and wife, stood on the other side of the room monitoring her son's progress.

She looked younger than Merinus. Brunette hair and gray eyes. Slender. Poised. She didn't look old enough to be an intern let alone the foremost authority on Breeds.

"You're crying."

Her gaze jerked down. Callan watched her through slitted lashes, his gaze flickering to his hand where a single teardrop had fallen.

"I've been doing that a lot." The half sob, half laugh had Seth wrapping his arms around her from behind, surrounding her with his strength.

She couldn't have made it without him. She had never faced anything so horrifying as watching her beloved brother die. Even the memories rushing back inside her hadn't hurt as much. God help her, if it had been Seth, she would have never made it.

"You never cry," he rasped, flicking a dark look at Seth. "It's your fault."

And Seth only chuckled.

"I hear I have parents." He grimaced, his gaze slicing to the mother across the room. "David's ecstatic."

He was off balance. Dawn could feel it, and she knew the other woman did as well.

"Yeah. He threatened to thrash Jonas yesterday." Dawn smiled, though tears still slipped down her cheek. "I offered to sell the tickets until he growled at me."

"I wanna buy one," Callan sighed. "Save it for me."

"I promise." She swallowed tightly, reaching out to touch his hand. "Callan . . ."

"Say *you're* sorry and I'll thrash *you*." He glared at her, though weakly.

"I was angry," she whispered.

His jaw tightened and she swore she saw the sheen of tears in his eyes. "I'd do it again, so save your breath."

"And I love you for it," she whispered. "You were right, Callan. I wasn't strong enough." Her voice broke and she shook her head tightly. "I didn't understand."

He watched her, his golden eyes somber, filled with his own pain at those memories.

"You were the important one," he finally whispered. "Even if you hated me for it. Protecting you mattered."

She leaned forward and kissed his cheek, before whispering, "Thank you for saving me. God sent you to me, and I've thanked him as well."

She straightened slowly and saw the surprise, the single tear that eased from the corner of his eye. He swallowed tightly, licked his lips, then glanced at the small woman who eased to the side of his bed.

"She won't let me hug you," he grunted. "I claim a rain check. And one of those tickets."

Elizabeth Vanderale was hiding her tears, but Dawn felt them, sensed them.

"He needs to rest now," she said softly. "And if I don't let Merinus in, he's going to start ignoring my chiding."

"My mate." He tried to glare at her, but his lashes drifted down. When they closed, Elizabeth's lips pressed together to hold back her tears as she nodded at Dawn and Seth.

Seth led Dawn from the room, his arm around her, and as they walked down the hallway, the last of the pain, the dark fury and the past eased away from her.

She had done as she'd vowed. She had washed her hands in Jason Phelps's blood. She had seen him defeated, broken. And she was walking away from it.

"I want to go home," she whispered as they stepped into the elevator, Stygian and Styx moving in behind them.

"The heli-jet can have you in Sanctuary within a few hours," he promised.

Dawn shook her head, turned to him and framed his face with her hands. "No, Seth. I want to go to our home. Now. Just the two of us."

The joy that lit his eyes flamed in her heart.

"We'll go home," he promised, his head lowering, his lips stealing hers. "Right now."

The kiss was a promise. A dedication. She had awakened to his love and she would never sleep without it again.

· E P I L O G U E ·

He slipped into the hospital room. And that was damned hard to do. There were so many Breeds positioned through the hallways, hard-eyed, merciless and waiting on blood to spill, that it was risking life and limb.

He was trained for stealth though, and he was trained to get in where others couldn't.

It was the sixth floor, a short climb up the shadowed wall. Cutting the window was a pain in the ass. And why the hell he was doing this he couldn't figure out.

Fine, she had gone down. Collateral damage, right? How many other Breeds had died for the sake of the community at large? He couldn't count how many dozen on two hands and all toes.

But here was his stupid ass, climbing up a sheer wall and cutting into a window as he struggled to activate the security rerouter.

This was a three-fucking-Breed job. He was one Breed. Insane crap.

But he just couldn't let it go. The memory of her crumpled on the floor of that damned ballroom, blood spilling around her head. It was just too much. He couldn't sleep for it. And when something messed with *his* sleep, then something had to be done about it.

Silently he eased the cut glass inside the room, inhaled slowly and grimaced. He'd disguised his scent as best he could, but it wasn't going to hold for long. They'd catch him in under five minutes flat and then all hell was going to break loose.

But he was in, and stepping across the short distance to the hospital bed where she lay.

Her parents must have dressed her in that immature neck-hugging gown. It was longer than he preferred. All prim and proper like some Victorian-era priss. She should be in silk thongs to display that fine ass, and nothing else. Because she had a fine curve to that ass.

He gritted his teeth and grimaced in frustration.

There was a bandage around her head, but all those beautiful curls were still there. They flowed around her like black silk.

He reached out and touched one, whistling soundlessly at the feel of it. Damn, it felt fine. And in that second his cock went hard as a rock as he imagined the feel of that hair against his sensitive flesh.

That would be some damned erotic sensation there.

As he stared at her, something besides arousal twisted at his gut though. Something like . . . regret?

Hell, had he ever felt regret?

He shook his head, rubbed the back of his neck in confusion and tried again to figure out what the hell he was doing there.

Cassandra Sinclair was none of his business. If her father, Dash Sinclair, had so much as a thought of the creature sniffing around her, he'd hunt him down and tear him limb from limb.

But this was almost worth it.

He reached out, ran his finger down the fine, ultra-smooth flesh of her cheek and knew he had never touched anything so soft.

I dare you. The memory of her pretty pink lips forming those words had his lips quirking.

He leaned close, feathered her hair from her ear and whispered. "Never dare me."

She jackknifed in the bed. Her eyes flew open, and a scream of pure terror erupted from her lips with such a suddenness that he couldn't counter it.

He cursed, jumped for the window, grabbed the rope he'd

secured beside it, and in the time it took for her screams to die he was on the ground and running.

Damn. Guess he shouldn't have warned her, he thought with a smile. But he had. And he hoped, for her sake, she remembered it.

Turn the page for an exclusive look at
the next title in the Feline Breeds series

Mercury's War

Now available from Berkley Sensation!

If she kept twitching her ass like that, he was going to fuck it. So help him God, he was going to take her to her knees, hike that plain brown skirt to her hips, and show her the folly of teasing a fully grown, hungry Lion Breed.

Mercury Warrant leaned against the wall of the small office Gloria "Please call me Ria" Rodriquez was using, and fought to maintain the same cool façade he'd held over the past week.

It wasn't easy. Especially when she moved from the desk to the table set up across from it to go through the files stacked there. She would lean over, sometimes studying each file's contents before choosing one, and the ugly brown skirt would mold to her ass like a loving hand.

Like his hand wanted to mold to it, clench it, separate the full globes as he watched his erection slide into the moist, silky heat below.

He was a walking hard-on, and after a week of it, it was starting to piss him off. He jacked off to the thought of her, the image of her face and of her naked body straddling him. The days he spent with her only fueled that desire until it was starting to pinch at his balls in hunger.

He wanted the little plain Jane. He wanted to throw her to the bed and rut in her until the need was obliterated and his mind was free of her.

"You were the mechanical specialist before you became part of Mr. Wyatt's team?" She turned her head, gazing at him through sharp, hazel eyes. "You were the one who set the specifications of the dirt bikes we shipped here?"

The *we* in question meaning Vanderale Industries, Sanctuary's more than generous benefactor.

He nodded curtly.

"Your lab files didn't hint at mechanical knowledge. Your specialty there was recon and weapons with a minor in assassination and torture."

He lifted a brow. "You make it sound like college."

She stared back at him silently, her expression unchanging.

"The ability wasn't listed because there was no chance to develop the talent." He finally shrugged. "When I came here, there were some old cycles in one of the sheds. I spent my time fixing them."

Jonas had said to cooperate with her. Fine, he'd cooperate. And he had to admit he liked that little flare of interest in her eyes whenever he gave her what she wanted.

"So you found the talent while you were recuperating?" She straightened and turned toward him, her hands sliding into the pockets of her slim skirt as she leaned a hip against the table.

Recuperating. Now there was a word for it.

He nodded. It was hard to talk to her when all he wanted to do was growl with lust. He could feel the urge rising in his throat and fought it back. Damn, he must have been too long without a woman. Maybe he should find one. Fast. Or he was going to end up in bed with a potential disaster. Vanderale's emissary was no one to screw around with. Literally.

"You requested six more of the cycles, with advanced electronics, weapons and power. Did you come up with the specifications?" she asked.

He nodded again. Those cycles would be a terror in the mountains the government had ceded to the Breeds.

The cycles were stripped down to only the necessary weight to allow for the small, mounted gun barrels and ammunition. GPS and advanced satellite links were contained in bulletproof shields, and the engines themselves were modified for a vast increase in power.

"And what would be the consequences if the cycles weren't approved?"

That question threw him. They needed those cycles.

"More Breeds will die," he answered her. "Keeping up with the tricks the supremacists use to get into the protected area is paramount. Those cycles will aid the teams that have to patrol the perimeters, which have grown in the past few years."

"The advancements you're asking for raise the price of the machines by several tens of thousands of dollars per cycle," she pointed out. "Not to mention ammunition and satellite time they'll be using. At this rate, Vanderale will need to place a satellite in orbit for Sanctuary alone. Do you know the cost of that?"

"Vanderale profits as well," he reminded her. "How many of our people do you already have working security for the new facilities you've placed in the Middle East?"

"People we pay an excellent wage," she argued. "There's no exchange of favors, Mercury."

Bullshit. He stared back at her mockingly. "Tell that to your executive we rescued from Iran last month, Ms. Rodriquez. The Breed community did for free what no other team could have done for any price. How much was his life worth to you?"

Her lips twitched at the point.

"You're right." She shrugged. "Mr. Vasquez is very important to Vanderale. He's doing fine, by the way. Considered it a hell of an adventure."

She shifted again, crossing one ankle over the other as she leaned against the desk, and he swore he heard the sound of silken flesh rubbing together.

God, he wanted to lift her onto that damned table and bury his head between her thighs. He wondered if she would taste as sweet as he imagined she did. If she would be as wet and hot as he was hard.

Would she scream for him? He wanted her screaming, begging, her head tilted back and that bun at the nape of her neck released.

"Sanctuary needs those cycles," he said instead. "With one of those per team going out, we'll have an advantage over the supremacists attempting to slip in and assassinate or kidnap the members of the Ruling Cabinet and their families."

In the past months, two more attempts had been made upon the main house.

She turned back to the files spread over the table before choosing one and turning back to her desk.

Mercury watched as she took her seat and opened the file. Her head bent, displaying the soft skin of her neck, the pulse beating heavily just below the flesh. He clenched his jaw at the need to scrape his teeth over it. To feel the delicate skin, to taste it, maybe bite it a little bit.

Fuck. At the thought, his cock jerked, his balls tightened with a shard of pleasure so sharp it was nearly painful. Mercury hastily ran his tongue over his teeth, checking for a swelling of the small glands, for any unusual taste in his mouth. Not that he expected it, but he had to be sure.

There was no swelling, no spilling of a mating hormone that would signal she was his.

What would he have done, he wondered, if it *had* been there?

He clenched his fists at the overpowering thought of mating her. Of having the choice taken away from him, of marking her, this one woman, as his own. The sexuality the mating heat produced was intense, fiery. The sexual need overwhelming.

Unfortunately it was something Mercury knew he would never know. He had lost his mate, years ago, in a life he fought daily to forget.

He hadn't marked the small Lioness his heart and body had claimed. He had never taken her, never kissed her, but he remembered the overriding hunger to do just that. The sensitivity in his tongue, the primal awareness of her and her scent, her lust. His rage and grief when she had been killed on a mission had nearly resulted in his own death.

She had been his mate. And Lion Breeds only mate once, just like their cousins, the lion. But he could still fuck. And he was damned determined to fuck his little plain Jane into screaming orgasm.

"Vanderale contributed more than twenty million dollars to Sanctuary last year alone," she murmured as she went over another file. "Mr. Wyatt has quite an impressive list of wants in the file he sent us for financial aid next year."

Mercury said nothing. He wasn't part of the Ruling Cabinet and at the moment, Jonas's wants were the last thing on his mind. He was too busy staring at the rise and fall of her breasts beneath her bulky blouse, wondering at the color of her nipples, and if the soft curves beneath were as generous as he was guessing they were.

The sound of her throat clearing pulled his gaze up. Mercury stared back at her, maintaining an even expression despite the fact he had been caught leering at her breasts.

Besides, he liked that little hint of a blush on her cheeks, the way her eyes chastised him from behind the small lenses of her glasses.

"I realize you're likely bored," she sighed, her expression resigned. "But that makes me uncomfortable."

"Why?"

Surprise glittered in her hazel eyes.

"Why?" she asked with a slight, uncomfortable laugh. "Perhaps because you and I both know it's not out of interest but merely your own boredom. Besides, women don't like to have their breasts leered at. You should know that by now."

"Doesn't mean I understand it." He shrugged. "The fact that I find your breasts interesting shouldn't be such an issue. You appear to have nice breasts. You should wear blouses that emphasize them rather than attempting to hide them."

Women were strange creatures.

"How would you like it if all I did was ogle your crotch?" she snapped. "It's insulting."

"Ogle to your heart's content." The very thought of it had his cock twitching in pitiful hunger to be noticed.

When her gaze dropped, her eyes widened and jerked back to his.

"Normal reaction when a man finds a woman attractive." He frowned at her displeasure. "Would you rather I had no reaction at all?"

"Yes." She slapped the folder closed. "I don't have time for affairs here."

"Did I ask you for an affair?" He frowned; he knew he hadn't. "I said I find you attractive."

"And you get hard for every woman you find attractive?"

Now that question made him uncomfortable. There weren't a lot of women he found attractive in that sense.

"Do you get wet for every man who comes on to you?" he questioned her instead. Because she was wet. He could smell her arousal, her interest. He had been smelling it for days and it was driving him crazy.

The sweet scent of dawn rising. That elusive, subtle scent of awakening, of moist warmth and adventure. That was what she smelled of, and Mercury loved the dawn.

Her skin was flushed a gentle pink now, and with the smell of her arousal, he could also smell her confusion.

"I'm not wet," she lied, shifting in her seat, most likely pressing her legs tight together.

Mercury let a smile tug at his lips. She knew the Breeds' sense of smell was stronger than that of a normal human's. She would also know that he would see the lie for what it was, an attempt to deny the attraction building between them.

He didn't call her on it. He kept his stance against the wall, his eyes on her, despite the fact that he wanted his hands on her.

She gave a little sniff of disapproval before turning back to the files and pointedly ignoring him. That was fine with him. Growing accustomed to a hunger of this strength took time anyway. Time and patience. He had both.

◆   ◆   ◆

Ria was flustered. She never got flustered, nor embarrassed, nor so turned on for a man. But she was now. She stared down at the file that detailed the dirt bikes Vanderale had originally supplied Sanctuary with, as well as the notes and captions of the modifications Mercury Warrant had made on them.

Modifications he had built into the specs for the new bikes they wanted. But her mind wasn't on motorcycles, attached weapons and the cost thereof, which was astronomical. Her mind was on the man.

Or the Breed. Of all the Lion Breeds she had met thus far, Mercury showed more of the physical characteristics than all of them combined.

High cheekbones and exotic brown eyes, almost amber but not quite. There was a faint darkness around the eye line and lids, as though someone had applied the smallest line of kohl. Thick, sun-kissed lashes framed them and gave him an erotic appearance. His lips were a bit thin, but well sculpted and sexier than they should have been. His nose long, with a flattened bridge more predominant than most Breeds.

Long, thick, brown-, black- and russet-streaked hair fell to his shoulders. Unlike Callan Lyons, with his golden brown hair

and handsome features, Mercury seemed to epitomize the
Breeds. A lion walking within a man's body. She could clearly
see the primal, feral qualities that she knew he fought to keep
subverted. As though he could hide what he was, at least to himself.

"I'm ready to go home." She slapped the file closed and stood.

She couldn't keep her mind on the file or the job she had
come there to do. She was too aware of him, too aware of the
sensuality steadily rising between them.

"I'll let Jonas know we're leaving." He nodded as he flipped
the mic of the communications unit down from the side of his
face.

"*We* aren't leaving; *I* am." She walked back to the desk that
held the files she had pulled to go through. "I don't need an
escort."

"That's not what I was told," he informed her before turning
his conversation to the link. "Jonas, we're ready to head back to
the house." He listened for a moment before replying. "My bag
is in the Jeep. I'll keep in contact from there."

Ria propped her hands on her hips as she stared back at him.
"Exactly what do you mean by that?"

His eyes narrowed on her. "There was another attempt to
breach the perimeter of Sanctuary's boundaries on the east side
of the mountain. Your cabin sits there. Since you're outside the
boundaries of Sanctuary, you're at risk."

"So?"

He restrained his smile. "So, from now on you have a guard
inside the house, namely me, as well as one outside whenever
you aren't at Sanctuary. We can't risk your kidnapping or death,
Ria."

"Namely you?" Oh no, that was not going to work. No way,
no how. "You'll have to tell Mr. Wyatt I've refused your charming company. You can sit outside with your buddy."

"That scared you can't resist me?" His brow arched as arrogant confidence curled at his lip.

"Excuse me?" He couldn't mean what she thought he did.

"You heard me," he said. "Are you that afraid you can't handle your own response to me, that you'd put your life in danger?"

Now that was a dare. She hated dares. A dare had landed her
there to begin with.

"I would have no problems resisting you, Mr. Warrant," she snapped, her voice cold despite the heat traveling through her body. "This has nothing to do with you, and everything to do with privacy. I like living alone."

He crossed his arms over his chest, his broad, powerful chest, and stared down at her with a frown.

"We aren't willing to risk your life for the sake of your privacy," he informed her. "You can accept the conditions or we'll be forced to call Vanderale and inform them of the danger and your lack of cooperation. We were assured you would cooperate with the protective measures we set in place."

Damn it. She was going to kill her boss. If Sanctuary complained it wouldn't just go through her own department, it would also hit the desk of the president and owner of Vanderale Industries. And no one, but no one messed with him over his favorite charity. Except her boss. Dane Vanderale might be the son and potential heir, but he was still answerable to his father, just as she was. And *he* had no idea she was here. She was trapped and she knew it.

"Don't you have a female enforcer you can assign to the house?" She fought back her irritation. "Someone who at least has a sense of humor?"

"I have a sense of humor." He shrugged again. "For example, I find it very amusing that you're afraid to be alone with me."

"Afraid?" She smirked. "You have an overrated opinion of your appeal, Mr. Warrant. I just don't want the aggravation of your hard-on bouncing around my house and invading my privacy. If I wanted that, I would have brought a man with me."

Yeah. Right. She hadn't had sex in years and wasn't likely to anytime soon. For some reason, she hadn't excelled in sexual relationships as easily as she excelled in her job.

She got along with her vibrator much easier than she got along with men.

"Regardless of my opinion or your wants, I've been assigned to the house. We don't have enough enforcers to go around as it is. You're stuck with me."

Oh, great. She stared at him, pursing her lips in displeasure as she met his gaze. His hot gaze. He watched her like the four-legged lions that patrolled the estate watched dinner being led in. It was nerve-wracking.

"This is not going to work," she bit out. "This is Friday. I don't even come in for the next two days."

He stared back at her silently, as though she hadn't even spoken. God, she hated it when he did that.

"I need to talk to Jonas," she snapped. "Now."

"Not possible. He's preparing to head back to Washington tonight for meetings this weekend and he's currently heading into conference with the Ruling Cabinet. You'll have to wait until Monday."

She snapped her teeth together. She wanted to stomp her foot and curse, but hated to give him a reason to be any more amused at her discomfort than he was already. He seemed to delight in throwing her off balance.

"This is not going to work." She jerked her purse from the corner of the desk. "Not in any way."

He straightened as she neared the door, all animal grace and sexual confidence. Dressed in the black enforcer mission outfit, a mini-Uzi strapped to his side, a knife sheathed at his thigh. He was too tall, too broad, much too sexy and way too dangerous.

"It's going to work fine. You'll be perfectly safe," he assured her as he opened the office door and allowed her to pass.

He made her brush by his body, her shoulder sliding against his chest, the heat of him surrounding her as she moved past him. God, she loved it when he did that. Loved the sense of strength and protective power she could feel surrounding her. That didn't mean she liked the thought of dealing with it all weekend. She used the time away from him for distance, to push back the attraction and the growing need. How the hell was she supposed to do that with him in her face 24/7?

"This is so not going to work," she muttered as she made her way down the sterile hallways of the underground offices.

"You worry too much." He followed her too closely.

"You're not the one stuck with an overgrown male all weekend," she snorted. "I like my privacy, Mr. Warrant."

"You'll survive, Ms. Rodriquez."

Maybe.

God, she wanted him. Wanted what she knew she couldn't have, because Ria didn't do one-night stands. She had learned long ago that they weren't for her, and she was determined never to be tricked into it again. And Mercury Warrant would never be anything else. Hadn't his file already stated that he was considered a surviving mate? The woman his heart and soul had chosen for its own had died. Mercury Warrant couldn't give his heart to another woman, because it was already taken. And Ria knew she couldn't bear walking away if she gave him the rest of her heart.